Front cover design by Simon Avery
Typesetting by Caroline Goldsmith

ISBN: 978-1-7395780-0-8

Also available as an eBook
ISBN: 978-1-7395780-1-5

LIKE ME

Katharine Light

Praise for *Like Me*

'Life-affirming and witty, page-turning and poignant, *Like Me* celebrates the friends that walk with us along the rocky path from first love to second chances. Reading *Like Me* felt like a homecoming—a chance to hang out with old friends. Scenes from this novel have taken on the status of memories, as if I really knew these characters and was part of their lives. It was refreshing to read a novel so warm and humane.'
Emma Claire Sweeney, author of *Owl Song At Dawn*

'A heartwarming exploration of love across the decades. Katharine skillfully unravels her characters' past to help them forge meaningful relationships in the present.'
Rebekah Lattin-Rawstrone, author of *Home*

Readers who loved the book

'I got completely involved in the story and the characters and found myself rooting for Jess and Sam…'

'…a complex, multi-layered, very relatable novel…'

'…loved the relationship between Jess and Sam from the start…'

'I thoroughly enjoyed reading *Like Me*… I measured out my reading stints because I didn't want to finish it. It's great that it's the first of a series!'

For my parents, Nicholas Light (1933 – 2023) and Ann Ford
and Roger Ford.

Thank you for everything.

JESS

Jess gazed round Caroline's cluttered, familiar kitchen and breathed a sigh. The two-hundred-mile drive had set her shoulders like rock and she made a concerted effort to tease them away from her ears. 'How can it be twenty years since we left school? It can't be.'

'The last time I risked a glance in an unfamiliar mirror, I definitely looked thirty-eight,' said Caroline.

'You look lovely.' Jess smiled at her oldest friend. They had met at primary school in Millingham, south of Manchester, a town sandwiched between the outer edges of the city and the Cheshire plain. Their friendship had been cemented when they passed the eleven-plus exam and found themselves in a class of strangers at Millingham Grammar School for Girls.

'I look haggard. Old and stern, my daughters tell me,' Caroline replied.

'Ah, the unfiltered comments of children,' Jess said.

'Of all family members, frankly.' Caroline shook her short dark curls. Grey threads at her temples hinted at the natural hair beneath the semi-permanent colour.

These were the somethings and nothings of a long friendship. Telephone conversations post nine o'clock watershed while Caroline's husband Philip was out, and once Jess's husband Tom had left. Children in bed, houses finally quiet, and each cradling a glass of wine, their chats would range across a multitude of subjects. Hair always featured heavily and hair colour was a recurring theme.

Jess didn't have the guts to colour her hair. During their marriage, Tom had insisted she kept her hair long—as it had been for most of her teens—and her decision to have it cut off after he left had been a tremendous shock. She'd been aiming for hip and trendy and instead she looked older somehow; fragile. Now, she didn't have the courage to cut or colour it, nor the financial means to do either.

'Why are we having a school reunion now?' said Jess. 'Couldn't it be twenty-one years? I plan to have my life so much more together this time next year.'

'It'll be fun. You said you liked the idea.'

'Did I? Was I being polite?' Although it was a warm July night, the air felt fresh, a slight breeze wafting through the double doors to the garden. Sometimes London air felt claustrophobic and stale to Jess, as if it had been breathed in and out too many times by too many people.

Caroline handed her a glass of white wine. 'Sit down. You've driven a long way on a Friday with two small children. You can relax.'

Jess slumped into a chair, propped her elbows on the kitchen table and took a gulp of wine. 'Relax? No. Can't place that word. Rings a vague bell.'

Caroline laughed. 'Philip won't be back until late, so it's just us tonight.'

'Thank you so much for putting us up. And putting up with us.'

'Don't be daft. It's terrific the children just pick up where they left off.'

'They were so looking forward to seeing your girls. Let's hope they're all still in their own beds. And that they've calmed down by tomorrow.'

'We'll hear them if there's too much leaping about.' Caroline narrowed her eyes. 'When did you last have a break from the children? Is Tom any use at all?'

Jess looked up from her glass. 'Oh. Mum has them now and then.'

Caroline shook a bag of salad into a bowl. 'Well, you'll never guess who's moved back into the family home on Woodham Road.'

Jess took another swig of wine. The only person she knew who once upon a time lived on Woodham Road was Sam Rushmore, and she'd convinced herself she'd stopped thinking about him years ago.

'Sam! Sam Rushmore. Brother of the more famous Will. His mother's gone into Barton House, the nursing home. He has the kids at least half the time. His wife's working in Leeds, or York, or somewhere.'

Before she could stop herself, Jess said, '*Ex*-wife. They divorced years ago, didn't they?'

Caroline regarded her. 'Can't be easy, juggling work and children.'

'I imagine not.' Jess rubbed her eyes.

'I see him occasionally, at the surgery.' Caroline put plates and cutlery on the table, along with the salad and a cheese board. 'Help yourself.'

'Thank you.' She took a plate. 'Is he your GP then?'

'No way. I'm not taking my clothes off in front of someone who once tried to get off with me. I see Dr Quinlan. She's very good.'

Jess gripped the stem of her wine glass. That was a jolt from the past. *When did that happen?* 'You and Sam? Did you—?'

'Oh no. He looks good though. Still has all his hair. Grey and sexy.'

'How's his mum?'

'Not so good, I hear. She must be well into her seventies. Sound in mind, but not in body.'

'How sad. I liked her. She always remembered our names.'

'We could ring him up. He could be your date for the disco tomorrow night. At least he'll know all the eighties hits. Just like old times.'

Jess's stomach plummeted. 'You promised me I wouldn't need a date.'

'You don't. It's mostly us girls. I couldn't persuade Philip to come.'

Jess contemplated the following day. It would be nice to see Anna, Ruth and Stella. Her thoughts swerved slightly over the possibility of meeting Sam Rushmore again, her mind fast-forwarding through a movie of improbable moments: 'Jess. My one true love. I've found you again. The woman I want to spend the rest of my life—' No. *No*.

She put her hand on her forehead. The backs of her eyes ached. 'How many people are you expecting?'

'At least eighty,' said Caroline.

'Wow.' Jess wished she'd had a chance to have a decent haircut. Why had she had it hacked so uncharacteristically short in the first place? The white hairs were becoming more and more noticeable. At least her face was relatively unwrinkled, and she weighed roughly the same now as she had before the children, even if it was less satisfactorily distributed. 'What are you going to wear?'

Caroline topped up their glasses. 'Something clean.'

Jess hauled herself off the hard futon mattress in the loft the following morning, feeling barely better than she had when she lay down. She was used to sleeping alone, and the close proximity of her children—six-year-old Ben, a jerky and nervous sleeper, and four-year-old Millie, clingy and decidedly hot-blooded—had not made for a restful night.

For a moment, she wished her mother and stepfather had stayed in Millingham, and that she was back in her old single bed, just a street away. Her mother had bought the house after her father left. When Martin moved in, they'd started looking for a house to buy together, but they'd never found another one they liked enough. Until a weekend in Gloucestershire two years ago. Despite the appearance of being practical and sensible, Martin had an adventurous streak which now found them in semi-retirement in a Georgian terrace in Cheltenham, away from family and friends.

Over breakfast with Caroline and the children, Jess did her best to persuade Ben and Millie they wanted to walk round the corner to say hello to her mother's old neighbours. The fact that East Street was close to Woodham Road—and therefore Sam's house—had nothing to do with it whatsoever. Besides, Woodham Road was pretty close to Millingham Grammar School for Girls, where she would be at two o'clock that afternoon. Not avoiding him. But not searching him out either.

She felt cold and clammy despite the sunshine that brightened the back garden and streamed into the kitchen. What did they say? Face your fears?

'Ben, we'll go and say a quick hello to Granny and Grandad's neighbours. Then we can walk across the common and back past the church.' She bit her lip.

Caroline eyed her. 'Or just retrace your steps.'

'What church?' said Ben.

'Barton Church. The one in the photos.' She shrugged at Caroline. 'Ben's become very interested in the family photo albums.'

'Ah,' said Caroline.

Ben gazed at his mother. 'The church where you got married?'

How different Jess felt from the hopeful twenty-eight-year-old who had married the man she planned to spend the rest of her life with, in that church. No, Tom was not controlling, he was caring. Not overbearing; considerate. Not selfish; single-minded. She had thought.

She took a breath. 'That's right, darling.'

'You and Daddy?' Millie slipped her small hand into her mother's palm.

Jess pasted a taut smile onto her face. 'That's right. To Daddy.'

In East Street, Jess knocked on the door of the neighbours, who asked after her parents, and exclaimed over how much Ben and Millie had grown in a year.

Up the street they walked, Jess's hands clammy, her shirt sticking to her skin. Nearer and nearer to Woodham Road, which backed on to Barton Common.

'Mummee,' wailed Millie as they toiled past the school. 'I need to go to the loo.'

'Oh, darling, can you hold on? We can have a run on the common.'

Millie stopped and tugged her mother's arm. 'I need the loo. Now.'

'Amelia. Please, darling.' Jess held both her hands. 'We can't stay here—'

'I *need* the loo.' She fixed her mother with an impassive look.

Jess looked up and down the momentarily deserted road, knowing the closest public toilets were opposite the church at the other end of Woodham Road, between the two pubs.

'Right.' She made a swift decision and marched them up to a large semi-detached house at the top of the road. Before she lost her nerve, she rang the doorbell.

A girl with long dark hair opened the front door and scowled at them.

'Hello,' said Jess. 'Are you Katie? I'm Jess. This is Ben and Millie. Say hello.' Unmistakeably siblings, with their fair hair and brown eyes, her children stood silent beside her. Jess swallowed. She felt at a disadvantage, on the steps below this tall child, who looked much older than she could possibly be. Surely she was only about ten?

'We came to say hello to your dad, if he's in?'

'I need the loo,' said Millie.

The girl said nothing.

Jess smiled desperately. 'He and I are old friends…from when we were in our teens.'

'Kate? Who is it?' Sam's voice—deep, more Northern than she remembered—called from the hall.

A tall man in jeans and a blue t-shirt appeared behind the girl. He took off his glasses and squinted from the darkness of the doorway into the sunshine. For a moment he reminded Jess of his older brother Will, but he still looked younger than his thirty-eight years. Thick greying hair, dark eyes, and smooth brown arms. He looked solid and dependable.

Jess took a breath.

'She says she knows you, Dad,' said Kate.

SAM

Sam's first thought on seeing the woman standing on his front step, flanked by two small children, was that she'd got the wrong house. In her navy trousers and cardigan, buttoned up over a white shirt, she almost reminded him of one of the better-dressed sixth-formers at the grammar school.

Then the doctor in him kicked in. She was terribly pale. Pinched of blood. Huge bruises of shadow smudged the delicate skin under her grey eyes.

Finally there was a flicker of recognition. But that short hair—no, it *was* her. 'Jess? Jessica Lamb? How the hell are you? What are you doing here?'

'Hi, Sam. I'm here for a school reunion.'

He walked down the steps, hesitated, and then gave her a quick hug. She felt tense and awkward in his arms, as if she wasn't used to physical contact, but it also felt like the right thing to do. She used to be a hugger. Maybe she'd lost the knack.

He turned to his daughter. 'Kate, Jess and I are old friends.'

Kate returned his gaze, unblinking.

'And who's this?' He crouched down, eyes level with Ben and Millie.

'I'm Millie,' said Millie, batting her eyelashes at him.

Sam looked up and winked at Jess, who shrugged in reply.

He turned to the thin boy who stood close to his mother. 'And you must be?'

'Ben,' mumbled Ben.

'I really need the loo,' said Millie, her hand already on Sam's knee.

'In that case you must come in.' He smiled at Jess. 'Have a cup of tea. Or something stronger. Katie, put the kettle on, would you?'

'Kate. It's Kate, Dad.' His daughter flounced down the hall.

'Sure we're not disturbing you?' said Jess.

'It's Saturday. I haven't had a word of adult conversation since I left work yesterday. It'll be great to catch up.'

He closed the front door behind them and pointed to the end of the corridor. 'Downstairs loo.'

Jess gave him a quick smile and hurried Millie inside.

'Ben, why don't we see if we can find Emma and Joshua? Josh's about your age, I should think. He's seven.'

'I'm six. Does he have a lot of Lego?'

'He most certainly does. More Lego than any other child I know.'

'Mummy says that about me.'

'In that case, I know you'll get on.'

Sam led the way through the large kitchen and opened the back door. 'Em? Josh?'

When Jess and Millie reappeared, nine-year-old Emma took Millie into the garden to meet the rabbit. Ben and Josh wordlessly kicked a football to each other at the end of the unmown grass. The grass Sam should have cut yesterday.

He glanced around the kitchen. Waking up again on the sofa in the sitting room at three in the morning, the heavy whisky tumbler still balancing on his chest, had done nothing for his mood this morning, and the chores remained untouched.

He turned to Jess. 'Please ignore the state of the place.'

'Really, not a problem. I don't want to put you out.'

'You're not. Tea? Coffee?'

He raised an eyebrow as Kate stomped through the kitchen, banging the door as she went. 'Hit adolescence way too early. Eleven going on seventeen.'

'She looks older. And so self-assured.'

'She's in a mood because she wants to go to a sleepover party tonight and I have refused to take her shopping for more clothes.'

'But it's a party. How could you be so callous?' Jess laughed.

For a moment, he caught a glimpse of seventeen-year-old Jess; a girl who giggled spontaneously, twisted her long hair round her fingers, blushed when he looked at her. A girl without the cares of the world.

'What would you like to drink?'

'Anything cold.'

He opened the fridge and extracted a carton of orange juice.

'Perfect.' Jess peeled off her cardigan. 'It's so warm. Even for July.'

'Please sit down. Ignore the mess.' He pushed away the piles of papers littering the ancient pine table to make space for their drinks.

The lethargy weighing him down since he'd left work the day before had ebbed away, leaving him feeling light and alert. He had known Jess when he was young and still hoped for more from life. Now he was facing forty on his own, trying to bridge the widening gulf between him and his eleven-year-old daughter, push work aside to focus on his younger children, and field the increasing contempt of his ex-wife.

For too many years he'd allowed life to wash over him. At medical school, Elizabeth had spotted him, snared him, married him. They'd had the children when it suited her, their careers competing until someone had to back down. Katie and Em had been easy, good girls, but it was hard to juggle childcare with two hospital schedules.

Sam had blinked first. Once Josh was in the picture—after a moment of reconciliation in a sea of hostility—one of them had to step back from the demands of a hospital doctor post. It was never going to be Elizabeth. Her ambition and drive—'I'm going in *this* direction, come along for the ride!'—had been hugely attractive in the beginning. The reality, though, was that for her to have it all, large sacrifices had to be made. Their marriage, the children, and Sam's career all suffered.

It was difficult not to feel that eventually Elizabeth considered him surplus to requirements. She'd got rid of him as quickly and efficiently as she did with any detritus in her life. Maybe that should have been a sign. The lack of clutter, the sharp capsule wardrobe, the aversion to sentimentality.

Now he found himself on the other side of a divorce. As a doctor, he knew he'd reached all the clinical thresholds for depression, which was why he had become expert at never putting more than two symptoms together in his mind.

'So,' he said. 'You're here for a school reunion?'

'Twenty years. Can you believe it?'

'You don't look much older than when we went off to university.' *Just faded. Drained of colour.* Or maybe she looked how he felt. Here they were, their orbits intersecting once more—even if briefly—while they still breathed in and out, got dressed in the morning, put one foot in front of the other.

Jess took a sip of juice. 'You know that's not true. Spot the grey hairs.'

'Don't talk to me about grey hair. I'm the expert.' Thank God he'd managed to have a shower earlier. His hair was clean, even if it needed a cut.

'I think it makes you look distinguished.' Her mouth twitched.

'Well. Thank you.' He smiled. He'd like to bet her life and her house were pretty cluttered, that she barely knew the concept of a capsule wardrobe, that she'd turn out to be one of the more sentimental people he knew. How refreshing. He put his glasses on. 'I can't see any grey hairs.'

'You need new glasses. I've got lots.' Her pale face brightened considerably when she smiled.

'You do still look remarkably fresh-faced,' he said.

'You know me. Never did like the sun.'

A moment came back to him. A summer evening under the oak tree on the common. A pink-faced Jess, who'd glowed under his gaze, and not just from the sunshine.

She cleared her throat. 'How's life?'

'Could be worse. Elizabeth and I share custody of the children. They spend a lot more time with me, now she's commuting to Liverpool. Consultant endocrinologist. I moved back here after Mum's stroke. Working at St Michael's Medical Practice.'

'I was really sorry to hear about you and Elizabeth.'

'Ah. Yes. Thank you.' He studied his glass.

'Is it strange being back in your childhood home?'

He grimaced. 'Much less weird than you might think. Will's settled in Oxford.'

'I heard. Did he really marry Diana?'

'He really did. They have two girls. After he saw what fun we were having raising a family…' He took a long draught of water. He had to stop guzzling whisky and passing out on the sofa. 'Who are you still in contact with?'

'Caroline, Anna, Ruth, Stella. Rob by email, very occasionally. You?'

'Still see Rob if he ever gets here. Nathan. A few people from school. I've seen a lot of James this year as he's been up to sell the house and move his mum into a home. We compare notes. I occasionally see him when we go to Will's in Oxford.'

Sam watched Jess worry the rings on her right hand round and round her fingers. He longed to reach out and still them. 'So, the reunion should be a laugh. What does Tom think about the whole thing?'

She stood up to put her glass by the sink. 'You didn't hear? We got divorced.'

'I didn't. Jess, I'm so sorry. When?'

'More than two years ago. He left at Christmas. The divorce came through last September.' She shrugged. 'It had been bad for a long time. Before we had the children.'

'How are you managing?'

'Oh, you know.' She glanced at him. 'Good times, bad times. Tom always thought I was obsessed with the past. Doesn't approve of me even coming. To the reunion, I mean. Do you ever think that we had such a great time growing up that the real world was always going to be a cold and lonely place?'

'I'm not sure we all had such a great time.' He could think of a couple of episodes in which his best friend James had featured—a foot stamping on small fingers, vicious words, deliberate lies—that were not so great. He stood up and moved to the sink.

'But it was easier. Innocent. Or something. Do you think it's unusual that several of the boys came out? Nathan.' She swallowed.

Sam saw the tension in her jaw as she observed the boys in the garden. 'Then James. That was a shock. And your friend from the boys' grammar. Matthew?'

'Yeah. And Tim.'

'Tim? I remember Tim. Really? And his sister, what was her name? Susannah. God. I haven't thought about her in years.'

Jess shrugged. 'I wonder what they're up to. Married? Divorced?'

'We're probably no worse statistically than any other group of friends.'

'Are you serious?' Her glance flicked towards him for a moment.

'Well, one in three marriages now ends in divorce.' He watched her profile, noted her rapid breathing.

'Are you saying it's just the way things are?'

'Mummy, Ben kicked me,' Millie wailed, from the garden.

Jess ran out and scooped her up. 'I saw. But it was an accident. Ben, we need to go now.'

'We haven't played with the Lego,' said Ben.

Seeing Jess hugging her daughter made a marked contrast to Elizabeth's reaction to the children's physical needs. As a doctor she was clinical and detached, and the role of mother had taken second place. She'd always been strong on maintaining consistency, had given the children clear boundaries and stuck to them. With Kate, Elizabeth would hold firm. In theory Sam agreed with it all. Maybe seeing Jess and Millie together was so affecting because he no longer saw affection demonstrated between his own children and their mother. He was sure there were hugs and kisses, but part of the anguish of divorce was that he no longer saw the complete picture, just a snapshot.

'Why don't you stay for lunch?' Maybe he could get Jess

to eat something healthy to give her some colour. Spinach. A large steak.

'Thank you, but we'd better go. I need to change for afternoon tea on the lawn, with the new headmistress.'

'How long are you here?' He was only proving himself to be a conscientious doctor when he wondered how best to encourage her to have a decent night's sleep, a balanced diet, a chance to relax… Any other thoughts were purely incidental.

'A week. It's a welcome break from London.'

'Come for lunch after church tomorrow?' he heard himself ask.

She smiled. 'Church? Don't tell me—'

'I sing in the choir. Is that so awful?' He was struck by the way her sweet smiles and soft blushes made his pulse kick up. He breathed a little deeper, stood a little straighter.

'No. It's endearing.'

Sam laughed off her unexpectedly tender expression. 'So. Church in the morning? See you there?'

'I don't know. Caroline and Philip go to St Cecilia's—the big Catholic one off the Manchester Road.' She put Millie down.

'No, Mummy, up, up,' said Millie.

'Darling, I can't possibly carry you. You'll have to walk.'

'Why don't you come to St Paul's, for old times' sake?' said Sam, as they walked down the hall.

'What about the children?'

'Great kids' activities in Barton Cottage. Really like old times.'

'I'll talk to Caroline.'

Was it ridiculous to think that Jessica Lamb appearing on this Saturday morning was the most exciting thing to happen since the last time Manchester United thrashed Manchester City?

Jess looked at her children. 'What would you like to say to Sam?'

'Thank you for having me,' they both managed.

'You're welcome.' He opened the front door as his elder daughter barrelled down the stairs and elbowed past. 'Kate? Come and say goodbye, would you?'

But Kate disappeared into the kitchen.

'Don't worry,' Jess said. 'It's not an easy age. Probably won't be for at least the next five years, maybe more.'

'Thank you for those words of encouragement. Listen, if you don't come to church, come for supper in the week. Ring me. I'll give you my mobile number.'

'Don't bother. I can always reach you on the landline.' She recited his home number.

He grinned. 'How the hell do you remember that?'

'Told you I was obsessed with the past.' She turned to him with the glimmer of a smile. 'Don't flatter yourself. I remember everyone's.'

JESSICA: age 14

The scout hut was dank even at the height of summer. Tonight, after Guides on the last Friday of September, it felt bone-chilling. Jessica shivered as she shrugged on her school coat over her blue Guide uniform. Any moment, less than a hundred yards away, Stella and the boys would finish church choir practice and emerge from the vestry.

She wound her dark green scarf round her neck and craned to see whether what fell down her back was the same length as what fell down her front. Shoving her dirty brown hair out of her eyes, she pulled it behind her ears. Why hadn't she washed it?

By contrast, her friend Ruth's dark hair shone, clean and smooth, in the strip lighting. Jessica watched as she stuffed her hat in her pocket and yanked her out of the Guide hut, into the cold darkness.

'Ow,' yelped Jessica.

'Shush.' Ruth walked fast. She conveyed such certainty, such confidence in where she was going.

Jessica sighed. As usual, she ran to catch up, the autumn wind forcing itself up her sleeves, down her neck. As they rounded the corner, the holly tree was silhouetted against the stained-glass windows of the church, the lights inside casting bright lozenges of colour over the gravestones.

'Beautiful.' Jessica's breath billowed into the clear,

cloudless air.

'Cold,' said Ruth.

Although she'd turned fourteen, Jessica was still in that mindset of not wanting things to change. If not comfortable with who she was, then at least resigned to what she knew. She had, perhaps for the first time, the understanding that she was on the cusp. That life was dissolving and reforming, never to be the same shape again. Her time spent at school—the biggest wedge in the pie chart of her existence—was in a purely female environment, and yet even there, her innocence was being eroded. Relentlessly. She could still feel the wave of heat that had swept through her in that first year at the grammar, caused by an older girl pointing and laughing, as she and Caroline held hands in the playground. Made even worse because of her total ignorance. The fear of doing the wrong thing, without the least sense of what that might be. Nothing seemed as bad as the shame of being ridiculous. She knew it had brought out the weak worst in her, causing her to laugh too long and loud—mainly with relief—as the searing pack attention veered away from her towards another unfortunate classmate.

Jessica and Ruth reached the small car park beside the church, and gazed towards the pub opposite, crowded with chatter. Smoke, and the yeasty reek of beer, wafted across the road.

'What time is it?' Ruth had no need for a scarf. She stood, thumbs hooked into the pockets of her open coat, looking as if she did this all the time.

Jessica pulled a hand from her pocket; shook her watch down her wrist. 'T—two minutes past.'

The door to the vestry burst open and a shoal of people flooded out. Stella reached them first. She'd done something amazing to her hair. Deeply glamorous, thought Jessica.

'Do you like it? I'm thinking of going really blond. It's Sun-In, so I can get it as pale as I like.' Stella's thick, layered hair had been teased into tousled curls, the front tendrils canary yellow. She wore her elder brother's discarded denim jacket, with a brightly patterned Indian silk scarf tied at the back, cowboy style, neatly filling the V of her jumper. Her jeans were moulded tightly to her legs.

The silhouetted shapes of three boys—two taller, one shorter—invaded her peripheral vision, coming relentlessly closer. In previous weeks they'd sauntered off, but not tonight. Jessica felt a rush of damp heat under her arms. She stamped her feet and pulled her hair forward to shield her face.

Stella stepped between the girls and the boys, suddenly formal. 'Right. Ruth, Jessica… Sam, James, Sebastian.'

Glances were flicked at each other. 'Hello.'

'Hello,' the boys nodded, their voices loud and deep.

Jessica raised her hand to her mouth, licked her dry lips. She had seen these boys several times at church, but the only boy she and Ruth had actually spoken to was Sam, Stella's boyfriend. He looked deeply sexy, maroon scarf tucked into the turned-up collars of a navy donkey jacket. An old one of Will's probably. William Rushmore, Sam's older brother, the boy they all admitted to having a crush on. A cool seventeen-year-old, he'd so far been devoted to the prettiest girl in the choir: blonde, petite Diana Westerham.

For Sam, surely having such a desirable brother was a mixed blessing. Both boys had thick dark hair and big brown eyes, good skin and teeth. Will, slightly taller, with John Lennon-type gold-rimmed glasses, glowed polished beauty which Sam had yet to attain.

Jessica sighed. Not for these smooth-skinned boys, the

desperate pondering over whether to leave that beacon-like spot alone, as *Jackie* magazine recommended, or to squeeze it enough to make her eyes water, knowing it would be red and fierce for days to come.

Sam looked at Stella, then turned to James. 'Are you going to tell them?'

Ever since the beginning of the autumn term, the lives of these boys had been a major topic of conversation in school breaks or during the lunch hour, so Jessica knew that James was at the same independent boys' school in Manchester as Sam. Also dark haired, he wore a thin anorak and what looked like black school trousers. But he did have full, generous lips, and a cute dimple in one cheek.

James looked straight into her eyes for a second before focusing somewhere between Ruth and herself. 'I'm having a party next Saturday night. Eight o'clock. Bring some cider.'

The shorter boy, Sebastian, said nothing. His cropped, straight brown hair made him look very young, which was comforting to Jessica. She longed to look older. To be older.

With that, the boys retreated along the road past the pub. Going to Sam's house, Jessica guessed, as he lived in that direction. He had a pool table in his cellar, another social claim to fame.

Stella walked a little way with the boys, did not kiss Sam, and then ran back to the girls.

'What's going on? Aren't you going out together anymore?' said Ruth.

They'd had lengthy accounts of evenings Stella had spent with Sam. Will and Diana had tutored them in the art of French kissing. The *Jackie* 'Ten Things You Should Know About Kissing' was not the same as actually doing it. It seemed Stella and Sam had become deft at it. After a giggling marathon, she had blushingly told them of when she and Sam had been left together in the dark and it had stopped being perfunctory and become hot and wet and exciting.

'Well, we've been seeing each other in a more serious way for a few months, and we'd like a change. You know, you get a bit bored...and there are some other people we like, too...' Stella tossed her hair.

Jessica and Ruth exchanged glances.

'Anyway.' Stella arched an eyebrow. 'He likes someone else. Someone not a million miles from where I'm standing, Jessie. He really likes you and wants to go out with you.'

Jessica put out a hand to steady herself, feeling as if she'd just been asked to step off a very tall building. 'He's very nice. But I just couldn't. I wouldn't know what to do.'

'Sure you will.' Stella linked her arm through Jessica's. She turned to Ruth. 'Let's go to my house and plan what to wear next Saturday.'

Stella lived in a pretty double-fronted Victorian house a short walk down the hill. Her spacious bedroom was painted bottle green, the large sash window hung with trailing spider plants in macramé pots, her bed a mattress on the floor. She went straight to the tape recorder and put on The Pretenders.

Jessica sat on the carpet. 'It's not Sam...I just want things ...I don't want to go out with anyone.'

'Crap,' said Stella. 'We're going to transform you for next Saturday. We can all meet and get changed here.'

'It's in a dark cellar. No one will even see,' said Ruth.

Stella laughed. 'Not that dark. Not all the time.' She searched for an eyeliner. 'Here's a green one, to draw attention to your eyes.'

Jessica tried some, inside the bottom rim of her eyelids. Her eyes looked huge and strange. She tried to blink away the fear.

She watched as Ruth took a blue eyeliner and defined her dark blue, long-lashed eyes. She blinked slowly and deliberately at her reflection in the mirror. A knowing, self-assured type of blinking.

'What?' Ruth met her eyes in the mirror. 'Don't look so petrified. They're only boys. Half the human race.'

With a black eyeliner, Stella achieved a startling Cleopatra look.

Ruth frowned. 'Doesn't go with your hair.'

Jess rubbed the make-up away with her fingers. 'Are you definitely going to the party?' The thought made her want to throw up. The only boys she spent any time with were relatives, or her younger brother Patrick's friends. These other boys were too big, too hard-limbed, too loud. She foresaw no delight in the frankly disgusting idea of French kissing. The exchanging of saliva was gross, and the idea of ever taking her clothes off in front of someone of the opposite sex brought her out in a red sweat.

She was dismayed by her own cowardice. The more worldly girls in her year—wise beyond their years—lived the other side of Millingham. They came to school by bus, chewing gum, wielding furled magazines and cans of Coke, twisting the waistbands of their skirts up and rolling their white socks down towards their chunky black lace-ups. Having bypassed teen bras, they'd negotiated their substantial chests into upholstered lace underwear, and exuded a cynical, knowing air. They would relish a party, a chance to get sweaty, drink cider, grind themselves against an even sweatier boy doused in noxious aftershave.

Kissing was too frightening—a painful clash of teeth, a

monstrous, invading, fat and heavy tongue, stopping her breath—with the lurking prospect of being found out, of not knowing what to do, of betraying her own ignorance.

Stella nudged her arm and smiled at her in the mirror. 'You'll be fine.'

She had to pray that no one would find out just how little she knew.

JESS

After lunch Jess changed her clothes, and she and Caroline walked up the hill to Millingham Grammar School for Girls, every step taking them closer to Woodham Road. Somehow the whole scene with Sam seemed surreal. Maybe because her senses had been poleaxed by the hug. She couldn't remember the last time she'd been hugged by an adult male to whom she was not related. He'd felt warm and safe. Nothing else. The stomach-plummeting stuff had been pure coincidence, she told herself firmly.

The distraction meant she didn't feel unmanageably jittery about the reunion. It would be interesting to see who turned up. What they were doing. What they looked like now. Her mind flicked through snapshots of her school career.

The vicar's wild daughter, who had once locked herself and her boyfriend in Jessica's parents' bedroom. Jessica had been outraged on her parents' behalf. That was way before anyone had actually Done It. She had thought.

Siobhan Frost, the scariest girl in the year, whose school uniform bore no resemblance to Jess's sensible below-the-knee navy skirt, white open-neck shirt, V-neck pullover, knee-length socks and brown lace-ups. Siobhan's look had been altogether tighter: bottom-hugging mini-skirt, high black lace-ups and white ankle socks, a too-unbuttoned shirt and non-existent cardigan. There'd been rumours about Siobhan being expelled from two girls' boarding schools. Group sex? Smoking pot? How shocking it had been, twenty years ago.

Or what about innocent, unworldly girls like Susan Hodge, Catriona Roberts? Catriona had been the only other girl to go to UCL as well, but they had not kept in touch. She had reminded Jess too much of herself.

And all the people she'd forgotten. And all the people who'd forgotten her. The fear, sometimes realised, of people saying, 'I'm sorry, who?'

Caroline disappeared to check on things as soon as they reached the school hall, and Jess flailed for a moment as she scanned the rows of seats, until she saw Ruth standing next to Anna.

'Hey there.' Ruth leant across for a kiss, her sleek dark bob shining in the sunlight. She had returned to her job in the city before her son was six months old, and her smart dark trousers and patterned top gave her an air of authority. 'You look absolutely knackered.'

Jess flinched. 'I'm sharing a room with the children. How's Andy…and Jack?'

Ruth's husband Andy was a wiry, shaven-haired computer expert from Birmingham. They'd met at university and been together ever since. 'Andy's fine and Jack's the chattiest one-year-old you've ever met.'

'Sounds like you're having fun!' Jess turned to give Anna a hug. 'How are you?'

'All the better for seeing you, love.' Statuesque in layered linen, Anna ran a successful women's clothing company, featuring natural fabrics. She lived near Bath in a beautiful Georgian house and maintained what seemed to be an emotionally exhausting long-distance relationship with Jonathan, who lived and worked in London. No children.

'Who've you seen?' said Jess, as they sat down, leaving space for Caroline, and for Stella, who had yet to appear.

'A few people from our class.' Anna smoothed a blonde curl off her face. 'There's quite a list of those expected.'

A tall woman in a cerise suit made her way onto the podium, followed by a familiar figure. She welcomed them, introduced herself as Mrs Hetherington-Small, the current headmistress, and launched into a series of bullet points about the school's critical role in raising the women of the future. Before Jess's eyes glazed over, she caught Anna's look and spent the rest of the speech trying not to giggle.

Then Mrs Kershaw, the head twenty years ago, added her own welcome, without the need for much marketing jargon at all.

'She looks exactly the same,' whispered Caroline.

'Identical,' agreed Jess.

Next, Mrs Hetherington-Small herself conducted a tour of the new Arts Block. The shabby extensions and portacabins had been replaced with architecturally sympathetic buildings to match the original Victorian school, the surrounding space converted into landscaped gardens. Everywhere looked manicured and uniform; no old trees to climb, mud to scuff new shoes in, bike sheds to hide behind.

After that it was tea, scones and cakes on the front lawn, bunches of chairs dotted among the daisies.

'This place has really gone up in the world since we left,' said Jess.

'It does look terribly smart,' said Caroline, surveying the front façade of the school.

'Is it true what the head said about being in the top fifty state schools in the country now?' said Jess.

'Yes, but it was good when we were here,' said Ruth.

'Not quite like this, though.' Jess surveyed the crowd. She did a double take. A girl who looked the spitting image of Susan Hodge, who must indeed *be* Susan Hodge—the straightest, shyest, stiffest girl in the sixth form—was walking past Jess wearing a t-shirt saying: *I have PMT and a pistol. Any questions?* Jess turned aside, shocked. It seemed so unlikely. In her world, most people didn't change. Not really. Yet here was someone who had thrown off the confining shackles of school and reinvented herself. And then some.

At the tea table, a blond, suntanned woman smiled at her, and Jess did her second double take. *Siobhan Frost,* said the badge.

'Hi, how are you?' Siobhan said, in the friendliest manner.

Jess took a breath. 'Fine, thank you. How are you?'

She worked her way back to Ruth, Caroline, Anna, and Stella, who had finally arrived.

'Doug's going to meet Andy and Jon for a drink,' said Stella, gorgeous in linen trousers from Anna's collection, and a funky t-shirt that was currently pulled up while breast-feeding baby Rosie, the newest edition to her family. Her long blond hair was piled into a soft, stylish bun. 'Where are your kids, Jess?'

'Philip's got all four of them. How are the boys?'

'Great.' Stella had done Fine Art and then jewellery design, and was now successfully creating pieces for various celebrities and members of the Royal Family. She had met her husband when he'd commissioned a bracelet for his then girlfriend. Said girlfriend was so put out it was not the engagement ring she coveted that they'd split up. Instead, Stella and Doug—well over six foot with impressive dark hair he wore longer than strictly fashionable—had a whirlwind romance and got married in Barton Church. They lived in a fabulous house in Islington, convenient for Doug's high-powered job in the City.

'Well done for organising a fascinating event,' Jess said to Anna. 'I'm humbled by my wildly inaccurate preconceptions. People really can change.'

'I *know*,' Anna replied. 'Siobhan Frost.'

'Susan Hodge.' Jess could see her having a perfectly civilised conversation with Mrs Kershaw, who appeared to ignore the t-shirt caption.

'Even you, if you have the strength.' Anna smiled.

'Or the courage,' said Jess. 'Gorgeous outfit, by the way. One of yours?'

'Yes, glad you like it. I do know I have more time on my hands than the rest of you.'

Jess turned to look at Anna, who was pouring more tea.

Whenever they got together as a group, Anna maintained she had neither the time nor the inclination for children. But Jess had seen the way she gazed at Millie, her god-daughter. Was she nursing a secret wound, untouched and unmentioned, even with such old friends? Old friends, but not necessarily close friends. There was a degree of intimacy to some of the relationships, but Jess knew her own tendency to romanticise was liable to imbue them with more depth than really existed.

As the single mother, Jess felt the strain of conversation around her. She wanted to shout: 'It's OK. I won't break if you mention your husbands' names. Or your impressive careers. Or both.' She clamped down on the thoughts that skittered over her unremarkable career in event management to date and what she would do to earn money, once Millie started school in September.

'What I find surprising is how we fall back into our old roles so easily,' she said, as they walked down the driveway. She was finding it hard to shake off those feelings of inferiority.

'What do you mean?' said Ruth. 'School was a long time ago.'

'Which doesn't stop it from being a very formative time of life,' said Caroline.

Jess smiled at her. 'With powerful patterns it's hard to resist.' All the old anxieties about where she was going to sit and who would deign to talk to her had reared their ugly heads, despite the fact that she was more confident now than when she was a teenager. She contemplated that thought for a moment. Not true. Her confidence had been steadily eroded throughout her marriage, and suffered a near fatal blow when Tom left.

More than two years later, she was still regrouping.

SAM

Somehow, having that unexpected encounter with Jess, and a brooding, drawn-out row with his elder daughter, Sam's Saturday was not the restful day he'd imagined. It never usually concerned him that he'd failed to make any type of social arrangement over the weekend. He justified this by focusing on the children. He didn't have them all the time, and when they were here, his attention was theirs. If he didn't switch on the TV to check the cricket score and become absorbed. Often he couldn't be bothered to leave the house except for work and essential errands, whether the children were here or not. Without his colleague Matt insisting that he have supper with him and his wife Jane now and then, and a couple of neighbours inviting him and the children for Sunday lunch, he had become a bit of a hermit.

Was it just seeing Jess that had made him uncomfortable? And was it worse knowing she was meeting up with so many from the old gang, on a Saturday night, and that his evening would revolve around cooking pasta for the children, getting Josh and Em to go to bed, trying to read the newspaper, and ferrying Kate to her party? He just had to concentrate on the children when he was at home, the day job when he was at work. Being distracted by one when he was immersed in the other was not helpful.

His mobile jolted him back into the messiness of his kitchen. *What must Jess have thought?* He scrabbled for the phone. 'Hi, James.'

'Sam. What are you up to?'

'Usual Saturday stuff. I've got the children.'

'Oh. I could do with a break, preferably over a beer. As well as needing some muscle to move Mum's writing desk.'

'Flattered you thought of me. Don't they have professionals for this kind of thing? Movers, I think they're called.'

'Ha ha. I haven't got time, and I need the desk shifted today. Can you give me a hand?'

'I can't just abandon the children.' Much as the thought might occasionally appeal.

'Bring them? If you have to?'

'No one else who can help? Stuart not around?'

'No. My brother is not in a fit state. I'm asking you.'

'Sorry to hear that. How's he getting on—?'

'It's a simple question, Sam. Can you help?'

Sam persuaded fifteen-year-old Suki from next door to hold the fort (really, the amount of cash that went her way, he was building her a college fund) and left her helping Kate apply purple nail varnish (purple?!) Then he walked up Barton Hill to James's old family home.

James opened the front door. 'Good. You're here.'

Sam followed him into the dining room, where the large oak desk sat in a sea of paper.

'Yeah. Lots still to do,' said James.

'You're making progress,' said Sam.

'Inch by inch. Let's get this out to the car.'

'Are you sure it's going to—?'

'It'll fit.'

With a lot of heaving, swearing, and shoving, they wedged the desk into James's estate.

'Time for a drink.' James led the way to the kitchen and opened the fridge. 'Beer?'

Sam followed. 'I should be getting back.'

James stepped onto the patio with two bottles of beer in his hand. 'Pressing social engagement on a Saturday night in Millingham?'

'The children. Taking Kate to a party.' He followed James outside, turning his shoulder, eyes trained on the house.

'It's a thank you. For helping me move the desk.'

'All right. A quick one.' Sam accepted the proffered bottle.

The Victorian terraced house was unremarkable, but the spacious back garden was graced by a large oak tree. The branches cast long swaying shadows in the late afternoon sunshine.

They swigged their beers.

'Looks like I'm confirmed for the Witney by-election,' said James.

'A safe Conservative seat then.'

'Thanks a lot.'

'Sorry. I didn't mean it like that. It's great you've got it.'

The sun faded behind a cloud. Sam shivered.

'Thanks. There are one or two things that could get into the press. You know how puerile they can be. It's possible they could find out about Stuart's head injury…so I just want to make sure things in the past…stay in the past.' James tilted his beer bottle at the tree.

Sam shut his eyes. For so long, what had happened on that hot July day—over twenty-five years ago now—had not been mentioned. It all came back to Sam as if it were yesterday.

Boys climbed trees. Boys fell out of trees. Accidents happened.

This had been dealt with. They'd been stupid kids.

He opened his eyes. 'You can't possibly think that—as a doctor I'd want to—'

'Good. Just making sure we understand each other.'

JESS

The evening event was taking place in Barton Assembly Rooms, built in the 1920s, close to the church. The building had an air of faded splendour, with its stained-glass windows and intricate brickwork.

Jess and Caroline walked, passing Sam's house on the way. Out of the corner of her eye, Jess managed to ascertain that there were lights on but no sign of life in the front rooms.

At the welcome table Jess was handed a badge with a photo. In the gloom she could barely make it out, but feared it was an unattractive image of herself in the sixth form. Permed hair—which of course she now knew never looked good on anyone—and a brown checked dress. At least some things have improved, she thought, smoothing down the creases in her long navy linen dress, silently thanking it for skimming her sagging midriff.

Caroline was talking to Ruth and Anna, her back turned. The old panic began to well up, but Anna looked over and smiled. 'Come on, Jess. Alcohol.'

They walked down the steps into the large room with its high vaulted ceiling and straight to the bar where Anna ordered a bottle of Rioja.

'Let's have a look at the wall of fame,' said Caroline.

'The *what*?' Jess took a gulp of wine.

They made their way past the throng already dancing to Duran Duran, towards a wall of photos. Everyone in their year displayed for all to see.

'Look.' Jess stared at the image of Camilla Jackson, a tall, striking girl who had started a nursing degree, and died of cancer before she finished it.

'Did you know about Andrea?' said Anna.

Jess studied the photo and the dates. Andrea Wilson was killed in a car crash just before her thirtieth birthday, leaving a husband, three-year-old daughter and baby son. Mousy hair, a round smiling face, small eyes.

She felt the tears start. Ever since being pregnant with Ben, her hormones seemed to have taken on a life of their own. Even the most sentimental or clichéd TV ads made her cry.

'Terrible, isn't it?' said Caroline. 'Poor Andrea. The slightest thing sets me off. Particularly if it involves children.'

They found a free table along the edge of the large room, and various people stopped to chat, without Jess having to seek anyone out. Which was good. She realised how tired she was, yesterday's drive and broken sleep catching up with her.

'Are you all right?' said Caroline, under cover of the clinking of glasses.

'It makes me feel as inadequate as I did when I was seventeen. Do you remember how desperate I always was to sit in the middle of the group?' Jess studied her toes in strappy sandals, courtesy of last year's Clarks sale.

'Yes.' Caroline nodded.

'I couldn't stop myself. I was convinced that without the spotlight of the group I would somehow fall into the shadows and disappear. I felt so plain and boring compared to the rest of you.'

'Jess, you weren't. You and I were friends from primary school.'

'I know. But then Anna was so much more entertaining. And Stella. And Ruth.'

'You had parties. The boys were always coming round to your house for coffee. Much better than my not terribly sociable parents, or Anna living with her grandparents on the other side of Millingham.'

'You'd have thought I'd have got over it by now.'

Caroline surveyed her for a moment. 'Did you know that if you've had a long-term relationship you're much more likely to find another than if you never did in the first place?'

'If I really wanted one.'

'You're considering it in a way you haven't for the past two years.'

'Says who?'

'Jess. Last time we were all together, you didn't even know the men were there. Being men. Now you notice them. That's all I'm saying.'

Jess considered mentioning Sam Rushmore to Caroline, but the idea gave her chest pains.

'Anyone nice in London?' said Caroline.

Jess shrugged. 'Not that I've noticed.'

'No potential at church?'

'You must be joking. There don't seem to be any unattached men, and there are a lot of much younger, more attractive women who go to the far hipper evening service. Who have midriffs they can bare. My midriff hasn't seen the light of day since before the children. The morning service is full of marrieds.'

'Not many divorcees, I suppose.'

'No.' She should ring Sam. Proper hugs from an unrelated man were not to be passed up. They could commiserate with each other. Not that he'd be short of companionship. He was bound to have a girlfriend. Maybe that would explain Kate's hostility.

'Jess?'

'Sorry,' she replied.

'You *have* noticed someone, haven't you?'

Jess gazed at the end of her third glass of red wine. 'Well—'

'Yes?' said Anna, falling into the chair on the other side of Jess. 'What are you talking about?'

'Shhh,' said Caroline. 'Jess has started noticing men again.'

'Excellent, I notice them all the time.'

Caroline eyed Anna. 'Go on, Jess.'

'There's this guy I used to see at the gym. I know nothing about him—I don't even know his name—but in my fantasy he's wonderful.'

'Have you ever talked to him?' Caroline asked.

'Not really. Our eyes meet occasionally, but it's got embarrassing because of the fantasy.'

'Why don't you invite him for coffee? Or a drink? You've got nothing to lose,' said Anna.

'Sure I have. I save myself some serious embarrassment. I get to go to the gym—on the rare occasions when I do go—without panicking about bumping into him the whole time.'

'He might say yes,' said Caroline.

'He won't. People don't say yes to nearly forty-year-old divorcees with kids and an ex-husband.'

'You're not nearly forty. You're thirty-eight,' said Anna.

Jess shook her head. 'Thirty-seven you can pass off as mid-thirties. Thirty-eight is definitely late thirties.'

'But you don't even look it. You look much younger than I do. No wrinkles at all,' Caroline put the pads of her fingers to her own cheeks.

'Yes wrinkles,' said Jess. 'It's lovely of you to be supportive, but it's not simple anymore.'

'You could always use him for sex,' said Anna. 'Well, hello.' She greeted Ruth, flushed from the dance floor.

'God, I need a drink.' Ruth helped herself to the Rioja.

'We're encouraging Jess to get out there again. Maybe even use fantasy gym man for sex,' said Anna.

Ruth raised an eyebrow at Jess. 'Fantasy gym man? Sex?'

Jess sighed. There was a tiny part of her that thought that if she had enough to drink, a night of wild passion might have its appeal. She certainly missed physical intimacy, as she'd been strongly reminded when Sam hugged her.

She set her shoulders. No. She didn't do that anymore. She was a Christian who believed sex was only for committed relationships. Her desiccated church-going habit had metamorphosed, after Ben was born, into a living faith, a God-given strength which helped her survive her toxic marriage. 'I couldn't. Not with the children.'

'You remove all children before you embark on anything,' Ruth said. 'Classic rule of dating.'

'I'm not sure I'm up for a casual fling. They always leave you feeling absolutely dreadful.' Not to mention the fact that she was never taking her clothes off in front of a man ever again.

'Not necessarily,' said Ruth.

'So,' said Caroline. 'How good looking? Details, please.'

'Short grey hair. Good eyes. Tall. Well put together.'

'All that time in the gym,' said Anna.

'And in the fantasy? Heart stopping sex?' said Caroline.

'What?' Jess blinked.

'Heart stopping sex. Not that I can remember.' Caroline grimaced.

'Sure you can,' said Ruth.

'I don't think sex is part of the fantasy. It's more about the physical male presence. Hugs from a man who doesn't belong to someone else.' Jess shuddered for a second.

'Remember what I said,' said Caroline. 'There's every chance you'll meet someone lovely and live happily ever after.'

Jess hesitated. 'Maybe.' But she would need to engage with the real world. She seemed to have lost the knack of starring in her own life. So gradually she didn't realise it.

The worst part—the part that yawned like a deep, dark pit beneath her—was that it didn't even bother her anymore. The guy-at-the-gym fantasy worked because it was unreal, just like those romantic films or books she wasted far too much time on. Safer than dealing with raw, messy emotions, in the real world.

Stella flopped down beside them. 'I'm exhausted. I can no longer function properly after ten o'clock at night—my body doesn't know what's hit it.'

'Story of my life,' Jess and Caroline said together.

SAMUEL: age 15

Early Saturday evening, Sam opened the door to Rob, head to toe in black, his thick dark fringe brushed forward. 'Vodka.' He tapped his pocket.

'Shhh!' said Sam, pushing him towards the kitchen, out of earshot of his parents in the front room. He had found a dark green shirt of his brother's and buttoned it to the neck over his best jeans. Despite having a shower and dousing himself in Will's deodorant and Aramis aftershave, he already felt sweaty.

They wolfed Marmite on toast and drank a pint of milk between them, to line their stomachs. Then they swigged the hipflask of vodka—too bitter and chemical for Sam's liking—and set off for James's, bottles of cider weighing down their pockets.

James greeted them with overpowering hugs that left Sam clammier than ever. The Aramis kept repeating on him. How much was too much? Had neither James nor Rob commented only because of the noxious fumes they themselves were covered in? Did girls have a better sense of smell? How sensitive was Jessica's sense of smell?

James took them down the stone cellar steps, into a room furnished with chairs, cushions, a bench along one wall, and shelves scattered with bottles, cups, baskets of crisps, a record player and speakers.

'You serve the drinks,' said James. 'I'll answer the door.'

When the girls arrived, Sam concentrated on what they were wearing. Stella's tight black trousers were set off by a pair of brown suede ankle boots, complete with fringing. A rust coloured shirt contrasted with her hair. She'd made her eyes look extremely dark, with the aid of a lot of eyeliner.

Ruth wore dark jeans and a grey sweater. She smiled at Rob and blinked very slowly. Maybe she had something in her eye. 'I'll have a glass of this one,' she said loudly, as she handed him her bottle of cider.

'Just cups,' Rob replied, decanting the contents into plastic cups.

Ruth took one and handed the other to Jessica. They gulped furiously, which made Jessica frown and cough. She looked slight and cold next to Ruth's substance, but she was wearing green. Was that a good sign? Her dark cords were almost the same shade as his shirt, and she wore a bright jade shirt underneath her navy V-neck.

Besides Jessica and Ruth, Stella had invited Anna and Caroline. Rob's younger sister Natalie had been dropped off by their mother. Sebastian and Nathan from school were the last to arrive. Stella had already decided they were going to play games. What else would they do in a dimly lit, slightly damp cellar, on a Saturday night?

David Bowie and Led Zeppelin LPs lay in a heap. Bowie's *Changes I* album played on the black turntable.

A game with partners was out, as the numbers were uneven. Sam let the discussion wash over him, eyes trained on Jessica, twisting her hair, coughing behind her palm. Her foot bounced. Maybe the cider would relax her.

'How about spin the bottle?' James said.

'Great idea,' Stella said.

'Somebody finish this bottle.' Rob emptied cider into

swiftly held out cups.

'Now spread out,' Stella said. 'We should be boy-girl-boy-girl. Jessie, sit beside Sam.'

Sam caught Stella's eye. Did she have to be so obvious? He wished he'd gone easy on the Aramis. Maybe he could ask about Jessica's sense of smell under cover of the general chatter. He smiled as she moved to the space made for her on the bench. She smiled back, and all the anxious planes of her face smoothed out.

'Right, I'll begin.' Rob laid the bottle on an offcut of carpet in the centre of the room and set it spinning. It came to rest, the neck pointing at Sebastian, who clutched his throat theatrically.

'You spin to choose now.' Stella pushed the bottle towards him. It stopped facing her. She glanced at Sam and stood up. 'Come on, then.'

'No,' said James. 'Outside. That way you get some privacy.'

Stella shrugged at Sebastian and walked into the hall, closing the door behind them.

Rob bounded over to the door.

'Can you see anything?' Ruth whispered.

'Not a thing. The keyhole's blocked.'

James looked smug. 'Leave 'em in peace.'

Stella opened the door straight into the boys. She looked slightly pink, but normal enough—all her clothes intact—and Sebastian was grinning.

'Nothing to it, lads,' he said in a low voice, as he sat down.

And so it went on. Rob and Anna, Nathan and Stella.

Then Jessica and James. Sam bit the inside of his cheek. She was coughing again. They were gone for maybe ten seconds. James came back grinning; Jessica's cheeks glistened red.

And then it was Ruth...and Sam. He stood up and grabbed her hand, not glancing at Jessica. Outside it was much colder, the light brighter. She kept her mouth shut. Sam moved closer. He let their lips touch—his were wet and hers were warm—hardly earth-shattering. He stood back as she opened her eyes, flashed him a fleeting smile and bolted back into the room.

Then they were off again. Stella and Rob. Ruth and Rob.

And finally it was Jessica and Sam. He took her hand as they stood up from the bench.

Stella shut the door firmly behind them. 'Let's not let them in for at least a minute.'

Jessica pulled her hand away, wide-eyed. 'Stella!'

'You'll have to wait,' Stella replied through the door.

Sam reached for her hand again. 'Jessie,' he said. Stella called her Jessie. Jessica sounded so formal. He was not much taller than she was. He stepped forward, front teeth against bottom lip. She closed her eyes. A soft pressure. He was about to tease her lips with the tip of his tongue when she pulled away and started coughing. She turned to the door.

Eventually Stella let them in. 'That obviously went well.'

Sam shrugged. Was it the aftershave? Would that stop her from kissing him back, if she really wanted to?

After that the game disintegrated and people talked in twos and threes. He stayed sitting by Jessica. Her thin, cold hand was just beside his on the bench. She even smiled and bit her lip. They talked about school. When he asked her questions, she didn't cough.

'I think the cider's giving me a headache,' she said.

'At least it's not making you giggle uncontrollably,' he said, glancing across the room at Caroline, Anna, Rob and Nathan.

Ruth was sitting beside James and seemed to be blinking slowly again.

By eleven the party was breaking up. They spilled out into the road, chatting.

Sam could have done without Stella shoving Jessica in his direction, but he took his cue. He knew there was a lane to her back gate. The surface was pitted and uneven: dark, away from the streetlights. 'I'll walk you home.'

'I'll be fine,' she said.

'Don't be stupid,' said Stella.

He took her hand, which was as cold as he'd imagined. Within seconds there was too much heat between their palms, turning to sticky sweat.

'You want to be with the others,' she said.

'They can wait.' He stumbled in the dark and she reached out her other hand to steady him, letting it drop without touching him.

'You know the potholes,' he said.

'You get used to them.'

At her gate, he leaned in to kiss her, but she was gone with the merest brush of lips, down a narrow brick passageway to her back garden.

'Don't you want—can you see where—?'

'Thank you, Sam, goodnight.'

He leant against the wall. Now his eyes were accustomed to the shadows, he could see the contours of the worn, grout-depleted, flaking bricks. He listened for her footsteps, the sound of a key in a lock, a door shutting, but all he heard was the movement of air through the leaves of the trees above him. He stood there for a while, in the creeping cold, until he turned back up the lane to the light of the road.

JESS

Sunday morning, Jess mentioned that she was thinking of taking the children to the family service at St Paul's.

'That's a good idea. Like old times,' said Caroline, echoing Sam's words. She stopped. 'Jess, I'm sorry.'

'Don't be. I've been back a few times since I got married. And there's a new vicar.'

So, after breakfast she persuaded her reluctant children to walk up the hill to church. Ben stopped on Woodham Road. 'Mummy. That's Joshua's house.'

'Yes, it is.'

'Is Emma there?' said Millie, swinging on her mother's arm.

'They'll be at church. Their dad sings in the choir,' she said, aware her voice sounded breathy. 'Come on. Let's see if we can find them.'

The cool air of the big sandstone building—the faintest moisture in the air, an echo of incense and candle wax—took Jess back to the many hours she'd spent here. Counting the beams across the vaulted ceiling above the choir; feeling the thin green velveteen pew cushions, flattened through years of being sat on; the tapestried kneelers that hung below the pew shelves; the rush matting underfoot. The reds and greens of Bible, prayer book, hymn book; the oak of the pews, dark and smooth, with more than a hundred years of use.

Hours had been spent thumbing these books, standing, sitting, kneeling, giggling, singing familiar hymns and unfamiliar psalms; always aware of the boys in the choir, wondering what they were thinking, how their robes and ruffs felt, what colour shirts they wore underneath. Trying to work out if that look was just in her general direction, or more meaningful.

Three pews in front of them, Millie pointed out Joshua and Emma, sitting with a young boy and a woman. Jess studied her lilac linen jacket and curly, highlighted, shoulder length hair, and wondered if this was Sam's girlfriend. How convenient. Same church, boys of a similar age.

On cue, the organ sounded and everyone stood up. 'I'm relying on you both to behave,' she whispered.

'Dear Lord and Father of mankind, forgive our foolish ways,' Jess sang. Eyes front for most of it, but like Orpheus preceding Eurydice, she couldn't resist a fractional glance to the right. Her eyes immediately met Sam's and caught a quick wink as he passed. She looked away, blushing guiltily, feeling so caught out that she didn't see if he did the same thing to his girlfriend three pews in front.

When it was time to take the children to Sunday school, there was a minor kerfuffle until Millie was allowed to stay with Ben and Josh in the older group, constructing plasticine loaves and fishes. But Jess's biggest shock was seeing mystery woman's face. Much older than her back view would suggest—fifty at least—and one of the Sunday school teachers, it turned out. Maybe not the girlfriend.

Back in the service, the words sung and spoken, ebbed and flowed around her while she concentrated on not thinking about Sam. She pulled herself away from alluring images of his hair falling over his forehead as he swooped to kiss her, and concentrated on singing, *'And our lips shall show forth thy praise.'*

Jess made a conscious effort to lower her shoulders, pull in her tummy, and maintain the illusion of being perfectly relaxed as she walked into Barton Cottage.

'Mummy, look at our models.' Millie grabbed her legs.

'Josh says we can go and play Lego,' said Ben.

'Millie, these are great.' She examined colourful piles of plasticine. Her son tugged at her arm. 'We'll see, Ben. Perhaps one day this week.'

'What about now?' said a deep voice behind her.

Jess let out her held breath and turned around. 'Hi, Sam.'

He grinned, the epitome of relaxation in jeans and a blue shirt. 'How was last night?'

'Could have been worse.'

'Is that code for, "Actually I enjoyed myself"?'

'I'll tell you about it sometime.' She met his eyes fleetingly.

'Come for supper one evening. The kids could eat together.'

'Will Emma be there?' Millie piped up.

'I expect so.' Sam smiled at her. 'Even Kate, if we're very lucky.' An almost imperceptible wink at Jess.

They headed for Woodham Road. The children ran ahead, catching up with Kate and her friend Alice.

'How was the party?' said Jess.

'Who knows? I'm staggered by how quickly she's stopped talking to me, and how fast she's growing up.'

'Time accelerates the older they get. The older I get. It's becoming a very precious commodity.'

'So, what are you doing this week?'

'Spending time with Caroline and the kids. A few day trips. You?'

'Work. Children are at tennis camp in the mornings and then being farmed out, most afternoons.'

'Must be complicated.'

'Usually it's not too bad. Elizabeth's on a course this week, though.'

They reached Sam's gate.

'Can we do Lego now?' said Ben.

'Not now, darling, but we will come back, sometime this week.'

'Promise?' said Millie.

'Absolutely. Sam, can I ring you? Are some nights better than others? Evenings. Are some evenings…?' She wiped her clammy hands down her skirt. He'd issued an invitation but maybe he was just being polite.

'Evening surgery Monday and Thursday. Otherwise anytime.' He kissed her cheek, smelling of fresh, clean soap.

She closed her eyes for a fraction of a second. An unrelated man.

That afternoon, Caroline and Jess found a moment to loll in deck chairs in the garden while the children jumped in and out of the paddling pool.

'Been invited to Sam Rushmore's for supper sometime this week,' said Jess, encouraged by an uncustomary glass of wine over a late lunch.

'What? No! When did you see him?' Caroline sat up in her deck chair.

'Yesterday. And today.' Jess pressed her lips into a line.

'Jess. You never said.'

'Yeah, well. Anyway. I thought we could go one evening if it's OK with you. Ben's desperate to play Lego with Joshua. And Millie just wants to flirt with Sam.'

Caroline laughed. 'Are you going for the Lego or the flirting?'

'No contest. The Lego.' She concentrated on the splashing children.

'Well?' said Caroline, after a while. 'Do you think he's still gorgeous?'

'Oh, he's definitely still gorgeous.'

'And?'

'And I will enjoy having supper with a man who is not my ex-husband, not my relative, not the husband of a friend. Someone I used to know a long time ago. All accompanied by three children and the hostile eleven-year-old chaperone from hell. Let's not complicate the situation any further.'

'So, she's a little frosty. Who wouldn't be?'

They sat in silence for a while, Jess pondering why Kate was hostile. Was this a usual level of hostility, or something more than that? She tried to remember how she'd felt, but the situation had been very different.

'How about Tuesday evening?' said Caroline. 'If it goes well, you can see him again later in the week. In fact, take the kids for tea, and I'll collect them and put them to bed, so you can have a proper evening.'

'In the company of his kids.'

'Yeah, but they're not your responsibility. Give him a ring.'

'What? Now?'

'Why not? He's unlikely to have made alternative arrangements since you saw him.'

'Maybe.' A long dormant fluttering in her stomach reminded her of occasional phone calls to Sam, or James, or one of the boys. The fear of not being recognised. The fear of sounding stupid. The terrible fear of not being able to stop talking.

It was a case of controlling her imagination. One of the problems in her teens had been trying to be normal with these strange beings, these boys who were bigger and louder, overwhelming the room with their physical presence, their testosterone. Then she'd felt self-conscious.

Convinced that she was ridiculous and stupid in the eyes of others. Bathed in sweat the whole time. Now she knew no one else was thinking about her half as much as they were thinking about themselves. And that she'd gather much more information if she could just manage to focus on what was happening beyond herself.

Jess swung her feet onto the grass. 'When is early enough for a Pimm's?'

'Now?' said Caroline, not bothering to look at her watch.

Jess poured Pimm's from the bottle she'd brought into two glasses, added ice, lemonade, and a couple of sliced grapes from the fruit bowl.

She took Caroline a glass. 'OK if I try now? Although who knows what I've done with my mobile.'

'Go ahead. Free local calls on the landline. Use the one upstairs if you want peace and quiet.'

'No, no. Here's fine.' She went inside, picked up the phone and dialled.

After two rings a very young sounding voice said, 'Hello, Emma speaking.'

'Hello Emma, it's Jess here. Ben and Millie's mum.'

'Hello. Are you coming to tea?'

'One day this week I hope. Is your dad there?'

Jess could hear Emma shout, 'Dad' and then immediately start talking in a normal voice. 'He's right here.'

'Thank you,' said Jess, taking a sip of her drink.

'Jess? How are you?' Sam's voice was close and intimate in her ear.

She transferred the phone to the other ear. 'We've been sitting in deck chairs in the garden, and I'm ashamed to say I already have a glass of Pimm's in my hand.'

'Really. I try and get through Evensong before I start on the booze on a Sunday.'

Focus on what he's saying. Not her dry throat, her hammering heart, the pulsing blood in her ears. 'Who looks after the kids?'

'Teenage daughter of my neighbours. When are you coming for supper?'

She took another sip of her drink. 'How about Tuesday evening?'

'I look forward to it.' His voice sounded deep and warm. She pushed the receiver away.

'OK, see you Tuesday.'

'Yep—oh, Jess? Why don't you give me your number in case I need to call you?'

She gave him her mobile, Caroline's home number, and put the phone down.

'What was the little squeal for?' said Caroline, when Jess sank into her deckchair again.

'What squeal?' She sat up quickly.

'You let out a little squeal as you put the phone down.'

'I did not. Don't you start.'

'What do you mean?'

'I mean I need to stay focused on the present. On the moment. Not on my imaginary life.' Surely it wasn't this easy? It certainly wasn't in London. Her social life had plummeted off a cliff when Tom left. Lone women didn't fit into the supper gatherings she had enjoyed and Tom had endured with several other local couples. She knew they continued, and once or twice—on special occasions such as New Year's Eve—she'd be included. There were the infrequent drinks with her girlfriends. It was not that she didn't want to go out with them, but by the time she'd paid a babysitter (even for the barest minimum of two hours, which meant she'd be walking home on her own, long before the others) and bought a bottle of wine, her carefully budgeted allowance for the whole month—dictated by Tom's meagre financial contributions—would have disappeared.

She'd done a smattering of freelance jobs since he'd left, but she had fewer and fewer contacts in the event management world, and anything that came up tended to be intense and time-pressured, hardly suitable for a single parent with two small children.

And none of these opportunities allowed for meeting new men. Jess knew several single women—unmarried, divorced, separated—and yet there weren't any equivalent men.

So, repressing that squeal as she put down the phone to Sam was too hard. A date, of sorts, with a man who had been in and out of her life for almost three decades, with whom she now had more in common than ever.

No. This tight ball of excitement lodged itself in her chest and threatened to escape in bubbles of laughter from deep in her throat. Only a long draught of Pimm's could keep it down.

'Tell me, this imaginary life. Taken all your clothes off already, have you?' said Caroline.

'What?'

'You heard me.'

SAM

As usual, the house was ablaze with lights when Sam returned from Evensong. 'Suki, I thought your generation was meant to be concerned about the state of the planet.'

'Sorry.' She didn't look up from the American sitcom she and Emma were watching.

'How long has this episode got to go?' He knew from long experience the challenge of extricating any of his children from the middle of a television programme. 'Time for bed straight after this, Em. I know there's no school tomorrow, but you're at tennis camp in the morning.'

'Da-ad,' said Emma.

'Don't you start. Where's your sister?' Josh would be glued to a screen somewhere.

He walked through the house switching lights off and found Kate lying on her bed in the gathering dusk. 'What's up?'

'Nothing.'

Sam leant against the door frame and folded his arms. 'Don't forget we've all got an early start in the morning. I need to drop you off before 9 a.m.'

Kate rolled to face the wall.

'You didn't tell me much about the party. Was it fun?'

'It was fine.'

'Katie, you could tell me if there was anything wrong. I might be able to help.'

'It's fine.'

'Or you could talk to Mum.'

'Yeah, right.'

'You know she'd listen,' said Sam, uncertain of what he was claiming for his ambitious ex-wife. He could make out Kate's thin shoulder blades and knobbly spine through her t-shirt.

'Shall I run you a bath?'

'I'll have a shower.'

He felt utterly useless. How had she closed up so entirely, so quickly? 'Well, I'm here if you need me.'

After he'd paid Suki, verified that all electronic screens were off and the children were in their respective beds, or at least in the right bedrooms, Sam grabbed a beer from the fridge and sat outside on the wooden bench. In the fading light, the unkempt areas of the garden took on a more picturesque aspect, and for once all was quiet.

Even with the rather grubby cushion, it was not a comfortable seat. Maybe it was time to upgrade his parents' heavy wooden garden furniture to something more modern—one of those garden sofas the girls could lounge on, perhaps.

Was it having Jess here that made him see the house through fresh eyes? Somehow any sort of house improvements plummeted to the bottom of his endless list. The house fulfilled a function, and there was enough space for him and the children to have their own bedrooms. That felt good, particularly as they'd lost the home they'd spent the first part of their lives in when he and Elizabeth separated. She had opted for a modern house which, while not too far from the schools, had small rooms. Or so he'd heard from the children.

He raised the bottle to his lips but it was empty. He sighed. Time to eat something rather than inhale another beer. His mobile vibrated in his back pocket.

James. He let it ring, looking down the garden, past the shrubs and hedge, to the Common beyond. In the darkness, he could still see the majestic branches of the large oak in the centre of the expanse of grass. He shook his head, walked into the kitchen, and locked the back door.

JESS

Jess spent two days striving to be present. Not wanting to indulge that growing connection with her younger, pre-married self. Slipping past the clichés of 1980s pop music—Duran Duran, ABC, The Specials, Madness—and creating a soundtrack to her memories that was being applied retrospectively. She had not heard any Nick Drake in her teens. And yet, no song better than 'Northern Sky' seemed to evoke her experience of first love, of longing and waiting and antipation, and the idea of holding emotion in the palm of her hand…

Late Tuesday afternoon, she changed into linen cut-off trousers and a cotton shirt. An outfit that was comfortable and covered a multitude of sins. Would make her feel good if she hadn't been so nervous.

She and the children walked up the hill to Sam's house. Supper with a man she used to know. With whom she had a lot in common. Divorce. Kids. Loneliness?

Emma opened the front door. 'Dad's doing a barbecue.'

Jess followed the children through the house into the garden.

'There you are.' Sam approached her, barbecue implements in his hands, as Kate pushed past and disappeared into the kitchen. He kissed Jess's cheek.

'I brought some wine.'

'Great. Don't mind Kate. She's very uptight about how I spend my time, and with whom.'

'Dad, are we having sausages?' Josh shouted, from the

bottom of the garden, where he and Ben were already deciding who should bat and who should bowl.

'Of course.' Sam turned back to the barbecue. 'Do you want to stick the wine in the fridge? Same place as always.'

Jess's mind raced back to an evening spent in Sam's kitchen, when something completely unexpected had happened that never happened again. Not with Sam. And in the end she began to wonder if she'd imagined it, although she knew she hadn't. She couldn't forget her surprise, so intense she'd almost exclaimed aloud.

'There's beer in the fridge. Pimm's, if that's your favourite at the moment. Soft drinks. White wine. Red on the side. Help yourself.'

'Thanks. You?'

He waved a bottle of beer.

The image stuck in her head as she retreated into the cool shade of the large kitchen: Sam grinning in faded shorts and a short-sleeved checked shirt, shading his eyes from the sun. Strong brown legs. Bare feet.

Emma must have taken Millie upstairs to see her room. Jess grabbed a bottle of beer and took it outside.

'Cheers.' He clinked his bottle with hers.

'Cheers. What can I chop?' she said, at the same time as Kate, standing just inside the kitchen, said, 'Dad.'

'Kate.' He shrugged almost imperceptibly at Jess. 'Come and say hello.'

'Hello,' mumbled Kate, staying firmly inside. 'How soon can I eat? I've got stuff to do.'

'It's nearly ready. What do you need to do?'

'Stuff.' She retreated into the hall.

'I'm sorry,' he said. 'Ordinarily I'd have bawled her out for interrupting you, but she's so angry at the moment, I'm trying not to alienate her completely.'

'It's fine. Shall we eat together?'

'I was planning you and I would eat afterwards, but—what do you think?'

'Might be easier if we all ate together. Then you spend less time slaving over a hot barbecue.'

'Yes. It's not…I don't know.'

'You're the host. You decide.'

He took a swig of beer. 'OK. Let's eat together. We can have pudding later.' He put his bottle on the table and turned back to the barbecue. 'You have no idea how refreshing that is. Elizabeth doesn't allow other people to make decisions.'

Jess winced. In the beginning, one of Tom's biggest complaints was that she would offer him a choice about something, already having a preference, and then try to sweep him into her way of thinking. She quickly learned that was not going to work.

Sam swung round to face her. 'What?' He watched her until she met his eyes.

'Nothing.'

'No, I'm not letting you get away with that. You used to stop talking just when things were interesting.'

'I did not.'

He raised an eyebrow and waited.

'I was petrified.'

'Of what?'

'Saying the wrong thing. Sounding stupid. Not being able to stop talking. Ever.'

'Why?'

'I don't know.' She interlaced her hands, left thumb over right, right over left, just for the sensation. 'I didn't like my voice. I sound too much like my mum.'

'That's bad?'

'Do you remember we rang you one Christmas Eve

when you were on call? You must have just qualified.'

'I do.'

She eyed him briefly. 'You recognised me within about three words.'

'I remember.'

Jess recalled the thrill of him saying, 'Hello, Jessica,' before she'd even finished asking to speak to Doctor Sam Rushmore. She had felt flushed and so alive, absurdly flattered he'd recognised her voice. She concentrated on her fingers, the air in the garden heavy and close.

They sat at the table in the garden to eat. Jess gave up talking after being interrupted by Kate for the fourth time. She totally understood Sam not wishing to alienate his daughter, but Kate was obviously feeling that things between her father and Jess were a little too cosy. As indeed they were. All that relaxed cooking and chatting, not to mention layer upon layer of sexy imagery—his husky voice, tousled hair, brown hands, deep dark eyes—and now he was nudging her with his knee. Too disturbing to her equilibrium, which had not been helped by the beer and two glasses of white wine. She moved her knee away. Knees again, she thought, catapulting her back to that Friday evening so many years ago, when, in a crowded kitchen, sitting drinking coffee, Sebastian had turned the lights off and Sam had put his hand on her knee.

She shook herself back into the present, the side of her knee still tingling. It must have been a mistake. (Had that other time been a mistake, she wondered for the zillionth time.) She didn't look directly at him, not wanting to give Kate anymore ammunition.

Caroline collected Ben and Millie so that Jess could stay a little longer, sitting on the bench, looking down the garden as the light slowly faded. They talked about her parents, his mum, summer holiday plans, and were now dwelling on the past. Whatever footing their rekindled friendship was on, the relative familiarity in their teens could fool Jess into thinking they knew each other better than they did.

The scents of the barbecue had blown away on the breeze, and Jess could smell the honeysuckle on the wall behind her. 'Do you remember all those parties in people's cellars?' She picked up her wine glass.

'What, four hour snogs without getting much past second base?' Sam laughed.

Jess grimaced. 'What does that mean, anyway? And why would we use American baseball terminology?'

'Second base was getting her bra undone, preferably one-handed.'

'Virtually impossible. You need both hands.'

Pause.

She laughed when he didn't reply. 'Wipe that smug grin off your face.'

He held up his hands. 'I'm saying nothing.'

Her eyes flicked to the dark blue sky. 'They were golden years. That's what they felt like.'

'Maybe that's what they feel like looking back on them.' He glanced sideways at her.

Jess said nothing.

'Anyway, what about Uni? Aren't those meant to be your golden years?' he asked.

'Not for me.'

'How many people are you still in touch with from college?'

'Two. Sort of.'

'And school?'

'Six.'

He waited.

'You know me. Obsessed with the past. Can't let go. Golden years. David Bowie was even the bloody soundtrack.' She twisted her shaking hands together.

'*Changes I*,' said Sam. 'Great album.'

She felt his eyes on her for a minute.

'College is in the past as well. Why not keep in contact with more people?' he said.

'Dad, Josh needs you.' Emma shouted down the stairs, easily audible from the open upstairs windows.

Sam sighed. 'Hold that thought.' He disappeared into the shadows of the kitchen. Jess stood up to take the empty bowls and glasses inside.

Get a grip. What was it about Sam? Was it just a physical thing? Or the novelty? The unrelated male again. Or possibly it was the history thing. The intensity of first love, or first lust. That had never quite been dealt with, got over, finished, put to bed. There was an analogy.

How many nights had she lain in bed in her parents' house, contemplating Sam Rushmore, analysing his behaviour towards her, his words, his look, his touch? But the question itself seemed dangerous. Not that she made a habit of re-examining the past. No point. It was all over and done with and the best thing she could do was forget about it and move on. All she had to do was stay focused on the here and now.

'Sorry about that,' said Sam, coming into the unlit kitchen from the light of the hall. 'How about coffee? Tea?'

The sudden light as he flicked the switch kept her frozen in the middle of the room, still clutching the bowls, the wine glasses shattered on the wooden floor. She'd tripped in the half-light, her unsteady hands too full, too late to save them, paralysed and unable to think what to do. She tried to blink back the tears illuminated by the sudden light.

He swivelled back to the door.

She shut her eyes, and kept them shut as she heard the door close, footsteps come towards her, then gentle fingers closed over her cold hands and pried the bowls from her rigid grasp. Warm arms moved her backwards, away from the broken glass, pulling her to a warm wall of chest, holding her, hands on her back, her neck, stroking her hair.

They stood like that as the minutes ticked by, Sam's hands soothing her like a frightened animal. She swallowed hard. She had to get out of there while she could still walk.

He began to stroke the nape of her neck. Lazily. Almost absentmindedly. Jess's heart beat fiercely against her ribs—so loudly, surely he could feel it—and she couldn't breathe, every inhalation and exhalation magnified. She could think of nothing but his steady breathing, the rise and fall of his chest, the warmth in his arms as he held her. She felt the sweat between her shoulder blades.

'Sorry.' Her voice sounded surprisingly normal as she peeled herself away. 'I'll replace the glasses.'

'There's no need. They were cheap.'

She felt in her pockets for a non-existent handkerchief. 'I think I'd better go.'

'I'll make us both a cup of coffee. Or tea.' He handed her a clean white folded handkerchief from his back pocket. 'Go and sit in the garden.'

'I'd rather—'

'You want to talk. Fine. You don't want to talk. Fine. But don't go yet. It's only half past nine.'

She considered contradicting him for a second. But she was so tired. Bone-tired. Fatigue had become part of her. Less effort to sit in the garden, in the last vestiges of twilight, watching more and more stars come out, listening to someone else make the drinks for a change.

SAM

Sam stuck his head out the window as the kettle boiled. 'What'll you have?'

'Do you have peppermint tea?' asked Jess.

'Hang on.' He found a fruit selection in the cupboard and sniffed the packet. It had been there for a while. 'Camomile and spearmint's the closest I've got.'

So, she probably didn't want to talk. He winced as he recalled those sobs. Well, he could do patience. But if she was a patient he'd want to rule a few things out. He wondered how much practical support she had from Tom. Did she get any time off?

Maybe it was stress and exhaustion. The reunion. Never fun when you're not looking your best. He tried to remember what she'd been like in her teens. Thin. Pale. Not much change there then. Now it was as if the life was draining out of her.

'Tea.' He put their mugs on the table and sat beside her.

'Thank you.' She nursed her mug. Her foot bounced under the table. He resisted the temptation to reach across and put his hand on her knee to still it.

'I'm sorry,' she said, eventually. 'I hate being weepy and clingy.'

'Don't worry.' He regarded her over the top of his mug. 'A bit of weeping, not much clinging at all.' He jolted in shock. What? The one that got away—was that why she fascinated him? That and general sexual frustration. His mind swerved over a still raw and painful incident in April, but he yanked his consciousness back to the present. *Don't go there.*

There was definitely something attractive about Jess. He didn't want to contemplate the idea that her pallor, her slight air of vulnerability might make him feel virile and manly again; useful in a way he no longer anticipated. He put his mug down and let out a long breath. The bouncing foot had stopped. For the first time since she arrived, Jess was sitting still beside him.

'Elizabeth's got the children this weekend. Come for supper Friday night.' Another opportunity to feed her some red meat. He winced. Sometimes he didn't like himself much at all.

She met his eyes for a millisecond. 'I'm driving home on Saturday.'

'I know. Leave the children behind and have a relaxing evening. Just sitting. No carrying glasses.'

She smiled at that.

'Dad,' said Kate.

Jess jumped.

How long had Kate been there? He walked her into the hall, telling her to go to bed. When he came back, Jess had bravely brought the mugs back in, gathered her cardigan and bag.

'I should be going.'

'Could I do one thing?' He took her arm to stand under the overhead light. 'Look up?'

She looked up and he put a light finger underneath each eye in turn, and pulled the lower lid down. Very pale.

'Do me a favour?' He looked directly at her.

'Yes, doctor?'

'Go and see your GP when you get home. Have a blood test for anaemia.'

She took a step back and he dropped his hands.

'Do you eat properly?' he said.

'When I get the time. It's hassle cooking for one.'

'I know. But you need to eat. Red meat. Green vegetables.'

'Hence the steak and spinach?'

He shrugged, palms upturned. 'I'm a doctor. If you look after yourself, you'll feel better. Not exhausted all the time. I'll be ringing you for updates, I'm warning you.'

'There's no need. Thank you for supper and everything.'

'My pleasure.' He followed her into the hall and opened the front door, conscious that Kate might be loitering on the landing.

'Ring me about Friday.' He kissed Jess's cheek. 'Let me know you're back safe.'

'It's only a few streets away. Ten minutes at the most.'

'But it's dark out there. If I didn't have a house full of children, I'd walk you home.'

'Which would be totally unnecessary.'

'Humour me. Call my mobile if you like.'

She pulled her mobile out of her bag and programmed his number into it, before she faded down the steps into the darkness.

Sam was putting the dishwasher on when Rob rang on the landline. He scanned for his mobile. Jess must be nearly back by now.

'I'm coming to Manchester to do an interview tomorrow and I'm buying dinner,' Rob said.

'Oh. Any chance you could give me more notice one of these days? I've got the kids this week.'

'Where's the bitch from hell? Can't she have them?'

'That's my ex-wife you're talking about. She's on a course.'

'Then get a babysitter. There's a new restaurant I thought we'd try.'

'I'll see what I can do. Who are you interviewing?' His mobile rang. 'Hang on, Rob.' He reached for the handset. 'Hi Jess. Back safe?'

'Yes. Thank you. For a lovely evening. Sorry about—'

'Don't worry about it. Call me about Friday.'

'OK. Good night.'

'Good night.' He put the other phone—held to his chest —to his ear. 'Rob. You were saying.'

'Who was that?'

'Jessica Lamb,' he said, before he thought.

'Really? What's she like now?'

'Tall. Pale. Very pale.'

'And interesting? Doesn't she have a husband and children? Not that that's necessarily stopped me in the past, but you're an ethical son of a bitch. What's she doing ringing your mobile?'

'She's divorced.'

'Really? Another one? This gets more and more interesting. Does she still live in London?'

'Yep. Here for a week's holiday.'

'That's my boy. I knew you could be a fast worker when you needed to be. Give me details.'

'There are no details. She came for supper. With her children. With my children. With Kate, for God's sake.'

'Oh. Maybe I should have a little talk with Katie. Tell her to chill out.'

'Thanks, but no thanks. And don't call her Katie. It's Kate now, or you're a dead man.'

'I see. When are you seeing Jessica again?'

'Who says I'm seeing her again?'

'Your tone of voice. But a word of advice. If you want to

score, remove all children and ex-wives from the scene. I speak as a man who's crashed and burned.'

'Exactly. Why would anyone in his right mind take any advice from you?'

Rob laughed into the phone. 'Admit it, you see me as a role model.'

'Do you want to stay here tomorrow night?'

'Nah. It's a profile for *The Sunday Times*. I get put up in a posh hotel. Well, a hotel, anyway.'

'And who's the lucky victim?' said Sam, reminded of some of the more scathing profiles Rob had written.

'Ask me tomorrow. I'll call to tell you where and when.'

Sam turned off the lights and loped up the stairs. The light was still on in Kate's bedroom. He knocked. 'It's nearly eleven.'

Kate was reading in bed. 'Who was on the phone?'

'Rob.'

Her face brightened. 'Is he coming here?'

'No, I'm going to meet him for dinner tomorrow night, OK?'

'Whatever.' She closed her book and turned the light off.

'Kate,' he began, but then thought better of it. Now was not the time to start an in-depth discussion. He kissed her right ear, the only place not covered by duvet. 'Good night, darling.'

Silence.

JESS

On Thursday, Jess sliced into her left index finger with Caroline's sharpest knife, while cutting onions to go into a bolognaise sauce. She refused to go to A & E, so Caroline zipped to the chemist at the bottom of the road for some steri-strips, which she applied to the wound.

Later, when her mobile rang and Sam's number came up for the second time, Jess swallowed and grimaced.

'Take it in here. There's your tea.' Caroline picked up the other two mugs and headed for the front room.

'I don't want to.' Jess felt about fourteen again. 'I don't know how to say no.'

'Say yes then. Go and have supper. No kids. Enjoy yourself.'

What does that mean? 'Sam. Sorry I didn't call you back.'

'No problem. How are you?'

Confused. Resisting change. 'Fine. You?'

'Fine. I had dinner with Rob, which was illuminating.'

'Is he still misbehaving?'

'I'll tell you all about it tomorrow.'

'About tomorrow. Could we do it another time, perhaps?' Her words echoed in her ear.

'You don't want to come over?'

'It's not that. It's—'

'Jess. Please come and have supper. No kids. Take a break.'

'I don't…' She concentrated on breathing in, breathing out.

'Is Caroline happy to have the kids?'

'Yes.'

'Is she happy for you to come for supper?'

'Yes.'

'Then there's no problem. See you here about seven?'

'OK.'

'Not feeling that I'm bullying you too much?'

'No. Not at all.' She couldn't swallow the lump in her throat. Tom would never have dreamt of asking her that.

'Good. If you're really lucky I'll tidy up *and* cook. See you tomorrow, Jess.'

She held the mobile in the palm of her hand. Encouragement. Persuasion. All on the right side of—but so close to—coercion. She shook her head. Sam Rushmore was a very different man to Tom Deane.

During the ensuing twenty-two hours Jess tried not to think about Friday night. Not entirely successfully. Her imagination veered from one extreme to the other. In one scenario, she confessed to Sam how she'd felt all those years as a teenager—or how she now thought she'd felt—and watched as he backed off rapidly from the sugar-coated Happy Ending of her fantasy. In the other, he confessed his undying love for her, but then insisted on having sex with her, while she felt nothing and the tears coursed down her cheeks. In neither version did the reality of Sam, especially the Sam who'd held her the other night, seem to match the cruel fantasy Sam.

By six-thirty on Friday evening she'd worked herself up into a jittery state. She smoothed down her navy linen dress and slung her navy cardigan round her shoulders.

Make-up or no make-up, she wondered, staring at her pale reflection. She found a lipstick and some blusher, but ended up feeling as foolish as Debra Winger dying of cancer in *Terms of Endearment*, and, like the character, took most of it off again. Better. A hint of blush on her cheeks, and the merest suggestion of colour on her lips. She applied some lipsalve, sprayed on some scent, and ran downstairs.

'Thank you so much for doing this,' she whispered. 'Are they…?'

Caroline looked up from her laptop and nodded towards the front room. 'A film has actually been agreed upon and all four kids are in a row on the sofa. Take a key.'

Jess raised her eyebrows. 'I plan to be back at a very decent time. I'm driving home tomorrow.'

'I know. But have fun.'

'You're so kind. You're not going to sit and work all evening, are you? Philip back soon?'

'I expect so. And I have wine.' She raised her glass, and Jess slipped out.

Walking along the familiar streets bathed in evening sunshine, calmed her down. So much so that when Sam opened the front door she smiled. Just Sam, wearing a blue linen shirt and a lopsided grin.

'You're on time.' He kissed her cheek. 'It saves me the hassle of deciding whether to come and find you if you didn't turn up.'

'Haha. I'm not *that* flaky.' She studied his face as he poured white wine. Was that what he thought of her?

They sat in the garden, and he told her about dinner with Rob and trying to talk to Kate.

'She's so angry with me when she's here. But that's nothing compared with the anger she shows towards her mother.'

'Well, it's a difficult time. She's about to start secondary school. And Elizabeth's job in Liverpool is fairly new, isn't it? Things are uncertain. Different.'

'They're not that uncertain. Elizabeth's made it pretty clear where her priorities lie. The children have always come second to her career, and Kate's not stupid. She can feel that.'

'And she obviously feels very protective towards you.'

'Yes. Thank God Emma picked up the phone when you rang on Sunday.'

'She loves you, and she's frightened. Of change. As we all are.' She looked up and met his eyes.

She looked down the garden. 'Sorry about Tuesday night.'

He waved that away. 'Nothing we can't cope with.'

She inhaled sharply, a gulp of breath—*we*, nothing *we* can't cope with—and blurted out the first thing she could think of. 'The idea of a holiday always seems so appealing, but in reality it's exhausting. Especially when you're sleeping in the same room as your children.'

'I'll bet. Next time, you're welcome to stay here.'

'Be careful, I may just take you up on that.' *Whoops. Internal thought, Jess, not out loud.*

'What happened to your finger?'

'Oh, that. Tried to cut it off while slicing some onions.'

He picked up her hand and examined the cut through the steri-strips. 'Bet that hurt.' He looked up, hair in his eyes.

Jess stopped breathing. 'Oh. Yes. I suppose it did,' she managed, after about a year and a half.

Sam stood up. 'Hungry?'

SAM

He had raced home from the surgery, shoved any extraneous kids' paraphernalia upstairs now they were at their mother's for the weekend, and thrust what clutter he could into cupboards. The kitchen looked pleasingly tidy, and he'd planned the meal with medical precision, to disguise his lack of prowess in the kitchen. Most of it came courtesy of M&S.

'Very impressive,' she said, over an empty bowl. 'Everything seems so organised.'

'Seems is the operative word… I'm constantly catching up, either with the kids or at work. Everything suffers, and I haven't had enough sleep since Kate was born.'

'I have no doubt your patients think they're very lucky you're their doctor.' A faint glow came to her cheeks. 'Anyway, Tom couldn't do all this.'

'What do you mean?'

'He's such a product of his upbringing. Public school, Oxford, straight into a graduate scheme in a big company. He's one of those people who thinks travelling on the tube is beneath him.'

'He never seemed like that. Well, not much.' Sam had only met Tom when the old crowd was back together—often for a wedding—and there had been too many other people to catch up with. He'd seemed pleasant enough, but then Sam recalled a quick image of Tom, his arm tightly around Jess, clamping her to his side. What should have been loving, turned out to have been something else…

'He thinks it's lowering in the way he thinks changing nappies or cooking and cleaning is women's work.'

'I didn't realise it was that bad.'

'Yeah, well, you never want to brag about what a misogynist pig your husband is. He's in a time-warp. Pre-post-feminism. Pre-feminism.'

'Another one of us who doesn't like change. More red wine?'

Jess hesitated, frowning slightly.

'Go on, you've had a meal, not that much left in the bottle.'

'Twist my arm then.' She held out her glass.

He took his eyes off the pouring liquid for a second to study the curve of her arm; shoulder to elbow, elbow to wrist.

'So, tell me more about the missing years.' He moved round the table to sit beside her on the bench, the darkening length of the garden stretching away from them.

'Which missing years?'

'Between Millingham twenty years ago, and now. Tell me about college.'

'Twenty years. Do you think the ties still feel strong because we keep coming back here?'

'Maybe. If I'd stayed in Birmingham when Mum needed more help, I'm sure I'd feel less tied to the place. But most old friends have moved away.'

'Maybe you're just ahead of your time. The first wave of a mass return from the big wide world, and we're all going to end up back here.'

'You feel settled in London?'

'I suppose so. Especially with Ben at school and Millie about to start. I've now lived there longer than I've lived anywhere else.'

'But you're in touch with hardly anyone from college?'

She straightened up.

'Sorry, I didn't mean to pry.' He watched her take a deep breath.

JESS

She glanced sideways at him. In a way it was easier to talk now that he was beside her rather than sitting opposite, but he was still a bit close. She laughed a tight little laugh. 'I look back at myself then and I don't like what I see.'

'Why?' Sam took a sip of wine and put his glass back on the table beside Jess's.

Jess sighed. 'I didn't handle being in London on my own very well. I was very immature.'

'You forget I knew you when you were at college. You weren't so bad.'

'I knew who I was at home. But London was a blank canvas. I didn't have to be me.'

'And you didn't want to be you?'

'You know what they say. If you always do what you've always done, you'll always get what you always got.'

'So what did you do?'

'I tried something different.' She took a big gulp of wine in the silence. Then she glanced at Sam, who caught her eye. As a GP, he must have learnt to suppress any looks of shock.

'Really,' he said, after a while. He seemed quite comfortable with silences. 'Who with?'

Jess's racing pulse had slowed during the silence. It kicked up again. *I've started, so I'll finish.* 'Just boys.'

'Did you like it?'

'It made me understand I was not a complete failure with the opposite sex.'

Sam frowned. 'You were never a complete failure with the opposite sex.'

'Yes I was. I couldn't work out how to have a normal relationship.' She stopped. 'I gave out the wrong signals. My mother started wondering if I was a lesbian.'

'Were you ever?'

She laughed. This wasn't so bad. 'I like men's forearms and solidity too much.'

'Ah.' Sam glanced down at his own forearms.

'Yep, you're right up there with the best of them. Tall, dark and handsome. Just my type.' She laughed.

Sam joined in. 'Yeah, right. The signal I remember was that you didn't want to go out with me.'

'My point precisely. I was either in love, or possibly in lust with you—I confuse the two—for about seven years.' She focused on her glass. Well, she'd said it now.

'No you weren't. You're bathing the past with a fictitious rosy glow.'

'Hey, you don't know.' She whipped round to face him on the bench. 'You don't know what happened. What I think. What I feel.' She jabbed his chest with her finger. Substantial, he felt, and closer than she had realised. She squinted back down the dark garden.

'So you're at Uni. Meeting all these boys who know nothing about you. Did you want a boyfriend?'

'First person I tried to get off with I really liked. But he was still madly in love with his girlfriend from home.'

'So then what?'

'I made some bad, stupid choices. But I was so pleased they liked me. Sounds so pathetic now.'

'No, it doesn't.' He picked up her hand and held it in his

own browner, warmer one. Flutterings of sensation shot up Jess's arm, radiated across her chest. 'Your parents had just split up, after years of your father behaving very badly.'

She turned in surprise.

'I think what you did is totally understandable.' He squeezed her hand.

She swallowed. How had he remembered that all these years?

'So how do you feel about sex now?'

'I haven't the faintest idea.' She laughed. Somehow talking about the past was less embarrassing. 'It's been far too long.'

'Really?'

'Well, Millie's nearly four and a half. By the time she was born, things were deteriorating on many fronts.'

Sam gave her hand another squeeze and let it go. He settled back in the bench, stretching his legs out in front of him, his upper arm now firmly against Jess's. Warm. There.

'So, serial monogamy through college?'

'What?' She hoped they might have changed the subject. 'Who's to say I was monogamous?'

'You're not the type to carry on while you're going out with someone, or married.'

'How can you be so sure?'

'Come on, Jess. I've known you for well over twenty years.'

'We knew each other a long time ago. I've hardly seen you at all for the best part of ten years.'

'And what's so horrible about you now?'

She sighed. 'Eventually I met Tom.'

'And before then? Boyfriends?'

'Yeah, the guy I tried to go out with at the beginning of my first term. Went out with him in my final year.' She swirled the last of the wine in her glass and took a sip.

'And?' Sam picked up the bottle and tilted it at her glass.

Jess shook her head. 'Wasn't so interested by then.'

'Is this a pattern? Like them until they like you?' He poured the end of the bottle slowly into his glass and finished it off.

'Possibly,' she said in a small voice.

'Tell me about Tom.'

'We met through work. He was a client, and he seemed so wise. Ten years older than me. He was so sure about what he wanted. Very attractive.'

'No hope for me then.' He gathered the empty bottle and glasses. 'Go on.'

'It was about lust. I mistook it for love. I think maybe that's our family failing.'

'Ah.'

'Anyway. Stop fishing.'

'Sorry?' He blinked at her.

'You know you're attractive to women. Bet all those receptionists' hearts beat faster when you're in the building.'

'Not my patients. Couldn't tell you.' Sam headed inside and switched on the kettle.

Jess followed him and leant against the kitchen cupboards while he assembled mugs and spoons. When he stretched up for teabags on the top shelf, revealing a smooth brown midriff, Jess's stomach disappeared as if she'd once again contemplated stepping off a tall building.

'So, what did you tell Tom?'

'About the past? Not enough. But that's another story.'

'While I think about it, give me your home number and email address.' He found a pad of paper and a pen, and put on thin metal-rimmed reading glasses. Very Clark Kent.

Jess distracted herself by concentrating on making her

writing as legible as possible, blue biro on lined paper, listening to hot water being poured into mugs. She had a sense of her heightened awareness, tingling nerve endings, flushed cheeks, fluttering fingers, full lips. Following him back outside, she admired the breadth of his shoulders, the way his hair curled over the collar of his shirt. Honestly, what was she thinking?

'What have you got to rush back for?' He put down their mugs.

'Sorry?' She tried to pull her mind off the beauty of his hands.

'Why are you going back tomorrow?'

'Back in time to go to church on Sunday, I suppose. And trying not to outstay our welcome.'

'You know you can always come here. I mean tomorrow, if you want to stay another night.' The way he focused on her was hard to resist. Made her think that her romantic life was not as dead as she'd imagined.

'It's a lovely idea, Sam,' she said slowly. 'But Ben in particular's not very good with changes of plan. He likes to know what's happening when, and we're going home via Tom's parents in Stratford tomorrow. But thank you.'

'What about the rest of the summer?'

'Ben's doing a tennis course next week. Then Tom's got them for a few days. I might take them to my parents after that, and then North Devon for a week, end of August.'

'Where?'

'Croyde. Friends have a cottage there.'

'I'm going to be somewhere between there and Padstow with the kids the Bank Holiday weekend. We could meet up.'

'Anna's hoping to come down for a few days, so it could be a nostalgia-filled reunion. Just like old times.' He was so close she could just turn her face and...she put a hand to her chest, as if she could still the thumping. 'And you?'

'Yes?'

'No girlfriend or anything?'

'Ah. Long story.'

'Too long?'

'I'll tell you about it sometime.'

'I'll hold you to that.'

'When you've been to your GP and had that blood test.'

She frowned. 'I feel fine.'

He raised an eyebrow.

'Well, nothing a week in bed—a week of sleep wouldn't cure.' She bit her lip.

'Quite.'

SAMUEL: age 15

Another Friday night and choir practice finished with a glorious Vaughan Williams anthem. They spilled out of the vestry, from light to dark.

'OK, what's the deal?' said James.

'We could go to my house,' said Sam. 'As long as we're in the cellar.'

'Cool,' James replied. 'Stella, what about you lot?'

'Let's find Jessie and Ruth—see if they could come for a while?' Stella turned to Sam.

'Great.' Sam grinned.

The wind was particularly fierce. Sam wrapped his scarf round his neck, tucking the ends into his jacket. The clock face on the square tower showed nine exactly.

Jessica and Ruth appeared, silhouetted against the glow of the streetlight. A proper smile when Jessica said hello. Progress.

He discovered—when they settled down in the cellar, mugs of tea or coffee in hand—that Jessica was much more animated while walking. Now conversation was stilted. She seemed too self-conscious. Ruth made more of an effort with him, although she was watching James—or was it Rob? No, Stella was watching Rob.

'Are you doing anything over the weekend?' Ruth said.

'Going to YF on Sunday,' Sam replied. 'With James, Rob, Sebastian.'

Youth Fellowship was run in Barton Cottage, beside the church, every Sunday evening.

Despite the name, YF had little to do with God. The extent of its involvement with the church seemed to be that two of its members would read the lessons at Evensong one Sunday a month, with, more often than not, one of the leaders having to fill in, due to lack of volunteers.

'Yeah, some of us were thinking of going along,' said Ruth

'You should…it's fun,' he said.

'What sort of things do you do?'

'Oh, play games, have discussions, drink coffee, that sort of thing.'

James stayed behind as everyone bundled themselves back into their coats to brave the October cold. 'What's going on with Jessica?'

'What?'

'Well, is it going anywhere? I don't see you getting any action any time soon.'

'As opposed to you, who has them falling at your feet.' Sometimes Sam wanted to punch James.

'I'm biding my time.' James pushed his arms into the sleeves of his anorak.

'Really.' Sam opened the front door.

'I can understand what you saw in Stella, but with Jessica…she's needy. Prick tease.'

'No, she's not.' He shook his head.

'We'll find someone who's right for you.'

'No, you won't. Go home. It's cold.'

'You'll see. I know you better than you know yourself.'

Once James was the other side of the door, Sam closed it and leant against it, caught off-guard by the cruelty of James's language. It made no sense. How had he made this judgement, about Jessica of all people?

Sam let out a long breath. He'd drunk too much coffee and hadn't even had a decent game of pool. Jessica had smiled in his direction as she left, but there had been no physical contact apart from the slightest touch of fingers as he passed her a mug of tea. When he handed her a cue she had not let their hands meet. Thinking about it, he couldn't work out if that was deliberate on her part or not. He raked his hands through his hair, which did not help his incipient headache. Time to go to bed.

On Sunday Sam and James walked into YF and saw Susannah Richardson for the first time. They turned and caught each other's eyes, grinning.

'Wow,' said James.

She was 'wow' all right. Small and slight, she had straight fair hair cut close to her head, a perfectly symmetrical face, blue eyes, smooth skin, and a great body. It wasn't that she had an amazing figure, but she was sexy somehow. The clothes certainly helped. She was wearing tight blue jeans, ankle boots, a turquoise close-fitting top and a pink bomber jacket. Definitely sexy.

'Who is she?' said Sam.

Stella was behind them. 'That's Susie. She's at our school. Been there since the beginning of term, and her twin brother Tim's at the boys' grammar.'

Sam looked for the first time at the boy beside her. Good looks obviously ran in the family. He had darker, sleek, shiny hair, and the same blue eyes and clear features.

'Twins?' said Sam.

'Yep,' confirmed Stella. 'They're really nice, and they live just off Lake Avenue.'

Lake Avenue was the cul-de-sac that ran from the church

down towards the golf course.

'Whereabouts?' James asked.

'The new houses, not far from you, Sam,' said Stella. 'Come and meet them. They don't know many people yet.'

The rest of the evening passed in a daze. Sam couldn't remember what they did, or who else was there. Did Jessica and Ruth come? He thought maybe they did, but he and James hardly left Susie's side. She giggled, but not in an annoying way, her blue eyes were strangely calming, and she didn't quite look up at them through her lashes.

There was no chance to talk to her properly; any attempts were constantly interrupted, not least by James. Having a brother, Sam couldn't insist on walking her home. All he could do was accompany them part of the way, before he had to turn off to his house. Tim eventually took his sister's arm to propel her away from Sam, along Lake Avenue.

'Come on,' said Sam, hanging up his cassock at the end of choir practice. Any moment he could find himself face-to-face with Susannah, after five long days.

James grabbed his anorak. 'Let's see who's out there.'

Sam hunched his shoulders against the wind as they walked over to Ruth, Jessica, Anna and Rob.

'Hi, guys, lovely weather,' James said.

'No. Weather is here, wish you were lovely,' said Rob.

They giggled inordinately.

Sam turned and saw Susie and Tim appear. They glowed as they walked across the circle of light created by the bright streetlamp.

By then Sam had given up listening to whatever Ruth was saying.

'So, where are we off to?' Susie said.

'We can go to mine.' Sam liked the idea of having Susie in his house.

'Or mine,' James said.

'We haven't got that long, so we don't want to go too far,' said the vision of loveliness.

They went to Sam's.

He was vaguely aware that Stella and the others joined them, and that Rob spent quite a while chatting to Anna. She was pretty, with bubbly blond hair tied back from her face. When she smiled or laughed, her eyes practically disappeared they became so crinkly and crescent moon shaped. She snorted as she laughed, which infected Rob and James with laughter too.

Sam spent most of his evening trying to teach Susie to play pool. It was a different experience to offering to help Jessica. Susie didn't mind people watching her. At one point he looked up and met Ruth's gaze. Beside her, Jessica was deathly pale and coughing. She and Ruth went upstairs to find a glass of water.

Sam showed Susie where to put her hands and how to hold the cue. 'Try it like this.'

'Show her.' Rob sniggered.

Sam put his arms about her, holding the cue in front of them both.

'Like this,' he said, his breath so close to her ear, he could see her golden hair stir. Together they bent over the snooker table, Susie warm underneath him. The soft pressure of her body beneath his was intensely arousing.

She was laughing now, her hands fumbling more than could possibly be necessary.

Sam flushed. He really needed some air.

'Who wants coffee?' He turned away and racked his cue.

'I'll help you,' offered Susie.

'After you.' Being polite, he told himself. Nothing to do with watching her backside as she climbed the cellar stairs to the kitchen.

JESS

By the time they arrived home to an empty house on Saturday night, Jess was ready to weep with fatigue. She'd slept very badly, not helped by Sam insisting on walking her back to Caroline's, kissing her on both cheeks, and giving her a full-bodied, and somewhat charged, hug before he left.

The visit to Clarissa and David, Tom's parents, had added to her nagging headache. Clarissa's immaculate, antique-filled house was quite unsuitable for young grandchildren. Jess spent every visit holding her breath. Today was worse than usual. The children were tired and crotchety and neither of them wanted to eat the fussy food Clarissa had prepared. Well, had *removed* from the Waitrose packaging. Salmon and cream cheese mini roulades, exotic cold meats, bread rolls covered in seeds and full of nuts. All of which were rejected by Ben, who, like his mother, just fancied a simple ham sandwich. His face lit up at the sight of mini Florentines until he was put off by the candied peel and nuts.

From an emotional point of view, Jess found these visits difficult because of her guilt. Guilt that she'd never been quite good enough for their elder son. Guilt that the marriage had failed. Guilt that she'd had the nerve to insist on sending her children to state school and vote something other than Conservative.

She'd almost been unspeakably rude to Clarissa, who kept telling Jess how very tired she looked, and how she really should have a proper rest. As there were never any offers of help with the children, only endless monologues about how busy she and David were, and the impossibility of fitting in even a weekend in Venice between now and Christmas, Jess found her patience wearing infinitely thin. It had been a positive relief to bundle the children, armed with Smarties from Granny—why did she insist on showering the children with sweets?—into the car and drive south.

The first half of August was very hot, but Jess didn't miss the school routine, or being ruled by the clock. The heat had her moving early most mornings, and she tried to take some proper exercise every day, jogging down to the park with the children on their bikes. She even had the occasional desire to do some sit-ups.

Sam did ring or text most days. Asking annoying questions about what she was eating and how much sleep she was getting. She tried very hard not to think about him all the time. Sometimes she lasted minutes without imagining what he was doing now this very second.

Tom's six days with the children—Sunday to Friday—turned into Sunday to Wednesday, because of some immoveable meeting on the Thursday. Jess had noble ideas about re-organising the children's bedrooms and sorting out their toys. But in the end she was so unimpressed with Tom—who told her about the immoveable meeting only when he picked up the children—that she lost any motivation she might have had, and spent a large part of each day lying in bed or lounging in the garden, reading romantic novels, missing the children, and trying not to eat chocolate and daydream about Sam.

She ignored the doorbell, kept the answer phone on the whole time, left her mobile switched off, and never even opened her ancient computer. When she realised it had been hours since she last ate, she would manage some cereal, a banana, perhaps some buttered toast.

Wednesday afternoon she had a shower, washed her filthy hair, and tidied the kitchen.

'Shame I have to bring them back early,' said Tom, when he returned the children.

'Yeah.' She knew she should summon the energy to tell him what an inconsiderate, selfish pig he was, but despite the fact that they no longer lived together, that she was no longer answerable to him, she had long ago realised it was kinder to her own sanity not to challenge him in person. It had taken long training to keep calm in his presence.

'Mummy, mummy,' the children shouted, hugging her legs, brandishing new Barbie dolls, boxes of Lego and large bags of sweets. She could feel a very distant anger bubbling low in her gut at the sight of her self-centred ex-husband who thought showering his children with gifts their mother couldn't afford equated to spending time with them.

She opened the front door. 'We're at my mum's next week and then on to Devon.'

'Fine,' said Tom, already checking a message on his beeping mobile. 'I'll see them in September. Bye, kids.'

Millie clung very tightly to Jess's leg. She transferred one arm to Tom's leg, forcing him to come nearer. 'Don't go, Daddy.'

'Got to, sugar plum. Send me a postcard.' He bent down and hugged her, his face in her neck for a moment, and then Ben, who was silent. There were some agonising moments as Millie began to howl, and Ben's face crumpled, while Tom got into his car, but then the three of them sat on the sofa in the front room, Jess's arms around the children until all was quiet.

Much later, once they were in bed, Jess returned to the kitchen and listened to her messages, while she hung the children's washing on the drying rack.

'You seem to have disappeared,' Sam said. 'Please let me know you're all right.'

She found herself pacing as she rang his home number.

'Hello?'

'The children have been with Tom.'

'Oh. OK. Are you all right?'

'I... It's like you said. The house is too big without them. Just wanted...to let you know...' She talked too fast, but he cut her off.

'Jess.' His voice was so gentle it brought a lump to her throat. 'How are you?'

She couldn't think of anything sensible and distancing to say. 'Tom was meant to have them for the whole week. But when he arrived he said he could only have them till today. I knew I should have gone away, then he couldn't have pulled this at the last minute.'

'You must be furious.'

She blinked, trying to remember what fury felt like. She'd battened down her emotions around Tom so successfully that proper anger felt like a distant memory.

'What did you do while they were away?'

She sighed. 'Nothing.'

'Was it relaxing?'

'Not really. I feel guilty I didn't use my time more productively.' She laughed bitterly.

'When was the last time you had a proper lie-in?'

'Apart from this week?' She tried to think. 'I had a long weekend at Easter.'

'So don't beat yourself up about it. God, Jess, if you didn't have a few lazy days you'd have a break-down. Everyone needs to do nothing sometimes.'

'Thank you, doctor.'

'I'm not being a doctor.'

The lump in her throat came back.

'Are you eating anything decent, or am I going to have to come and feed you?'

'I'm fine. Perhaps you don't realise I'll have to wear a swimming costume on the beach.'

'Proper food for the next ten days. And I expect you to return my calls a bit quicker next time. I'm going grey here.'

'What do you mean, going grey?'

'Even greyer than I am already.'

SAM

Sam pulled open the front door. 'What's the big hurry?'

'What took you so long?' James stepped past him into the hall.

'Sorry, I was on the phone. What's going on?'

'Last night in Mum's house. The agent gets the keys in the morning.'

'Oh. How do you feel about that?'

James stared at him. 'Are you going to offer me a beer or what?'

'Sure.' Sam followed him into the kitchen, grabbed two bottles from the fridge and handed one to James.

James nodded and took a long draught. 'How do I *feel* about it? What the hell's wrong with you?'

'How do Alison and Stuart feel about it, then?'

'Everyone's used to the idea. Mum's settled. She's warm and fed and has company.'

'My mum's better where she is, too.' She was well cared for, and if a quick hello during a GP visit to Barton House often felt rather like an after-thought, at least he saw her regularly. He should make more effort to take the children, but that was another stress to shoehorn into a busy weekend, and just the sort of thing that might put him even more at odds with Kate. Not what he needed.

'We need to go back to the house. Now.'

Sam looked at his watch. Twenty to four on a Sunday afternoon. 'I've got Evensong.'

'They don't need you for another hour.'

'Look, James, it's all good. We can sit in the garden in peace. The kids are at Elizabeth's—'

'I thought you'd understand. We need to go back.' James held his gaze until Sam put down his beer and turned away.

Why did he feel the need to stay on the right side of James after all these years? Wasn't it time he relinquished the role of eternal peacekeeper? He took a breath. 'For Stuart?'

'Don't be stupid. You and me. Now.'

Fifteen minutes later, they stood on the patio and surveyed the oak tree.

'Come on.' James set off across the grass and Sam followed. It was much cooler under the shadow of the large branches above them. The blue sky filtered in and out of Sam's vision as he looked up through the green leaves, some already papery, rustling in the slight breeze.

'Stay there.' James backed up and took several photos on his phone of Sam under the tree.

Sam swallowed. Shook his head fractionally. 'You could have warned me, I'd have put on a more flattering t-shirt.'

James shrugged.

'Do you really think that's necessary?' said Sam.

'Insurance policy. Conservative Central Office doesn't like skeletons in closets. So. Who were you on the phone to?'

'What? You're not making any sense.'

'Voice from the past? I bumped into Stella. She told me about the reunion. Seemed to think you might have bumped into Jessica.'

Sam clenched his hands into fists. 'I did. It was good to see her again.'

'Really. She's not a needy divorcee?'

'No. Really not.'

'Too much hassle for you, though. Single mother and whining kids. Still living in London?'

'What about you? I know how hard it's been since Raoul…since he died…but that was a long time ago...'

James walked towards Sam, into the shade of the tree. 'That was a *very* long time ago. Things are entirely different now.'

'OK.' Sam stepped back. 'Is there someone new?'

'There is. Say goodbye. It's time to go.'

Having the bass part to focus on during Evensong, including two Purcell settings and a tricky Psalm, took Sam's mind off his surreal afternoon.

He hoped James had found someone who could stand up to him. Really, he was becoming weirder and weirder. Maybe it was just that Sam didn't see as much of him as he used to. They'd gone through school and university as close friends, and even when he'd been consumed with staying alive as a junior doctor, they'd spent time together. But now James was commuting between Oxford and London, and finally had his mother settled, he was less likely to spend much time in Barton. Perhaps—given this afternoon's events—that was a good thing.

The way James had questioned him about Jess made him feel uncomfortable. Not to mention taking those photos.

Hopefully he could get back into a safe routine this week. No interruptions. Work. Cricket on the TV. Peace.

JESSICA: age 15

'Whisky's better. Gin's disgusting. Tastes like aftershave,' Jessica said.

'How do you know what aftershave tastes like?' James moved away from Jess. 'I hope you don't have a really strong sense of smell.'

'Why? What are you wearing?' She leant forward and sniffed. A boy. A male body. *Keep talking. Stop thinking about what Sam and Susie might be doing in the dark sitting room next door*.

James exchanged looks with Ruth. 'How much has she had to drink?'

Ruth grinned. 'I think she's on a mission.'

Jess took another swig of cider. Tried hard not to choke, swallowed, pressed her chest.

'Good job we're on the heavy stuff.' He drained his paper cup of cider. 'I'm going to find some more.'

They were in the hall of Caroline's house. Her parents had wisely retreated upstairs, and the downstairs rooms thronged with teenagers.

Jessica watched James stop to talk to Stella and Anna, in the doorway to the kitchen. Sebastian squeezed past them and approached. He spoke as someone opened the door to the sitting room, which pulsed to the beat of Blondie. People were dancing, mostly girls, although Jessica spotted Rob among them before the door closed.

Sebastian spoke again. 'Thursday.'

'Thursday?' Jessica stared at him.

'Yeah, what was your Dad doing on Thursday?' Sebastian said.

She blinked.

'Where was he? What was he doing?'

'I don't know—working?' Her dad was a television director and producer.

'Oh—he wasn't out with anyone?'

James returned with a nearly full bottle of cider. He handed it to Ruth and made for the sitting room.

'What do you mean?' Jessica's head began to pound. What secret was Sebastian about to spill?

He took a swig of cider and shoved his cup against the bottle Ruth held for some more.

'I thought maybe I saw him…' He hesitated.

Jessica focused on him. 'Where?'

'Well, I went to the Royal Northern College. They had a concert performance of *Idomeneo*.' He paused. 'Mozart opera, idiots. Anyway, I thought maybe I'd seen him and the woman who works for him—what's her name?'

'Diane?' Jessica pressed the flat of her hand against her forehead.

'It was a bit odd… I would have said hello but he looked like he didn't want to be seen or something… I wondered—'

Jessica stared at him, aware of Ruth's focused scrutiny. She moistened her dry lips, took another sip of her drink.

'I'm sure there's a perfectly good explanation,' said Ruth. 'They were working…'

'But she's his PA. Why would they go to a concert?' Jessica's bottom lip quivered, so she swiftly bit down on it.

'I'm sure it's fine. Your parents are all right, aren't they?' said Ruth.

Jessica blinked several times. 'They're having an affair, aren't they?'

Sebastian said nothing.

'Why don't you sit down?' Ruth took Jess's arm and led her to the stairs, where they both sat down.

The throbbing pain had moved to the back of Jessica's head. 'I'd like another drink.'

'I'll go,' said Sebastian.

Jessica stared at the floor. It looked like cork, but was actually lino.

'You don't know it's true,' said Ruth. 'Sebastian could have got it totally wrong. Your dad may not even have seen him. How good's his eyesight?'

'He does wear reading glasses.' Jess rubbed her eyes.

'There you go. He probably didn't even see Sebastian,' said Ruth.

They sat there until a wary Sebastian reappeared. He brought Jess a glass of water. 'Sorry. No alcohol left.'

'Thanks.' She downed the water. 'I'm going to dance.'

It was dark in the sitting room without the shaft of light from the hall. Human League's 'Don't You Want Me' pulsed on the stereo. Jess began to make out the shapes of couples sitting on chairs and sofas pushed back against the walls.

She had only said that thing about the affair because, in some distorted way, it made her worthy of attention. Her parents weren't going through a bad patch. Marriages did that and survived, didn't they? Her dad was not having an affair. Diane had even babysat occasionally. She was friendly. Anyway, she had a husband and a little girl. That meant her dad and Diane were just colleagues and there'd be a perfectly rational explanation about why they were out together.

Not that she'd ask anyone. She was not about to talk to her dad, and Mum would just laugh and change the subject. And if Jess stayed within earshot, she'd find herself having her hair stroked, and her mum saying, 'I love you, Jessica,' which was the most embarrassing thing ever. It wasn't as if she didn't love her mum, of course she did, she was her mother, but why did she have to say it out loud?

Jess hugged herself in the pulsating gloom. She was acting a part without the plot or the lines, not knowing what to say or think. Except that it hurt. An indefinable ache under her ribs, a low weight in her abdomen, mostly noticed only when she lay on her back in her single bed at night, feeling that only then could she unclench the tight fist of her existence, breathe fully, release her weight into the mattress, and try to sleep.

She gave up trying to identify Susie and Sam. She didn't even know why she was standing there. They weren't anywhere else and she hadn't seen them leave, so they had to be in here, together. Just then the door opened again, and in the corner she saw a glint of reflected light on Susie's shiny trousers. So perfect they looked as if they'd been sprayed on.

Even if Jessica hadn't recognised Sam's shape, his hands and dark shirt, she could have identified him from the glint of white socks between black jeans and sturdy Doc Martens.

She watched in fascination as Sam's hands stroked Susie's back and moulded her bottom. Then she turned away, clenching her fists. When would this bloody song *finish*?

The hall was full of people chatting and starting to leave. Caroline stood at the door, saying goodbye. The kissing of cheeks seemed to have caught on. Ruth made space for Jessica to sit beside her on the stairs.

Sam and Susie appeared, practically doing up buttons and tucking in shirts as they walked. He took her hand and whispered in her ear, then disappeared down the hall. Susie talked to Caroline, her back to the stairs.

Jessica felt she was watching from a great height.

Sam returned with their coats. Then they were gone, out into the darkness, with Tim on one side of Susie, Sam on the other.

JESS

Even the stunning views on the coast road to Croyde couldn't hold back the wave of exhaustion that broke over Jess when they finally reached the house. Always a moment she missed Tom, in spite of herself. Having to pack the car, do all the driving, and unload at the other end, was a marked contrast to the times he'd done the loading, unloading and most of the driving. For the first time in a long while she thought eating something would make her feel better.

They ate cheese on toast on the patio at the back of the house, which belonged to her friends Claire and John. Re-energised by food and fresh air, Ben and Millie were desperate to go to the beach. The sun was hot, even at four o'clock. Laden with towels, they took a hazardous walk down the narrow roads to the beach. Jess sat with the heat on her back, watching the delight on their shining faces as they ran in and out of the sea.

Later, she rang Sam's mobile with her feet up, in front of the television. An August Saturday night of tired, forgettable action movies and repeats.

'The kids and I came down from Oxford yesterday,' he said. 'Guess who's here?'

Jess cradled the phone between chin and shoulder—which did her neck no good whatsoever—and stretched for her glass of wine. 'Tell me.'

'Sebastian and his lovely wife and baby.'

'Oh.' Impressive, successful Sebastian. She slumped back into the sofa.

'Did I say we're staying in his house? They were going to be in Nice for the weekend, but thought better of it with the weather so good in the UK. So we're all in the house in Cornwall together,'

'Wow.' Jess felt old. New wife, new baby.

'Anyway. You're all invited. Tomorrow. Will you come?'

'I'll have a look at the map.' Dear God, she needed strength. To steel herself for Sebastian's scrutiny and Sam's physical presence.

'Sebastian says an hour at the most. There's plenty of room for you to stay the night. Bring things for the children to sleep in, just in case.'

She felt something more than nerves at seeing Sam. Meeting him again had made her lonely in a way she hadn't allowed herself to feel. There had been huge relief—as well as many other emotions—when Tom left. But now it was as if she'd opened a door, and no matter how hard she tried, she couldn't quite shut it.

Her shoulders tensed at the thought of seeing Sebastian. He'd been 'one of the boys' for so long while they were growing up. But once he embarked on a high-flying career at Oxford, Harvard and the BBC, he'd entered another realm. He'd come for lunch with Stella, years ago, when Jess and Tom were first married. Stella had been considering whether her little crush on him was just that or something more significant (it was just a little crush). He'd been charming and attentive, dressed in a deep blue shirt that matched his eyes, driving a sports car the men admired, and had seemed untouchable somehow.

She told herself she remembered him when he was a little

squirt. That didn't help. He probably remembered her when she was spotty, greasy-haired and wore braces on her teeth.

Did he remember the first time her father's long affair with his secretary had been put into words, at that distant party at Caroline's house? She'd somehow known there was something amiss between her parents, that Diane's status was all wrong, but it had been Sebastian who'd cemented her own fears, even before she properly believed them.

And there was the Japanese wife and baby. Hadn't there been a previous wife? French; impossibly beautiful. She should ask Sam what happened to her.

Sam. He'd been lovely to her in Millingham, and still seemed interested in her welfare: ringing to find out what the blood test showed (low iron count, but not so low that it couldn't be corrected with proper diet), making her feel noticed. As he would do for any friend he met up with again. He was a doctor, for God's sake. But her mind veered back to those few moments—how he'd held her in his arms after she'd broken down over the smashed glasses, and they'd sat together on the bench in the garden —when the electricity vibrated between them.

Jess parked outside Sebastian's spectacular glass house overlooking the sea. She retrieved a freezer bag from the boot which contained a more expensive bottle of supermarket wine than usual, and strawberries, clotted cream and scones. Having agonised over what to pack, and even more over what to put on, she was wearing old khaki shorts, and an aqua t-shirt. She'd brought fleeces for them all, not that she'd worn a cardigan for over a week.

Just in case, there was an overnight bag with all the things they might need if they stayed. It was already hot and cloudless.

Before they reached the huge front door, Sam opened it.

'Hello.' He smiled at the children and bent to kiss Jess's cheek. 'That colour suits you.'

An elegant open-plan living area and sleek high-tech kitchen led to a sun-drenched terrace with stunning views out to sea. Ben and Millie headed straight for Joshua and Emma, who were down the hill in a wooden playhouse. Kate was sunbathing on a sun-lounger, in the farthest corner of the garden, consciously or unconsciously putting as much distance as possible between herself and everyone else.

'Jessica. Fancy meeting you here.' Sebastian emerged from a cream cushioned wicker chair wearing nothing but shorts. Although not much taller than her, he had filled out and was startlingly good-looking: bronzed, with dazzling blue eyes, a smooth brown cheek against hers as he kissed her.

'Hello, Sebastian,' said Jess. 'This place is amazing.'

'We'll give you a tour later. This is my wife, Tamiko.'

A slim, dark-haired girl stood and shook hands with Jess. 'Call me Tami. Come and meet Ava.' She indicated a ravishing baby, asleep on her back in a shaded Moses basket, her fists either side of her head.

'She's gorgeous,' said Jess. 'How old?'

'Nine weeks, and a dream, most of the time,' said Tami.

'A model baby as far as I can work out,' said Sam.

'Drinks,' said Sebastian. 'What do you fancy?'

'Could I use your loo?' said Jess.

She was shown to an ultra-modern downstairs cloakroom that was so high-tech she struggled to locate the loo paper. She looked in the mirror. Her face stared back, grey and miserable. A complete contrast to all those shiny, glowing people. Hell, she hated her hair. She should have taken the time to have it trimmed properly.

It took several minutes to summon up the courage to unlock the door.

Sam was leaning against the uncluttered kitchen island, checking his phone. He took her hand firmly. 'Come and sit down; you get to be waited on today.'

She pulled her hand away as they stepped into the sunshine, but not before she'd caught Sebastian's eye and flushed. Forever the gawky teenager.

Jess smiled at Tami. 'You look so well, for having a nine week old baby.'

'I keep waiting for it to be awful, but she's an angel. I'm very lucky.'

'I'm going to check on the roast,' Sebastian said. 'We're having lamb, Jess. Will your kids eat that?'

'I hope so.' She followed Sebastian with her eyes, ignoring Sam because he made her feel too hot. Her gaze flickered briefly over Kate, on her stomach, reading a book.

Sam stretched, revealing brown midriff, transporting Jess back to his kitchen for a moment. 'Going to see if I can help the chef.'

SAM

'What's going on?' said Sebastian, as Sam joined him in the kitchen.

'With what?'

'Don't give me that. What's going on with Jess?'

'Nothing.' Sam grinned.

'Really. And what are your intentions?' Sebastian wielded the knife he was using to cut up potatoes.

'Who are you? Her father?' Their eyes met at the thought of Jess's charismatic father. He'd appeared at Jess's parties now and then, memorably flirting with the girls, Anna especially. Sam remembered Jess—a sad expression on her face—once saying that her dad wanted her to call him Nathaniel, not Dad.

'God, I hope not,' said Sebastian.

'There's nothing going on. We met up again and she was finding life hard. I optimistically thought a day in your company might cheer her up.'

'You mean she looked worse than she does now?' Sebastian glanced towards the terrace.

'She looks much better, you have no idea. She's got colour in her cheeks. She's wearing a top that actually suits her. The things she wore in Millingham made her look like an ancient pupil from the grammar school.'

'Wow. You're hooked.' He slid pieces of potato into a saucepan.

'No I'm not. I'm being a friend. Her husband left her in the lurch with two infants. Give me a break.'

'Yeah, right.' Sebastian sliced into an onion. 'Don't string her along. She looks as if she might fall to pieces.'

'Do you really think you are the person to give me advice?' He indicated a bottle of wine on the counter. 'Shall I open the red?'

'Yeah, try that drawer for a corkscrew. Look, you got divorced. I got divorced and have now re-married. What makes you think you're so much better than me?'

'I don't think that. But I don't think you have a totally unblemished record when it comes to behaving well towards women.'

'As opposed to you. Who obviously does.'

'Let's not get into this. I don't want to treat her badly. I want her to smile.'

'I never thought I'd say this, but be careful. Do not lead her on if you don't intend to follow through.'

Sam turned away from Sebastian to put the opened bottle on the table. From there he walked over to the fridge, to calm his nerves.

He and Jess really needed to have a proper talk.

JESS

After spending the afternoon on the beach, they gave the children tea on the terrace. Jess, who had been pressed to stay for dinner, was still talking about driving home, but when Tami and Sebastian went to put Ava to bed upstairs, she found Sam in the kitchen.

'What can I do?' said Jess.

'Ah. I'm not altogether confident about you and sharp knives,' said Sam. 'Do you want to make a salad dressing?'

Jess glanced down at her finger. The healed wound was surprisingly painful when pressed. She explored the cupboards for ingredients and a small bowl.

'You OK?' He unwrapped the meat and fish. Sebastian had already lit the built-in barbecue beside the terrace.

'Yes,' she said, gradually adding oil to the mustard she was stirring.

'You seemed to go into a decline when we were on the beach.'

She opened her mouth and shut it again, absurdly flattered he'd noticed.

'Go on, you can say it.'

'Tami looks amazing for someone who's just had a baby!'

'She's young.' Sam started chopping peppers for the kebabs.

Jess smoothed her t-shirt down over her shorts, wishing she made more effort to eat healthily, walk, do all those sit-ups. Yes, young, with a pelvic floor, a smooth tummy, and a killer figure, she thought as she whisked vinegar into the olive oil. 'And unmarked by life.'

'Yet.' Sam glanced round, knife in hand. He grinned. 'Besides, nothing wrong with a few cracks here and there. As the great Leonard Cohen said, it's where the light gets in.'

Jess smiled back and tried to ignore the sliver of steel that caught the light. 'Hallelujah.'

He smiled appreciatively. 'Quite.'

'What can I do now? Lay the table?' She blushed. It must be the sun.

'You can do something about all that, you know.'

'I know, but you're not at work. I'm *not* talking gynaecology with you.'

He ran his hands under the tap, reached for a tea towel and turned to face her. He looked fabulous in shorts and a red t-shirt, his feet bare. 'All I'm saying is, there's a lot of good in your life.'

'Mm,' she nodded. *I'll say*.

They ate outside, watching the last glows of the sun disappear into the sea and the stars emerge. Apart from the faint whisper of the waves, it was quiet and still, the sun-baked stones of the sheltered terrace and the heat of the barbecue keeping them warm as the air cooled down.

'This really is a stunning house,' said Jess.

'Why don't you go and explore?' said Sebastian.

Sam re-filled the glasses. 'I'll show you.'

They passed the children, curled up on huge sofas in the living area, watching a large-screen television. On the first floor were four big bedrooms furnished with lavish cream bedding, blonde wood floors, pale mats and sheepskin rugs, plus a couple of bathrooms. Upstairs was the master suite—Ava asleep in a cot in the smaller room—and a spectacular roof terrace with a panoramic view. Sam took Jess's hand, and pulled her out of the door.

'Let's look at the stars.' He kept hold of her hand. Just as right as it had been that other night, all those years ago, when they'd looked at the stars, in the snow. Not that he'd remember. No one remembered.

She gazed upwards but after a while it hurt her neck.

'Lean back on me,' he said.

She hesitated, but then leant back, her head against his shoulder, his arms around her, holding on to the balustrade in front of them.

'That's better,' he said, warm breath on her cheek.

She saw more and more stars, the longer she looked.

'Did you know your head weighs about eight kilos?' he said.

'What?'

'It's just a fun fact.'

She turned in his arms. She could see his face clearly now she was used to the faint moonlight. His look made her flush. Slowly, slowly he bent his head towards her upturned face.

He kissed her, smooth pressure on her lips, while her stomach disappeared.

She didn't consider it a first kiss. A first kiss since her husband left. A first kiss as a divorcee. But not really a first kiss from Sam.

His arms tightened around her, pulling her against his chest. She opened her mouth on a gasp and he kissed her deeply, his tongue circling hers, hot hands in her hair, cradling the back of her head, as her arms snaked around his neck. His lips were soft, his skin warm, incipient beard gently prickling her cheek.

He leant his forehead against hers, while they caught their breath. 'The others will wonder where we've got to.' He had a glittery, heated look in his eyes.

She shook her head. How long had they been out there?

Sam leaned away to see her better. 'You're not going to go funny on me, are you?'

She looked down. *That wasn't meant to happen*. But how could something that felt so right be wrong? Yeah, right. That would be lust again. Out of control. And with Sam, who had been so kind to her. Who'd been such a good friend this summer. Oh hell. Now it would get weird, it always did.

'I'm sorry.' She studied her feet. Her flip-flops were nothing like as sexy as his bare feet.

'I'm not sorry. I've been wanting to kiss you since this morning. Probably long before that. You're going to have to stay now.'

'I can't stay. I can't sleep with you.' Her voice rose in panic.

'And I can't sleep with you,' he said, deflating her like a pin.

The lust curling around her stomach evaporated. She lifted her eyes to meet his gaze.

He grinned. 'Well, not tonight.'

SAM

Apart from an arch look from Sebastian, their absence was not commented upon. Jess sat in one of the wicker armchairs on the other side of Tami and filled the space and silence with praise of the house. Sam watched her knee twitching under the table and longed to stretch across and stop it with the flat of his palm.

Jess paused to draw breath, and he took his chance. 'Did you say Anna was coming down this week?'

'Anna?' said Sebastian.

'Don't tell me.' Tami laughed. 'Another of his old flames?'

'No, more like another of Sam's,' said Sebastian. 'But watch out, memories are deceptive. So many of those romances rekindled via social media have ended disastrously.'

'Have they?' said Jess.

'Coffee,' said Sebastian. 'Tami, why don't you go to bed? You're going to be up feeding in the night.'

'Ah.' Sam eyed Sebastian. 'That's why you were so supportive about breast-feeding.'

Tami raised her eyebrows. 'And he has the capacity to sleep through anything. None of you are racing off in the morning?'

'I do think—' Jess began.

'Well don't.' Sebastian spoke over his shoulder as he went into the kitchen. 'Tell her, Sam, she has to stay here now. She's had far too much to drink.'

'I haven't.' She met Sam's eyes for only the second time since they'd sat down.

'I know, but you're driving on roads you don't know. Go back in the morning.' *And you get to sleep next door to me,* he nearly added.

'I'd better get the stuff from the car,' Jess said.

'Give me the keys, I'll go. Then we'll put the children to bed.' He held out his hand for the keys until she went to find her bag.

The children went to bed without a murmur. Millie was already asleep on the sofa, and Sam offered to carry her up to the bedroom opposite Jess's, where they tucked her into bed.

He didn't even have a moment of protest from Kate. Kate who'd avoided him all day. Kate who'd stayed silent almost all day. The only person she'd talked to had been Emma, and then only when it couldn't be avoided.

Nothing would be gained by challenging Kate's attitude towards Jess. He knew his elder daughter could sense the rapport building between him and Jess and that she didn't like it. He could understand that. But it didn't mean he had to indulge it. She would be seeing more of Jess. Whether she liked it or not.

JESS

Jess couldn't sleep. The bed was firm for her back, and the house was quiet, but she couldn't stop imagining the soft breathing of all the people nearby. She'd checked on the children, sleeping with their limbs outflung in a bid to stay cool.

She opened the pale curtains and watched the patterns of light and shade on the ceiling, as if the air were revealing itself in monochrome. She imagined flitting into the other quiet, darkened rooms and watching the sleeping forms. Feigning death, Shakespeare said. No tension in Kate's face, no enquiring glances from Sam. She squirmed, imagining his smooth brown skin under cool sheets. *Bet he doesn't wear much, if anything.*

This was not helping her sleep. But it was novel. She had not thought about sex much at all, since Tom left. She'd been telling the truth when she told Sam she'd practically forgotten it. Not that she couldn't remember, but she just didn't. There wasn't any opportunity for it. The children took up so much of her time, and she was so tired. A few well-meaning friends had told her all she needed was the love of a good man. Someone even told her that her problems stemmed from sexual tension, and she just needed a good seeing to. That comment—a throwaway remark from the friend of a friend—had made her angry in a way she hadn't felt for years, almost making her wonder if there wasn't some truth in it.

So here she was, lying alone in a huge bed, the man who'd kissed her sleeping less than five metres away. She sighed and turned on her side. *I'll just pray. That'll help. Our father in heaven…*

But she relived the heat in his eyes, the erotic pressure of his tongue teasing her lips, the feel of his hands cradling the back of her head, his hard torso pressed against her breasts.

She rolled onto her back, smoothed the light cover over herself, arms by her sides.

Eventually she put the light on and reached for the book she was comfort re-reading: Dodie Smith's *I Capture The Castle*.

She felt for her watch. Nearly eight o'clock. Someone must have taken Ben and Millie downstairs.

The next thing she knew, there was a knock on her door and Sam appeared.

'Peppermint tea,' he said.

'Oh, thank you. I meant to get up.'

'Don't worry, they're fine without you.'

She scrabbled to sit up, self-conscious in her pink strappy nightie. 'It's twenty past nine,' she squealed.

Sam grinned. 'Thought I'd better bring you something in case you need to be back. We never did get around to when Anna's arriving.'

'Not until tomorrow. But I must get going.'

'Take your time.' He looked out the window. 'We're driving to Oxford later, but thought we might come as far as Croyde with you…it's meant to be a great surfing beach.'

She swallowed. 'That's a good idea…'

'Great. You look very cute, by the way.' With a wink he was gone.

A split second later she leapt out of bed and bolted for the bathroom. She'd caught the sun yesterday, her face almost rosy, and although her hair was a bit over-tousled, the overall effect was not too bad. No streaked make-up, no sleep in her eyes. Even her old nightie was passable, in a pretty rather than sexy way.

She scrutinised her reflection. Parted lips, dark, pupil-dilated eyes, the blood pumping to her cheeks, pumping to parts of her body she'd forgotten she had. Masturbation—the idea she'd quelled in the night—flickered through her mind again.

'For God's sake.'

That was the problem with sex. Nothing for more than three years. And now, after one kiss, she was calculating how quickly she could get him into bed.

No. She would have done. Before. Things were different now. She was a responsible single mother. A Christian who didn't believe in sex outside marriage. Perhaps if she repeated it enough, she'd stick with the programme. 'A cool shower,' she said out loud.

Ten minutes later, she was dressed in shorts and the highest-necked t-shirt she had. There was nothing she could do about the fact that Sam was a wearing a similar shade of blue.

After a late breakfast, the two families thanked Sebastian and Tami, and headed up the coast. They set up camp on Croyde beach with all the accumulated gear of five children, two adults and two car boots. Jess brought her book to enjoy in the breezy sunshine. The boys, Emma and

Millie were constructing sandcastles and digging moats. Sam, in dark board shorts and t-shirt, was stretched out beside Jess, flicking through the News and Sports sections of the Sunday papers. Kate, as far away as possible, studied the magazines.

Sam turned onto his side, head propped on his hand. 'Fancy a swim?'

'Not without a wetsuit, or the temperature rising another ten degrees.'

'A paddle?' He rolled to his feet in one fluid movement, and pulled his t-shirt over his head, revealing more taut brown skin. He's in very good shape, she thought, before averting her eyes in case elder daughter saw.

'Who's coming for a swim?' he said, expecting the bursts of, 'Me, me, me,' that had the children flinging down their spades and racing for the water's edge. 'Katie?'

Brave, thought Jess.

'I'm reading.' Kate didn't bother to lift her eyes.

'Come on, Jess. Race you,' he said.

Sam ran into the water, performed a sleek surface dive, and appeared beyond the breakers.

Jess splashed with Millie, in and out of the shallows, amazed at how much warmer the water felt after the initial shock. *Head up, shoulders back, tummy in.* Emma, Josh and Ben did their best with body boards, running for the waves, while Sam dived between them.

'Hi,' he said, blocking out the sun, his hair dark and sleek from the sea.

'You're showing off, right?'

'Of course. Are you impressed?'

'Not in the slightest.' She laughed.

'Come in. It's great.'

'I'm sure it is, but I need to keep an eye on the children.

And before you ask, I'm not going in on my own. Not even to impress you.'

'Oh, I'm impressed.' He backed into the water.

She felt hotter and hotter under his gaze. Maybe she would go in, just to cool off.

Millie's teeth chattered.

'Come on, darling,' said Jess. 'Let's warm you up.' They ran up the beach, leaving the others splashing.

Kate was propped on her elbows, reading *I Capture The Castle*. She closed it and pushed it away as Jess sat on the rug, pulling out towels for the girls. She wrapped one round Millie, who snuggled into her mother's lap.

'You're welcome to it,' said Jess. 'I only discovered it a few years ago, but I wish I'd read it at your age.'

Kate glanced in her direction briefly, and reached for the book.

'Have you seen the film?' said Jess.

'No,' mumbled Kate.

'That's worth seeing too.'

Well, it was a conversation of sorts. OK, an exchange. A word.

Jess found a bit of newspaper to skim, resting her chin on the top of Millie's head. From the corner of her eye, she could see Kate turning the page.

'Cassandra's the most wonderful heroine.' Jess smiled at Kate, who met her eyes, fleetingly. 'But I also love the character of Topaz, the stepmother. The one who likes to take off all her clothes to commune with nature.'

Kate's eyes turned to flint, while Jess cursed herself. Stepmothers. The perfect subject to raise with Sam's hostile daughter. Jess flushed red, cheeks still burning when the others came to shake cold water all over them.

'Josh,' shouted Kate, furious.

'Been having fun?' said Sam.

By three-thirty they were by the cars, with all their wet, sandy gear.

Kate lolled beside the Volvo.

'Why don't you finish the book?' said Jess.

'No thanks.' Kate turned away, busying herself with the contents of her bag.

Jess and Sam exchanged looks.

'Come on, you lot, in the car,' he said.

Jess pushed the beach paraphernalia into the boot and strapped the children into the car, jittery with nerves. Would he kiss her? Would he not kiss her but want to kiss her?

He came round to the driver's side of the car, and gave her a hug. A moment when their bodies were pressed together. 'Assume I'd be doing this differently if we weren't in public. Say hello to Anna for me.'

SAM

'Give me a clue, little brother. It must be serious if you're meeting on holiday. With all your children,' said Will.

'Mm.' Sam scanned the front page of the newspaper, and wished he hadn't gone into the details of who had been at Sebastian's house. Will's kitchen was momentarily quiet while the children played in the garden, and he'd hoped to have a couple of minutes to himself.

'This is Jessica Lamb, right? Do I remember her?' Will dunked teabags, and plonked a mug beside his brother.

'Friend of Stella's.'

'What did she look like?'

'Tallish. Thinnish. Brown hair—longish.'

'Very descriptive! And now?' Will sat down at the table opposite his brother and propped his head on his hand.

Sam sighed. 'About the same, except her hair's shorter.'

'What's attractive about her?'

Sam put the newspaper down. 'She came up to Millingham for a school reunion. We had a couple of suppers. We were both going to be in Cornwall at the same time, so arranged to meet up.'

'Great.' Will grinned. 'But what's she like?'

'You're being really annoying.'

'Looking out for your welfare. I don't want to have to piece you back together again.'

'You didn't.' Sam clenched his jaw. 'And you won't have to. Jess is kind. She's nothing like Elizabeth.'

'Good sense of humour? Attractive? Sexy?'

Sam released a breath. 'Really. You're not helping.'

'Did you ever get together in the past?'

'What makes you ask that?'

'So you did. When was this? Did it last?'

'The timing wasn't right.'

'And now?'

'Who knows? She lives in London. I'm in Manchester. Blah, blah, blah.'

'But you want to see her?'

Sam examined the question he'd been circling since the drive from Croyde to Oxford. His senses heightened, skin tightened by the cold splash of the sea, the fresh whip of the air. That intense rush of adrenaline when she laughed and said, 'You're showing off, right?' The pleasure of causing that much joy on another person's face.

In spite of their circumstances.

JESS

Jess and Anna sprawled on one of the two sofas in the house in Croyde. The children were safely in bed, tired out by more beach adventures, and the two old friends finally had glasses of wine in their hands.

'Do you have regrets?' asked Jess.

'Yes. But I try not to think about them. It's too depressing.'

Out of the corner of her eye, she saw Anna pick up Millie's crumpled red gingham sunhat from the arm of the sofa and smooth it into shape.

'Do you think about Millingham much? When we were growing up?'

'Sometimes. More so when I'm there.'

Jess picked at a loose thread on one of the cushions. 'Did I tell you about Sam?'

'You know perfectly well you did not! Sam who?'

Jess grinned.

'Sam *Rushmore*?' Anna sat up sharply, and narrowly averted tipping over her glass.

'We spent yesterday on the beach with the children.'

'I've been here nearly four hours and you haven't said a thing.'

Jess liked to think that she and Anna had the sort of shorthand friendship that even sporadic get-togethers could weather. Jess's domestic life was so different from Anna's brilliant career, that they probably met no more than four or five times a year, sometimes with Caroline, Ruth, and Stella. Occasionally they'd spend a Sunday together, Anna combining it with a weekend in London at her boyfriend Jon's flat. Jess worried that she didn't make more of an effort to see Anna, but somehow, when they met, the gap shrank.

'It's a surprisingly long story,' said Jess. 'I'm going to cook.'

'What do you mean, 'surprisingly long'?' Anna followed her into the kitchen, carrying her glass.

'It began the weekend of the reunion.' Jess took fish and salad out of the fridge.

'What began? You never mentioned Sam.'

'I knocked on his door and had a chat. Then I saw him at church. We went for tea with the kids. And then we had supper.'

'All in that week?' Anna met her gaze, her blue eyes wide in her round face, framed by curly blonde hair. She'd always had curves: an impressive bosom, a slim waist, a body that flared in and out in a way that was totally unfamiliar to Jess, with her straighter, more boyish figure.

There had been a time when they'd both liked Sam. Jess had married and had children and Anna had not. And now Jess had met him again. Guilt rose like bile in her throat.

She heated a splash of oil, emptied salad into a bowl. 'He came to Cornwall for the bank holiday. Guess whose house he was staying in?'

Anna finished her glass of wine and opened the fridge for the bottle. 'Surprise me.'

'Sebastian Cameron and his wife Tami—she's Japanese—and their baby.'

'What happened with Sam?'

'Nothing.' Jess concentrated on the fish in the frying pan. 'Well, not exactly. We kissed.'

'You *what*?'

'I'm sorry. Déjà-vu. I mean, I'm in London and he's in Manchester.'

'So? Tell me about the kiss.'

Jess squirmed, recognising the feeling of perverse enjoyment at being grilled for details. 'We'd all had a few—'

'What do you mean, déjà-vu?'

'I feel as if I'm seventeen again. Confessing to you.' She had a clear picture of Anna collecting her in her Fiat Uno, a present from the Polish father she never saw, soon after she'd passed her test. They'd drive along the quieter roads of Barton, and as far as the National Trust property the other side of the golf course, while Jess unburdened herself. Much easier to do, somehow, sitting side by side, and able to gaze out of the window.

'Tell me about the kiss. Then we'll deal with the recurring theme of guilt.'

'I'd had a couple of glasses of wine. Champagne to start. And you know what a cheap date I am, never been able to handle much alcohol. Anyway. Sam and I went on a little tour of the house—which is incredible—after supper.' She stopped, her stomach doing a little somersault. 'We looked at the stars. And then we kissed.'

'And?'

'He's still a great kisser.'

After supper they flopped on the sofas, opposite each other this time.

Jess, her long fringe in her eyes, caught sight of her reflection in the mirror, the silver threads in her brown hair catching the light. 'Stella told me she thought I was very brave letting my hair go grey.'

'It only shows in certain lights.'

'You can't imagine how much grey I saw yesterday morning in Sebastian's guest bathroom.'

'Oh, you poor thing.'

Anna's dry tone of voice made Jess look up. 'Sorry. Am I making it all about me?'

'It's not that…'

Anna had fixed her gaze to the left of Jess. What was she looking at? Absently, Jess gathered Millie's hat and a stray frilled ankle sock onto her lap. 'You know you can say whatever you're thinking.'

Anna set her glass down on the low table between them, and took a deep breath. 'You got married, you had two beautiful children. When your marriage imploded, which we could all anticipate because Tom's a shit—don't you remember I was the most lachrymose bridesmaid in history?—then you grieved. Now you meet Sam Rushmore again, and he kisses you. But you'd like me to feel sorry for you because your hair is going grey?

'I'm sorry. Tell me about you.'

Anna leant back again. 'The usual. Work is manic.'

'How are things with Jon?' The temptation to keep talking was overridden by what Jess had learnt from Sam. *Listen.*

Eventually Anna sighed. 'I'm alone. I've always been alone. No. That's not right. I have a boyfriend who assured me he was moving out of London with me, but he's never made the move. You were with someone. Then you were alone. And now you're not alone.'

'Not even when I'm at my most ridiculously romantic do I imagine that one kiss means we're together.'

'So, take a risk.'

Jess stared at her. What was she saying about being alone? 'I thought the situation with Jon suited you both? If I hadn't been so self-absorbed—'

'Don't, Jess. It's fine.' She folded her arms across her stomach.

'But friends are meant to know what's going on in each other's lives. If you can't say it how it really is, there's not much point, is there?'

'You'd rather we were honest? Are you sure?'

Jess contemplated that thought. No! And yet. Yes! At what point would a long friendship buckle under the weight of such truths? Wouldn't it be put under more strain if they were each clambering over untruths? Even if it was painful?

Jess took a deep breath. 'When things got really bad with Tom, I turned in on myself. And I've been like that for a long time. It's been just me and the children. Trying to keep our heads above water. I'm sorry if—'

'Don't apologise,' said Anna. 'You're right about honesty. About trying to say what you really feel. If you can't with your oldest friends…'

'Do you think there's something special about friends you've known since you were a child? Something more profound?'

'I have no idea,' said Anna. 'Are things more profound with Sam?'

'Don't ask me that,' said Jess. 'I'm over-thinking things anyway.' She had to stop. She'd end up not being able to answer his phone calls—even his texts—if she wasn't careful.

'Is he just the same?'

'He's lovely. I think he's been finding it hard to keep *his* head above water. But life's getting easier, finally.' She saw his big grin, hands shielding his eyes from the bright sunlight. Spinning away from her into the surf. Hugging her. Watching her, suppressed emotion in his dark eyes…

'Maybe you'll rescue each other. Is it getting chilly in here?'

Jess stood up and yanked Millie's pink stripy towel off the back of the chair where it had been airing. She handed it to Anna 'This is dry.'

Anna unfolded her arms, pulled the towel around her shoulders and buried her face in its folds for an instant.

Jess had found the stray thread on the cushion to pull at again. 'You know, one of the things I've learnt—no, I'm trying to learn—is to take responsibility for myself. I never felt equal to Tom; the balance of power was always in his favour. It wasn't good for either of us. I thought putting him first, allowing him to make all the decisions was selfless and would make him happy, but he ended up despising me.'

Anna looked up. 'You disappeared.'

'Yes. Now I'm trying to understand what I want. To be honest with myself.'

'That sounds healthy. So is Sam what you want?'

Jess exhaled. 'I'm in London. He's in Manchester.'

'That's just geography.'

'And you and Jon? How do you keep it going, if you're in different places most of the time?'

'Ah.' She drew the towel tighter around her neck. 'That's a whole other story. Absence makes the heart grow fonder and all that.'

'Does it? Or do we just learn to rebuild our lives without them? God, it's gloomy in here.' Jess reached out and switched on the standard lamp beside the sofa. The bulb was dim and gave out very little light.

Anna stretched to the lamp on the small table beside her,

but the bulb was just as weak. Somehow both pools of light only drew attention to how night had fallen outside.

'So, if you're so keen on God and keeping to the rules, how are you going to keep him at bay after over twenty years of longing?'

Jess winced. 'Do you know what surprised me most at the reunion? You remember the photo of the five of us?'

'With the girls?' said Anna.

'Yup. Did you spot who's tallest?'

'Caroline? Ruth? Not Stella.'

'Me. Not by much. Caroline was always the tallest, right through school. But I'm the tallest now.'

'You were a late developer.'

'This is true.'

'Well, you've caught up. You can finally have Sam Rushmore.'

SAMUEL: age 17

Sam grimaced at his reflection in the small mirror, in his room under the eaves. Dark eyes, dark hair that he pushed out of his eyes. He could pass for eighteen. Unlike Jessica, who had been humiliatingly asked to leave the pub the previous Saturday night.

They'd walked down to Barton Village, at the bottom of the hill, over the level crossing, past Safeway and the brand new video rental shop, to the pub beside the railway, houses on one side, fields on the other. He'd stayed on with James and Rob, but the girls—Stella, Ruth, Caroline and Jessica—had gone home.

For some reason, he'd agreed when Stella had suggested meeting up again this Saturday. The other option was a party in Manchester, but it had been such a hot day he didn't have the energy to take the train and couldn't be bothered to stay sober enough to drive.

Midsummer, give or take a day. Balmy. Cloudless. Exams finally over.

He wandered along Woodham Road to the church and sat on the low wall. Ruth, Caroline, Stella and Jessica swept up the hill, and stopped in front of him.

Stella eyed him. 'Didn't think you'd show.'

He stood up. 'Why wouldn't I?'

'Better things to do?'

He shrugged. Stella wasn't usually this obvious. 'Where's Rob meeting us?'

It was her turn to shrug.

They walked down Lake Avenue towards Barton Common. Ruth wittered about Nathan while Caroline listened. Stella walked a little apart. Beside the bigger personalities of her friends, he noticed that Jessica faded out of focus.

Susie and Tim joined them as they reached the common. The air felt soft and heavy; warm still at eight-thirty. He'd gone out with Susie for a few months, but she'd finished with him, saying she didn't want to get too serious too young. He still thought of her sometimes: her weight on his knee, the press of her breasts against his chest through their clothing, her silky hair slipping through his fingers.

'I told Rob we'd be at the oak tree,' said Stella.

'Yeah, Nate might join us,' said Ruth.

Sam glanced up and caught Jessica's eye. *Nate*?

'She does know he's not interested in girls?' Jessica fell into step with Sam, as they walked towards the huge, lone oak on higher ground in the middle of the heath.

'Not at all?' Caroline watched Tim, walking ahead with Susie.

'Says he never has been. James told me.' Jessica turned to Sam. 'I heard it freaked him out.'

'Interesting,' said Caroline.

Jessica stopped. 'Why is it interesting that it freaked James out?'

'Well. Why was James freaked out? If he was completely comfortable with his own sexuality, then it shouldn't bother him.'

'Are you saying James is gay?'

Sam studied a particularly fascinating leaf on the path.

'He doesn't behave as if he is,' said Caroline. 'He and Ruth were together for quite a while. He's always got girls interested in him, hasn't he?'

'Sam?' said Jessica.

He returned her look. He didn't want to talk about James. Sometimes he was a little too intense, stood a little too close. He had a clear snapshot of James handing him a cigarette, high up among the oak branches, the end damp when he put it between his lips.

Then, last weekend, on the way back from the pub, James had jumped on him and taken too long to extricate himself from the heap they'd landed in. Rob had looked on in amusement.

For Sam, it was as if their easy equilibrium had been disturbed. Meant that what had been a lads' friendship—a physical, joshing running commentary between two boys —had become weightier, uneven somehow. It made Sam feel uncomfortable and self-conscious. But had he tipped things over into murky waters? Was James still in the sunny, teasing past, and it was only Sam's suspicions that clouded things?

'Come on, you lovely creatures.' Tim pulled a bottle of white wine from the depths of the mac he was wearing, relieving Sam of the need to answer Jess's question. 'Drinks, darlings?'

Stella giggled. 'What on earth are you going to open it with?'

'This.' He scythed the air with a corkscrew. 'Hope my parents don't miss it.' He placed the tip of the corkscrew in the centre of the top of the cork and began twisting. It was a practiced performance. He glanced up. 'Glasses?'

'Had we known,' Sam said, catching a small smile from Jessica.

They sat under the tree, passing the bottle back and forth for swigs, as the lights came on in the surrounding houses. The sky was huge and clear, the faintest, palest of blues, slowly darkening, eventually scattered with pinprick stars. Sam liked the idea of the stars—which were always there, had been there all along—slowly being brought into focus by the disappearing light. He found it comforting.

'I like the romantic idea of lying on my back to look at the sky,' said Jessica. 'Dancing, maybe, like in *Gregory's Girl*. But the reality is damp and muddy.'

'That's films for you,' said Ruth.

'About bloody time.' Stella stood up and walked towards two figures on the path from Woodham Road.

'Just in time.' Tim tipped up the empty bottle.

James and Rob wielded bottles of cider and cheap white wine, and passed round thin plastic cups.

'Goodee.' Stella wound her arms around Rob, who French kissed her while his free hand moulded her backside in the skimpy shorts. Sam looked away.

'Where's Nathan?' said Ruth. 'He said he was coming.'

'Yes, well. Something came up.' James took a packet of cigarettes out of the top pocket of his short-sleeved shirt. He put two between his lips, lit them and offered one to Susie.

Several expressions flitted across Susie's face. Her hand came out to take it, her thumb travelling over the tip of the cigarette before she put it between her lips and inhaled.

'Not a clever idea,' said Tim.

Good, thought Sam. Some of his parents' entreaties must have rubbed off. He'd never got the hang of smoking. Despite its undeniable sexiness.

'Try stopping me.' Susie raised her chin as she moved away from her brother. In silhouette, the red tip of the cigarette glowed between her first two fingers.

'Oh no,' said Ruth, as the tree was illuminated for a brief second. 'For God's sake, Jessica, do you have to?'

'You'll all love to see them when they're developed, and you'll moan if you're not in them.' Jessica wound the film on, raised the camera to her eye again.

'Want a bet,' Rob said under his breath, as the flash exploded.

They tottered in a sort of elongated group hug for the camera. Then Tim took a photo while Jessica joined the group. She wriggled into the shot between Sam and Rob, smelling faintly of something floral. Her hair tickled Sam's cheek.

They loosened their grip on each other's shoulders and ambled away from the tree. Jessica walked ahead of Sam, talking to Caroline. James pushed in between them, linking arms with them both.

Sam thought about calling goodnight, but in the end he turned away to take the other path, across the Common to his back gate.

The evening ending in anti-climax reflected his own secret fear that he'd not made the most of this group of friends, and now it was too late. Because he'd been seduced by the shiny, groomed girls at the private high school close to his in the centre of Manchester, he'd let these local friendships founder, untethered, until he couldn't remember what had bound them in the first place. Was it only proximity?

Or was it more than that, especially with James? A shared, shameful guilty secret. Too late to do something about it. Stuart was OK now, anyway, wasn't he? And there were things he didn't want to challenge James on. Like a TV lawyer, never ask a question if you don't already know the answer. He feared the direction a conversation with James could veer if they found themselves on their own together.

JESS

Once Jess had wrestled the children into bed, she climbed upstairs to the study and hunted until she found the box of diaries. She arranged them in date order, brushing the dust off, scraps of paper and locks of her own hair falling out.

'Top of the Tops and Mash. No one sat with us in Latin... Did some art and read Wuthering Heights. Discussed Wales in dinner...hair...'

It was either prosaic or incomprehensible. Reading the words her younger self had so lovingly—so self-consciously—written, but finding them meaningless, was like a body blow.

She worked back until she found Sam's name, after that first party in James's cellar.

'Everything gets complicated, and then people start being different. Why can't we all just be friends? ...Sam walked me home and we were not quite relaxed... What I don't like is the others teasing me...!'

Her writing stared out at her, tight, legible, in sharp contrast to her scrawl nowadays which was large, spiky and bordered on the illegible. Did that reflect a difference in her personality since then? Was she less repressed?

Not so she'd noticed.

She opened a later diary, rubbed her fingers over the paper to feel the indentations made by the pen. Sam was mentioned here and there, among the cryptic entries. *'YF... Sports night... indoor games, musical chairs...his knee!!'* She dredged her brain for memories. *'Met Stella, Rob, James... I HATE him, he uses hateful words! Sam and me.'*

This was harder to decipher. Why would she hate James? What had happened to make her write that? And what did the next bit, *'Sam and me'* refer to? There was so little of her own reaction to any of it.

The phone rang. She rushed downstairs to quieten it, not wanting the children out of their beds again.

'Hello, Jess. I've missed you.'

Her heart leapt against her ribcage and her mouth went dry. 'You have?'

'Yep.' There was a pause. 'I have.'

Her eye caught the winking clock on the front of the cooker. 'Sam, why are you home at nine o'clock on a Saturday night?'

'I've been out. It's my weekend without the kids. Just got back a bit early.'

'How much have you had to drink?' She poured a glass of wine and opened a packet of nuts.

'A few beers. At my colleague Matt's. Anyway. The point is. When can we meet?'

'What did you have in mind?'

'You. Me. A bottle of wine. A bed if you're up for it. More to the point if I'm up for it.'

She heard him inhale sharply.

'Sorry. More pissed than I thought.'

'Did something happen?'

'I'm being morose. Remind me next time I want to drink too much, would you?'

'Tell me about today.'

'Sophie, one of our practice nurses was there. Recently

married. New baby. Full of the joys of spring. Asks after the kids, wants to know how I am.'

'And?'

'She brought a friend.'

'A friend?' she prompted, into the silence.

'Don't you hate people looking concerned, trying to fix you up with unspeakably dreadful dates? And don't you hate that word? I've never been on a date in my life. We all just went out together in the old days, didn't we?'

'Well, was she at least pretty?'

Sam sighed. 'I guess...I'm sure she's very nice... but that's not really the point. There was a desperation to it all...and Sophie, bless her, watching us to see how we were getting on. You can't imagine.'

'Oh yes I can,' said Jess, with feeling. 'I know just what you mean. I'd hate being set up. So, what was she like?'

'Her name's Amanda. Radiologist. Flat in Manchester.'

'Convenient,' she said, with a touch more resentment than she'd intended.

'Younger than us. But a bit too keen. Or intense. Or something.'

'She sounds great. I can't imagine why you wanted to leave.'

'Can't you? Do you think I go around kissing just anyone?'

'Of course I don't.' She thought about it. It still seemed too surprising that Sam—lovely Sam—would be interested in her above anyone else. 'I'm here and you're there.'

'So is that an insurmountable problem?'

Jess tried to see into the silence.

'Are we talking about the distance?' she said eventually.

'There's something I should tell you. Before we go much further.'

Dread solidified in the pit of her stomach. She knew it. There was someone else.

'Yeah, there's something I should tell you, too.'

'Go on, then.'

'You first,' she stalled, hoping to break the tension.

'I'm not sure I can on the phone. Maybe we can work up to some phone sex. You're much more attractive than Amanda. Even if your hair's brown.'

'I'll take that as a compliment, shall I?'

'I did like you in that blue top at Seb's house. Could barely keep my hands to myself. Let alone sleep, knowing you were lying there, practically naked, next door.'

'Is that so?' She took a large sip of wine.

'Tell me what you're wearing. And if you're not sure, have another glass of wine.'

She laughed. 'I'm on glass number one. I know exactly what I'm wearing.'

'Is your underwear pink?'

'I'm not telling you!'

'I thought we were building up to phone sex. The least you could do is describe your knickers. You can tell me, Jess, I'm a doctor.'

'Actually, that would be quite an incentive not to leap into bed with you.'

'What? Why?'

'Too gynaecological. You'd know too much about where everything is.'

'And that's a bad thing?'

She thought for an instant about his long, expert fingers driving her to heights of pleasure hitherto unreached. 'It's irrelevant, as I'm not about to leap into bed with you.'

'Oh.' He stopped, stretching the distance between them. 'Is this what you wanted to tell me, Jess? Don't you want to?'

'Like you, I'd rather not be having this conversation over the phone.' She twisted the stem of her glass between her thumb and forefinger.

'But…as we *are* having this conversation…?'

'Going to bed with people did me no good at all at Uni. I'm better not doing that. I've got kids to think about now.'

'Well, for a start, let's hope we're not talking about people. Only me. We've known each other a long time. You can trust me.'

She sighed. 'I do trust you.'

'So, if we met, do you think—?'

'It's also because of God,' she blurted.

'Because of God?'

'I think sex is for marriage.'

'I see. What if you were engaged?'

'If I was engaged, I might as well wait until I was married.'

'So you're not one of those ex-wives who have sex with their ex-husbands?'

'What? No, I'm not.' She concentrated on the withered plant on the surface in front of her. She'd tried watering it earlier, but it still didn't show much sign of life.

'You?' she asked eventually.

'No. Not a possibility.' His voice was flat.

'What did you want to tell me?'

'Irrelevant now. Jess, would you forgive me if I rang off and went to bed? The booze is finally catching up with me. I'll call you. OK?'

'Sure, Sam. Look after yourself.' She put the phone down and drained the glass. *Shit. Shit. SHIT.*

SAM

Sunday afternoon, after Sam had walked past the phone sixteen times, he picked it up and dialled Rob's mobile. It clicked straight on to the answerphone. He left a brief message.

Then he rang Matt. 'Thanks for yesterday. Did it go on very late?'

'Midnight-ish. How was the lovely Amanda? I saw Sophie handing her to you on a plate.'

'Not you too, Matt. Leave me alone.'

'Fair enough. Pretty though. Good body.'

'I have nothing to say on the subject,' Sam said, wondering what sort of displacement activity had made him ring Matt in the first place.

'Why not? You're over Elizabeth, aren't you?'

'Too right,' said Sam, with feeling.

'You're ready then.'

There was a pause.

'You never did tell me what happened on the course with that doctor—Bethany, Beverley, what was her name?'

Sam let out a breath. 'Briony. That was six months ago.'

'Not so raw that you can't tell me what happened.'

'It's a very boring, humiliating story, and one I'd rather not go into.'

'Well, you know where I am if you want to talk, or need something more practical.'

'Yes. I do. See you in the morning.'

Sam put the phone down, picked it up again, dialled Jess's number from memory, listened to it ring, and put it down when it clicked on to the answerphone.

He stared at it for a long time.

JESS

By Friday night, Sam had not made contact, and Jess, twenty years wiser than the last time, rang him. It had been a relief having the children at school and being able to sort out the house, but he hadn't rung. Six days of silence. No email or text message. There had been a silence on the answerphone when she came in on Tuesday night, a hiatus before the line went dead. Part of her desperately wanted it to be Sam, but wouldn't he have left a message? Oh hell, why had she told him? Why hadn't she waited?

She listened to his phone ringing, to his recorded voice, and then stood up and took a deep breath. 'Hi, Sam, it's Jess, just checking you've recovered from Saturday. Hope you've had a good week. Speak to you soon.'

She put the phone down. Eight-thirty on a Friday night. He'd be at choir practice. She wondered if he'd go to the pub afterwards, or be home in time to ring her.

Think of something else.

JESSICA: age 18

In an increasingly unusual moment of unity, her parents had agreed that she could have some friends round, that New Year's Eve. Her brother Patrick insisted that he, and their younger sister Julia should be allowed to stay up too, and that the parents should be banished upstairs with plenty of wine.

Sometimes—rarely—everything came together. That's what it felt like, that evening.

She'd given up thinking anything was going to happen with Sam. For three long years she'd understood she'd missed that boat. Bad timing.

But that night in her kitchen, he looked at her, his eyes crinkling at the edges. Their fingers brushed as she handed him a beer. He leant towards her, his thigh grazing hers, their eyes met and she knew.

Other people tried to join in their conversation, but eventually gave up and melted away. When he drank the last of his lager, he set down the can, took her hand and led her out of the kitchen, along the hall to the front room.

It was dark in there, relatively discreet, despite several couples on sofas and chairs, snogging to Roxy Music. He pulled Jessica onto the carpet in front of the gas fire.

'Your hands are cold,' he said, to which she made the stunning reply, 'Yours are warm.'

When he kissed her, the yearning of those teenage years

rose to her throat and she started hyperventilating.

'Take it easy,' he said, hugging her tight, his hard body pressed along the length of her. 'We've got all night.'

The hours dissolved as they lay on the floor in front of the fire, Sam on top of Jessica, her arms tight around him, his hands in her hair, thumbs stroking her face, kissing her open-mouthed, and her kissing him back. It was the most erotic experience of her life. To date.

Eventually they wandered back along the hall to the kitchen, catching the end of a conversation between Caroline and Anna.

'…getting along very well on the floor of the front room.'

'Wow. She's a dark horse. I thought there was something going on with James?' said Anna.

'Not for ages. I'm not sure she ever really liked him, and she's always had a bit of a thing for Sam,' said Caroline.

'Morning all,' said Sam.

Caroline blushed. 'Eeee…'

Sam glanced at his watch. 'I'm starving. Is 5am too early for breakfast?'

'Food? Fabulous idea.' Ruth came into the kitchen with Rob. 'How about some toast? I'll put the kettle on.'

Jessica opened the fridge. 'Eggs?'

'Delicious,' said Sam, grinning.

Jessica located the frying pan and fried all the eggs. Her brother Patrick found another loaf in the freezer. Stragglers who'd not gone home—Stella, Anna, James, Sebastian—ambled into the kitchen, attracted by the cooking smells, and they all sat down to a very early breakfast.

James leant back in his chair and pulled the curtain away from the window, peering into the darkness. 'It's snowing.'

It had threatened to snow a couple of times over Christmas, the temperature plummeting and then creeping back up for a short shower of bitter rain. Now plump, flurrying flakes of proper snow were settling on the glass roof above the window.

'Snowing, it's snowing!' Patrick, who'd been hovering because of a shortage of chairs, jumped around.

'That's right, Patrick.' Rob slapped him on the back, unable to stop grinning.

'We need to go and play in it,' said Ruth.

'Let's walk up to the Common,' said Stella.

'Along to Lake Court,' said Rob. 'The Lake might be frozen.'

Lake Court was an imposing mansion used as a hospital for the elderly, with gardens open to the public. There were a couple of tennis courts on one side of the house and a vast shallow pond, with a fountain in the middle, on the other, which gave the building and Lake Avenue its name. In bright sunshine, Jessica found its atmosphere benign, but she could imagine how creepy it would look at night.

As if he read her thoughts, Sam grinned.

'I need to find my boots,' Jessica said, trying not to smirk.

Sam lounged against the piano while the others retrieved their coats.

She came back and handed him his donkey jacket and maroon scarf, then sat on the piano stool to lace up her boots. When she put on her huge green coat, a hand-me-down from her grandfather, she tied her scarf under her chin before doing the buttons up to the top and turning the collar up, like Sam. She pulled navy woollen gloves from her pockets and put them on. Then Sam took her hand.

But when they walked up the garden into the lane, Jessica took her hand away, pulled her glove off and stuffed it into her pocket. Sam reached for her hand and slipped them both into his pocket, pulling her close.

'Look at the stars.' Sam stared upwards, stopping them all in their tracks, while they peered into the darkness. Then he propelled Jessica forward a few steps, away from the bright pool of streetlight. 'There's the Plough.' He pointed his index finger up from the constellation. 'The North Star.'

She pointed to the 'W'. 'And Cassiopeia.'

They walked in time, a mirror image of each other, as if bound for a three-legged race. The snow muffled the sounds of their footfalls to a scrunch, their prints symmetrical and brightly compacted. It was cold enough to make her teeth ache.

The white of the landscape brightened the dark night. Five forty-five on the church clock as they reached Lake Avenue, the first footfalls on virgin snow that was growing thicker all the time. Jessica blew upwards, to dislodge the flakes settling on her fringe.

'Allow me,' said Sam, his free hand gently shaking her hair.

'Thank you.' She looked up into his dark brown eyes.

'You're welcome.'

She stumbled and he righted her, taking their held hands out of his left pocket and giving her balance. They walked close together, his head bent towards her, their linked hands between them. Somehow this public display of affection made her heart swell even more than rolling around on the sitting room floor with him.

In bunches of twos and threes, they crept through the imposing Victorian gate with its roofed porch and covered benches, into the grounds of Lake Court. It was even more of a fairy landscape than the ghostly, snow-laden beeches of Lake Avenue. A blanket of the crispest, purest white lay pillowed on every surface. Stella, James and Sebastian lead the way past the house towards the pond, the snow silencing them. Jessica and Sam fell behind, arms wrapped around each other, kissing under the grand portico of the house.

Rob slid across the surface of the pond towards Sebastian.

'Will it hold?' Patrick stood on the edge.

'Even if it doesn't, it's not very deep,' said James.

'Are you sure?' said Caroline.

'Don't you believe me?' said James. He turned away from the ice towards the bank of trees and shrubs, a pattern of green latticed with heavy blobs of snow.

'Weird, isn't it?' said Jessica, her hand still held by Sam. 'To think that most of the time you can't stand there at all.'

'You could,' said Sam. 'You'd get a bit wet, though.'

'You know what I mean,' she said, smiling.

'Course I do,' he said, looking into her eyes.

They walked to the centre of the pond, where Sam sat on the stone fountain, and pulled Jessica on to his knee.

'Take that, and that,' yelled Stella, emerging from a rhododendron, throwing snowballs towards their legs. Rob and James pursued her and chucked more snowballs until James fell heavily on the ice and there was a loud crack. Patrick, who had ventured onto the pond's icy surface, leapt back onto the bank.

'Come on, Jessie.' Sam helped Jessica up and they walked towards the edge.

Back on the grass she stamped her feet. 'I'm freezing.'

Sam eyed her. 'But not wet or dead.'

'Chilly wind picking up,' said Stella.

'It's gone six o'clock,' said Caroline. 'Anna, we should head home. I'd rather we were in bed when my parents get up.'

'We'll all head back. We can walk Jessica back, can't we, Seb?' James looked straight at Sam.

'Mm,' said Sam, his arm around Jessica.

James swerved into Sam, speaking as he passed. 'I warned you…'

Jessica tried to catch what he said, but it was blown away on the wind. She found it more difficult to walk in step with Sam with his arm around her. Holding hands had been easier, and somehow more intimate.

It was no longer so magical now they were retracing their own footsteps in the snow.

At the church they stopped, Sam turning one way, Jessica the other. Suddenly he seemed hurried. 'Goodnight.' He pecked her briefly on the lips.

She watched his hasty lope down the road, until James gripped her arm. 'Come on, Jessica, this way.'

Was it just the cold that made her shiver? Or was it that peculiar expression about someone walking over her grave? She felt that something irrevocable had happened without her seeing it coming. She'd had tonight with Sam, but it was already slipping away from her.

She walked down the hill with Sebastian on one side, James on the other, followed by Rob and Stella, Caroline and Anna, and last of all Patrick.

JESS

On Saturday Jess returned from a painfully busy trip to buy the children new school shoes, to three messages on the answerphone. First, her mother looking forward to seeing them at half-term. Shame, thought Jess. Had her relationship with Sam lasted longer than one kiss, maybe she could have persuaded her mother to have the kids for a couple of days. Second, Tom confirming that he would pick the children up at five rather than two. Jess was unsurprised—this was standard behaviour from her ex-husband—but an intriguing sliver of fresh anger sliced into her conscious mind. This was so unexpected she almost missed the third message.

'Mummy, how tall would this Bionicle be in real life? As tall as this room?' Ben held up his Lego toy.

Jess dropped her bags and swooped to the phone to re-play the message. 'Hang on, darling.'

'But would it?'

'I'm hungry.' Millie opened the cupboard in search of biscuits.

'Hold on,' Jess said. 'Just let me listen—'

'Was it Daddy?' said Ben.

Jess flushed. 'Yes.'

'Can we listen?' he said.

'Benedict, darling. Just give me a minute.'

'Hi, Jess. Sorry I've been…'

'Mummy, is that Sam?' said Millie.

'Millie. Darling. Let me listen,' said Jess.

'…incommunicado, and sorry for that phone call last weekend. I got your answerphone a few times and I've been too embarrassed to leave you a message. Please give me a call.'

'Why's he sad?' Millie said.

'Would Josh know how tall Bionicles would be in real life?' said Ben.

'I don't know. Would you like to listen to Daddy, darling?'

'When will he be here?' said Millie.

'This afternoon.'

'After lunch?' Ben stood beside his mother.

'A bit later.' She smoothed the back of his hair down. 'Shall I play you the message?'

Millie pressed her hot hands round Jess's jeans-clad thigh. 'Can we listen to Sam too?'

'Yes, darling.' Jess's shoulders descended a millimetre.

'Glad you're still talking to me,' said Sam, when she rang after lunch. 'Please erase that phone call from your mind. Whatever I said, I didn't mean it.'

'All of it?'

'Well, the bits you didn't like.'

'What's not to like?' Jess said. She had the same feeling she'd had last weekend; that they were somehow talking at cross purposes.

'Look, I've got to drop the children at Elizabeth's now… Are you in later?'

'Yes. Tom's picking Ben and Millie up later this afternoon.'

'And this evening?'
'I'm meant to be going to a drinks party.'
'What time?'
'Eight, eight-thirty?'
'We'll speak before then. OK?'

They spent the afternoon in the garden, Jess trying to mow the grass, and cut back the rampaging climbers. Tom arrived just after five.

'Hi,' he said, stiff and formal, after he'd bent down to hug the children.

'Hi.' She was too tired to argue with him about the blatant way he'd changed the arrangements for the children. Again.

It had taken her a long time to recondition her body's instincts in Tom's presence. At first she'd been unable to stop the palpitations, the dry mouth, sweating palms, shortness of breath. Her friend Claire—a trained counsellor—had been invaluable at offering just the right amount of support and advice. It was learning to concentrate on elongating her breath that managed to break the pattern. Now she could stand in the confined space of her hall and not flinch or fall or run in his presence. Maybe she'd send him an email telling him what she really thought of him.

'I might need to bring them back about three tomorrow,' he said, not quite meeting her eyes, his thin shoulders stooping in her narrow hall.

'No.'

'I have to go—'

'No.' She stepped in front of Ben and Millie so that she could speak quietly, moving closer to him than she had for years. 'It stays at six o'clock, as arranged.'

Tom's eyes flickered for a second. 'Would Lucy—?'

'No.'

A deadening silence settled between them.

'Mummy?' said Millie.

'Goodbye, darling, have a wonderful time.' She picked up her daughter to give her a hug. She turned to Ben, bending down to hug him fiercely. 'Bye, darling, look after Millie for me.'

'I miss you, Mummy,' said Millie.

'Me too, darling. See you tomorrow.' She let go of Ben and gave Millie a kiss, not looking at Tom as he ushered them towards a silver Mercedes.

'New car?' She clenched her fists by her side.

'Company car,' he dismissed.

Tom's charmed life—marketing director, new house in Fulham—had him driving to work each day. He still avoided public transport.

With the children in the back of the car, she watched as he raked his hands through his thinning hair and opened the driver's door.

'Six o'clock,' Jess said.

'Six o'clock,' he said.

He slammed the door, started the engine and swept out into the street. She waved to the children as she went inside. Then she climbed the stairs to her bedroom, pulled the duvet back, and lay face down on the white sheet. She pressed her face into the mattress, counting in for six, out for seven, in for seven, out for eight…

At six o'clock she removed the smudged mascara from her eyes and rubbed it off the sheet as best she could. Alone again on a Saturday night. Did she really have the energy to shower and change to go to Lucy and Dan's drinks party?

She pulled the stopper off the half-empty bottle of white wine, found some not completely stale crackers and took them into the garden.

Half an hour later she went to find a cardigan and realised someone was standing outside her front door. She opened it to find Sam, poised to ring the bell.

'What are you doing here?' Her heart hammered against her ribs. She'd meant to be so smooth and silken next time she saw him.

'I said we'd talk. Just thought face-to-face might be easier. May I come in?' He handed her a cold bottle of champagne.

She ran the back of her hand across her hot, no doubt shiny forehead. 'When did you leave? Are you mad, driving all this way?'

'That's your fault. I used to be a perfectly rational human being.' He followed her down the hall and surveyed the large kitchen with French windows open to the garden. 'This is great.'

'Thank you,' she said, trying not to hyperventilate. *Breathe*. 'I take it you'd like some champagne.'

'One glass would be lovely, if you'll have one too.'

She wiped her damp palms on her jeans and put them on the cool granite surface, either side of the bottle. 'How long's it taken you?'

'Left shortly after two-thirty. Stopped briefly at Warwick services. Got lost only once, coming off the A3 into Wimbledon.'

She found two flutes, holding one under the bottle as it made a quiet exhalation, pushing the cork into Sam's hand. Sam's brown, steady hand. Unlike her own shaking, jittery ones. He was taking years off her life, turning up like this.

'Olives?' She searched the cupboard. 'I've run out of

crisps and those crackers are stale.' She pointed to the remains of the packet on the surface. She felt wrong-footed. Thrilled, too, but the last thing she needed was a knight on a white charger. She pulled the top off a tin of olives, drained and shook them into a bowl.

They sat on the garden bench and surveyed the scene. The back fence needed vital repair work and the grass was a mess, but she'd hidden the empty pots, and round the patio, the lavenders and nasturtiums ran riot.

'This is lovely.' Sam sipped his champagne.

Jess took a deep breath. 'What are you doing here, Sam?'

'Would you rather I wasn't?'

'No.' She stopped. 'Not necessarily.'

'I wanted to show you I haven't lost it. That I'm still sane.'

'Don't you think driving from Manchester on the off chance might make me think the opposite?'

'I should have rung. I felt bad about last weekend…'

She waited for a bit. 'Are you going back tonight, or were you thinking I might offer you a bed for the night?'

'It doesn't matter. Whatever you like.'

'Did you bring a toothbrush?'

'And a change of shirt in case you wanted me to take you to that party.' He grinned for the first time since he'd arrived.

'You want to go on a date?'

'Why does everyone keep calling it that?' He pushed his hand through his not thinning hair.

She laughed. He'd offered to take her to the party. She could go with him, introduce him, see the thinly disguised looks of pity from all those married women transformed into interest or shock or even envy. She'd spent too many evenings trying to fill the void a husband left in her shrinking social life with her own best impression of a single mother. Coping-admirably-given-the-circumstances. Looking nice enough that no one would try to commiserate with her over how tired/drawn/pale she was, but not so nice that the wives would start treating her with suspicion and intervene any time their husbands talked to her. A thin line to travel, particularly at Lucy and Dan's where she would know a lot of people not terribly well—hello in the street, isn't our Harry in the same class as your son, sort of acquaintances—and just a few people properly. Only Lucy to whom she talked honestly.

'What's so funny?' he said.

She blinked. 'I was thinking you might come in useful to scupper any potential Amanda situations.'

'You don't think she'll be there.' He tried not to smile.

'It's very kind, Sam, but you don't need to do this. Tom and I split up a long time ago—three years this Christmas—and I'm managing—'

'Jess. I am not here to rescue you. I'm here to talk to you. I fucked up on the phone and fucked up even more when I didn't reach you all week. I wanted to see you. That's all.' He ran his hand through his hair again. He frowned, looked up, following her eye line.

She cleared her throat. 'Sorry.' What the hell did it matter why he was here?

'Look. If you want to go to the party, fine. If not, fine. I'll go home as soon as you like. You decide.'

'Well, I can't send you back straightaway.' She reached for her glass. 'The least I can do is feed you.' She smiled, until she questioned how that sounded. 'Food. Would you like to go to the drinks thing?'

'As long as we can have a proper conversation somewhere along the way. Before, after, during…'

'Mm.' Maybe he would tell her what he had been going to say on the phone. She focused on a clump of missed weeds between two paving stones.

'I do remember what you said on the phone. I'm not expecting you to invite me into your bed. The spare bed will do just fine.'

The ambiguity of the phrase brought her out in a hot flush. Oh, Lord.

He stood up. 'Shall I get the bottle?'

Just keep breathing. And go to that drinks party. If he's staying the night, don't spend the evening alone with him.

He re-filled her glass.

She took a couple of olives. 'I think I might just ring Lucy, and check it's OK to bring a strange man with me.'

Jess sat down on the bench. 'All good. Drinks, and food as well. Eight o'clock.'

'Great. Where?' Sam picked up his half empty glass.

'Lucy and Dan live in the next street. We can walk. Their daughter's in Ben's class, and their son's in Millie's. She's been a very good friend the last couple of years.'

'Glad I brought a clean shirt.' He put down his glass and turned to look at her. 'And my toothbrush.'

'OK. Well, I should have a shower. I've been gardening all afternoon. Shall I show you where you can change?' She knew she was talking too fast.

He was very close, and getting closer, blocking out the light, until his lips brushed hers.

Her stomach fell away.

'Are you sure about this?'

'Absolutely. We *must* go.' She couldn't possibly keep him at bay for the next five hours unless they were with other people.

'About me coming with you.'

'Honestly?'

He nodded, encouraging her to continue.

'I'm a little freaked out about it. But in a good way. And it's going to be a far more interesting Saturday night than I had envisaged. Which can only be a good thing.'

Sam winked. 'Certainly spicing up my Saturday night.'

'Wow.' He stepped into the kitchen, his hair damp from the shower. 'That's a great dress.'

'Thank you.' The red linen sleeveless dress—a present from Anna—seemed absolutely the right outfit to go out with Sam on a Saturday night. The gardening had brought colour to her cheeks, and the tops of her arms.

He stood in front of her. 'You're taller too.'

'One of the two pairs of shoes I possess with a bit of a heel,' she said, showing a wedged sandal.

'Mmm.' He leant one arm either side of her on the work surface, stepped closer. 'Means you're nearer.'

His lips found hers, his tongue caressed her mouth, his weight pressed hard against her. She grabbed hold of his shirt to stop from dissolving into a puddle at his feet.

The ringing phone made her jump.

Sam stepped back.

'Sorry,' she said. 'It might be the children.'

SAM

Sam leant against the sink, his back to the garden, watching Jess talk to Millie and Ben. He felt that familiar wrench of being apart from his children. It didn't matter how many times it had already happened, his heart sank every time they left to stay with their mother. Despite all the challenges of dealing with an increasingly closed-off, monosyllabic Kate. Jess was agreeing to take all the forgotten toys into bed with her and look after them until the children returned from their overnight stay with their father.

He wondered what uncharacteristic spontaneity had made him drive to the M6 and keep heading south after he'd dropped the children off.

He stopped. Not uncharacteristic spontaneity. Forgotten spontaneity: he had been spontaneous before children. He pondered that thought for a moment. Before Elizabeth. For so many years she had controlled so much of their lives, and he had let her. And before Elizabeth there was James, deciding what they did, who they saw. It felt a very long time since he had made his own decisions, without deferring to anyone else.

Jess was saying goodbye. God, he wanted to make love to her. Even thought he'd be able to. Contemplating it only aroused him more.

'How are they?' he asked.

'Fine now. It doesn't get any easier, does it?'

'Just what I was thinking.' He turned around to look down the garden, holding out an arm for her. 'How are we doing for time?'

She stood in the circle of his arm. 'Twenty to eight. Do you fancy walking up the hill? I want to buy some crisps and then we could go through the park.'

'Fine by me. I like the idea of getting to know where you live.'

JESS

'Jess, hi, come on in.' Dan held the door wide for her, kissing her on both cheeks.

'Hi, Dan.' She tried to pull enough breath into her lungs. 'This is Sam.'

'Hello, Dan.' Sam smiled.

'Sam. Pleased to meet you.' They shook hands, while Dan looked as if he was trying to remember if they'd met before.

'Go on through,' Dan said, pointing to the kitchen and garden beyond, where several people milled around, glasses in hand. Lucy walked towards them, tall and slim in a swirly purple skirt and beaded top.

'Lucy, this is Sam,' Jess squeaked. *Breathe.*

'Hello, Sam, so glad you could come. What would you like to drink?' She looked from one to the other. 'Wine? Beer?'

'Wine,' they said together.

Sam winked at Jess as their eyes connected.

'So, you're the doctor?' said Lucy.

'That's right.'

Lucy smiled at Jess. 'By the way, Claire rang just after you and said they *would* be able to come after all.'

'Oh, good.' *Thank you, God.* Presenting her with her conscience at a moment like this. Always good to have a vicar's wife on hand. She sipped her wine.

'Hi Jess.' She turned to see Louise, a mum from school, with her carefully waved long blond hair, high flowery mules, designer jeans, tight top and impressive cleavage. She wore a shrewd expression and serious red lipstick. Her husband Jeremy, snazzy in black, stood at her elbow.

Jess tucked a stray lock of hair behind her ear. 'Hi. Sam, this is Louise and Jeremy. Parents from school.'

'Hi,' said Louise. 'And you are..?'

'An old friend.' Sam's tone was calm.

'I see,' said Louise. 'Honestly, Jess, you never tell us anything.'

Jess opened her mouth and then caught Sam's eye. She took a breath. 'Sam just happens to be in London…'

'I see.' Louise surveyed them.

'And what do you do?' said Jeremy.

'I'm a doctor. GP in Manchester,' Sam said.

'Interesting?' said Jeremy.

'Has its moments.' Sam smiled. 'You?'

'I'm a director. Commercials. Films.'

'Busy?' said Sam.

'Been a quiet summer,' Jeremy said.

'But some very interesting projects coming up,' said Louise.

'And do you work outside the home?' Sam asked Louise. 'Or is your focus children at the moment?'

'I couldn't possibly do just children, I'd go out of my mind with boredom. Sorry, Jess. No, I'm a television producer.'

'Louise works for CBeebies,' Jess couldn't help interjecting.

'Actually it's mostly CBBC now, among other things,' said Louise, smiling exclusively at Sam.

'My kids love CBBC,' he said.

'Really. How many?' she said.

'Three.'

'We've got three as well. Very close together,' said Louise.

'Louise puts the rest of us to shame,' said Jess.

Sam met her eyes, the beginning or the end of a smile tracing his lips.

'I enrol a lot of help,' said Louise. 'I have a fabulous au-pair. What about you, Sam? How does your family manage?'

'My children are a bit older, which helps.' He drank his wine.

'And your wife? Does she work?'

Jess inhaled. Sam put his hand on the small of her back. 'Ex-wife. We share custody, Does anyone fancy some fresh air? It's a bit warm in here.' With his hand he steered Jess past Louise and Jeremy and stepped into the garden, lit with flares and lanterns. For September, the fast falling dusk was still and warm.

'Whatever you do, don't turn around,' he whispered in her ear. 'And breathe, for goodness' sake.'

'She is so impudent.'

'Good word.'

'Don't you mind?'

'Not half as much as you do.' He smiled at her. 'Now what's the problem with Claire coming, and what does Dan have against me?'

'What?' She looked up at him, in the half-light. 'You're perfect.'

'As are you.' He waited. 'So? Tell me about Dan.'

'Nothing to tell.'

He shrugged. 'I must have imagined he had some hold over you.'

'No hold at all,' she said, meeting his eyes.

'Good. Now who's Claire again?'

Something made Jess turn around as Claire and John stepped into the garden, glasses of wine in hand.

'This is Sam,' she began. 'Old friend from Manchester,' she added, to avoid the inevitable question.

'John Hardy. This is my wife Claire. Good to meet you.' John extended his hand to Sam.

'Likewise,' said Sam.

'Do you still live in Manchester?' said Claire.

'He lives in the old family home,' said Jess, before she could stop herself. She braced for a steely look of disapproval. Tom had hated the way she used to butt in and finish his thoughts. Once she'd learnt, she'd never got a word in edgeways. But there was no warning grimace from Sam.

'What brings you to London?' John said.

'Just passing through and thought I'd drop in on Jessica,' Sam said diplomatically.

'So you're going back tonight?' John said.

'Oh, stop giving him the third degree.' Claire beamed at Sam. 'I do apologise. Vicars are notorious for asking too many questions.'

There was a short, interesting silence during which John appeared to struggle to keep his mouth shut.

'Jess is kindly putting me up in her spare room,' said Sam.

'So you managed to get out of going to that thing?' Jess said to Claire.

'Is your church local?' Sam asked John.

'Yes, and I'm so glad we did,' said Claire, under cover of the men's voices. 'Otherwise I'd never have met the gorgeous Sam.'

'Claire!' said Jess, wondering whether he'd heard.

'Quick, tell me more,' she whispered. 'You met up with him when you were back home, and then again in Cornwall. And now?'

'He's there. I'm here. There are five kids involved. An ex-wife. An ex-husband.'

'It's got absolutely nothing to do with Tom,' said Claire.

Jess smiled at her with gratitude. Being able to behave relatively normally in the same space as Tom had been achieved in part through many helpful conversations with Claire, who, as well as being a trained counsellor, was a perceptive listener. 'Except it has. If I was there, he'd see far less of the children. I couldn't do that.'

'There's high demand for doctors everywhere. Especially London.'

'And then he wouldn't be around for his mother, or his children. He shares custody with his ex. He couldn't move, and I wouldn't ask him.'

'Well, pray about it. These things can all be worked out.'

'Another glass of wine?' Sam asked.

'Yes, please,' said Claire. They handed him their glasses.

'I'll find some water,' said John. 'I'm driving.'

Jess and Claire watched the two men going back into the house.

'How do the children feel about him?' said Claire.

'Oh, they're at Tom's this weekend.' She realised what she'd just said. 'They like him. Millie loves him. They both get on well with his kids. Two of them anyway.' She ground to a halt.

'So you're telling me it's just the two of you in your house all night? That's quite a temptation.'

'Oh, it's fine. Millie rang to tell me about all the stuffed animals she'd left behind, so I've promised to look after them in my bed. There won't be room for anyone else.' *Where's my wine?*

'But plenty of room in the spare bed,' said Claire.

'Claire!' Jess said.

They moved indoors to eat Thai green curry and rice. Not before time, Jess thought, hoping it would soak up the alcohol. Which was good, because it lessened the chances of flinging herself into Sam's arms shouting, 'Take me to bed or lose me forever,' as soon as they crossed her threshold.

She found his presence more and more distracting, her stomach twisting into knots. She wondered what she had missed in that unguarded phone call last Saturday night. He'd had a few glasses of wine tonight, but was it enough to get him to say whatever it was he'd wanted to say?

'More?' Sam took their empty plates and stood up.

'No, thank you.'

'Wine?' He turned back when she didn't reply, and crouched beside her. 'Jess? Anything? Water?'

'Yes. Water would be lovely.' She followed him down the hall towards the kitchen. Half-way he stopped. 'Tired?'

'A bit.' A definite answer suddenly felt loaded.

Claire and John were helping themselves to seconds, chatting to Lucy.

'You OK?' Claire said, scanning Jess's face.

'Beginning to flag. Need some sugar or something.'

'Cheesecake,' said Lucy, as if on cue.

At half-past eleven, those guests with children began murmuring about getting home to relieve the babysitter.

'Of course that is one of the big bonuses of having a live-in au-pair,' said Louise.

'So's being divorced,' Jess whispered to Sam. 'Sometimes the children aren't even there.'

'Behave.' He grinned. 'Why do you dislike her so much?'

'I don't dislike her. I just feel inferior. As if I have to apologise the whole time.'

'So, don't see her. If that's how she makes you feel.'

'But she's been really kind to me since Tom left,' said

Jess. She'd thought about this before. It was not a revelation that Louise made her feel worse, not better about herself.

He raised an eyebrow.

'Is that something they actively teach you at medical school?' she burst out.

'What?'

'The silences. Leaving them long enough for the other person to fill.'

'Jess, what are you talking about?' He looked dead serious until she detected that ghost of a smile again. 'Shall we go?'

'Oh. Yes. It's getting late.' Strange how life was made up of instants—this way, that way—which could be clarified and concentrated into a key moment. Would she take this path, or that?

'Bye, Sam, it was good to meet you.' John shook his hand.

'Let us know when you're in London again, we could have dinner.' Claire reached up to give him a kiss.

'Thank you, I will.'

'I take it we won't see you at church tomorrow morning?' said Claire.

'Whatever makes you think that?' Jess's words sounded slightly strangled.

'Be good,' Claire said. 'Don't do anything I wouldn't do.'

'But you're happily married,' Jess protested. 'You've got someone to kiss.'

This last sentence was said into a surprised silence.

'And I'm very grateful,' said John. 'Come on, Claire, early start tomorrow.'

Walking brought on a sense of panic. Jess glanced sideways at Sam, his long strides falling into step with her own.

How fast was too fast? Would he think her rude if she sprinted home and slammed the door on him?

She looked up to find him watching her.

'You've got that look in your eyes, Jessica.' He seemed so ready to be leaned on, metaphorically as well as physically.

'What look?'

'Like you're having an argument in your head.' He reached for her hand. 'Stop it.'

She shivered. Now he had that cheerful look on his face. She waved her free hand at his face. 'Definitely don't do that.'

'What?'

'That smiling in the moonlight.'

'You don't want me to smile at you?' He stood stock still, forcing her to stop too.

What would her genetics teacher have told her? This is how genes work. Attraction to others, to something new, a natural physical response felt by many species, not just humans.

Her stomach plummeted as she thought about the kiss in the kitchen. All these years—years of waiting—and they were on their way back to an empty house. She knew it. She should have shut the door in his face the second she realised who it was. There were some people you could never be sensible about.

He dropped her hand and searched her face. 'What is it? Would you rather I left?'

'Don't be silly. You can't drive back to Manchester at this time of night.'

'I'm not expecting sex, if that's what you're thinking.'

At least he wasn't charming her with talk of making love.

'Which is not to say that making love to you has not been on my mind.'

'You've got to stop this.'

'Stop what? Give me specifics and I'll do what I can.'

'The smiling. The being absolutely perfect with my friends. The talk of…you know…' She made a wave with her hand.

He mirrored the movement. 'Are we talking about what I think we're talking about?'

'Just don't.'

'Why? Find me irresistible, do you?' He laughed. When she said nothing he began walking along the street again. 'I'm joking, Jess.'

'Anyway.' She followed. 'Aren't we supposed to be having a conversation?'

'As opposed to what we've been doing all evening?'

She took a deep breath. 'Didn't you want to talk about something, on the phone last Saturday night?'

'Actually, what I thought might be a problem is no longer a problem. So, no, I don't need to talk about it.' He wore that cheerful look again.

Why can't I just enjoy him while he's here? Enjoy his company while he's here, she corrected herself. There'd be time to scourge her conscience later.

He smiled at her as they turned the corner. 'I promise not to pounce. So take that look off your face.'

'Sorry, Sam—'

'It's all right. You always were a deep thinker.'

She sighed. 'High maintenance. *When Harry Met Stella.* Tom always thought I was the worst type of woman. High maintenance, but thinks she's low maintenance.'

'Always? Right from the beginning?'

'I guess he thought it was worth the effort in the beginning.'

'Well, don't beat yourself up about it. Elizabeth would win any competition on this issue you care to have.'

SAM

By the time Jess unlocked her front door, Sam's ardour, which had been successfully fanned into flame at regular intervals since he'd arrived—and re-ignited by holding her hand on the walk home—was once more under control. Just. He wanted to give her a hug, but decided against it when he caught her eye.

Tricky. She looked like she could do with a hug.

'What would you like?' Jess walked down the hall to the back room.

She switched a couple of side lights on and he enjoyed seeing her move while he imagined several of the things he'd really like, and his ardour rose again. Hot and tight. 'Are you having anything?'

'Water. Maybe some mint tea. Do you want a coffee?'

'No, thanks. Water please.' He watched her stretch for the glasses, the curve of her shoulder and neck heating his blood. Then he pictured her in black underwear, his weight on her, the softness of her body underneath him.

Time to get up to that top floor, before he broke his promise and lunged.

He swivelled on his heels. 'Thank you for letting me stay.'

'No problem.'

He reached the end of the hall and dumped his glass down on the stair. Then he marched back to the kitchen.

Jess was motionless by the sink.

'Come here.' He reached her in five strides, taking her in his arms and hugging her. He held her until she started breathing again, until she began to melt against him and fire up the blood in his veins. He kissed her open mouth. 'Sleep well. I have plans for tomorrow.'

He retrieved his glass and headed upstairs. In the spare room he opened the window wide, and dropped onto the bed. It was going to be hard staying up here alone, knowing Jess was so close. He wondered if she'd be wearing that strappy nightdress.

Yep, staying here was hard. Actually everything was hard. And wasn't that something to be thankful for?

JESS

'Of course, in the old days, I'd never have rung you. And you'd never have appeared unannounced.' She pushed her plate away and looked over the edge of the sunny balcony to the river below. 'Doesn't the Thames look perfect?'

Sam regarded her. 'Perfect. What old days?'

'You know. Twenty years ago. If I'd heard nothing from you for almost a week, there's no way I'd have rung you up.' She relived the shocked relief at opening the door to him. The divine way he'd coped with Louise and her friends. She couldn't work out if it was that, or the hard kiss pressed against the kitchen cupboards, which was more of a turn on. She'd been perversely disappointed by his quick disappearance when they got home.

'Maybe we're clearer about what we want now.'

She felt hot under his gaze. 'It's not just that. It's having the courage to communicate directly. I found out more about your state of mind from…from James…than I ever did from you.'

'What are you talking about?' Sam leaned back in his chair.

She swallowed. 'Giving me the brush off. Via him.'

'When was this?'

'It's all right, Sam. It was a long time ago and I got over it.'

'When was this?' he repeated.

'After that New Year's Eve. It was just before your A Level mocks. I did understand.' She examined her hands, unable to meet his eyes. 'I know you weren't interested.'

'I *was* interested. I'd always been interested,' he said, a look of grim concentration on his face.

They stared at each other as Jess envisaged another fork in the road, the road less travelled.

'Oh.' She was less surprised by this revelation than she might have been. 'If we'd really been that keen, a bit of misinformation on his part wouldn't have stopped us.'

'But it would. That's what you just said about ringing me on Friday. Twenty years ago you never would have.'

Jess shrugged. 'You know, at the time I did wonder whether…James…was intent on keeping us apart because he was interested in me. But now I suspect it was someone altogether different.'

'I don't know about that,' Sam said. 'I think he was putting his oar in because he could. He's always liked being in control.'

Jess took a gulp of water, to relieve the dryness in her mouth. 'What did you say he does now?'

'Something very suitable. He's standing as an MP.'

She laughed, feeling the prickles of sweat on her body, the tension in her neck easing fractionally. She didn't want to know what Sam had really thought about her.

'There was definitely something about you then. Even if you were pretty intense. You're a lot more relaxed now.'

'Relaxed?' she snorted. 'I'm so relaxed I may shatter into a thousand pieces.'

'OK. You have the potential to be more relaxed. In fact, I've been having some ideas about how to help you with that.' He ducked as Jess's arm swung in his direction and he neatly caught her wrist. 'And fun to be with. I can see it in your eyes.'

She flapped the neck of her top, trying to breathe. 'This is definitely not about sex.'

'OK.'

Without thinking, she smacked him on the arm, his reflexes blunted for once. 'Don't wrong-foot me the whole time. Being so bloody reasonable.'

'You don't want me to be reasonable? Tom has got a lot to answer for. And don't think I'm going to disappear. This time I'm going to be a lot harder to get rid of.'

She lifted her chin. 'Is that so?'

He cleared his throat. 'What are you doing the last week in October?'

Jess pulled a face. 'I don't have plans after next weekend, let alone two months' time.'

'Half term. Assuming you have the same week.'

She shrugged. 'Possibly go and stay with my mother in Cheltenham.'

'Find out which week, would you? I may have plans. Involving you.'

JESSICA: age 18

The first Sunday of the new year, Jessica dragged herself up to the youth club, YF. Anything was better than being in the same house as her parents. Or alone with her thoughts. Visions of Sam pinning her to the floor of the sitting room kept crashing into her mind.

Now, in the main room of Barton Cottage, they were coming to the end of a game of charades, veering from mildly interesting to inspired; inexplicable to hilarious. Jessica strived to pay attention, but the scene at home was repeating on her, and she kept missing the punchline. She'd taken the coward's way out by leaving the house.

Caroline approached Jessica. 'Everything OK?'

'Fine.' Jessica avoided her eye.

'Must be difficult.' Caroline looked to where Sam and Rob stood talking.

She followed Caroline's eyeline. 'That,' she spat. 'That's *nothing*.'

'Oh. I imagined…?'

Jessica stood perfectly still for a second, gauging how fast she could reach the front door. 'Do you know what I had to do before I came here tonight?'

'I've no idea,' said Caroline.

'My father sat us all down. My mum, Patrick and Julia and made us watch the promotional film he's just finished editing. Marketing three new hotels.' She closed her eyes.

'Jessica. You don't have to tell me.'

'At the end there's a soft-focus romantic music bit with two lovers. Guess who?'

'Who?'

'My father. And that woman. His secretary.'

'What happened then?'

'I left. I didn't have the guts to tell him what a fucking outrageous thing that was to do to my mother.'

'And to you.'

Jessica blinked. 'He denies it. He thinks we're fucking stupid.'

'I'm so sorry. Maybe it's all a horrible mistake.'

Jessica met her eyes for the first time. 'Do you really think that?'

James materialised in front of Jessica. 'It was definitely your dad. And that woman.'

'Shut up,' she said.

'You know you've got to talk about it. Now's the perfect time.'

'Now's the worst time, James.' She shook with rage.

'Jessica?' Caroline put out an arm, but James was there before her.

'Don't touch me!'

He calmly folded his arms. 'Just because you're upset, too.'

'Don't you dare,' Jessica whispered.

'What's—?' Caroline began.

'This I do not need. Sorry.'

She dodged down the hallway to the door but James followed her and drew alongside.

Broad, dark-coated; his shape similar to her father's. Nathaniel Lamb. The charmer.

Jessica was slowly developing a sense of how others saw

him. The life and soul of the party when he chose to be, particularly when surrounded by pretty girls.

How long ago had Ruth come round to find Jessica's mother calmly picking up pieces of her husband's trousers? He had lost his temper with a sticking zip so badly that he had hacked them up and strewn them all over the hall.

Jessica had shrugged and turned away, and said her dad had anger issues.

Luckily Ruth never mentioned it again.

Three days later, the evening before they went back to school, a bunch of them walked into Millingham to the cinema. They were days away from their mock A Level exams. Rob and James already had their university places lined up. Caroline had taken the Oxbridge paper. There would be no let-up in studying, with the real exams in May and June, and then the long summer.

Already, there was talk of separate plans, a sense of scattering to different places.

The roads were eerie in the orange streetlight reflecting off the grubby snow, reminding Jessica once again of that walk through the grounds of Lake Court to the fountain, and what had gone wrong with Sam. They hadn't spoken since that night and her dreams of him ringing her up and asking her out had been well and truly crushed.

It was so much worse than before. Then they were friends. Now they were strangers, sitting well apart in the group. Jessica found herself much further along the row, wrestling James's arm from around her, and shoving it back at him with her elbow. Twice. The second time. he'd stared at her until she glanced away from the screen.

'Prick tease.'

She felt the hairs rise at the back of her neck, her mouth

dry. The rushing in her ears distorted the film's soundtrack. 'Why would you say that?'

'You know that's what you are.'

Jess gazed, unseeing, her face raised towards the screen. Blinking now and then, but never shedding a tear. When the film finished and the lights came up, she had a moment, her face in her scarf, as she turned away to put on her coat. She managed not to turn around as they edged out of the row, knowing he was right behind her, but perhaps wisely, not touching her. And then Stella was asking her about the film, and helpfully not waiting for her answer, prattling to Caroline, drawing her into their conversation.

They climbed the hill, as far as Woodham Road, where they would have usually splintered off to walk home.

'I have a better idea,' said James. 'Can't miss this opportunity.' He cut down towards the Common, Sam and Rob behind him.

Jessica desperately wanted to go home, but she also didn't want to walk the length of Woodham Road, past the church, down the hill to her house, on her own. By the time the girls joined them, the boys had arrived at the locked gates of the sixth form centre, which was still surrounded by pristine, glistening snow.

James climbed over the metal railings—easy to do with their smooth top edge—and they all followed. Jessica exchanged looks with Caroline. Law-abiding middle-class children—because that's what they were, even if they were pretty much eighteen—getting their kicks from a little light trespassing.

Jessica boosted herself up on the railings and watched James roll a snowball, criss-crossing the wide lawn, until it was too big to push. Rob stood in the centre of the snowy expanse, cigarette glowing. Beside him Sam declined a smoke, standing hunched into his jacket, hands deep in his pockets.

One by one they were harangued into joining James—even Jessica, who had no desire to draw attention to herself by dissembling—pushing the vast snowball until the ground was green again, rolling it into place across the double doors of the sixth form centre with a resounding and satisfying thud.

From beneath her fringe she scanned the group. Caroline and Stella were speculating about essay questions on *Middlemarch*. James was trying to persuade Sam to invite him and Rob in for a drink. Whenever she spotted James staring at her, she flinched. His attitude in the cinema hadn't been deterred by her emphatic no. And when she fleetingly looked at Sam, she felt a cold absence that made no sense. Their moment together had been so brief, how could it hurt this much?

She shuddered. Why did James use that hateful term, prick tease? What had he said to Sam? What had she failed to hear, blown away by the wind?

She'd thought they were an ordinary group of friends. Friends who looked out for each other, at least most of the time. But James seemed to have a completely different idea about what friendship was. Generally, or just in his attitude towards her, she didn't know.

Maybe this was just what happened to friends who grew up in close proximity to each other. The quality of the relationships changed. They had all spent such a lot of time together over the last four years, but increasingly had other interests, other friends.

And yet here they were, standing in an untidy circle in the snow. Was it just the unique snowclad landscape that gave the scene finality, as if this was the end of an era?

JESS

Tuesday night, Jess was still trying to shrink the large piles of paperwork spread all over her kitchen into one small pile, when the phone rang.

'Can you talk?'

'Only if I interrupt the very important filing I'm doing.'

'When does Tom have the kids next?'

'End of the month, I think.'

'Good. That's my free weekend too. Can you come here?'

'Where? Your house?'

'If you trust me.'

She could hear the grin in Sam's voice. 'Of course I do.'

There was a brief pause. 'Maybe you shouldn't.'

'What?'

'I'll organise the ticket.'

'No. I'll organise the ticket. If I come.' The phrase hung in the airwaves.

'You know you want to,' he said.

She had a dangerous feeling they were no longer talking geography. 'I'll think about it.'

'OK, but not for long. Ring me tomorrow to say yes.'

She spent the following day agonising about going to Millingham, and had almost definitely decided that it was just too much of a temptation. She knew exactly what she was unable to resist, as far as Sam was concerned. Until Tom rang.

'I can't do the last weekend of the month.' She'd thought it odd enough that he didn't bother to say hello on the phone when they were married, but now she thought it downright rude. Really, Clarissa had a lot to answer for, making her elder son believe that the world revolved around and slightly below him.

'I'm away from Friday to Sunday,' said Jess.

'What? Where? You never go away.'

The impulse to scream, 'None of your fucking business,' almost overcame her, but she swallowed hard. 'I know. Which means you feel totally at liberty to change the arrangements at a moment's notice. I hate being in London, knowing the children are here, but not with me. I'm going to Millingham to make it more bearable.'

There was a long pause. Breathe. In. Breathe. Out. Jess felt the blood pulsating in her ears, waiting for the counter-attack. This was why she didn't do confrontation.

'Why are you going? Can't you change it?' he said eventually.

'What's so important that weekend?' She was surprised by the normality of her voice. Tom said nothing.

'Nothing is that important, or nothing you can tell me?' She waited. *You gave me two wonderful children. We have a history. No one can change those facts.* No one could change the fact that he'd once asked her to marry him—and she'd said yes.

How had it come to this?

'Fine. Leave it as it is. Go to Millingham.'

With that he put the phone down and she was left to stare at it. *Don't feel bad. This is not your fault.*

SAM

After several rings, the phone was answered. 'Rob Randall.'

'Bloody hell, you're difficult to get hold of.' Sam was itching to ring Jess, but he didn't want to hassle her into a no.

'Sam. Sorry. Absolute nightmare. Only been back in the country a couple of hours.'

'Anywhere glamorous?'

'Brussels. So, no. How are the kids? How's Katie?'

'You realise you're taking your life in your hands calling her that?' Sam thought about it. 'In fact you may be the only person who can get away with it.'

'Still stroppy, is she? Any particular reason?'

'I think it may be something to do with hormones. I did read about it somewhere.'

'Very funny,' said Rob. 'You'll have that for at least five years.'

'That's exactly what…'

'What's exactly what?'

Sam swallowed. 'That's exactly what Jess said.'

'When?'

'In the summer. July.'

'Then you saw her in Cornwall.'

'Did I tell you this?'

'Bumped into Sebastian at Heathrow. He said you definitely needed rescuing.'

'From what?'

'Jess. She's sweet, I'm sure, but—'

'Sweet is not the word I'd use to describe Jess.'

'What is, then?' Rob's question sounded like a challenge.

'I don't know. She's feisty. She manages to raise her kids on her own, with virtually no support from her ex-husband.'

'So you're stepping into the breach? Are you insane?'

'No, I'm not insane.'

'Couldn't you find someone closer to home, without all the baggage and the children?'

'I'm not sleeping with her. We're friends—'

'Is this about Briony?'

Sam seriously contemplated putting the phone down, and deeply regretted—for the hundredth time—telling Rob what had happened. He'd only told him because they'd spent a very long, alcohol-fuelled evening together, and mostly because he hadn't told anyone else.

'Rob, just forget it would you? Forget I ever told you.'

Rob sighed. 'Tell me about Jess then. You haven't had sex yet, but you—?'

'Just because you want to shag anything with a pulse. OK, anything female with a pulse.' Sam found Rob's tone of voice deeply annoying.

He heard Rob swallow, then take a breath. 'Explain it to me.'

'There's something about her.' As he said the words, he realised there really was. He loved looking at her, talking to her, waiting to see what she'd say next.

'What? Sebastian said she's not that attractive.'

'She's lovely. She's got great eyes. So, she's not a babe in his sense of the word, but I'm—'

'You've lost me, you really have. Empirically, you are an attractive man. This I know. Briony was attractive. Single. No kids. Living in Manchester.'

'Rob, think about it. I need someone like her like I need a hole in the head. They'll want to get married and have their own kids. I don't want any more kids.'

'But Jess has some. Two? Three?'

'Two. Sweet kids.'

'So, what's the difference?'

Sam tried to formulate the words to explain to Rob what it was about Jess that made him want to see her, but he wasn't convinced he understood it himself.

'She makes you feel virile. You can protect her, it's her vulnerability that attracts you.'

Sam opened his mouth to say something but couldn't think of anything. Was that it?

'I still think it's mainly about sex,' said Rob. 'Face it, most things are about sex.'

'You're unbelievable. One day you're going to wake up and realise half your life has gone and you're alone.'

'But not lonely. I like my own company.'

'Good. You may have to get used to it.'

'When do you see her again?'

'End of the month. I hope.'

'Keep me posted.'

'Sure.' Not a chance.

He disconnected, filled the kettle, and picked up the phone again to dial Jess's number, but there was no dialling tone. 'Hello?'

'Sam?' said Jess.

'I was just about to ring you. For your answer.'

'OK.'

'OK you're coming, or OK you're going to give me your answer?' he asked, dimly aware of his surging pulse, clammy hands, dry mouth.

'OK, I'll come.'

'Good. That was the correct answer. What time do you get in? I could meet you—'

'I'll drive up during the day.' Her words sounded rushed to Sam.

'Do you really want to drive? It's a long way.'

'I know precisely how long a drive it is. Don't patronise me.'

'Sorry. I'll have surgery till six, so I can leave a key somewhere, if you arrive before I'm home.'

'Fine. It will depend on when I leave. Hopefully before lunch.'

'Good. We can do as much or as little as we like, once you're here. Is there anything in particular you want to do?'

There was absolute silence on the line between them for a moment. A silence which morphed into an atmosphere. Sam tried to remember the exact words he'd just uttered. 'Have a think about it. OK?'

JESSICA: age 18

Jessica used revision as the excuse to spend less and less time with the girls. But one afternoon she bumped into Caroline by the door to the sixth form centre and told her she was going to the deer park.

'Shall I come with you?' said Caroline, to Jess's surprise.

It was a bright, blustery April day, but despite that, Jessica hunched into her jacket and scarf. 'I still think of the vast snowball every time I open this door.'

'I know.' Caroline followed her out. 'The look on Miss Portman's face.'

They swept along, past the turning for Susie's and Tim's house, into Lake Avenue.

'Shame the boys missed it,' said Caroline. 'Although they did have the satisfaction of knowing they disrupted the first morning of school.'

They cut through Lake Court and across the Manchester Road, Jessica keeping up a fast pace. When they reached the golf course, she said, 'I think my father's going to leave.'

'Oh God. Jessie. I had no idea it was that bad.'

She shrugged. 'I've been sure he was having an affair with his secretary for ages, although I couldn't quite believe it when Sebastian mentioned it at your party.'

'How long ago was that?'

'Three years ago. The night Sam and Susie got together.' She spotted Caroline's sharp look from the corner of her eye.

'You've been thinking this for a while?'

'Yep. When I came in from my piano lesson on Tuesday night, Mum was ironing.' She examined the short tufts of grass by the toe of her shoe.

'Ironing,' Caroline said.

Jessica shrugged. 'She said she thought Dad was having an affair and I said, yes, I thought so too. It's what you'd call a pivotal moment. Once you've said those words, you can't un-say them.'

'Oh, Jessie. I'm so sorry.'

'Yeah. Actually, I think they'd be better apart. Especially if his taste in women has changed from my mother to that…woman.'

Objectively, she could see the difference between her mother, a highly organised head-teacher, in her Jaeger suits and Russell and Bromley shoes, and Diane in her clinging chain-store mixed fibres and stilettos. Fifteen years younger, with her pert bosom and tight skirts.

Sex. The unknown. For herself, and, she was pretty sure, for Caroline too. There was the possibility that Stella had Done It. She was heavily involved with a friend of her older brother's, who, in the throes of passion, had laced his fingers through Stella's hair and whispered, 'Love you, Stella.' The thrill of hearing about it, at the back of the classroom when they were meant to be studying the finer ironies of Jane Austen's *Emma*.

Caroline shook her head. 'Maybe there's been some horrible mistake.'

'Mum told me about going to the theatre with them and realising they were holding *hands*. Right in front of her.' Her shoulders heaved.

'I don't know what to say.'

'There's nothing to say. He's gone already, even if he's still living in the house. Let's run,' she said, feeling the need to move. She set off along the tree-lined path towards the deer park.

When they reached the vast beech at the beginning of the magnificent avenue of trees down to the house, Jessica stopped to lean on its smooth trunk. Caroline caught up with her and they listened to themselves catch their breath, the rustle of the new leaves far above them. Maybe it was all the sap-rising, leaf-burgeoning images that made Jessica think about sex. This heavy breathing was just the sort of exertion people seemed to go through when they Did It. She couldn't quite picture that. What exactly did they do that was so physically tiring? They were lying down, weren't they? She still had visceral images of Sam's weight on top of her as they kissed on the sitting room floor. Surely they'd fade eventually, wouldn't they?

After a couple of minutes, they walked to the end of the avenue and then turned for home. Much of the time they were silent. A silence that was less difficult than she would have thought possible, given the subject they'd been discussing.

When they reached the top of the lane to Jessica's house, Caroline said, 'I won't tell anyone.'

'Thanks.'

'You can ring me anytime.'

'Thank you.'

Jessica watched Caroline's tall figure walk away from her, and wondered what it felt like to be naked and horizontal with another human being. The weight of somebody on top of her, inside her. And how that act could make the difference between being a virgin and having lost one's virginity. Another almost physical memory of Sam's weight on her. A sharp intake of breath.

If her father no longer wanted to be with her mother, but with Diane, why didn't he leave them to be with her? Why spend his life miserable?

Her sensible-school-shoe-clad feet crossed the line of slate-coloured cobbles forming the gutter at the edge of the lane, her footsteps a practiced navigation of the rivulets and potholes that led to her back gate.

JESS

On the last Friday of September, Jess dropped the children at school with much kissing and hugging. Then she packed, which took forever. She longed to be able to toss wisps of gorgeous silk underwear and dresses into an elegant leather holdall. Having none of the above, she made do with a few clean clothes, her diary and her Bible.

She'd stayed away from the hairdresser's all summer, convincing herself that she was finally growing out the layers and would go back when she could have it cut into a definite style. It was wispy, with bits sticking out, even after careful blow-drying.

Although the traffic was slow and heavy in places, she turned off the M6 before half past five. Once on the dual carriageway, she began to shiver. Her mouth went dry. All the thoughts about why she was really going to spend the weekend with Sam surfaced and she felt dizzy with the effort of keeping the car on the road.

Now what? Turn and go home?

No. Not even she was that mad.

Talk to him. Ring Caroline. Maybe she could stay there. And still see him.

There was a turning to the left up ahead. A straight, field-flanked road, and then a garden centre. She pulled into the car park, stopped, wiped her sticky palms down her jeans, and drank from her bottle of water.

She picked up her mobile and texted: 'Came off at J19 and having a wobble'. Then she wound the window down and sat, concentrating on breathing slowly and deeply. In. Out. In. Out.

Six minutes later her mobile rang. 'Jess? Are you OK?'

'Just having a little panic attack.'

'Where are you?' Sam's voice warmed the pit of her stomach.

'I turned off the dual carriageway. I'm in some garden centre.'

'OK. I should be able to meet you soon after six-thirty. You know the little church in Rossington?'

'I'm sorry to—'

'Don't be. Remember, we don't have to do anything you don't want to…'

'That's the problem. I want to.'

'Oh.'

She could practically feel Sam assimilating this new information.

'Hold that thought.'

Jess re-joined the main road and took the little right-hand turn to Rossington. Immediately she was plunged into a high-hedged country lane, fragrant and autumnal. She could see blackberries in the hedges and thought of the 1980s' television adaptation of *Brideshead Revisited,* some of which had been filmed here. She caught a glimpse of the mirrored water of the mere, and then she was in the pretty village, and there was the church on the left-hand side, the square towered building a modest twin of Barton church. She parked, walked through the greying wooden lychgate, and picked a path across the ancient gravestones. The church door was locked, so she walked round to the bench that looked across the mere towards the hill, topped by Barton church in the distance.

She sat and watched the still water and listened to the distant murmur of motorway traffic, the backing track for swooping birds calling to each other overhead.

SAM

At twelve minutes past six, Sam had seen everyone on his list and persuaded Matt to see the extra patient, on the understanding that he would be given an explanation on Monday.

'What's her name? Not Amanda, I take it,' Matt said.

'See you on Monday.' Sam flew out of the door, into his car and out on the road towards Rossington.

No sign of her in the graveyard, so he walked around the church and found her sitting on the bench gazing at the mere.

'Jessica.' Saying her name caused a lump in his throat. He stood still to recover. Did he want to marry her? Or was this a baser desire? Was it about sex?

Jess turned to him and her clear grey eyes filled with tears. 'I'm sorry, Sam, I think I've...sorry I dragged you out here.'

'I haven't been here for ages. Isn't it glorious?'

She looked more alive, and her hair was prettier round her face. He sat beside her on the bench. 'Cold feet?' He took her hand. 'Cold hands.'

'I'm not sure I'm ready for... It's not you, it's me.'

He leant back against the bench. 'I've seen this before.'

She jerked her head up to meet his eyes.

'Desperate parents planning precious time away from their children, so desperate and precious that it's a hopeless situation. Nothing you arrange can ever live up to your expectations.'

'It's not that. I'm quite sure you'd live up to my expectations.' She clamped her mouth shut.

'Thank you.' He smiled.

They watched the changing light on Barton Hill. 'What do you want to do?'

'I'm an idiot. I should never have come. You don't need this.'

'You're not an idiot.' He rubbed his thumb over the back of her hand. Smooth. Soft. 'If this is about sex, we don't have to go there at all. I thought you might like the spare room anyway.'

'It's just being able to resist everything except temptation. There's a part of me that's still not ready to be tempted. Does that sound pathetic?'

'No. None of this is an ideal situation. If you didn't live so far away, it would be easier.'

'I was thinking of ringing Caroline, seeing whether she'd put me up.' She stared at his face. 'Just to sleep there. You hate the idea.'

Sam shook his head to clear his thoughts. 'No. I wanted it to be just us, but if you think that'd work…'

'I haven't rung her, she may not even be there…'

'Go ahead. Find out.'

JESS

Jess left her car at Caroline's and walked to Sam's for supper. He produced chicken breasts in a white wine and mushroom sauce and steamed green beans. They ate in the kitchen, and lingered over the end of a bottle of red and some delicious cheese.

'I've eaten far too much,' Jess said, eventually.

'So've I, but nobody else need ever know.' He filled the kettle. 'Tea? Front room, or do you want to stay here?'

'I'm fine here.' *I'm definitely not having sex with you. Definitely not tonight.* She smiled at him as he sat beside her at the table. On a wooden dining chair. Not a squashy sofa where the possibilities of becoming horizontal were far greater.

She watched the movement of his arms as he put down the mugs, and then the light was blotted out as he kissed her. The lightest of touches, lips to lips, so tantalising her stomach disappeared and she felt a rush of heat between her legs. He moved his hand up the back of her neck, bringing her face against his, and she put her palms on his chest, clutching at him, needing his weight against her.

Her thoughts cascaded…*we're safe, as long as we don't move to a sofa…if I keep my clothes on…however up for it he might be, I can't believe he has a condom in his pocket…he'd have to find one… I'm quite prepared to believe he has one in the house…gives me a moment to regain my balance, to escape…*

'Jess?' His voice was deep and husky.

She looked up, trying to focus, his face was so near.

'Relax. Stop over-thinking.' Then he leaned in and kissed her in earnest, the hand at the back of her neck moulding the shape of her head, his other arm pressing her body against his.

She tried to dredge a coherent thought from the soup of her mind…*he's really good at this… I can stop any time…just like old times…hours of kissing…he knows I'm not going to have sex with him… I know I'm not going to have sex with him…*

He pulled back slightly, that glint in his eyes.

Where had she seen it before?

'Jessica. Really. Stop thinking,' he whispered against her cheek, kissing his way down her neck.

She knew he'd just said something. *What?* Her mind was addled with the effort of trying to remember. She could think of nothing but the weight and heat of his hand travelling by increments along the curve of her neck, across her collar bone, to the soft cotton of her t-shirt, down, down to the heaviness of her breast, his thumb gently brushing across the material of her top and bra.

'Sofa. We'd be so much more comfortable.'

Jess sat up, fighting the realisation that this was the reason she'd put on her only good bra with the need to get up and leave before she took off all her clothes. 'Much as I'd love to progress to your sofa, I should think about going.'

'I've never liked the word should,' said Sam, his arms around her. 'You just know it's something you'd rather not do.'

'I should like to see you tomorrow, though.'

'In that case, I should like to sit on the sofa with you.'

'I know. But I'd better go.'

Sam dropped his arms. 'OK, I'll walk you back.'

From the moment she woke from a broken night, Jess suffered a tight feeling in her stomach. Dressing took forever, her trembling hands fiddling with buttons and zips. She made herself eat some toast, although it was the last thing she wanted.

They met under the railway clock and took the tram into the centre of Manchester, teeming with Saturday shoppers. She was thankful Sam didn't put his arm round her or try to hold her hand. For some reason, embarrassment kicked in just thinking about it. Tom had never been much of a hand holder. He seemed to think any public displays of affection—sometimes even with the children—were signs of weakness.

'Time for a coffee?' she asked.

'Why don't we go and look at clothes?'

'You're a man. You don't want to look at clothes.' She felt hot under the collar and elsewhere.

'You forget I have a fashion-conscious elder daughter who is just young enough to bear shopping with me, as long as I'm paying.'

'And it would be totally understandable if you didn't want to set foot in a clothes shop at any other time.'

'Indulge me. And give me that hand. I know you're still trying to get used to it all, but I'm growing old waiting for you to catch up.' He took her hand. 'Harvey Nichols first.'

On the first floor, Jess draped cashmere and gossamer fine wisps of silk—just the ones she'd imagined packing so elegantly the day before—against her body and fantasised another reality where she didn't mind what it had become since bearing children. She picked up a couple of tops.

'What about this one?' He held up a coral pink top.

'Not sure about the colour.'

'Try it.'

She tried it on and realised the pale pink and grey-blue tops she'd chosen for herself made her look greyer, whereas the coral brightened her skin.

'How were they?' he said, when she came out of the fitting room.

'You were right, annoyingly. The bright one is much better.'

Never breaking eye contact, Sam came towards her and kissed her, his tongue darting into her mouth, short-circuiting her brain, heat flooding through her.

'Give me warning if you're going to do that when I'm standing up. I don't think my knees can stand it.'

'But it's so much more fun if I take you by surprise.' He stopped, as if struck by what he'd just said.

Hooray, Jess wanted to shout. He struggled with all the double-entendres, too.

He cleared his throat. 'I'm going to buy that top for you if you'd like it and you may as well save your breath, because I'd rather not listen to any protests. You'll just have to get over it if I'm offending your principles or sensibilities or whatever.'

'Only if I can buy you something in return.'

'Coffee. And you wear it tonight. Trust me enough to spend the night in my spare room?'

The mattress in Caroline's loft was as uncomfortable as it had been in July. And she'd never been upstairs in Sam's house. 'Possibly.'

Jess reminded herself that she'd been invited, as she followed Sam up the stairs. There was no ancient aunt who would disinherit him when she heard he'd rambled over the whole house with a completely unchaperoned female. Maybe it was possible to read too much Jane Austen.

Sometimes she had to remind herself that guilt—once her default setting—no longer had to be her way of life.

He showed her to a bedroom papered in a faded Laura Ashley print. It had a wide sash window overlooking the back garden, the tennis courts and Barton Common beyond.

'This is lovely,' she said.

'Bathroom next door. All yours.' They passed Kate's room and the family bathroom. 'I'm in here. Mum's old room.'

Jess stood on the threshold of the front bedroom. A couple of novels, a Bible, medical journals, a radio alarm, and framed photos of the children sat on the bedside cabinet. More photos of Sam's parents, and Will and family ranged across the mantelpiece.

'Is your house always this immaculate?' she asked.

'Absolutely. Especially when the children are here. Haven't had the time or the energy to re-decorate, sadly. I grew up with most of this furniture. New mattresses, though. Your bed's got a really good mattress.' He turned away abruptly, but not before Jess thought she spotted a red flush. Ha.

'My study.' He pointed to a square room next door dominated by a large wooden desk, Sam's father's medical certificates framed on the wall, beside his son's.

He put his arms round her and kissed the side of her neck. 'Next flight up to where Josh and Em now live. Where I spent my teenage years and had all sorts of dreams about you.'

'You did not.' She shivered at the warmth of his lips on her skin.

'I did. You used to wear very tight trousers.'

'You don't remember that.'

'You'd be surprised. You don't have a monopoly on all that.'

Jess decided this was not necessarily a safe conversation, not with his hands on her ribcage, able to feel the bumpy beat of her heart.

'OK.' He let her go.

She followed him back downstairs. 'This is a proper grown-up house.'

'I only moved in here as a temporary measure when Mum had her first stroke. But the more I lived here, especially with the children here a lot, the more it felt like our home. Helped by Will taking some of the furniture, so we had space to move. The only other thing I've bought is the sofa in the front room.'

'I envy you. Although I hadn't lived at the house in East Street for many years, I felt that my links with Millingham were being irrevocably severed when Mum and Martin sold up.'

'I can understand that. But Caroline's here. And me.' He led the way to the kitchen. 'Tea? Too early for a glass of wine?'

Jess swallowed. 'Tea please.'

SAM

By the time Jess walked into the kitchen after having a bath, Sam was holding two freshly poured glasses of white Burgundy. 'Wow.' He put the glasses back on the work surface too heavily.

'I may never take this top off again.' Her cheeks flushed pink.

'Unless I have anything to do with it.' She looked more alive than he'd ever seen her.

'Is that so?' She tilted her chin at him.

'That is so. Cheers.' He handed her a glass, watched her take a sip, their eyes connecting.

She set her glass on the counter. 'Sam, have you mentioned anything about me being here this weekend?'

'What do you mean?'

'I don't know. Friends maybe?'

He smiled, amused. 'I didn't realise I had to ask permission.'

'That's not what I meant. I have helpful friends who want to know what's going on.'

'So, don't tell them. Or only what you want to.' He looked into her eyes, grey and huge in the soft light, and concentrated on not studying the curve of her neck.

'I think you're better at that than I am.'

He raised an eyebrow.

'You see what I mean?' She raised both eyebrows.

'I'm going to have to teach you to raise one at a time.' He lifted his left eyebrow expertly.

She grinned. 'That's just annoying.'

'Is there anyone in particular you feel you must justify your plans to?'

She sipped her wine. 'Maybe. My friends Claire and John. You met them.'

'And?' he prompted, after a moment or two.

'Claire gave me a little lecture about temptation. And a rock song.'

'A rock song?' he said, not expecting that.

'A Christian rock song. "Don't pop the lock till you've got the rock".'

'What?' He laughed outright. 'They sing songs about this stuff?'

'I'll send it to you. You could play it to Kate.'

'Don't. You think very differently about sex where your daughter's concerned.'

Jess nodded. 'So much angst to look forward to. And Millie's such a flirt already.'

'Millie's adorable.'

'Quite.'

He laughed, breathing in her heat. Maybe Rob had a point. Was this attraction about feeling better about himself? More virile, more macho?

He spent the meal watching her fill the space on her side of the table with laughter and movement and light. It was so ironic. Here he was, convinced he had the confidence to perform sexually again, with a woman, who—for whatever reason—wouldn't. He kept his eyes on her face. The temptation to let his gaze fall to her breasts was almost overwhelming. He recited times tables in a bid not to lunge across the table for her mouth. And he still couldn't quite believe it. Jessica Lamb—sorry, Deane—had breasts. OK, so she must have had them in the summer—in fact, he knew she had—he'd been lucky enough to have them pressed against him once, but not like this. Nothing like this. She'd always been so slim in her teens. Thin even. But now, although she was still slim, she had curves. She was *womanly*.

'Real aphrodisiac, watching you eat,' he said.

'You'll put me off my food. No looking at me like that.'

He dropped his eyes, catching a glimpse of round smoothness through her top. 'Fair enough, but brace yourself for when we've retired to the comfy sofa.'

'OK.' She grinned. 'You've given me fair warning.'

He re-filled their glasses. 'Do you feel very settled in London?'

She frowned. 'Yes. No. I don't know. Tom's there. I couldn't take the children too far away from him.'

'How often does he see them?'

'Not often enough. We try and stick to an arrangement, but as you know he's not wholly reliable. I had to fight for this weekend.'

'Which I appreciate. How did it all go wrong? Or would you rather not talk about it?'

JESS

She scrutinised her wine glass.

'You don't have to.'

She shook her head. 'It's just so boring. Things weren't right for a long time. I accused Tom of having an affair with his assistant Denise, which he has consistently denied for years. That gave me a real sense of déjà-vu. I just knew, like I did with my father. But this time I guess I also felt like my mother. As if I was going mad and maybe he was telling the truth.'

She stopped for a breath.

'Go on,' said Sam, after a minute.

'It started going bad a long time before that. Before the children.' She met his eyes, warm and brown, in his open, familiar face. So few people knew much of this. And Sam liked her. She'd made him laugh tonight. She wanted him to think well of her.

But he hadn't been scared off. Maybe honesty really was the best policy.

She studied her hands. 'To begin with I was flattered. He was this tall, certain man who noticed me. I felt seen properly for the person I was trying to be. As if I had found the one person in the world I was destined to be with.'

She looked up, her eyes connecting with Sam's. 'I discovered later that Tom was incredibly skilled at mirroring and matching. At saying all the right things. I don't think he could help himself. It was a strategy that worked very well for him, with his almost entirely absent father and passive aggressive mother.'

'Mm,' said Sam.

'We got engaged very quickly. Several people—not least my family—were alarmed by how quick it was, but I felt so sure it was what I wanted. I don't think I'd felt that safe for any length of time since I was about twelve or thirteen.' She caught her breath. A moment when she had just turned eighteen. A sudden picture of her hand in Sam's, of him tucking their clasped fingers into the warmth of his pocket, the bracing cold of the snow, their mingling breath in the night air. 'It turned out they were right. What I loved—the protectiveness, the caring concern, the interest—tipped overnight, virtually the day we returned from honeymoon, into a compulsive need to know what I was doing—and with whom—every second of my life. To begin with I pretended I loved it.'

She looked up. Somehow, when she was talking, she couldn't look at him, only at his lovely hands on the table in front of him. She didn't want any of those old feelings to seep into this precious time. 'I didn't help things. I stopped being me—having opinions—because nothing was ever right. I didn't buy anything because it was always wrong. Clothes, food, things for the house…he made every decision, and I told myself that was OK because I no longer had to apologise for my mistakes. Handing over control about everything seemed more bearable. But I can see now that all it did was tip power in his direction so firmly that he came to despise my spinelessness.'

She clasped her hands in front of her. Left thumb over right. Right thumb over left. 'Funnily enough, when he decided we'd have children, I had more freedom than I'd had for a long time. Antenatal exercise classes are definitely women only. That's how I met Claire. She was my guardian angel in so many ways. And Tom behaved better in John's presence.

'After Ben was born he made me give up work. I was so overcome with love for this new life that it suited me to be with him all day, every day. And when Millie was born, Tom had his perfect family, a boy and a girl.' She bit her lip, traced the smooth surface of her thumbnail with her index finger.

'Would you have liked to have more?' said Sam.

'Yes. No. Yes. It was probably just as well we stopped at two. I might have killed one if I'd found myself on my own with three little ones.'

'Not much of a hands-on father, then?'

'He wanted all the best bits—good cop—and I was painted into a corner—bad cop. The one who disciplined. Who was consistent.'

'So what happened?'

'I don't really know…his assistant Denise? By that point, things were terrible between us. Being ridiculed by him in front of our friends finally became unbearable enough to do something different. Parties when I turned up in the wrong clothes, totally underdressed, without a present, when Tom had deliberately withheld information and misled me, and then publicly mocked my stupidity. When he repeated the story at a Sunday lunch in front of Ben—who must only have been about three at the time—and I could see that he was beginning to catch something of the dynamic between us, I accepted I had to do something.'

Sam reached across and put his palms over her hands.

'I think it would have been virtually impossible to have

persuaded Tom to leave, had there not been somewhere else he'd rather be. Which only cemented my suspicion about Denise. But even now… I don't know.'

'God, Jess, the things you've been through.'

'Yes, but I can now look back and take some responsibility. I was not honest. Not with Tom, not with myself. Not for a long time.' She looked up and gazed at him.

'Come here.' He pulled her round to the chair beside him and gave her a full-bodied hug. 'I think you're amazing.'

Calm down, she told her pitter-pattering heart, in thumping overdrive. 'Deeply flawed,' she said.

SAM

He contemplated Jess, sitting beside him, a finger tracing the contours of her glass. 'Do you think people start out being wrong for each other or just become so? I can't decide. Are long-term relationships all about compromise?'

She sipped her wine. 'Among other things, I hope.'

'I was convinced Elizabeth and I were right for each other, from the start. But I think we got the timing wrong. She's two years older than me, and I didn't realise quite how driven she was. She was pregnant before we got married.'

'I don't think I knew that,' said Jess.

'She was aiming to be the youngest consultant in her year. I was a Senior House Officer, and hoped to do paediatrics, but then Kate arrived and we couldn't both be at the hospital and on call all the time. We tried. We nearly killed each other that first year. Then Elizabeth pushed for another baby, and I said OK, if she took a break for a year, instead of six months this time. I believed her, until I took a phone call at home, when Em was about four months old. She'd already arranged her next rotation and a nanny.' He shrugged at Jess, a hand in his hair.

'So we tried an older nanny. She was fine, until she said the ghosts in our house were making her feel uncomfortable. Then we tried a younger nanny, until we started missing things—earrings, bottles of wine—finally Elizabeth's new leather jacket. At that point I signed up for the Vocational Training Scheme, to become a GP, and the rest, as they say, is history.'

He knew he was generalising. There had been good pockets of time with Elizabeth. But they had somehow been blurred into the overall arc of a failed marriage. Sometimes, when the children were looking at old photo albums, it was important to remember that.

'What about Joshua?'

'Ah yes. We were on holiday and fell into bed after too much Sangria. I think Elizabeth used sex as a weapon.' He cleared his throat. 'I'm going to have another glass of wine after all this heartfelt honesty. Do you fancy some of last night's cheese?'

'I don't think I could. But present it to me on a plate, and who knows what might happen.'

'I'll bear that in mind.'

After such revelations Sam was not at all sure Jess would be interested in kissing on the sofa. But then again, the least he could do was offer to take her mind off things. So, when they'd finished the cheese and he'd re-filled their glasses and motioned towards the front room, he breathed a silent sigh of relief as she stood up and walked in front of him, no questions asked.

She hesitated inside the door, before sitting on the sofa.

Sam switched on some side lamps and sat down beside her.

'Thank you for a lovely day, and for my top.' Jess sounded breathless.

He stretched his arm along the back of the sofa. 'My pleasure.'

'It's been very relaxing.' Her foot tapped madly.

'You don't say.'

She grinned. 'OK, relaxing is not the perfect word.'

'What is?'

A slight frown played across her face. 'My life hasn't been this exciting in years.'

'I agree.' He hadn't been this turned on in years.

'Oh, please. I find it hard to believe there haven't been others, apart from Amanda.'

He raised an eyebrow. 'Let's just say the timing wasn't right. Rather than anything about people who come across as too intense or desperate.'

That made Jess laugh. 'As opposed to me. Mrs Horizontal. To coin a phrase.'

'You're already considerably more relaxed than you were earlier. Perhaps it's the drinks? Finish your wine.'

She laughed, and he pressed his back into the sofa to stop himself lunging for the curve of her neck. In this light, her skin was golden, a smooth sheen across her cheeks.

'It's delicious.' She took a sip.

'It certainly is. I mean it. Relaxation therapy coming up.'

'What's in it for you?'

'Come here and I'll show you.'

JESS

I knew this was going to happen. Who am I trying to kid, thinking I can stop? Would I even want to stop? As she admitted this, several other thoughts clicked into place. It felt as if her mind had been out of alignment and now the strain and tension had dissolved. She was breathing deeply and fully, something she probably hadn't done for months. Hell, try years. She shook her head. No pain, no tension. Everything felt great.

I've been here before. How long ago exactly? Why had it taken such an age to get back here, when it felt this good? She looked into Sam's eyes and saw a hesitation.

'Jess?' he said, his hand frozen on her breast. 'You shook your head.'

'Did I?' She blinked. Of course it had taken this long. After that New Year's Eve twenty years ago, she had had to amputate her feelings for Sam.

'Oh, I see,' he said.

She kept looking at him. Dark eyes in this soft light, his hair ruffled, lips parted, a moment of uncertainty until he grinned and swooped, blotting the light out again.

His hand moved over her breast, teasing at the bra cup with his fingers. His other arm kept her connected with every part of his body, his hand at the small of her back, finding her skin with his hot hand.

The heat between her legs built steadily, her arms twisting around his neck. Her hands felt the contours of his shoulders, the landscape of his back—skin, spine, sinew, strength—learning his shape, his substance, so different from tall, thin Tom. His scent—fresh, clean, the faintest hint of citrus—made her stomach disappear.

His hand was at her waist now, pushing up the fabric of her t-shirt and she shuddered. He could have found her wrinkly tummy above the top of her trousers—thank God she was underneath him, not on top for it all to hang out—but he caressed the side of her waist, his fingers quick on her breast again, pushing gently, feeling for her nipple, pulling the bra aside, letting the weight of her breast out into the heat of his hand, making her gasp as nipple connected with palm, the exquisite pressure of gentle fingers cupping and circling.

She clenched her inner thighs against the heat of his leg, thinking, she was really going to come like this, fully clothed, and then her attention was triggered by his other hand, pushing into the back of her knickers, stroking downwards, which to Jess was much further than she would have imagined possible.

'You are so beautiful, Jess,' he murmured against her mouth.

She put her hand up to cup his cheek, to kiss him, feeling that the perfection of this moment needed to be anchored. But it slipped into the next moment as he paused to focus on undoing her trousers.

'Sam—' she said, but he was quick. He'd undone the top button and his lips were on hers again, his fingers on her zip.

'Please,' she gasped and he stopped.

'Jess?' He braced the weight of his chest off her with his

arm, enough air between them to let her focus on his face. He looked as dizzy as she felt.

'I'm…I'm feeling doubtful,' she said.

'About this?'

'No! About me.'

'Don't be doubtful. You're beautiful. How could this not be what you want to be doing, right now?

'I don't want to disappoint you.'

'You couldn't.' He dropped back on top of her. 'Words escape me,' he whispered into her ear. 'You are incredibly sexy.'

The heat flooded through her. E*njoy this moment, God knows, it's been too long*…aaagh! Why did she have to think of that turn of phrase right now?

Sam kissed down the side of her neck, along the v of her top, between her breasts, his hands underneath the soft fabric, caressing softer skin. He undid the ribbon ties, a man on a mission, revealing pink bra and an expanse of white tummy.

The rush of air made her whisper, 'Don't look.'

'You're lovely. Your body's lovely,' he said, fingers delving inside both bra cups, sending waves of heat down her body as they found both nipples.

She tensed. 'It's too much. I can't—'

'Are you sure?' He stopped moving his fingers, cupping both breasts in his palms and raised his head to her. 'You've given birth to two children. Give yourself a break. Concentrate on how good this feels.' His eyes were so dark they looked black.

His mouth trailed down the slope of her breast, his tongue circling her nipple, making her arch against him. 'See?'

She was intensely aware of the wet warmth between her legs. She pushed her hips against his and he responded, head still bent to her breasts, finding the other nipple with his tongue, minutes caressing her with expert fingers and mouth.

Then he put his arms around her and moved, so that they were facing each other, on their sides. 'I knew it was a good idea buying the largest sofa.' He buried his face in her neck.

'Done this before, have you?' she said, before she could stop herself.

'No. We're christening it.' He brought his mouth down on to hers, kissing her thoroughly, easing down the zip of her trousers, pressing his hips to hers against the back of the sofa, easing his hand inside the back of her knickers with no trouble at all this time.

'Sam,' she gasped.

'I know. We can stop anytime.' His fingers caressed the curve of her bottom, each time moving lower and lower. 'Your skin is so wonderfully smooth.' He plunged his tongue deep into her mouth, his thigh between her legs, pushing her apart to find her wet heat. 'Oh, Jess, you are so lovely.'

She had the feeling she should say something, but she couldn't think of anything except the touch of his fingers stretching her against him as she clenched her thighs around him, her hand finding his hardness against his chinos, pressing and hearing his sharp intake of breath against her mouth.

'I can't…' she gasped, on a breath.

'You can.'

'I can't stop.' She gripped him tightly, wrapped around him, his arms around her, his fingers slipping deep inside her, pressing her against him, holding her while the waves of heat rose and rose and rose and she gasped for air before shuddering against him again and again while he held her and kissed her.

He manoeuvred on to his back, holding her curled against him, her head on his chest, his hand smoothing her hair behind her ear. 'I've been wanting to do that for you for the longest time.'

Jess blushed, wondering why she felt such embarrassment about sex. 'What about you…?' she said eventually.

'Plenty of time for other things,' he said, caressing her shoulder in lazy circles.

'It's been such a long time,' she whispered.

'I know. You and me. Who'd have thought?' He laughed against her hair.

They lay like that until Jess's body began to twitch. 'I'm falling asleep.'

'Come on then.' He disentangled their legs. 'Let's go to bed.'

Her eyes flew to his face.

'Would you rather sleep in the spare room? There's only so much self-control a man can have, if you get into my bed.'

'Oh.' She felt as if she was in a car hurtling towards the back of an enormous lorry, much too fast. She wanted to stop. No. To pause.

'How do you feel?' He turned off the lamps.

'Different.'

'Different is good.'

In the bathroom she splashed her flushed face. Sam knocked on the door. 'Glass of water by your bed. You know where I am if you want me, but I cannot guarantee to behave so well with you in my bedroom.'

She opened the door. 'I understand. Sleep well.'

He gave her a hug. Their bodies knew exactly how to fit together. 'I hope so.'

SAM

Sam lay on his side for a long time, listening to the breeze in the large beech tree in the front garden, thinking about Jess. OK, thinking about sex. Not actual sex with Jessica. But the hot excitement of that sofa. She'd been so warm and wet and lush beneath his fingers and he ached for her. Think of something else, he told himself. And then he thought of her again.

He wondered how long he could keep up not actually having sex. At some point they would talk about God and adultery and marriage, but not now. Anyway, this old-fashioned heavy petting was fulfilling a very useful purpose for him. Could have been tailor-made to ratchet up his confidence. He was convinced that however far they'd gone tonight, he could have performed.

Having Jess as the other person made things much easier, especially when he considered how turned on she became. How lubricated everything was. He winced: no matter how hard he wished to romanticise sex, his medical training came to the fore. He had a fleeting snapshot of Elizabeth demanding sex when he was at his most depressed and exhausted and then laughing in his face, followed by the hideous failed coupling with Briony slicing across his memory in full technicolour glory.

He shook his head to dislodge the images. They were in the past.

With Jess, it was different. Everything was different. He had a sudden, almost physical memory of the heavy softness of her breast in his cupped hand. Two nights. Two nights rolling around, with Jessica, kissing and breathing and touching.

So far apart. And yet, after tonight he could visualise that other night, over twenty years ago, so clearly.

He rolled over. He wasn't going to make the same mistake twice. Night number three was coming a lot sooner.

JESS

Jess lay in bed summoning the will to get up. How could she have been so stupid? Maybe she'd only been living a fraction of her life—far less than a half-life—before she met Sam again, but it was one in which she knew the rules. She channelled her feelings into safe, romantic bubbles, in the films she watched, the books she read, which bore no resemblance to reality, and cut herself off from actually experiencing anything real. Now she felt like a ridiculous adolescent in the first throes of passion. She shook whenever Sam appeared. Her mouth dried, her hands felt clammy and the blood pounded in her ears.

She remembered the moment she'd accidentally sliced into her finger at Caroline's. A peculiar wound. At the time it hadn't hurt that much. Later it had begun to throb. Now, two months later, it really hurt if she pressed it.

Then there was the sex thing. She felt such guilt, lying here, in the harsh light of day. If she'd known she was going to feel this shitty, she'd have gone all the way. Why the hell not?

Her mind flickered for an instant over a happy ending, where she and Sam and their children lived a life together. But where would that be? She couldn't take the children away from Tom, nor could she see Sam moving to London to be with her.

A long-distance relationship? People did it. Anything was possible if you wanted it enough. But that seeping dread was taking over. Sam could do without the painful complication of her and her children. She shuddered to think of all the stuff she'd told him last night. A real turn-on. Which he'd managed to get past at the time. But what about now? As long as she didn't blurt out how she felt. There really were situations where honesty was not the best option.

She got away with it while they ate breakfast and browsed through the papers. But then Sam reached across the table, took her wrist and said, 'How are you, this morning?'

She tried to stand up and wriggle away from him, but he said, 'Jess, it's me. Talk to me.'

And then she made the mistake of looking into his eyes. 'I miss you,' she said. Not good. But better than saying, 'I love you.'

'Come here, love.' He pulled her onto his knee. 'Let's go out for a walk and then lunch.'

'I need to leave by two.'

'We've got four hours before then. Let me find my car keys.'

He wanted to drive her, in *his* car. *It'll be fine.* But she dreaded the intimacy of a car. Just the two of them, his hands on the steering wheel. Gynaecologically expert hands.

An unwelcome memory crashed into her conscious mind of a fellow student with his hands in her knickers, rubbing desperately. A long time ago, she'd thought that sex—even bad sex—would stop her from feeling the pervasive emptiness.

Now she'd turned down great sex and was facing the void again.

'Jessica.' Sam said. 'It's just lunch and a walk. A chance to relax.'

She shook her head free of the unwanted memory. Here she was now, with a man who definitely knew how to turn her on. It was time to blot out all those shameful feelings and replace them with something so much better.

SAM

'I'm still counting on you, last week of October,' Sam said when Jess rang to say she was home.

She sighed. 'Tom's just told me he has to be in New York on business that week.'

'I thought you were taking the children to your mum's? You only need to get from Cheltenham to Oxford.'

'Oxford?'

'We could stay with Will and Diana. Think about it. Even if it's just for a couple of nights. Closer than Manchester.' He imagined the concentration on her face, white teeth on pink bottom lip.

'Sam, are you sure about this?'

'What do you mean? Aren't you having fun?'

'Well of course, but it's hassle for you…'

'And for you.' His palms turned sweaty. *You may be the only person who can help me solve my problem.* 'But when you're there, we have a great time.'

Jess laughed. 'Your certainty is very attractive.'

He hadn't thought of it as certainty, and yet, he was fairly confident that his performance issue was really not going to be a problem with Jess. Just thinking about her biting her bottom lip turned him on.

As soon as he came to the end of morning surgery on Monday, there was a knock at his door. Fellow GP Matt bounded in. Grey-haired, energetic, he'd been at the same school as Sam, a couple of years below.

'So? Tell me everything.'

'God, I hope you're more empathetic towards your patients. For all you know I might have had the most dreadful weekend.'

Matt sat down and surveyed Sam. 'Nah. Start with the basics. Name, appearance, vital statistics—'

'What surprises me most is that your wife is so lovely. Does she have any idea you behave like this?'

'I'm waiting.' Matt lounged back in the chair.

Sam leant back too, stretching his legs. 'Jessica. Tall. Brown hair. Grey-blue eyes. They can look quite different in certain lights and they change colour by the sea.'

Matt grinned.

Sam tried to remember the exact words he'd just uttered.

'Good in bed?'

'Right. Out.' Sam turned away to hide a grin. There was something infectious about Matt's enthusiasm.

Matt held up his hands. 'So when are you seeing her again?'

'Half term, I hope.'

'Not till then? Where does she live?'

'London. I know. It's complicated.'

They sat in silence for a moment.

'How did you meet?' said Matt.

'She's an old friend. We knew each other in our teens.'

'What's her name again?'

'Jessica Lamb.'

'Patrick Lamb's sister. I remember her. Tall and thin.'

'Not that thin.' Sam had an almost physical memory of

her curves in his arms, the weight of her breasts, her hips.

'Is that so?' Matt laughed until Sam threw him out.

By Monday night, the house was full of three children and various school bags, water bottles, grubby lunch boxes, damp PE kit and musical instruments. Sam spent a frenzied couple of hours trying to referee several squabbles between Emma and Josh, and not have a stand-up row with Kate, whose anger seemed to radiate off her in furious waves. He couldn't get to the bottom of it, but Emma's innocent enquiry about his weekend—and mention of the name Jess—had certainly not helped. By nine o'clock, the children were upstairs. Sam gathered the various piles of paperwork and post and settled down at the kitchen table. Four minutes later he rang the telephone number at the bottom of a heavy, embossed card.

'What the hell?' he said into the phone, when a deep, precise voice answered.

'The traditional response is, "Congratulations, I hope you'll be very happy".'

'I just didn't expect… You're getting married. To a woman.'

'Well thanks a lot for those warm words of encouragement.'

Sam swallowed. 'Sorry. I'm surprised. I thought—'

'Yes,' said James. 'I know what you thought, but things change.'

'Do they?'

'Yes, Sam, they do. You'll like Fiona. No-nonsense girl. Took me back many years to those three-hour snogging sessions in various cellars.'

'In that case, I'm very pleased for you,' Sam said, hoping it sounded genuine.

Perhaps it did, or perhaps James just let it go. 'Met her through the parliamentary party.'

'Wow.' Sam regrouped. 'Fiona.'

'She's Welsh. Reminds me of someone.'

'Welsh.' Sam rubbed his forehead. 'How nice.'

'Breath of fresh air, frankly.'

'I don't know what to say.'

'You're delighted for me. You hope we'll be very happy.'

'I am. I do.' He reached for the drinks cupboard and extracted the whisky bottle.

'She's already been so helpful in my selection process. I'm in the right place at the right time for once. People are keen on MPs who've held down real jobs, who are not just career politicians.'

'I'm sure you'll be very good at it.'

'It's all coming together. Especially with Fiona. You understand I need to make the right impression, don't you, Sam?'

'Of course.' Sam wrestled the top off the bottle and poured himself a hefty measure.

'With an impeccable background. I can't afford to have even the slightest hint of controversy in my past.'

Sam took a stiff swig of whisky. 'No. Of course not.'

'And I need to make the best choices for my career.'

'OK. Are we talking about anything specific, here?'

'Are you still in touch with Jessica?'

'I am.'

'And are you planning to see her again?' James asked.

'I am.'

'Is she still as much hard work as she used to be?'

Sam pulled the phone away from his ear and stared at it.

'Sam?'

He switched to his other ear. 'Actually, she's lovely,' he said, surprised by the strength of his conviction.

'So it's serious?'

'It's…it's not casual. I'm not—'

'Is it serious for her? No. Don't answer that. Stupid question. Do you talk about the past much?'

Sam clenched his free hand; released his fingers. Once. Twice. 'No more than usual.'

'And you don't talk about anything in particular?'

'Not really. I don't think those years were so easy for her. Having Nathaniel Lamb as a father must have been a challenge.'

'Memory can be unreliable.'

'Can it?'

'Definitely. Anyway. I'm counting on you to come to the wedding. I need you there.'

Sam wondered what serendipity already had him staying in Oxford the last Friday of October. 'Have to sort logistics out, but I'll be there. And I'm bringing a plus one.'

'Jessica I assume?' He laughed, fractionally too long.

'I'll let you know.'

'Good. I'll give your love to Fiona.' He put the phone down, just like those long phone calls they used to have on Saturday mornings, interrupted when either of them went to make more tea, or go for a pee, or answer the door. Endless, stream of consciousness calls, which James usually ended without warning, only to turn up at Sam's house, barely ten minutes later, to carry on where he'd left off. What he had thought of as a straightforward boys' friendship had been tainted at the edges somehow. And was he disingenuous to label it straightforward? Something else now permeated these recollections.

James had always managed to be so cut and dried about things.

Why was Sam so surprised that James's life was heading in a new direction? He swallowed hard.

Jess. He dialled and left a message on the answerphone.

JESSICA: age 18

May was wet and rainbow-filled, with Jessica surviving the atmosphere at home by furiously revising in her room. At school she found it difficult to talk to anyone. She had a terrible fear that someone might ask her a kind question and she would be unable to stop talking.

It was better not to start. At YF, she spent her time avoiding James and Sam, but one night James followed her to the loos. The problem was that too many of their parents' friends knew each other, and the news was seeping out. He wanted answers to questions she didn't know how to tackle.

'But why would your mother still want him in the house? If he's having it off with another woman?'

She turned her back on his tirade and wrenched open the tap. 'Go away!'

'Don't you have an opinion? Would you want a man to treat you like that?'

Jessica just wanted it to stop. All of it. She held the backs of her hands under the jet of water until they ached with cold. 'I don't want to talk about it. It's none of your business.'

'Head in the sand again Jessica. Only see what you want to see. It's pathetic,' he spat.

A wave of nausea swept over her, saliva flooding her

mouth. She concentrated on the pain radiating to the ends of her fingers. Refusing to look up, knowing he was still behind her, willing her to meet his look in the mirror above the sink.

She heard him slam the door and charge down the hall.

'Jessica?' Caroline appeared in the doorway. 'Are you all right?'

'He has no…no fucking right.' Her voice sounded ludicrous to her ears when she swore. Like a little girl wearing ankle socks and her mother's high heels. She scrubbed her hands under the tap, water spurting everywhere.

'What did he do?'

She avoided Caroline's eye in the mirror. 'I am quite entitled to think that my father is a complete tosser, but I really don't need it from anyone else.'

'What did he say?'

'Oh, you know James.'

'Well. Ah. I've been meaning to ask. How are things at home?'

'Don't ask.' She turned off the tap. 'I'm sorry, please don't ask.'

Despite her exhaustion, Jessica slept badly the night before the first A Level exam. Maybe it was to mark the end of an era that Jessica decided to take her old route to school the next morning. When Caroline had started spending more time with Anna, Jessica had gradually stopped walking with her.

Once on the Avenue, she saw Caroline walking towards her, still a distance away. She would reach the turning for school sooner.

Caroline stopped and waited. 'How are you feeling?'

Jessica gazed at her.

'About the exams?'

'Who cares?'

'Of course you do, Jessie.'

'Well, at least I have the perfect excuse when I fail everything,' Jessica muttered.

Caroline sighed. 'What's been going—?'

'Did you get any post before you left?'

'Post?' Caroline blinked at her. 'I don't think so.'

'Me neither. I did however get a dozen red roses. I don't even like red roses. They're vast and blood-sucking. That deepest of reds that looks as if it's going to absorb everything else.'

'You got a dozen red roses?'

'Well, as he couldn't actually be present, he somehow thought they might make up for his absence. How wrong can you be?'

'Who? Your dad? Where is he?'

'Not at home. At least not at our home. He may well be at *his* home.' Jessica focused on placing one foot in front of the other, staring at the pavement.

'When did he go?'

'Two weeks ago. Perfect timing. Two weeks before your oldest child's first A Level exam.'

Two weeks. There had not been much socialising. No trips to the pub. Jessica had seen nothing of the girls after school, making a point of not being around when arrangements—to walk home, meet up, revise together—were being made. There had been some whispering in the library, but it had mainly involved discussing English essay questions with Anna and Stella. Caroline and Ruth didn't have the same free periods.

Caroline turned to face her. 'Jess. I'm so sorry—'

'Yeah, I know. Nothing you can do. Nothing anyone can do.'

JESS

Although she tried to focus on other things, Jess spent most of her time having imaginary conversations with Sam about half term.

That problem was solved by her mother Felicity ringing. 'Darling, is it still all right for me to come and stay on Thursday night?'

'Yes, of course,' Jess lied, wondering what else she'd forgotten.

'I thought I'd come for about five. Then I can see the children and bring something for supper. How would that be?'

To her horror, Jess couldn't reply, choked by silent sobs. She'd felt on the edge for days, so a part of her wasn't surprised at the swift onslaught of tears.

'Oh, darling, what is it?'

'Nothing. That would be lovely.'

'Good. Now about half term, you *are* coming down aren't you?'

'Yes, please.'

'Why don't you think of going off and doing something for a couple of days, spend some time away from the children and have a proper break?'

'Um...'

'Think about it, darling.'

'Have you got something smart to wear to a wedding?' Sam said when he rang.

'Whose wedding?'

'James Gorton is getting married.'

Jess sat down on one of the high stools at the kitchen island.

'You still there?' said Sam.

Jess prised her dry lips apart. 'You're joking?'

'No. I want you to be my plus one.'

'Oh no, Sam, I couldn't.' She tried to lick her lips with her parched tongue. 'You're the one he invited.'

'And I'm asking you. Aren't you the slightest bit interested to know what's happened to him?'

'Only very slightly,' she said, her palms slick with sweat.

'Jess, I can't see you but I know you've got that look on your face.'

'You don't know me that well.' She stood up and bent across the sink to open the window. Her body remembered the clash of unyielding edge against hip bones. She recoiled and sat down abruptly.

'You really love your children and feel torn every time you're apart. You feel guilty about the break-up of your marriage, and really guilty about sex. You're confused about how you feel about me, but I know you really like me and are dying to say yes.'

She forced herself to laugh. Underneath his bravado she had a feeling he was holding his breath. 'OK, maybe you know me a little,' she conceded.

'Can you get away Wednesday to Saturday? The wedding's on Friday, but we're invited to a Scottish dancing practice on the Wednesday night. Apparently that's what we'll be doing at the reception.'

'Oh, God. Who else is going to be there?'

'I'll find out.'

At the end of supper, her mother would be put off no longer and asked how things *really* were. Felicity was still a force to be reckoned with—grey-haired now, slightly stooped but almost as tall as Jess—cultured, well-groomed, never to be seen in public without a decent haircut, handbag and shoes.

Jess squared her shoulders and took a deep breath. 'Well, the first thing to say is I'm sorry I lied to you. When Tom had the children last weekend, I didn't stay with Caroline the whole time.'

'Were you in Millingham?'

'Yes. But I stayed somewhere else on the Saturday.'

'I sometimes wonder what life might have been like if Nathaniel had left me when you were all as young as Ben and Millie.'

'Don't, Mum. We're OK.'

'I hope you were somewhere having fun. God knows you need it. Darling, when did you last have your hair cut?' Felicity reached across and tucked some stray strands of hair behind Jess's ear.

'Mum, honestly, I'm not six years old.' She inched backwards. 'Remember I told you I'd met up with some friends from home again?'

'Yes. Sebastian Cameron, Sam Rushmore…'

'I stayed with Sam.'

'Oh. I see.'

'He wants to meet me in Oxford the week of half term. James Gorton is marrying Fiona somebody.'

'James Gorton? I thought he was gay?'

'Apparently he's changed his mind.'

'I'm not sure they really change their mind. They might think it politically expedient to get married, but do people change that much?'

'Did you know he won the Witney by-election?'

'How fascinating.' Her mother regarded her. 'Tell me about Sam.'

'He's lovely. But he's there. I'm here.'

'I always thought he was a nice boy. Did you and he ever get together in your teens?'

'No. Not really.'

'You were always so secretive about who you liked…'

Jess shrugged.

'And now? He's divorced?'

'Yep. Three kids.'

'And you're talking your way out of it.' She put her hand over Jess's. 'I'm going to write you a cheque, but only if you spend it on a proper haircut and something to wear to the wedding.'

'Oh, Mum.'

'Do you know what? I still wish you'd call me Mummy. After all these years.'

Her mother went to Brussels to visit Jess's brother Patrick and his pregnant Spanish wife Maria, and Jess rang Sam and said she would look for something to wear to a smart autumn wedding.

Two weeks before half term, she and Lucy set off for the King's Road. Jess saw all sorts of things she'd like to buy, but nothing that was at once suitable for a smart wedding, and something she would actually wear again. 'I just can't justify spending two hundred pounds on a posh suit I might only wear once a year, if that.'

On the tube home, Lucy said, 'What about that boutique around the corner? They have all sorts of interesting labels in there, stuff that's a bit more unusual.'

'And interesting prices.'

'Have a look. Nothing else has inspired you.'

So, the following morning, after dashing through the weekly shop, Jess walked to the boutique. It was crammed with lovely pieces from several European labels, and almost immediately she found a fine wool skirt in charcoal grey, and a stylish pink wool top. The top was neither a jacket nor a cardigan: unstructured, fastened with a large pin. Jess tried on both skirt and jacket and knew she had to buy them. The skirt hung beautifully. For the marriage service she could wear it with her black boots, and change into shoes later if she felt the need. The top was surprisingly flattering too, and just the right shade to wear over the top Sam had bought her. In the evening, she could just take the outer layer off.

She felt a frisson feather down her spine as she stared at her reflection, catching a glimpse of the person she could become. Not just a daughter, a mother, an ex-wife.

Then she arranged a visit to her hairdresser Kurt, who used to cut her hair when she was still working and could justify the trip into town to see him. He greeted her like a long lost but much-loved client. He cut quickly, with certainty, and started by taking a good inch off the length, making her hair look thicker and healthier. Then he trimmed her fringe and softened the remaining layers, blow-drying it smooth and shiny, which made the grey less obvious.

Her mother would be delighted. A decent haircut. And that was nothing to what Jess felt. She felt grown-up, serious, attractive even. No longer a bit player in her own life. With a haircut like this, she was definitely the lead.

'Excellent,' said Lucy. 'Takes years off you. Sam won't be able to keep his hands off you.'

'He better had.'

SAMUEL: age 12

James pulled himself up from his full-length sprawl on the lawn. 'I know.'

'Yeah?' Sam lay on his front, his cheek cushioned by the springy grass, the sun hitting the backs of his arms and legs.

James shoved Sam with his foot. 'Let's see how high we can climb.'

Sam flopped onto his back, hand over his eyes and squinted up at James through his fingers. At thirteen, he was already a head taller than Sam, sporting incipient dark stubble on his chin, and grappling with body odour. Several months younger, Sam felt far behind him, alternately relieved to have been noticed by James, and glad not to bear the brunt of his sharp tongue.

James faced the large oak tree at the end of the garden. 'I reckon we can get higher than we did last time. Get a move on.'

James's nine-year-old brother chose that moment to appear, silhouetted in the kitchen doorway, stretched hands steadying himself between the door frames.

'Get lost, Stuart,' said James.

'What are you doing?' said Stuart.

'Nothing that concerns you.'

'Why not?'

Sam could see the tension in Stuart's arms as he held onto the wooden architraves.

'You're too weak,' said James. 'You need to be much stronger to get up the tree.'

Stuart glanced at Sam, who smiled and shrugged.

Sam rolled to his feet. 'What's the plan?'

James pulled himself up onto the lowest branch without too much difficulty. For a moment he balanced on his stomach, his upper body counterbalanced by his legs, until he kicked himself onto the branch lengthwise. Easing towards the trunk, he knelt and then stood, reaching for the next branch, making it look easy.

Sam, after a lot of straining, managed to haul himself up onto the bottom branch, aware of how little upper body strength he had. The muscles in his arms and shoulders juddered from the effort. He felt red-faced and embarrassed, with James goading from above, Stuart cheering from below.

'Give us a hand up.' Stuart stretched up and grabbed Sam's ankle.

Sam looked over his shoulder at him.

'Please, Sam.'

'Piss off, Stuart,' said James.

Sam held onto the branch with one arm, leant down with the other, and pulled Stuart up beside him. He tried to catch his breath from the physical exertion.

'Come on, Sam,' James called from above.

'Hang on tight, Stuart.' Sam smiled, his confidence boosted by Stuart's admiring looks. He edged his way towards the trunk, wide and thick, feeling upwards for the next branch, not wanting to lose contact with the tree at all. He knew not to look down. The pattern of the bark became fascinating, filling his vision.

'What are you doing, Sam? The view's great up here.'

Sam searched for purchase with his trainer-clad feet.

At last a foothold, and once he'd begun, his limbs unfroze, found a rhythm, following the sound of James's voice. Always one foot and both hands or one hand and both feet clinging to the rough bark. A heart-clenching moment when he almost lost his grip, as he reached the branch James was straddling.

Only the sweat beaded across his forehead belied James's relaxed tone. 'At last. What took you so long?'

They surveyed the view as far as the girls' grammar school in one direction, the church in another, the tops of the huge beech trees in Lake Avenue and the green expanse of Barton Common spreading into the distance between the two.

'Wow.' Sam clung on tight. Not looking down. Clenching his fingers around the branch to stop the shaking.

'Relax,' said James, smiling.

'I am.' He would be. When he returned to earth.

James lounged against the trunk, reached for a packet of cigarettes in his shorts pocket. 'Ciggie?'

'Thanks. No.'

'Go on.' He stuck a cigarette between his lips, sucked in air as he struck a match, threw it away as it blew out, tried again. 'Shit.'

Sam concentrated on the horizon, saw the cigarette glow finally from the corner of his eye.

'I reckon we can get higher.' James took a long drag and held the cigarette out to Sam.

Gripping the branch tightly with his knees, he raised one arm slowly towards James and took the cigarette between his thumb and first finger. The end was damp from James's mouth when he raised it to his lips and inhaled gingerly. It wasn't that he'd never had a cigarette before, but with his dad being a doctor, he and Will had the dangers of smoking regularly drilled into them.

He managed not to cough aloud, and returned it to James, who put it back between his lips. 'Come on.' He manoeuvred to stand on the branch and reach upwards. The branches were thinner up here, the leaves less dense.

'I need to be home by five.'

'Wimp.' James felt for the closest branch, but even though he could touch it, he couldn't quite grip it enough to lever himself up.

Sam started his backwards descent and nearly trod on Stuart's fingers on the branch below. 'Stuart, what are you doing up here?'

'What the fuck?' James said. 'Mum'll kill you.'

'I'm really good at climbing,' said Stuart.

'It'll be the death of you. Get down,' said James.

'What are you doing? Are you blowing a cigarette? You know you're not allowed.'

'Shut up. It's none of your business. That's not what you say, anyway. It's smoking a cigarette.'

'You'll get cancer.'

'Shut up. Get down now.'

'I like it up here. I'm not moving.' Stuart crawled further along the branch, away from the trunk.

Sam carried on climbing down, his fight for breath easier with every step towards the ground. He concentrated on his points of contact with the tree, the feel of his hands, his fingers digging into the welts of bark, his feet finding any bump or gouge in the trunk to hold his weight. At the lowest branch, he eased himself down to sit, push off and jump to the ground. He crouched there, palms on the parched earth.

'Stuart, I said get down!' James shouted.

'Get off me!' Stuart yelled.

'You will get down, now.'

'Go away!'

Sam heard scrambling, looked up to see Stuart shinning towards the end of the branch.

'Don't be so fucking stupid.'

'You said a bad word. I'll tell. I'll do what I want. You can't make me.'

'I bloody well can,' James grabbed the waistband at the back of his brother's shorts. 'Fucking idiot.'

Stuart slumped backwards onto his brother, but James pushed him upright. 'Just get a move on.'

They shifted, caterpillar-style, back to the trunk.

'You first,' said James.

Stuart edged down, inch by inch, shuffling his feet, as he clawed from branch to branch. 'I'm stuck.'

'No fucking way, I'm sick of this.'

Sam saw James's foot connect sharply with his brother's fingers on the branch below.

'Ow,' Stuart yelped, flinging his hand away as if burnt, wrenching him off balance.

In sharp relief, Sam watched as the fingers of Stuart's other hand slipped inexorably until he could hold on no longer, arms flailing, falling through the lower branches onto his back on the hard, cracked earth, his head crashing onto the ground with a sickening thud.

'Stuart,' Sam crouched beside him, his voice hoarse, his breath shallow.

'Fucking hell.' James slithered down the trunk.

Stuart's body lay still, exactly where he'd fallen, arms stretched wide.

Sam felt slick with sweat and an urgent need to pee. 'Stuart. Stuart, please wake up.'

James jumped onto the ground. 'Stu! Say something.'

'Stuart, can you hear me?' Sam leaned closer, searching for signs of life.

'We're going to be in such deep shit we're not going to—'

'Shut up,' Sam hissed.

He resisted the urge to slap James while he concentrated on the first aid he knew. If it was a spinal injury, moving him would make things worse. But if he was having trouble breathing, turning him on his side into the recovery position could save his life. He didn't know what to do. He felt around the sides and back of Stuart's head, bringing his hand away warm from the blood. With gentle fingers he sifted through Stuart's hair until he found a wound.

He pressed the heel of his hand against it and focused on Stuart's face.

Eyes closed in repose, he looked as if he were asleep.

James shook Stuart's arm. 'We're never going to…my mother will never…'

'Stuart, can you hear me?' Sam bent his head closer to Stuart's face, his chest, scanning for signs of breathing—a pulse, the slightest movement—but his own blood pumping in his ears stopped him from hearing anything. His hand was becoming slippery with blood.

Stuart's eyes fluttered open, unfocused.

'Oh my God, thank Christ,' said James. 'He's alive.'

Sam slumped onto his front beside Stuart. The sun was too hot, the parched grass too prickly, but the ground was firm beneath him.

'Pull yourself together, Sam.' Wham. James punched him hard on his upper arm just below the sleeve of his t-shirt, connecting with bare flesh.

'Ow. What's that for?' He put his free hand up to the hot, stinging skin. The metallic smell of blood—Stuart's blood—blind-sided him.

'Get some colour back into you. You've gone grey.'

Sam felt as if he were watching the whole scene unfurl from the wrong end of a telescope. He opened his mouth to say something. Anything.

He knew there was an audacious element to James. He'd witnessed—in awe—James shoplifting from Woolworths. Not a modest chocolate bar, but a large Easter egg casually slung under his jacket.

But they were no longer dealing in chocolate contraband.

'When are your mum and dad back?'

'Stu's going to be fine. You're going to have to get used to a bit of blood if you want to be a doctor.'

'James. He didn't fall—'

'Yes, he did. He missed his footing.'

'I saw you stamp on his fingers—'

'No, you didn't. No. You didn't.' He emphasised the final word.

'My head,' Stuart moaned.

'Lie still. You're OK.' Sam turned to James. 'When are your parents back? We need a doctor. Now.'

JESS

Sam was already waiting, looking at a street map, when Jess met him in the centre of Oxford.

'Jess.' He blinked. 'Your hair.'

'Do you like it?'

'Do I?' His eyes roamed over her. 'You look so…'

'I decided to try to brighten myself up.' She wore a stripy scarf, a riot of salmon, scarlet, aqua, and jade.

'Good.'

'Good?' She laughed. She'd shocked him into monosyllables, making her heart sing.

'Good.' He pulled her into his arms and kissed her.

After lunch they walked along the High Street to Magdalen College, over the bridge and back to the Botanic Gardens.

At six o'clock they arrived at the North Oxford Victorian semi where Sam's brother Will and family lived. His wife Diana, still blonde and fresh-faced, opened the door. 'Come in. Jess. Hi.' She kissed her cheek.

'Thank you so much for having me.' That sounded too intimate. 'Putting me up.' She handed Diana a bottle of wine.

'Thank you. You're very welcome. Come through, the kettle's just boiled.'

They followed her down the hall to the kitchen, in which two blue-eyed, blonde children sat at the end of a large table eating their tea.

'This is Freya and Natasha,' said Sam. 'Girls, this is Jess.'

'I have two children about your age,' said Jess, meeting the curious stares. 'Are you six or seven, perhaps?' she said to Freya.

'I'm seven,' said Freya.

'I'm five,' said Natasha.

'Tea,' said Diana. 'Or would you like something else, Jess?'

'Tea. Would be lovely.'

'Will should be back soon and we can have a drink before you go out.' She turned to Sam. 'What time have you got to be where?'

'Eight o'clock. I've got the details upstairs.'

'You must tell me what you think of Fiona,' Diana said.

'Have you met her?' asked Jess.

'A couple of times. James has been keen to show how very supportive he is towards higher education. He's always turning up at College functions and clapping Will on the back.'

'I suppose an ambitious politician wants to keep in with everyone,' said Jess.

'You can say that again,' said Sam.

'Do you want to have a bath, or anything?' Diana asked. 'We've put you on the top floor for a bit of peace and quiet.'

Jess's eyes flickered towards Sam. She'd assumed they'd be in separate rooms, but this house was not as big as the house in Millingham.

Sam lifted an eyebrow.

'I'll have a quick wash and change. Thank you, that's so kind.'

'Not at all. It's a treat to see Sam.' Diana put her arm round him and reached up to kiss his cheek. 'We don't see him nearly enough.'

'Mum, I want a Kit-Kat,' said Freya.

'Not now. What fruit would you like?'

'A Kit-Kat,' said Natasha.

'Let me just do some fruit, and I'll show you upstairs,' said Diana.

'I can do that, if you like,' said Sam.

'I'm definitely still hungry,' said Natasha, reminding Jess of Millie.

They walked back down the hall and Sam picked up her bag.

'Mum,' they heard Freya ask. 'Is she Uncle Sam's girlfriend?'

Jess felt a wave of embarrassment sweep over her and avoided Sam's eye.

'That's right. Isn't it nice Sam's found someone he likes?'

'But why's he in the little bed? Doesn't she like him?' came Natasha's shrill tones.

At that point Diana closed the door.

'The little bed?' Jess asked.

On the first floor, Sam showed her a study, with a futon along one wall, already made up into a double bed.

'Doesn't look too little to me,' said Jess.

'Not too little at all,' said Sam, eyeing it and then her. 'Little, as in close to the ground.'

'I see. Are you going to be all right in here?'

He looked her in the eye. 'I don't know.'

She turned away to break the look.

'This way.' He led the way up the stairs to a spacious loft room and adjoining bathroom. The front part of the room housed a desk and crammed bookshelves, the other end a large double bed and chest of drawers. She cast an eye over the books—this must be where Will worked when he was at home—and wondered about the other study. 'Does Diana work?'

'She's a primary school teacher.' Sam looked calm and relaxed, his shoulder against the doorframe. She was a jumble of jangling nerves, feeling that if he touched her she might spontaneously shatter. Or combust.

'I feel bad making you sleep downstairs,' she blurted. 'Why don't you sleep up here?'

'Is that an offer?' he said, his eyes dancing.

'Or we could swap.' She tried to turn the conversation smoothly.

'But I'm not interested in sleeping up here on my own, and it wouldn't be fair to let you take the futon.'

He had that look in his eyes again. That cheerful, I'm-about-to-get-what-I-want look. She turned away and picked up a book on Will's desk. Hobbes' *Leviathan*. She put it down, fearing she had nothing intelligent to say about it.

Sam crossed his arms. She could see the movement out of the corner of her eye and felt his eyes on her. 'I was thinking we were getting pretty good at having-sex-but-not-actually-having-sex, so we could sleep in the same bed, all night.'

'It's still having sex.'

'Not technically. I was thinking of a few other variations we haven't tried yet.'

She cast about. 'What about Diana? She's gone to the trouble of making up the futon.'

'I may have mentioned that the sleeping arrangements might have a degree of fluidity to them. We wouldn't want the girls to think you didn't like me.'

She heard Sam push himself away from the doorframe, come and stand behind her and wrap his arms round her waist, pulling her back against him. He felt warm and substantial and safe and all the things she didn't have.

He kissed her cheek. 'Just a thought.'

She turned in his arms, pressing against him, lifting her face to meet his lips, erupting as he kissed her back, his tongue hard in her mouth. Had he not had his arms around her she would have crashed to the floor with the intensity of it all. Between them—her pushing, him pulling—they fell on to the bed. Immediately he rolled, his weight on top of her, and she wrapped herself around him, tight and close, feeling the hard heat of his erection pulsing against the hot wetness, the layers of clothes between them insignificant, his hands in her hair, his tongue in her mouth, mirroring the movement of his hips.

'Uncle Sam, Mummy says here are the towels,' said Natasha, climbing the stairs.

Sam sprang off Jess, shoving his fingers through his hair, trying to breathe, while she sat up, a hand over her mouth. In two strides he met Natasha at the top step and propelled her back down the stairs. 'Great. Jess is just going to change. Let's put these in my room.'

She tried to bring her breathing back to normal, touched her palms to her flaming cheeks.

Footsteps sounded on the stairs. 'That was close.' Sam handed her two blue towels.

Jess clutched them. 'I feel like a naughty teenager.'

'Fantastic role reversal, isn't it?' He winked before he descended the stairs two at a time.

'Thank you so much for letting us stay. Letting me stay.' Jess addressed Will as Sam handed her a glass of white wine.

'You're very welcome,' said Will.

Really, it was a crime to have two George Clooneys in the same family. She imagined Will's philosophy lectures crammed with pretty undergraduates, undaunted until they saw his attractive wife and daughters, and perhaps not even then.

'Good to see Sam with a smile on his face again.'

Jess didn't know quite how to respond to that. She took a sip of wine. It was cold and delicious, and before she knew it, she'd finished her glass, sitting beside Sam, listening to the brothers talking about work, football, their mother, plans for Christmas. Diana joined them, having got the girls into bed, reaching for the proffered glass of wine.

'Best moment of the day.' She smiled at Will. 'I said you'd go and say goodnight.'

'OK. How was Freya today? Not too lippy?'

'No. Nothing like last night, I think she worked it out of her system,' said Diana.

'That's good.' Will turned to Jess. 'There are times when she seems keen to emulate her older cousin.'

'Ah, that's not fair,' said Sam.

Will shrugged. 'You rise to it every time, little brother.'

'Kate's…Kate can be perfectly civilised when she makes an effort,' said Sam.

Will raised an eyebrow. 'What about you, Jess, what do you think of Kate?'

'Not a fair question,' said Sam.

'I try and keep her and Freya as far apart as possible.' Will grinned. 'Already Freya hero-worships her anti-social behaviour.'

'I can imagine,' said Jess.

'We need to make a move.' Sam finished his glass and stood up. 'I'll drive.'

Jess swallowed. 'Don't you want a drink?' That was all she needed. The intimacy of a car journey, Sam driving with his expert gynaecological hands, there and back.

'I'll drop you, if you like. Then you can take a cab back,' said Will, looking at Diana.

'I'll start supper,' said Diana.

Sam and Jess walked down the wide corridor, following the babble of noise, until they reached James and Fiona, who stood at the entrance to a large room with a wooden floor, and chairs and tables round the edges.

Jess realised she'd faint if she didn't concentrate on breathing.

'Jessica Lamb, you look exactly the same as you always did.' James grasped her upper arms and kissed her on both cheeks.

She stood absolutely still while he touched her.

The same could not be said of him. He was still a big, good-looking man—dark hair, with only a touch of grey at the temples, now receding from a wide forehead, same dark brown eyes, that dimple that Ruth had been crazy about—but there was a heaviness to him. Not that he was conspicuously overweight. But he wore a well-cut dark suit, with a white shirt and loosened tie, and the flatteringly long jacket skimmed a bigger stomach than twenty years ago. She felt Sam's taut, lean torso on her two hours before, and her stomach disappeared, which detracted from the shudder James' touch induced.

'And this is Fiona,' he said.

'Delighted to meet you.' Fiona smiled but her look was shrewd and assessing. 'I've heard such a lot about you.'

Jess unstuck her tongue from the roof of her mouth. 'How nice to meet you, congratulations on your engagement.'

Sam shook hands with James and kissed Fiona's cheek while James handed them a flute of sparkling wine each.

Jess concentrated on Fiona, a sturdy curly-haired woman, wearing a navy jacket. For a moment Jess felt insignificant in her cardigan, the sign that she was not a woman of substance. Even Sam was wearing a jacket over a white shirt, unbuttoned at the neck. Looking *really* good. He put his hand on the small of her back.

'So how did you meet?' Jess blurted, after a gulp of fizz.

'Through work.' Fiona laughed. 'I do PR for constituency MPs and I'd seen him at a few party conferences.'

'And you're based in Oxford?'

'Yes. We're buying a house in the constituency, in Witney hopefully. Of course we have the flat in London. I work in Victoria.'

'The flat's in Pimlico, so we can both walk to work,' said James.

'Of course,' said Jess, thinking there is not enough alcohol in the world.

'What about you?' said James. 'Are you just very old friends, or something more than that?'

Jess studied her almost empty glass. If she focused on her breathing she'd get through the evening without fainting. Or screaming.

'Yes to both.' Sam seemed as relaxed as ever.

'And all those children. That must be interesting,' said James.

'How many?' said Fiona.

'I've got two and Sam has three.' Jess bit her lip to stop herself from laughing out loud at the expression on Fiona's face.

'Can't say I've ever wanted children,' said Fiona, and the slightest movement made Jess look at James properly for the first time. Something—she couldn't decipher what—

passed over his face. Well, at least we won't be invited over, she thought. She glanced at Fiona. She could be thirty-five or forty-five, it was difficult to tell.

'So, are you going to make it an even number?' said James.

'Excuse me?' said Jess.

Sam spread his palm on her back. 'It's not something we've discussed.'

'But you have absolute confidence in your contraception? I suppose you would, being a doctor. Though I seem to remember that Elizabeth was pregnant when you got married. Two doctors getting it wrong.' James laughed.

'You're making a lot of assumptions,' said Sam, his voice ultra-calm.

James swallowed the rest of his drink. 'Oh, I see. You're not sleeping together? Well, that makes sense, given your —'

'We're holding you up, there are people waiting to say hello,' said Sam. He propelled Jess towards the table of drinks, swapped her empty glass for a full one.

She took three quick sips.

'Are you OK?' he said.

She put her hand on his lapel. 'I am. You're here.'

At a break in the dancing, Jess left Sam to find the loos. Once in the furthest cubicle, she heard voices.

A high, posh voice she didn't recognise. 'Fucking terrible to marry someone who wasn't into adventurous sex.'

A fit of giggles ensued, as doors were banged shut.

'How adventurous?'

'I'm not saying a word, you might blab.' A voice she *did* recognise.

'Fi, darling, of course I won't. But I am seeing James in a whole new light. He has the confidence of the well-endowed.'

Another explosion of giggles.

'As if he might suddenly push you over a chair and roger you senseless.'

'That is the general idea,' said Fiona.

'Lucky bitch.' Toilets were flushed, doors unlocked. 'I expect you to come back from honeymoon absolutely fucking knackered. In the true sense of the word.'

'Bella!'

Doors opened and closed, bringing the throng of chatter into the echoing, high-ceilinged room. Then silence.

Jess flushed the toilet and unlocked her door.

Fiona was still standing in front of the basins, mopping her red face with a paper towel. She shrugged at Jess in the mirror. 'Old school friend. Gosh, it's hot work, all this dancing.'

Jess hauled herself back to the present and started washing her hands. 'Yes.'

'Look. Don't worry about it.'

'Sorry?' Considering the way the evening had started, she'd been feeling better than expected. This was helped considerably by the exhilaration of increasingly uninhibited dancing as the room filled, encouraged by the caller and the lively band. Having done Scottish dancing at primary school, Jess was pleased some muscle memory had stopped her from making a complete fool of herself. Sam turned out to be an excellent dancer.

She realised Fiona was speaking.

'...most men get over it. Happens a couple of times and then never again.'

Jess gave her a blank look.

'And if they don't there's always the little blue pill. Works wonders, I'm told.'

'I'm sorry?' She shook her hands and turned to the paper towel dispenser.

'Sam's little problem. James mentioned it.' Fiona caught Jess's eye in the mirror. 'I'm sorry. I didn't mean to pry.'

'No problem.' Jess walked out of the Ladies. By the time she reached Sam her jaw ached. She put her hand on the side of her face and consciously opened her mouth to separate her teeth.

'All right?' Sam put his hand on her arm.

She reached for another glass, obliging him to let go. The alcohol had been blotted only slightly by the buffet of cold meats, salads, and cheese. She drank, knowing the children in the house would not require her attention in the morning.

'What is it?' Sam slipped his arm around her.

'Get off,' she said.

'Trouble in paradise?' James stood behind them.

Jess swung round, freeing herself from Sam's hold. She stepped backwards, feeling the table against the back of her thighs.

'There you are,' said Fiona, newly coiffed and lipsticked. 'Come on, let's make up a set. They're about to start the next dance.'

Sam eyed Jess. 'I think we might call it a night, if you don't mind.'

'Oh, that's a shame,' said Fiona. 'See you on Friday, then.'

'I hope all the last minute preparations go well,' Jess found herself saying.

'I'm sure they will.' James kissed her on both cheeks.

Really, anyone would think they were old and civilised friends.

James slapped Sam on the back. 'Just get on with it.'

Sam cleared his throat. 'Jess?'

'I'm going to find my coat.'

Jess stared down the dark road. It was much colder, away from the heat of many bodies dancing. 'I suppose you think I'm stupid.'

'Why would I think that?' Sam stood opposite her on the pavement.

'Don't you think you might have mentioned something like that? Did you really think I'd be thrilled hearing it from *Fiona*?'

'What did she say?' His voice was calm; quiet, but his expression was worried.

Jess clenched her fists into tight balls. 'What the hell does it matter? What matters is what *you* should have said.' Her knees started to shake. She lurched from foot to foot. 'You were happy to roll around with me on your sofa, but you didn't trust me enough to tell me. Do you know how awful that makes me feel?'

Sam's expression relaxed, the furrows of his forehead smoothing away. 'I'm sorry I didn't—' He reached for her.

'Don't.' She batted his arms away, blotting the tears with the back of her arm. 'I don't understand. You can't tell me, and yet *James* knows? *James*? I wouldn't trust him further than I could throw him.'

'I didn't know he knew—'

'Yeah. Right. It may surprise you to know that I'm not as stupid as I obviously look.' Above her, the streetlamp began to flicker.

'You have to believe me. The only person I told, at the end of a long, alcohol-fuelled evening, was Rob, and that I regretted immediately.'

'So you should. He obviously told James, who then told Fiona!'

'I can't help that now. But I should have told you. I tried to, but I didn't want to let you down. I so wanted to be who you wanted me to be.'

'What are you talking about?'

'On one of those evenings I spent with you in July, you told me you'd been in love with me for all those years in our youth. And you were a shadow of the person you used to be. I wanted to help you—'

'You think I need your fucking charity?' she shouted.

They stared at each other.

'No, I don't. It's tough being a single parent. You didn't need my problems on top of it all.' In the sallow streetlight he looked all of his thirty-eight years.

'You felt pity for me. You thought I wouldn't be able to cope with knowing that you couldn't get it up, so you decided not to mention it.'

He winced. 'I was going to tell you. Then you told me you weren't going to sleep with me. So the problem was not going to come up.' He drew breath. 'As it were. It was cowardice on my part, but I thought I could not mention it.'

She shoved her hands deep in her pockets. 'So, were you ever going to?'

The failing streetlight died, darkness seeping between them. Sam became an outline; she couldn't read his expression.

'Of course I was. But things seemed to have changed…'

She concentrated on the contours of the pavement.

'I daresay you've noticed that not being able to get it up has never been a problem when I'm with you. Quite the opposite, in fact.'

A thought occurred to Jess, and she had a horrible moment of thinking she was going to be physically sick. She swallowed hard. 'I couldn't believe you kept wanting to see me. But I understand now. I fulfil a therapeutic need for you.'

'Jess, no. I respect your wish not to sleep with me. It's fine.' He pushed a hand through his hair. 'I'm not sure fine is the right word. I seem to think of nothing else. But I would see you even if you wouldn't do what we've been doing. I want to see you for you. Which is not to say that I don't want to make love to you more than anything.' He grabbed her arm, holding on to her coat while she tried to shake him off. 'Look at me.'

'Stop it, Sam, just stop it.' She stood still.

'I will stop. Just look at me. Once.' He was so close.

She knew the quickest way to end this would be to look at him. She raised her eyes, hit by the tenderest expression she'd ever seen on Sam's face.

'Jess, you have to believe me. This is not about pity, or kindness, or sexual therapy or any of those things. I'm here because I'm interested in what you'll say next. What you think. What you feel. None of the other stuff matters.'

Jess woke up on Thursday morning with the worst hangover she could remember. She was used to one, possibly two glasses of wine an evening, and she must have had at least three times that amount. Her mouth was as dry as sandpaper, her head throbbed. She crept to the bathroom for several glasses of water, brushed her teeth and returned to bed, groping for her watch. Ten past nine. Diana and the girls would be at school, having had half term the previous week. Will would be in college, presumably. Which left Sam.

As she lay there, nursing her pounding head, parts of the evening fell into place in her mind. Fiona's expression at the thought of having five children; her open mouth when Jess sprinted out of the Ladies. James. Smiling at her, telling her she hadn't changed a bit, alluding to Sam's problem, telling him to go for it. And Sam. Kissing the life out of her on this very bed. Winking at her. Smiling at her in front of Will. Grey and anxious in the streetlight.

They'd got back to Will and Diana's somehow, most of the walk conducted in silence. She'd been overwhelmed by fatigue, exhausted by anger. Every time he tried to speak she'd stopped him. 'Not now, Sam.'

How could she have cut him off like that? Yes, he could have mentioned his little problem earlier, but hadn't she had a pretty good suspicion? Wasn't this anger much more to do with hurt pride that somehow James knew? Why did she fall into the trap of feeling and behaving like a damaged teenager when James was near?

Too many repeating patterns. No learning from the past.

Her lack of wisdom depressed her. She seemed to have lost the will to pray anything other than the briefest of prayers: *God give me strength,* or *Have mercy on me, a sinne*r.' She repeated the words to herself as she lay, wide-eyed and sleepless, in the darkness.

SAM

Sam sat in the silent kitchen, most of his attention straining for sounds of Jess descending the stairs.

Finally he heard her footsteps. He straightened up. 'Tea?'

'Thanks,' Jess answered, not quite meeting his eyes.

He flicked the kettle on, busied himself with a mug, teabag and milk. 'What would you like for breakfast?'

'Um.' She rubbed her eyes. 'Have you had something?'

'Not really. Well. That's to say, I had the rest of Tash's toast, but not properly.'

Jess pleated her fingers this way, that way. 'So, what are you…?'

'Whatever you fancy.' He stopped. Unfortunate turn of phrase. 'Yogurt, cereal, toast, eggs, probably other things for a cooked breakfast…'

'Maybe some yogurt? And toast?'

He longed to hug her. This morning she looked tired and pale, almost as pale as when they'd met in the summer.

'Good choice. Sit down, I'll do it.'

'Really. You don't have to. I'll—'

'Please, Jess. Breakfast is the least I can do.'

She subsided into a chair on the other side of the table. 'Thank you.'

'You're welcome,' he said, keen to keep the conversation going. 'Did you manage to sleep?'

Her eyes flew to his face, skimmed away, dropped to scan the tabletop. 'Eventually.'

The kettle filled the silence with gurgling and hissing until it clicked off. He turned away from the table to pour water into the waiting mug.

'You?' she asked.

He placed the steaming mug in front of her. 'Eventually.'

She kept her eyes lowered.

Sam found yogurt and honey and put them on the table. He cut two slices of bread and slotted them into the toaster. Then he sat down opposite her.

'Thank you for the tea,' Jess said, her hands cupped around the mug.

'Are you warm enough?'

'I will be.'

'I could put the heating on. I'm sure I could work out how to do that.' He paused. 'Well, I could have a go.'

'It's fine. I'm warmer already.'

'Good.' He pushed the yogurt pot towards her. 'Honey?'

Her eyes met his. Lingered briefly this time.

'Or jam? Sugar?'

'Honey's good.' She dolloped some into a bowl, squeezed a wave of honey over it, but when she brought a spoonful up to her lips, she replaced it in the bowl without touching it. 'Sam. I'm sorry I was so angry.'

'No, I'm sorry. You had every right to be angry.'

'I don't want to fight with you. I don't mean to descend into angry teenager mode around…around James.'

At last Sam could smile. 'Don't worry. Reminds me of Kate.'

After drinking several cups of tea, they took a bus into the centre of town, wandered through the pedestrianised shopping area and had lunch in one of the cafes. He didn't reach for her hand or try to kiss her. He missed her touch, like a dull ache settling between his shoulder blades.

After lunch they walked down the hill, over Magdalen Bridge, along the river Cherwell.

Finally he said, 'Are you too cold to sit down?'

'No.'

He sat beside her on a bench, staring at the river. 'I'm sorry I didn't tell you about…the technical term is erectile dysfunction… I've been trying to work out my exact motives for not telling you. I used the not having sex thing as a convenient excuse, but under it all, you're right, I did think I might get away with not telling you.'

Jess nodded.

'I also thought that if I told you it would take on a bigger significance. That by not talking about it, I might be able to cure it.' He raked a hand through his hair. 'It happened two or three times with Elizabeth. When things were really bad. She used sex as a power tool. Withholding it or dishing it out as she saw fit.' He stopped and shook himself, almost as if he were physically separating himself from the memory. 'Anyway. I assumed it was purely to do with that situation. I didn't go and see anyone of course. GP, too embarrassed to talk to anyone. All rather pathetic. Then the situation didn't come up. I didn't need to think about it for ages. Until I was at a conference in York at Easter. I met a doctor there. Briony. We talked in a way I'd not talked properly for years. One thing led to another after a few glasses of wine. Everything was fine until she took her clothes off. Then suddenly nothing was OK and she was crying and I was crying. Dreadful.' He shuddered. 'So. Cowardice. Fear. You name it.'

She reached over and took his hand. 'Courage. Guts.'

At last he turned his head to look at her. 'Thank you.'

They sat there, hand in hand, watching the trees being buffeted by the wind until Jess roused herself. 'I can no longer feel my feet.'

'Shall we go back?' said Sam.

'Yes.'

When they reached Will and Diana's, Jess pleaded a headache and went upstairs to lie down. Sam took the opportunity to ring Rob.

'I can't believe you,' Sam said, angrier than he'd felt for a long time. 'You're a fucking journalist, for Christ's sake.'

'I rest my case,' said Rob.

'But I told you in confidence, as you well—'

'For fuck's sake. Grow up. Get some therapy,' said Rob.

'God, Rob, listen to yourself. I don't have the problem with Jess. Quite the contrary, as it happens.'

'Then what are you complaining about, man? Get a life.'

When Sam put the phone down, he sighed. Difficult to stay pissed off with someone who displayed such a spectacular lack of contrition.

An hour later, Sam climbed to the top of the house and handed Jess a glass of wine. Had he been honest with her from the beginning, he might have spent last night in this bed, not on that shockingly uncomfortable futon. 'How are you feeling?'

'Better. I'm afraid I just can't handle large amounts of alcohol. Don't let me drink like that this evening.' She took a sip of her wine and laughed at the contradiction. 'On second thoughts I'll keep myself in check.'

He let his shoulders sag in relief. The first proper laugh all day.

'Sit down,' she said, leaving him a space at the end of the bed, still warm from her feet.

He wondered what it was about her he was drawn to. She was not conventionally beautiful, hadn't even been particularly pretty in her teens, and yet, right from the beginning, from when he'd first noticed her as a fourteen-year-old, there had been something. Her clear and expressive face, the way her emotions played across her features, her nervous energy, had all been attractive. Her hair was mussed up and her right cheek was red from where she'd been lying on it, but her eyes shone. Now she was a fleshed out, gloriously technicolour, fully paid up member of the human race. She had come back to life, since he'd met her again in July.

'You look—' he started to say, at the same time as she said, 'Thank you—'

'Go on,' he said.

'I just wanted to say thank you for telling me.'

'You're welcome. I was thinking how alive you look.'

She swung her legs over the side of the bed to stand up. 'Can I do anything towards supper, do you think?'

He stood up, wanting to put his arms around her, hesitating a fraction too long so the moment was lost.

Another dreadful night. Sam woke every couple of hours, wrapped in damp covers, convinced something had startled him out of his vivid dream, shaking with the force of the violence he felt towards James as he pursued him from ward to ward of a labyrinthine hospital.

He wondered if Jess was getting more sleep than he was.

He rolled onto his front, away from the damp sheet, to the other side of the futon. Maybe it was wrong to invest such hope in Jess. Maybe it was unwise—dangerous even—to give one other person such responsibility. Weren't such expectations bound to be disappointed? He prayed, something he did fleetingly, when he was not in church. *Help me. Help Jess. Stop this from happening, if it's not meant to be.*

He woke to sounds of the family surfacing, the girls running in and out of the bathroom, pausing to converse in loud theatrical whispers on the landing.

'Shhh,' Diana said. 'Sam's sleeping.'

'Why's he in the study? Why isn't he upstairs?' said Natasha.

'Good question,' said Diana.

'Because Jess is upstairs,' said Freya.

'Yes, but why…?'

JESS

Jess was relieved that she still liked her outfit. The skirt and wool top fitted beautifully, and the coral top was as flattering as ever. What was Sam going to read into her wearing it? She shook her head. What did it matter anymore?

It was as if the re-ignited relationship with Sam was a fragile and guttering flame that needed constant protection. The question was whether all these confrontations, revelations and disappointments—triggered in no small part by the lurking presence of James—had completely snuffed out the flame, never to burn again, or whether, despite receiving a severe dousing, it could recover…and strengthen, even.

Sam was waiting for her at the bottom of the stairs, wearing a beautifully cut dark suit, shirt and tie. 'Ready?'

They took a bus into the centre of Oxford, and walked to the chapel of James' old college through a persistent drizzle. Jess huddled into the warmth of her wool coat and boots.

The male half of the wedding party stood outside, impressive in full morning dress, sporting deep red roses as buttonholes. James kissed Jess and shook hands with Sam before they were ushered to their pew, already occupied by a smart looking couple.

'Who are the ushers, I wonder?' Jess said, not recognising anyone.

'The party faithful, no doubt.' Sam took his glasses out of his inside pocket and put them on to read the Order of Service.

Clark Kent. Let me introduce myself. Lois Lane.

The other couple, Jess discovered, were Alasdair and Isabelle, thrilled to talk about themselves and their children. Sweetly—or nauseatingly—his tie matched the exact colour of her dress. Within two minutes, Jess knew that Alasdair had worked with James and still worked in the City, and that they had two exceptionally bright and musical children named Titus and Tabitha.

Jess found herself gripping Sam's hand to keep from laughing.

'PCLT,' she whispered.

'What?' He looked at her over the top of his glasses.

'Tell you later.'

'There's Rob,' he said, catching his eye. He was being marched to a pew two rows in front, and smiled broadly at them. 'I gave him a bollocking, by the way. Wanted to say it before today.'

'How did he take it?'

'Couldn't work out what I was so worked up about.'

'No remorse?'

'None.'

Sebastian and Tami walked past, on their way to a pew three rows from the front.

'No children, the invitation stipulated,' said Sam.

'That figures.'

'I'm sorry you're sitting this far back,' he whispered in her ear, sending shivers down her spine. 'Lowly GPs obviously count for less than top print journalists and media tycoons.'

'You only save lives, after all.'

'Life isn't everything,' he agreed.

The organ began, and Jess pressed her face against his shoulder to stop herself from laughing out loud.

'What?'

'*The Arrival of the Queen of Sheba,*' she gasped.

'I understand now why they didn't want any children here,' said Jess, nearly an hour later. 'My bottom's far too bony for these pews.'

'Not that bony.' Sam smiled down at her.

Jess ignored her skipping heart. 'Why do they need to have communion as part of the marriage ceremony, anyway?'

'So that we are made wholly aware just how devout their devotion to God really is.'

'And it separates everyone out neatly. You're either with us or you're not.'

'True. However we pass this particular test. We're in their club.'

'Exactly, although I'd rather not be in their club.' Rob, Sebastian and Tami had not gone up for Holy Communion.

'Groucho Marx.'

'Exactly,' she beamed.

'PCLT?'

'Shhh, later,' said Jess.

SAM

'Why aren't you Best Man? You're the obvious choice.' Rob addressed Sam above the hubbub of wedding guests that filled the large room overlooking the college quad.

'Not anymore. I'm not the correct shade of blue.' Sam scanned the crowds. He really wanted to say hello to James's brother Stuart. Sam didn't see enough of him, considering they both lived in Millingham. He was also looking for a particular shade of pink. Jess had said she needed to change her shoes, but he liked being beside her.

'Who gives a bugger about that? You were always his best friend.' He paused. 'Or maybe he didn't want to hurt my feelings, so he didn't choose any of the old crowd?'

'Yep. Must be that. But lining up Andrew must have been a coup.'

'Why are you so morose? Anyway, who cares about the Tory chief whip, when he could have had you?'

'I'm not morose. He sees everything through a political lens—as he must now—and a wedding is a vote winner.' Out of the corner of his eye he was aware of Rob rubbing his jaw.

'So… I had a brief word with Stuart earlier. Have you spoken to him?'

Sam glanced at Rob, who looked straight at him, unblinking. 'Not yet…'

'I knew he'd had some problems…'

'I think there was a moment when he might not have come.'

'Does it still go back to that head injury?'

'What?' Sam scanned the crowds for Jess. *Where was she?*

'Sam,' Rob pressed. 'You were there when Stuart fell out of the tree, weren't you? What happened? Did he really fall?'

Sam kept his gaze on the crowd, fists tight in his pockets. 'Yes.'

'Nothing happened with James?'

'No.' Sam stared into the throng of wedding guests.

'Are you OK, Sam?' Rob swung round to face him.

'We were stupid kids. It was a very long time ago.'

'Then nothing happened that shouldn't have? You've never wanted to talk about it—'

'There's nothing to talk about.' Sam literally felt hot under the collar. The men were not taking off their jackets. Yet. Maybe when they sat down to eat, it wouldn't be frowned upon… Or there would be some more air… 'I felt responsible because I helped Stuart onto the bottom branch. He was only nine. I never imagined he'd be able to climb up so high.'

'So, he turned out to be a good climber. Why do you think he fell then?'

Why did Rob have to be an experienced journalist who was always on the lookout for a story? Sam had managed not to think about this, and about Stuart's subsequent stay in hospital, and the consequences of his head injuries, for many years.

He really didn't want to think about it.

Stuart was here today, and that was a good thing.

'Shhh. Here comes Jess.'

JESS

Jess came back from changing out of her boots into her shoes, to find Sam shaking his head at Rob in the middle of the crowded room.

'Everything OK?' She put her hand on Sam's arm as she fiddled with her ankle strap.

'I can't think what she reminds me of.' Rob swigged his champagne.

'Hello, Rob. Don't you mean 'who'?' said Jess.

'What, darling.' Rob grinned at her. 'You really do look exactly the same as you always did, Jessica. No, on second thoughts you look better. Must be the love of a good man.' He kissed her cheek.

Jess blushed, not convinced by Rob's tone, acutely aware of Sam's eyes on her.

Rob snapped his fingers. 'That's it. She looks like a majestic ocean liner at full speed. Look at her.'

Jess and Sam watched Fiona's progress, in her long white, billowing dress and train, leaving admiring smiles in her wake, neatly fitting Rob's description.

'Have you met her properly?' Jess asked.

'Oh yes. I've been networked.' Rob grinned.

'How impressive.'

'What's your verdict, Sam? Doesn't she remind you of Ruth?' said Rob.

'Yes,' said Sam.

'Are you all right?' said Jess.

'Fine. Glad you're here.'

'Here come Sebastian and Tami. I'm going to try out my one useful phrase in Japanese,' said Rob.

'Which is?' said Jess.

He winked at Jess. 'I love you.'

'Jessica,' said Sebastian, kissing her on both cheeks. 'Looking much better.' He raised an eyebrow at Sam and gave him a back-slapping hug.

Jess laughed. 'I'll ignore the patronising tone.'

'Do. I'm hoping by ignoring it, it might disappear altogether.' Tami kissed Jess and Sam. 'You both look so well.'

'Well, we've already decided that with Jess it's the love of a good man. We're just hoping that the same applies for Sam.' Rob stopped a passing waiter and swapped his empty glass for a full one.

'Absolutely. The love of a good man,' said Sebastian.

'Speaking of which.' Sam looked beyond him to the approaching bridegroom. 'Congratulations, James.'

'Should have done this years ago,' said James.

'Yes, but then he'd have had to have sex with a woman,' Rob said in Jess's ear.

'You're dreadful.' She smiled at him.

'That's me. Same as ever.' He tucked a stray strand of hair behind her ear. A jolt of lust shot through her. She was so sexually frustrated, even dedicated flirt Rob could turn her on. Masturbation was beginning to look like her only option. What did the Bible say about that?

'Less of that.' Sam handed Jess a fresh glass of champagne. She met his eyes, so pleased he was standing close to her. *Don't leave me alone with Rob. Protect me, love me, make love to me.*

Whoops. A momentary aberration. She focused on his face. He didn't look as laid back as usual. Not that he looked nervous. He looked…

He backed away from the others and she followed to stay close. 'No flirting with Rob,' he said.

'I wasn't flirting. Not deliberately.'

'Well don't. Not in that outfit.'

'You're managing proper sentences again?'

'Just about.' He frowned.

'Sam, don't be ridiculous. You think I'd ever choose him over you?'

'Just like to hear you say that.' He cleared his throat. 'Anyway. PCLT?'

She followed his eyes and saw Alasdair and Isabelle in earnest conversation with another couple a few metres away. That is to say, Isabelle was speaking while the others gave her the attention she required.

'People carrier, leather trousers. It's a marketing category, apparently,' she said—accompanied by Sam's burst of laughter, the anxiety finally wiped off his face—aglow at making him laugh so hard.

At last they were summoned to the wedding breakfast. 'Bloody funny time, six o'clock in the evening,' Rob came up behind her and spoke into her ear.

'Stop it.' She moved closer to Sam, who put an arm round her waist as they walked into the adjoining room. They were sitting with Sebastian and Tami, and Alasdair and Isabelle. 'Well, at least we won't have to worry about any awkward pauses in conversation,' Jess said.

'What's that?' said Rob.

'You'll see.'

After the smoked duck starter and the accompanying Chablis, and the beef with a full-bodied Burgundy, Jess sat back and surreptitiously loosened her waistband.

'I have to pace myself,' she said to Sam.

'Tell me about it. I'm giving up alcohol for a month when I get back.'

'A month?'

'OK, a week. Hold me to it.'

She didn't want to think about tomorrow, about their separate paths and how and when they would converge again. She turned to Rob, sitting on the other side of her. 'I've got a bone to pick with you.'

'Go on then.' He grinned.

'How could you betray a confidence like that?'

'I assume we're talking about Sam, and what I believe is his recovered manhood? Congratulations, by the way.'

'That's none of your business. You know he told you in confidence and yet you told James.'

He sat back and drained his glass of red wine. 'First, it is my business if Sam tells me these things, and second, what is your problem with James? What did he ever do to you?'

Jess tried to work out exactly how the conversation had taken this turn. 'This is not about me, Rob. This is about Sam.'

'He and I talked about it. Fully and frankly, thank you very much.' He glanced towards Sam, who was talking babies with Tami.

'Why did you tell James?'

'Apart from anything else, because he is a friend of mine, and of Sam's. I refer you to the previous question, Miss Lamb. What did he ever do to you?'

She couldn't think of anything to say. Her memories of what James may have done had been worn away by too many unreliable but much scrutinised twenty-year-old images, so what could she say? And how long was she going to carry this burden? Why not lay it down, close the door, walk away?

Rob leant forward, lowered his voice. 'If you have such a problem with him, what exactly are you doing at his wedding, drinking his wine, eating his food?'

She took a deep breath. 'I don't have a problem. I'm happy for them both, if it's what they really want.'

'Isn't it?'

'I don't know. I don't know anything anymore.'

'A good starting point for the rest of your life.'

'What's this?' Sam looked round.

'Rob's saying that knowing nothing is a good starting point for the rest of your life,' said Jess.

'That's a bit profound for you, Rob,' said Sam, catching Jess's eye.

'You know me. Read it in a fortune cookie.' Rob collared a waiter for more red wine.

'Are you OK?' Sam whispered to Jess.

'He was giving me a hard time for being negative about James.'

'What? You don't have to take it from—'

'No, he's right.' She met his intense gaze. 'Here I am enjoying his hospitality, at his wedding, for God's sake, and I'm… I can't… Oh, I don't know.'

'So…your feelings for him may be clouded by the past—'

'Yeah, but isn't it time I grew up?' She stopped, caught in his look. 'I think we're saying each other's lines.' She swallowed. 'Do you know the most frightening thing about meeting up with the people you grew up with, twenty years later? You forget that half your life has been lived without them. You step straight into the emotions you felt all those years ago.'

'Why do I have a bad feeling about how this conversation's going? You're going to tell me that all you feel for me is a schoolgirl crush.'

'I don't think it was ever a schoolgirl crush.'

'What do you remember? Accurately?'

'I have diaries. Written evidence.'

'For how many years? The whole lot?'

'No. Bits and pieces. Most of it's extremely banal, with only the odd glimmer of interest.' She reached for her water glass and took a long drink.

'And?'

'Do you remember that night?' She didn't look at him.

'New Year's Eve?'

She nodded. 'Did it feel like it felt to me?'

'Yes.'

The bustle and hubbub of the room faded as she met his eyes. Darker than ever. She licked her dry lips. 'I don't know why I put myself through the same mental hoops over and over again. What's the point in thinking about it? Worrying about what ifs?'

'What does the diary say?'

'Who knows? Can't find that one.'

After the speeches, the bride and groom cut the cake before leading the way to the hall for the first dance, Fiona's head against James's shoulder, tucked under his chin, their arms about one another. For a moment Jess glimpsed a happy life. It made her think of her own first dance with Tom—he'd insisted on stopping the band to make them play a different song—and Sam's dance with Elizabeth. Both of them dark-haired; Elizabeth tall and strikingly beautiful, just as a bride should be.

Then the Scottish dancing caller started giving them

instructions. They were to form sets of six couples for *Strip The Willow*. Jess was very glad she and Sam had gone to the practise session on Wednesday—despite the other secrets and lies that had swilled around that evening—and managed to get by. After nearly an hour and a half of strenuous dancing, there was a supper break. The guests fell upon the food, despite the filling meal earlier.

Half an hour later, a swing band started up. This caused Jess some trepidation. Somehow it was far easier to follow the Scottish dancing rules than it was to go freestyle. She danced like this so rarely now that it took all her time to get over the embarrassment, and when she started to relax it was invariably time to go home. Tom refusing to dance with her, even in the beginning, should have been a warning sign, but she'd ignored it.

Sam raised an eyebrow at her and nodded towards the dancefloor.

'Oh no, thank you, Sam.'

'Sure?'

Sebastian and Tami joined them, Tami twisting her skirt in delight. 'Come on, Seb, please, I love this music.'

'Not a chance,' he said, holding on to his glass.

'Sam'll dance with you,' said Jess.

He glanced at her, raised an eyebrow. She nodded, thrilled that he checked with her. So very different to Tom.

'It would be my pleasure.' He held out his hand.

'Really? I'd love to,' Tami said.

He led her into the throng of dancers, Jess's hands slick with embarrassment for them both. But Sam manoeuvred Tami skilfully across the floor, twirling her this way and that, catching her hand neatly, passing her from one arm to the other.

'Bloody hell,' said Sebastian.

'Say that again,' said Jess.

'Fuck me,' said Rob. 'Watch out, mate, your wife's impressed.'

'Is there nothing he can't do?' said Jess, realising she'd said it out loud when Sebastian and Rob turned to look at her.

'Oh, for fuck's sake,' said Rob.

'You should have danced with him,' said Sebastian.

'Thank you for pointing that out,' she said, mesmerised by the two of them. Tami laughed up at Sam, as he smiled down at her, and her heart twisted.

'Patience,' came Rob's voice in her ear. 'Your time will come.'

'I have to go to the loo,' she said.

'Be quick, or you'll miss it.'

She fled to the loo, amazed at her calm reflection in the mirror. There was no sign of her inner turmoil. Interesting thought. Maybe there was no inner turmoil, maybe she just enjoyed being with Sam…

Back in the hall, the people watching the dancers were silhouetted against the whirling colours on the parquet floor. She searched for Sebastian and Rob, and saw Tami, close beside her husband. She couldn't see Sam. Maybe he was dancing with someone else. Fiona or Isabelle, or…

A hand on her arm.

She turned, her body recognising his touch.

'Want that dance now?'

He led her into the crowd and propelled her away from him, anchored by his hand, and brought her back into his chest. An arm around her, twirling her, swapping hands to bring her round his other side, hands above her head, then arms across each other's shoulders. His face close to hers, smiling, twisting her into his arms, beside him, holding her securely, swooping her backwards so that the whole room tilted, light into darkness, darkness into light, his eyes shining above her.

She began to get the hang of it. This way, then that, back and to the side, arms up, across, down into the swoop, his lips so close to hers, his hands on her waist, guiding her, spinning her away and bringing her in close, always her hand in his, his arm about her, his strong body to be propelled towards.

Another dip, his face above hers, and she said, 'I love you.' She gasped. 'I mean I love this. I love *this*.'

'I love you too,' he said, dark eyes smiling down at her, holding her in his arms as he pulled her back into the light, and sent her spinning again.

When the music stopped and everyone clapped, he kissed her on the lips and said, 'Say it again.'

'I can't believe I press-ganged you into saying it.'

He held her chin, tilting her face up. 'Say it again.'

She gave up. 'I love you, Sam Rushmore.'

'I love you, Jessica Lamb.'

SAM

Sunday evening. Sam could hear the phone ringing as he put his key in the lock on his return from church. He grabbed the receiver and settled on the bottom stair.

'Thought it might be you. How was your journey?'

He listened to Jess's voice as he turned over the problem of how to keep going while they lived two hundred miles apart. Switching the phone to his other hand, he wiped his palm down his trousers. 'Jess. Do you think maybe we should talk about getting married?'

'What?' she yelped. 'On the phone?'

'I'm not proposing. Not on the phone. But couldn't we talk about how we might make this work? Here. Or there. Or somewhere in between.'

'How? How can we make it work? We can't take our children away from their other parent, and neither of us is prepared to leave them behind. It's not solvable.'

'Don't you think we should discuss it, at least?'

'I would if I thought I could see a way through.'

'But you can't?' The handset slid in his sweaty palm.

'What's this really about, Sam? Is this so you can score?'

'Are you talking about sex, Ms Lamb? Since when do you use Americanisms?'

Jess laughed. 'That's not even a grammatical sentence.'

'It's not about sex. It's about many other things. Although

that is an additional benefit, it has to be said. Don't you miss it?'

'No point in asking questions when you already know the answer.'

'Think about it, would you?'

Sam had the impression that neither of them thought about much else. Life went on. Christmas preparations were in full swing. His children were spending Christmas with Elizabeth, and Will and the family were coming to Millingham to see Sam and his mother. Tom was having the children for Christmas and Jess was going to Brussels with her mother and stepfather.

'The cruellest part about being a single parent is only having your children every other Christmas,' she said, when he rang her one evening. 'I can't contemplate the idea of being near the children, but prevented from seeing their faces when they discover the full stockings on their beds on Christmas morning.'

'Why don't we meet in Oxford? I'll do a house-swap with Will. Don't know if I can stand them playing Happy Families, anyway.'

'It's a nice idea, Sam. But I'm going to see Patrick and Maria, and hopefully their new baby by then.'

'Well, the offer stands.'

JESSICA: age 18

'I still can't quite believe it's all over,' said Jess, pushing away images of her parents yelling at each other in the back garden. On Tuesday, her father had come to pick up some stuff. She'd holed up in her room at the top of the house, but when the shouting got so loud she couldn't think straight, she'd charged downstairs and yelled at them to shut up. Not such a great idea. Her mother, in floods of tears, pounded up the stairs after her, and wouldn't go away until Jess opened her door. All Jess wanted to do was sink back into the fictional world of *Emma*. Anything not to think about how her capable, strong mother had become this sobbing woman with hair in her eyes.

Still. That was all in the past. Thank God. As were the exams, and tonight, Friday, they were all going to a *Brideshead Revisited* party at Tim and Susie's house.

Jess wore a bright pink dress of her mother's that was big enough on her to have a dropped waist, round which she'd tied a pink and purple silk scarf. This outfit was complimented by a home-made black velvet choker, her hair curled and pinned in place with the help of a solution of sugar and water. High black shoes, and brand new underwear including stockings and suspender belt, completed the outfit.

Stella wore a sumptuous black lace creation that had belonged to her great aunt.

It was still ridiculously light as they left Stella's house and walked past the church to Lake Avenue. Half past seven, and almost midsummer. Nearly two hours of sunlight still to go.

'I hope we don't meet anyone we know.' Jess ran her palms down her thighs, feeling the unfamiliar loops and buttons of the suspenders. She felt even more self-conscious than usual. 'Or anyone we don't know, for that matter.'

'I hope we do,' said Stella, never in danger of impersonating a shrinking violet.

As they walked past the entrance to the tennis club, Will Rushmore and two friends ambled down the steps. He waved at Stella, and Jess blushed a violent red to the roots of her hair, her body slicked with heat.

By the time they got to the party she understood the sentiment about being desperate for a drink, and when Tim, their exuberant host, greeted them with a glass of red wine each—'So much more sophisticated, my dears!'—she gulped hers down on an empty stomach.

A group of them—Stella, Caroline, Anna, Ruth and Jess, Tim and his friend Matthew—sat in garden chairs on the lawn, admiring each other's outfits, particularly the boys' dinner jackets. Caroline's short dark curls made her look authentically twenties, a band across her forehead, a bow at her ear.

Jess let the talk of exams waft over her as she sipped her second glass of red wine. Barbecue smells stole across the garden in the bright, light dusk. Everything seemed lilac-tinged. Magical. She pulled her mind back to the discussion. Ruth and Anna wailed about the shocking second economics paper. Jess shuddered, thinking about the European history exam. Minutes of reading the questions, trying to work out which were the least awful ones to answer. But, despite the palpitations, she'd had a heightened sense of being alive in that exam, almost able to grasp the enormity of the firing synapses of the human brain being transferred into coherent, strategic human thought. Creative. Stimulating. The feeling that only this moment—only this series of thoughts—mattered, that everything else was of the utmost insignificance.

'Earth to Jess. Come in, Jess,' said Tim.

'Tim. Our host.' She smiled.

'Glad they're over?' He topped up her glass.

'You bet.' Glad and a little fearful. Fearful of results day. More fearful of exactly how she was going to fill her time between now and October, assuming she got the results she needed to go to her first choice, University College London. Up till now she'd had the perfect excuse not to think about her parents. Such a useful crutch.

She drank steadily as the light faded. Someone had a black and white film in their camera and she remembered the flash, the moment in time she was captured for posterity. Anna on one side, Caroline and Susie on the other, Tim and Matthew standing behind them. One flash. Then another.

There was food, but somehow Jess missed it. Not hungry. She sat and talked to people or sat and watched. A lurch as Sam and Sebastian appeared, dashing and unavailable in their dress suits. Sebastian golden, blue-eyed and assured. Sam remote, as if he'd already moved on, talking about going to another party. Not drinking in case he needed to drive, handling his mother's Peugeot with such assurance, as he had from the moment he passed his test.

Jess, who had never drunk more than two glasses of wine at one time before, didn't realise quite how drunk she was until she stood up. Previous encounters with alcohol had involved mainly sweet cider, and even after that long ago party at Caroline's, the worst she'd suffered was a bad headache. Now, she badly needed the loo. Fragmentary thought was all she could manage. *Get to the loo…don't fall over…whoops.* She landed hard on her bottom, totally unused to the red wine and high heels. She got up, ignoring the giggles and stares. *Loo…desperate…hold on… loo.*

Tim and Susie's house had a long, thin utility-come-downstairs-toilet, with a washing machine. She negotiated the step into the house—too bright, too light—through the kitchen to the hall. She lurched for the door handle, knowing there'd be a catastrophe if the door were locked. Instead it swung open hard on her grasp, and she fell against the door as it connected with the wall. Shit. She shut the door and held on to the wall for support, reached the loo and sat down. Blissful relief.

Afterwards she washed her hands and focused on her reflection in the mirror. She looked surprisingly normal. If out of focus. Flushed pink lips and cheeks. She turned her head to admire her neck, the novelty of her pinned up hair, but the room span alarmingly. Slowly she turned back to face herself. The door opened.

'Jess.' James shut and locked the door behind him.

Jess's stomach cramped. Not James. Why didn't he understand that she didn't want to go out with him? He was too big and slick and invading.

Her brain jolted. A thought hurtled into her consciousness. Why had he locked the door? 'James.' Jess stared at him in the mirror. 'What are you doing? You need to move!' Surely she'd locked the door when she came in. Hadn't she? Why hadn't she?

'Come here.' His large frame filled the mirror, as he advanced towards her.

She edged around, hands in front of her chest, acutely aware of his sour odour. He still wore a dinner jacket over his sweat-drenched white shirt. An ordinary thing, a white shirt; no harm in a white shirt.

'Move, James, I need to—'

'That's not what you need. Prick tease.' He grabbed her hard—forcing her to stop before she collided with his chest—fingers in her hair, his mouth on hers, thrusting his tongue into her mouth, tasting of bitter beer, making her retch.

'No.' She wriggled away, feeling the room tilt, putting her hands out sideways, hoping to connect with a wall, clutching at thin air. Why would he say that? She'd known him for years. He'd sat at her kitchen table and drunk coffee and made her siblings Patrick and Julia laugh. Why hadn't she locked the door?

He followed her, hand on her jaw, pinning her down with his hands, but she wrenched away, gasping for breath, shutting her eyes to steady the spinning, opening them again because that made it even worse. *Got to get out. This is madness. This is not happening. This is unreal.*

He grabbed her again, and this time, as she twisted away from him, his overwhelming strength held her fast. A wall. Immoveable. She clawed behind her, but he held her shoulders, an arm on her back, a hand on her neck, pushing her against the hard, cold front of the washing machine, a dense thud as they smashed against the metal.

This is ridiculous. It makes no sense. The phrases overlapped in her brain, but as she squirmed he pushed her right over the washing machine, kicking her legs apart, pulling at her dress.

'No,' she screamed. 'No, no!' Knowing the door was locked, that she'd never be heard over the loud music. He was too heavy and too engrossed. She could feel his erection, his hard legs against the backs of her thighs.

She gasped in air, fighting to stand upright but he was too strong. All of him pressed against her, pushing her again and again, her hips, her pubic bone slamming against the angles and corners. He pressed his thighs between her legs, trying to push them wider apart, and for an instant she thought, 'At least I'm wearing knickers,' until she realised her new black lace-trimmed cotton underwear and her mother's dress would offer very little resistance in protecting her virginity. Such mundane thoughts: knickers, stockings, dress. White shirt.

The cold metal of the top of the washing machine connected with her ear, her chin, as she twisted her head. *Why hadn't she locked that door?*

His body was immensely heavy, the damp hand at the back of her neck like a noose that wouldn't loosen. She flailed behind her with her arms, but it felt as ineffectual as a fluttering of wings against a trap. She couldn't make sense of it. Bile rose in her mouth. If she turned her head—not that she could move an inch under the weight of his palm, his fingers and thumb—could she vomit on him? Would that cause the madness to stop?

She struggled to pull air into her lungs, knowing she was hyperventilating, but he leant his forearm hard between her shoulder blades, slamming her against the cold, unyielding surface until she stopped resisting. She felt bruised everywhere.

His other arm grabbed at her thighs, pulling the dress

up, tugging it hard. She could feel it resist, despite his frantic yanking, the fabric taut.

'Fucking hell!' Still leaning heavily over her, he pulled his hand away from her neck and she flung herself backwards, falling sideways off her heels, straight into him.

He grappled with his belt buckle, irrevocably caught on the pink fabric, as she lurched towards the open toilet.

'No,' he said. 'You're not going anywhere.'

'James, stop it,' she yelled, clawing at his arms, trying to free the back of her skirts from his grasp.

'Fucking bitch!' He slapped her, catching her left ear as she ducked away from him. The sound reverberated through her head, a shock of heat spreading across her face, chased by searing pain from ear to cheekbone to jaw.

For a moment their eyes locked and a frozen mask of shock covered his face as he turned to look at his palm.

She arched away from him, ignoring the tearing of fabric, the spinning room. That terrible rush of saliva in her mouth. Nothing could stop it and now she knew how to try to end this nightmare. She twisted round and vomited red wine down his white shirt.

The ordinary white shirt looked like the aftermath of a bloody injury.

James recoiled, hands raised, staring at his front. 'What the fuck?'

She sank onto her hands and knees, shivering.

'Bitch. Prick tease. I told you. You're unfuckable.'

She hunched over, her forehead on her arms.

The stamp of feet, a wrenched lock, the slammed door.

Silence.

She was alone.

The silence echoed on and on in her ears. What had happened to the music?

Slowly she uncurled, reaching for some loo paper to wipe her mouth. Pulling herself up, she limped on shaking legs to the basin and splashed the right side of her face with cold water. Her icy fingertips explored the other cheek, not daring to touch her ear, which still sang with pain. Then she raised her eyes to her mascara-streaked reflection and prised apart the Velcro fastenings of the black velvet choker round her neck.

Don't cry. You're pathetic. You only have yourself to blame.

She whispered her fingers up her arms and throat, carefully over her face, but nothing bore any outward evidence of the force with which she'd been held down. Her left ear glowed magenta, but she knew no one would notice. Nothing to show for it. Except that her knickers were still where they should be... She discovered new aches and pains as she turned her head and bent her bruised body to examine the long tear at the back of her dress. She'd have to think of something to tell her mother.

Stupid, stupid, stupid. Why the hell hadn't she locked the door?

The door was still unlocked. She leant against it, shot the bolt across.

Her right ankle throbbed from being thrown off her heels as she tried to escape James's reach. Could she leave through the house, never return to the garden? How long would it take to get home if she couldn't walk properly?

SAM

James's mobile rang and rang before he answered.

'How was the honeymoon?' Sam asked.

'Splendid. Greek island hopping in the sunshine when it's a wet and rainy November at home.'

'How's Fiona?'

'Marvellous. I hear she's plotting—with Rob of all people—a little dinner party in London soon.'

'So marriage is suiting you?'

'It certainly is. Maybe you should try it again.'

'Ah, a real conversion. You've changed your tune about Jess and me?'

'Yes. Well. Keep your friends close...'

'What?'

'How are things going in that department? Like old times?'

Sam wondered about the wisdom of making this phone call. It had seemed the right thing to do. 'I realised it was Stuart's birthday. It was good to see him at the wedding. I bump into him in Millingham of course, but it was great he made it.'

'Yes. Mum was very pleased.'

'How's he doing?'

'Everything's fine, Sam. Alison's a complete star looking out for him. Of course she's close by, so the burden of Mum falls more to her.'

'Ah.' Sam fiddled with the cuff of his sweater. 'Do you… do you ever think about the accident?'

'It's best left in the past. How are things in Millingham?'

Sam surveyed the piles of stuff, most of which belonged to the children, on every surface in the kitchen. It was a long time since this room had been as tidy as it was when Jess came for the weekend. Maybe it was better to leave things as they were. What could he hope to gain? 'Busy as ever. The kids are less and less keen on being shunted back and forth between two houses. Kate especially.'

'It just takes organisation. Fiona's marvellous about what's needed in town and in Witney.'

'That must make life easier,' said Sam.

'Yes. Can't imagine why I left it till now to find a wife.'

'Really? You never wanted to be completely honest with another person?' said Sam.

'No. Not really.'

Sam listened for a sign that James was still there.

'The only person I was ever…who loved me unconditionally… died…' A sharp intake of breath.

'James.' He spoke into the gap between them. 'I didn't mean to—'

'No. Never been a fan of talking therapies. Good of you to ring though.'

'Well, I'm glad I phoned then. We've had some very happy times with Stuart. Do you remember that dinner in Manchester? Raoul was there, it must have been just before he got sick—'

'Yes. Good of you to understand. About Andrew as Best Man.'

'I know you have to make certain choices now.'

'Yes. Fiona understands. She knows when to leave things in peace. See you at the dinner.'

Sam laid down his mobile. He craved Jess's unconditional love. But would she love him if she knew everything?

Secrets. They rarely left you in peace.

JESS

'Hey, babe. Missed me, I trust?' said a voice, when Jess picked up the receiver.

'Rob?'

'The very same. How are you, sweetheart?'

'Fine,' she said, her stock answer to anyone who asked her that question.

'When are you seeing Sam next?'

'Um, why?' They hadn't met since Oxford. It wasn't that she didn't want to see him—she did, desperately—but she couldn't figure out how to make it work. How could they get married—if it really had been a serious suggestion—when they couldn't work out where to live? She fell into bed exhausted each night, only to wake at four in the morning, unable to get back to sleep, thanks to the persistent internal dialogue about Sam, sex, and geography that she managed to suppress during the day. He hadn't mentioned the 'm' word again, for which she was grateful. There was always the danger that she might say yes, in spite of everything.

'How about next Friday? I'm in London and we're getting together at James and Fiona's flat. I'll make sure Sam's there.'

Jess moved the phone away and leant her forehead on the back of her hand. Then she put it back to her ear. 'Rob, I thought you lived in London.'

'Yeah, I'm based here. When I'm not elsewhere. Friday week. You can organise a babysitter, can't you?'

'Yes, but I'm…' *Too emotionally damaged to see Sam? Too sexually frustrated to see you? Too bitter to see James?*

'So? Eight o'clock? Or do you want to meet even earlier so you can go to bed early?'

She stared at the phone. A smackable offence? 'Since when did you start having cosy suppers with James and Fiona?'

'Come on, babe, aren't you intrigued to see how they're enjoying marital bliss?'

Jess contemplated this. There was a certain fascination, and she did want to see Sam. The drug of which she couldn't get enough.

On the Friday night she left the children in the care of Holly, her next-door neighbour, and took the tube to Pimlico, wrapped up in her coat, her hair freshly washed, lipstick on her dry lips. In her bag, a bottle of red wine clinked against her keys.

She told herself that the past was all over and done with. There was no reason to even go there anymore. Not that her unconscious mind paid any attention. Only this morning, she'd woken—hot, tangled in the duvet—the sensation of James' hand hard on the back of her neck so physical she had to turn on the light to banish the idea he was in her bedroom.

Telling herself she'd got through the wedding without vomiting or otherwise causing embarrassment didn't help. This was an intimate evening where it would be far harder to avoid physical contact with James, even if Sam was there. Sam, who was such a rock of dependability at the end of the phone. Sam, who—against the odds and her track record—she was beginning to trust.

She pushed away the recurring thought that she should tell him exactly what had happened at that post-A Levels party. If she didn't, if she wasn't honest with Sam, she ran the risk of allowing the past to drive a permanent wedge between them. But she didn't want to put herself between Sam and James; they continued to be good friends. Throughout their teens, they had been bound by childhood adventures and mishaps, shared experiences that went back to a time when they were trying to work out what sort of people they would become.

The flat was easy enough to find, on the fourth floor of a mansion block, interior-designed into an order that would not have been possible if children lived there. Sam's train arrived at Euston after eight o'clock, so he would meet her there. Jess was greeted by James and Rob, who were almost at the bottom of a bottle of champagne. Fiona waved from the kitchen.

'You look well. Married life must suit you.' Jess made herself look James in the eye.

'Absolutely,' he smirked. 'Though the best part of a month in Greece helped.'

'Sun, sand, sangria and sex?' said Rob.

'Something like that.' James handed Jess a brimming glass of champagne.

She sank into one of the capacious sofas ranged round a glass coffee table, gulping quickly, realising she'd practically drained her glass when James gave her a whopping top-up. Devouring most of the designer crisps and olives didn't do much to mop up the alcohol.

James received a brief text from Sam saying the train was delayed, and they should start without him.

Jess felt light-headed. She had left her mobile in her coat pocket. Perhaps she should check her messages too. But levering herself out of the plethora of cushions, standing, walking, locating it, would be too much of an effort.

'The fish pie needs to be eaten sooner rather than later. Horrid when it's dry and overcooked,' said Fiona.

'Food would be good,' said Rob, finishing his glass.

Jess had to agree.

She had become hyper-conscious of all her movements, carefully balanced as she walked, easing herself into the space between the dining table and the chair with precision.

Unlike at the wedding, and in previous encounters with James, Jess did not feel a sense of detachment from the situation. She couldn't observe herself, or focus by counting her inhalations, her exhalations. This time, it felt as if all the seamless functions of her nervous system had crashed into her consciousness. She had an awareness of the incremental expansion of the spaces between her ribs as she breathed in, the sensation of a pulse at her neck, her wrist, topped by the steady throb of blood in her ears.

Her top lip felt cold caused, she knew, by the rush of sweat to the surface of her skin. Her mouth felt dry and drained of saliva. The moisture of her mouth on the surface of her skin, a sheen of sweat prickling her scalp.

The taste of fish pie passed her by. It smelled good, but she was slightly overwhelmed by the enormous portion she was served by Fiona, and ate what she could, because it was in front of her. Every time she wielded her cutlery she had to stop drinking the wine James assiduously topped up.

Conversation flowed around her as they moved on to the cheese: the honeymoon; the by-election triumph, James's maiden speech in the House of Commons, the new house in Witney; Rob's recent broadsheet character annihilations and accompanying press fall-out.

In an unexpected pause in the chatter, Jess swallowed a mouthful of Beaujolais, which sounded absurdly loud in her ears.

'Tell me, Jess,' said James. 'How are things with Sam?'

She blinked. 'I'm here. He's there.'

'So?' said Rob. 'Move.'

'Nice idea.' She focused on Rob, sitting beside her. 'But there are children and exes involved. It's not so black and white.'

'You're over-thinking it,' he retorted.

She shrugged; took a long draught of wine.

'You want to make it work,' said James.

'Somehow.' She could feel his scrutiny. Why did it have to be James asking questions? Rob wouldn't annoy her half as much, and he could be forgiven for lapsing into work mode. Underlying the irritation was the sense that, no matter how she viewed the situation, there was a two-hundred-mile distance she couldn't manage to bridge to everyone's satisfaction.

'Why are you so worried about what everyone thinks, Jessica?' said Rob. 'Go for what you want for a change.'

'Maybe a way out will present itself,' said James.

'Yes, I'm sure it will,' said Fiona, glancing at her husband.

Jess refused to look at James. 'I wouldn't worry about it. We'll probably manage to fuck it up on our own, this time.'

Silence. James put a hand on his wife's arm.

'Holy cow,' Rob said. 'She swears.'

'Was that just a general observation?' said James, his voice liquid and even. 'Or were you alluding to anything specific?'

Years of pretending to be in control of her life, in control of her emotions, in control of her mind, snapped deep inside Jess. She sat back and faced him across the table. 'You know I was.'

'Would you care to elaborate?' he said, proving his mettle as a trained politician. Provoked, but not rising.

'I don't think you want me to. You know what I'm talking about,' she said quietly.

Fiona gripped her linen napkin in both hands. 'James?'

He held up a hand, his eyes never leaving Jess's face. 'Explain yourself.'

She took another swig of red wine, the glass almost sliding out of her clammy hands. 'I know you lied to us. Both. But it was a long time ago. I've forgiven you.' Maybe, if she said it aloud often enough it might become a sort of truth.

'Really. Is that so?' said James.

Jess flinched.

'I don't need your *forgiveness*. There's nothing to forgive.'

'James?' said Fiona.

'What exactly are we talking about?' said Rob.

Jess turned to him, gripping her glass. Keep it simple. This was about Sam. Nothing else. 'Sam and I got together one New Year's Eve. The last year of school. It was James who told me Sam wasn't interested in going out with me.' Her voice sounded surprisingly normal, but she felt as if part of her, long-buried, was about to erupt, words she'd never uttered spewing out of her mouth with such force they couldn't be stopped.

She swallowed hard, clenching her teeth together. She had to get out of there. Now. She was drenched in sweat, her clothes damp, clinging to the heat of her body.

'New Year's Eve? Was I there?' said Rob.

'Are you really going to dwell on something that happened twenty years ago? Can't you move on?' James said with a sneer.

'I'm not dwelling on it. I'm just interested in the truth.' *Some of it.*

'You want the truth? He wasn't interested,' said James. 'I told you exactly what he told me. No, I was probably gentler on you. He was about to do his mocks. He needed going out with you—the self-centred, over-emotional hard work that you'd have been—like a hole in the head, and wisely decided not to go there. You both had a good time. Why spoil it?

'What are you talking about?' Fiona stared at her husband.

Rob exhaled. 'Fuck's sake, James.'

Jess blinked hard, trying to stay in the room.

Vivid memories sliced across her mind.

Tom laughing, putting his arm round her, squeezing her shoulder, a vice holding her firmly against his upper chest. 'Jess, honestly, you didn't really think that, did you? I know I told you, silly girl. Honestly, what are you like? I can only apologise for my wife's forgetfulness…'

The snap of mood from jovial to vitriolic as soon as they left whatever social occasion she'd misjudged with the wrong clothes, the missing present, the forgotten dish of food. The silences that lasted for days, mediated only through the children.

Stay in the room. This was not about Tom. He no longer held sway.

She shook her head to dislodge the images, carefully put her glass down and stood up. No point in breaking what might have been a wedding present.

She addressed Fiona. 'Sorry, I hope you'll excuse me if I go home.'

'Oh no you don't. The least you could do is apologise to me.' James stood up.

'You want me to apologise to you? Did I commit some horrible offence? No, I don't think I did, James. It's not you who's still waiting for the apology, after all this time.' Saying his name aloud made her feel stronger. She focused on reaching the door, leaving the flat before she broke down.

Keep it simple. This was not about Tom, not about James. This was about her and Sam. Where was her coat?

'So? What's the big deal, Jessica? Who cares what happened then? Who even remembers?' Rob followed her into the hall, James and Fiona behind him.

'Don't you get it?' she said. 'If James didn't lie to me—and of course he's a politician, so we must trust him, mustn't we?—then Sam did.'

'Oh, fucking hell,' Rob exclaimed. 'What planet do you live on? People lie to each other the whole time. You've probably told ten lies today—'

'I haven't.'

He looked her up and down. 'No, I guess you haven't. But give Sam a break. He's crazy about you. He probably didn't want you to feel bad. He may not even remember—'

'Sam let me believe something that wasn't true. I have to go home now.'

'James, stop her.' Rob shoved his hands through his hair, the gesture reminding her of Sam.

She couldn't face meeting him.

'Jess,' said Fiona. 'You don't look well, let's order you a cab. Why don't you sit down?'

'Thank you, but I have to go.' She didn't look at James.

James retrieved her coat and held it out for her.

Jess took it, not touching or looking at James.

'What the fuck are you doing, James?' said Rob. 'Why can't she stay and deal with it?'

'Leave it.' James opened the door for Jess. 'It's OK. Go.'

The door shut, but not before she heard Rob. 'What the fuck are you going to tell Sam?'

'Think about it, Rob. Think about Nathaniel Lamb,' said James.

She plunged down the stairs, the blood rushing in her ears, praying that she would not meet Sam. He lied to me, was all she would allow herself to think. He let her believe he felt like she felt. She refused to think about James and his lack of apology, even after twenty years. She broke out into the cold night air, all the chillier on her wet face, scrubbing the tears away with her sleeves, as she ran for the tube. How long would it take Sam to travel from Euston on the Victoria line? She turned the corner, the blood pounding in her ears, ready to duck into a doorway if she saw any tall men with overnight bags. Every new figure that swung into view fitted his description until she blinked and focused properly and they became business women in heels, or men with briefcases.

She rushed to Pimlico station and fumbled for her travel card. This was not how the evening was meant to end. She had anticipated taking a cab back along the river with Sam, their arms round each other, Albert Bridge and all its lights looking suitably romantic. A fresh wave of people came through the barriers and she kept her head down, hands shaking, expecting a tap on her shoulder any second. No one touched her. Eyes down, she headed for the escalator, leaping into the air at the sound of her phone ringing in her bag. She scrabbled for it: Sam. She switched it off. She'd be home soon enough.

Fragments of conversation flashed through her head. Sam saying, 'You've had a lot to deal with… You didn't need my problems on top of it all.' She tried to remember his exact words, when they had apparently realised that James had lied to them. 'I was interested, I'd always been interested,' was that what he'd said? Her head throbbed with the effort of trying to reconstruct that conversation and not re-live a long-suppressed scene in a downstairs loo.

Tears of fresh, hot embarrassment scorched her face as she thought of asking Sam whether he'd felt the same as she did, that New Year's Eve. His perfect answer. Telling her exactly what she wanted to hear. Embarrassment crystallised into anger. How could he? She didn't want his pity. She needed his honesty. Nothing else would do.

She was aware somewhere—at the back of her mind—that it had been foolish to pin all her hopes on Sam. They'd grown silently, without her paying any attention, into a verdant forest of plans and dreams. It hadn't worked out before. Why did she think it would work out now?

Try as she might, she couldn't stop her mental slide into the abyss. *This is how men behave. They lie. They cheat.* And this was what she deserved. It started with her father. It continued with Tom. So why would she even doubt it would carry on with Sam?

Stupid. Stupid. Again.

Even if it was more existence than life, when she was alone, at least she only had to count on herself. Focus on the children. Being their mother. Staying in the room, rather than in her Mr Darcy fantasy life.

She locked up after her neighbour Holly had gone home, turned off all the lights and unplugged the downstairs phone. Then she went upstairs and unplugged the one in her bedroom. She left her sodden coat over the banisters, her mobile still switched off in the inside pocket. She kissed the sleeping children and fell on to her bed, fully clothed.

It was a long night. At three o'clock, Millie woke her up, needing the loo. Jess got up, stiff, still in her clothes, her face dry and grubby from a combination of slept-in make-up and tears, her teeth furry and her head throbbing more than ever. She put Millie back to bed, pulled on her pyjamas, washed her face, cleaned her teeth, drank several glasses of water and kept reluctant and increasingly frustrated vigil for the rest of the night. *Keep it simple. James has nothing to do with it.*

At seven she heard Ben stirring. He came in and asked to go and watch television.

'Fine.' She drank the water by her bed, too weary to go and make a cup of tea.

At eight Millie surfaced and joined Ben.

At nine, the doorbell rang. She was out of bed like a shot, but Millie was there before her.

'Mummy, it's Sam,' she called, delighted.

Several possibilities streamed through Jess's mind, but she didn't want to have a scene on her doorstep. Neither did she want to have a stand-up row in front of her children. So, impersonating a civilised person, she said hello to Sam, walked into the kitchen, and switched on the kettle.

After some rather excited chatting—during which Jess studied the back garden—Millie wandered back into the front room to see what was on CBBC and Jess was left with Sam. She kept her back to him and made tea.

'You weren't answering either of your phones,' he said, when she passed him a mug without meeting his eyes.

She stepped over to the phone and plugged it back in.

'You're angry,' he said.

'No, I'm disappointed. And I'm sick of being patronised and protected and *lied to*.' He had the decency to wince at the last words.

'Do you have any idea how humiliating it is? You let me believe that James was the villain of the piece, that he'd somehow kept us from getting together, and worse than that, he's the one who puts me right. Do you know how he looked at me last night? *With pity.* It was unbearable. I won't be pitied by any of you.'

She sat down, as far away from him as possible, her hands over her face. 'It's not even about what did or didn't happen twenty years ago. You made me believe that you felt the same way I did when you didn't even have to. That's what I don't understand.' She kept her hands pressed over her eyes, willing herself not to cry. 'You had me at hello,' she said, under her breath.

'What?'

'Nothing. *Jerry Maguire*.'

'What?'

'Forget it. Don't you have anything to say?'

'I have plenty to say. Just wanted to make sure you'd said what you wanted to say.'

She opened the cupboard above the kettle and riffled around for a bottle of paracetamol, extracted two and took them with a glass of water. She felt Sam watch her until she sat back down.

'I didn't mean to suggest that I felt something I didn't back then. I was interested in you. I did feel like you did about that night. I was not just saying that at the wedding. Didn't I know exactly what night you were talking about with virtually no information?'

She shrugged, studying her hands, holding her cup of tea. Maybe she'd take up coffee. This was not the sort of conversation to be had over peppermint tea. It was a bit early to accompany it with a large tumbler of gin.

'But James is right. I was also a coward, and he very

helpfully volunteered to put you right about my lack of intentions. He simplified it though. It was not that I didn't want to go out with you. It was much more about timing. And I repeat what I said on the phone. I was interested. I was always interested.'

'Just not that interested.'

He sighed, hands in his hair. 'Yes, I suppose so. At that point in time, I was not interested enough.'

'It's not as if I expected you to fall madly in love with me. But realising this through James tipped the balance.'

'I know. I'm really sorry. You'd have thought I'd have got the message by now. Disastrous things happen when I'm not entirely honest with you. But you know the worst. There's nothing else.' He put his hands flat on the surface, either side of his cup. 'There's nothing else to do with you and me.'

She took her hands away from her face and watched his hands. 'I'm so sick of being lied to. For me it is the worst sin.'

'Yes.'

'I've told you things I've never told anyone. I've been honest with you and you didn't have the decency to tell me the truth. It's the only thing I'm interested in.'

'I know.'

She shook her head. She *had* been honest with him. There were just some things that were better left alone. What good could it possibly do? There was no way she wanted the responsibility of jeopardising Sam's friendship with James. There was a difference between honesty and cruelty. She sipped her tea and contemplated making some fresh coffee in the cafetière she kept for her mother's visits. But she was too weary to stand up.

'Bad headache?' Sam rested his head on his hand and looked at her.

'Millie woke me in the night. I couldn't get back to sleep.'

'I'm sorry. If it's any consolation, I hardly slept either.'

'Not much,' she said, still not meeting his eyes.

'I wondered if there was something else you wanted to say.'

Jess pressed the heels of her hands against her closed eyes. 'About what?'

Sam turned his mug around and around with his free hand. 'Everything all right between you and James?'

She stood up to flick the kettle on again, to remove her face from his sight. 'Why wouldn't it be?'

'I don't know. Just a feeling.'

SAM

Sam concentrated on his mug of Earl Grey and willed himself to say the right thing. Funny how saying what he thought was the right thing kept coming back to blow up in his face. He'd allowed himself to be persuaded to stay the night at James and Fiona's when he'd finally got there about ten, after a long delay on the track the other side of Watford. He assumed Jess was having such fun that she hadn't heard her mobile. So, when James met him at the door and Rob immediately launched into a tirade about her departure, he intended to understand as much of what had taken place as he could and then follow Jess home to plead his case.

It was soon clear he'd fucked up, again. Rob, ever the opinionated journalist, couldn't work out what Jess was so blown away by, but James got it. James got it perhaps even more than Sam did. *What was that about?* A recurring thought.

He tried to remember exactly what had happened with Jess's father. He'd finally left the family home some time around her A levels, that much Sam could reconstruct. A distant memory of an enthralled James telling the story, clouded in equal parts by outrage and admiration for the selfish arrogance of pushing one's child to the edge.

They'd all been convinced Jess would flunk her exams

with equal passion, but she stunned herself, her friends and certainly the boys, with straight A grades. Neatly letting her father off the hook, James had observed.

Sam looked up and saw Jess's eyes slide away. 'Do you see much of your father?'

Her eyes flew to his and then away. 'Not much. He had a little girl with Denise, but they split up—'

'Denise? Was that her name?'

She blinked at him. 'Diane. He had a daughter with Diane.'

'Denise…that's Tom's assistant. The one you think he's having a relationship with?'

She shrugged. 'I don't know anymore.' She opened the fridge to stare at its contents, cutting herself off from him. He could tell nothing from her hunched back.

'Have you thought of—?'

She rounded on him. 'Don't. Just don't. I couldn't bear a pop psychology analysis of the shocking state of my relationship with my father, and my ex-husband, and…'

'Jess,' he said, desperate to cradle her in his arms.

'Please don't,' she said, meeting his gaze for a split second before her eyes focused on the door.

'You're going to ask me to leave?'

'I can't work out how to make it work. I wasn't having much of a life before I met you again, but at least breathing—existing—wasn't painful. I just felt numb most of the time. All of the time. Now I feel bereft and frustrated and way out of control. It's too much.'

'Can't we discuss it?' Sam knew that now would be a really great time to exercise patience and understanding. Instead he felt overwhelmed by the itch of his fists, the rigidity of the muscles in his forearms.

'I've been over and over it in my head. You need me and

my kids like a hole in the head, as everyone keeps telling me, and telling you too, I'm sure.' She held on to the fridge door.

'You are a lot of things, Jessica,' he said, his thumbs wrapped tight in his palms. 'But I didn't have you down for a coward.'

'Fine,' she snapped, slamming the door. 'Call it what you will. It's doing my head in.'

'Never mind what anyone else wants for you, or what you think you should do. What do *you* want?'

He watched her blink at him. She put her hands on the counter as if to steady herself. 'It's not about me anymore. It stopped being about me when Ben was born. There's a family to consider now, not just my own selfish desires.'

'Don't you think your children might be happier with a mother who actually enjoyed life?'

'Don't you dare! I don't have to listen to this. Not in my own house.'

He stretched his hands out on the counter. 'Jess, I don't want to leave. Not like this. If I go now, I won't know how to put it right between us. I'm so sorry about not being absolutely truthful with you, and I'm not going to make that mistake again.'

She stared at the fruit bowl in front of her.

'Tom still having the children at Christmas?'

She nodded.

The hell with it. 'Come to Oxford.'

She shook her head.

'Would you really rather I left?'

'Yes,' she whispered.

He got up and walked round the island that separated them, and tried to take her in his arms, but she felt tense and brittle against him. 'Jess.'

'Don't.' She shook him off, her pale, bluish eyelids lowered.

He dropped his arms and retreated into the hall. There was no sound at all from Jess. When he turned round, she stood motionless beside the kitchen island, head bowed. It felt so wrong to leave. He hesitated for a minute by the door to the front room, desperately wanted to open it to say goodbye to Ben and Millie, but knew he'd be unable to keep it together. Upsetting them would make matters infinitely worse for Jess. He made himself walk to the front door, open it, step outside and quietly close it behind him.

Sunday, 9.30 p.m.
Dear Jess
I've been thinking about what you said ever since yesterday morning, and I thought it might help (it can't make things worse) if I wrote down what I remember.

I looked forward to that New Year's Eve. I knew a party at your house would be fun, with all the old crowd, and the possibility of snow. That's one of the things I remember most about being with you that night. Walking in the perfect snow together.

I remember the loud music—David Bowie, Duran Duran, The Cure—and raucous laughter in the kitchen. You had your curled hair pinned back, and you wore a silky top that glinted in the low lighting. When you met my eyes, your long lashes seemed to blink in slow motion and when I reached for your hand, you knew too.

I kissed you and you felt familiar and right, as if it were not the first time. Of course it wasn't; three years before, I'd tried to kiss you properly, after James's party, but you'd run away like a startled foal. Now you lay under me on your sitting room carpet, pressing through your clothes as much as I pressed against you, my fingers in your hair, minutes of open-mouthed kissing, exploring each other. Your eyes caught mine in the firelight. It was magical.

By five o'clock, we were hungry. You fried eggs and Patrick raided the freezer for a sliced loaf for toast and Marmite. Jess, you sat on my knee, until we couldn't resist going outside, bundled up against the cold. The snow was still falling, but gently now, big thick flakes landing on the good eight inches already settled on every surface. I laced my fingers with yours, pulling our hands into my pocket to keep them warm, as we walked up the path, virgin footprints in the scrunching snow. Golden pools of floating snow around the lampposts as we walked past the church, along Lake Avenue, and onto the wide, frozen pond. The cold air was absolutely still, the snow still falling softly as we parted outside the church.

Thinking about it, the pictures in my mind seem so vivid, although I could tell you very little about that Christmas or January. It was the first Christmas without my Dad, but I know that because of the date, rather than what I actually remember.

I'm sorry James kept us apart. He didn't want us to be together and I allowed him to wield too much power over me, I can see that now.

I can't change the past. But this time I'll fight for you.

All my love

Sam

JESS

Despite the sleepless nights, she survived the weekend by allowing the children considerably more screen time than could possibly be healthy. By Monday evening, there were several messages on the answerphone. None of them from the one person she wished would call. The sensation that she might at any moment vomit words she'd never uttered subsided to a dull, low-level nausea.

When the phone rang, Jess tried to interrupt the internal dialogue spiralling through her mind and haul herself back to the present. She listened to Sam leave a message on the answerphone.

He sounded terrible. She re-played the message. Brief. Asking her to ring him if at all possible, because he really wanted to talk to her. She wandered into the front room and turned on the television, but five minutes later she was back in the kitchen and snatched the phone up the second it rang.

'Hello?'

'Oh, Jess.' Sam's voice broke, and she heard him steadying his breath, fighting for control.

'What's happened? Is it the children?'

'No. Nothing like that. We're fine.' His voice was flat.

She waited.

'I'm so glad you're there.'

'I'm here.'

She heard him swallow, gasping in air. 'I lost a patient.'

'Oh, Sam.' She listened to him fight for calm, try to regulate his breathing. 'What happened?'

'She was thirty-three. She shouldn't have died. She's left a husband, a two-year-old daughter, and an eight-day-old baby boy.'

'Oh my God. Sam.'

'She didn't feel well over the weekend, complaining of abdominal pain and fever, but somehow…' He stopped to gulp in air. 'She came to the surgery this morning. I took one look at her and rang for an ambulance. She died on the operating table.'

'I'm so sorry.'

'It was too late. If I'd seen her earlier, or over the weekend… She obviously had a uterine infection. At the first hint of it, she should have been admitted and put straight on a drip. She shouldn't have died.'

She listened to him breathe. 'Sam, it's not your fault. As soon as you saw her you did what you could. Immediately.'

'I can't believe it.' His voice broke again. 'I think that's part of the shock. She looked dreadful when she came in, but even I didn't think she was about to die.'

'I'm so sorry. Those poor children. That poor husband. What can I do?'

'Give me a hug,' he said, and her heart lurched. 'Why the hell are you in London?'

'It's where my life is.'

'Thank you for talking to me. I didn't think you would. If tragedies like this teach us anything, it's that we should seize any opportunity to be happy with both hands.'

'Well, that's one way to look at things.'

'Come to Oxford for Christmas. No hassles. No children. Just you and me and an empty house.'

'No. I have no willpower where you're concerned.'

'Jess, we don't have—'

'I'm here to talk to. Anytime. But I'm not coming to Oxford.'

'I'm warning you I may ask you again. Oh, and I wrote you a letter.'

'A letter?'

'Yes. It might reach you tomorrow.'

'You posted it?'

'I did. It couldn't make things any worse. And it worked for a few Jane Austen heroes, I believe.'

'I don't know what to say.'

'Just read it.'

On Tuesday, she came home to find a white envelope with Sam's looped black writing on it. She scrabbled to unfold two sheets of formal white paper with the address printed in black across the top, a legacy of his parents she supposed. Now the letter was open in her hand, she felt the intense thump of her heart, her dry mouth, her damp fingers.

She slumped into the armchair in the front room and read his words, imagining him bent over his pen, hair falling across his forehead, the slash and dash of his strong writing across the thick paper. *Dear Jess… All my love Sam*, and all the phrases in between. The perfection of his descriptions, how the pictures he painted enhanced the images in her mind, the irresistible, *'But this time I'll fight for you.'*

He'd taken the time to write her a letter. The pain in her chest eased a fraction. Even the mention of James couldn't burst the little bubble of hope that hovered there. And there was comfort in Sam's admission that he'd been swayed by James. That he'd been manipulated by him. That she had not been alone in being mistreated by him.

On Friday night, Jess sat down to open the package that had arrived from her mother. She'd have opened it earlier, but she'd met Ruth for lunch and the District Line had been up the spout when she tried to get back in time to pick up the children. She'd rung Lucy, who'd taken the children back to her house, and persuaded Jess to stay while she gave them all tea.

Which worked out very well, as it turned out, as Jess had been having small, exploratory fantasies about what might happen with Sam if she *did* move to Millingham. But there was no Lucy there. Who would she ring if she couldn't pick up the children? Caroline, said her sub-conscious. Or, daring as it might be, Sam. Husband. Stepfather. She shoved these dazzling thoughts into the darkest recess of her mind.

She opened the package and smoothed out the thick cream paper.

Dear Jess

Found the enclosed when I was sorting out the last of Patrick's stuff to take to Brussels, and thought you might want them, knowing how you like to hang on to the past.

Our neighbour Geoffrey, who lived next door but one with his wife Eileen, died yesterday. He just never woke up. They think it was his heart. He was sixty-nine. Spoke to your father about it, who was shocked, being sixty-nine himself. Do give him a ring sometime, darling.

Looking forward to seeing you and the children in less than a month, and to our trip to Brussels,

Love Mummy

Jess picked up two exercise books and flicked through them. They contained several pages of her own earnest writing, filled with sentences such as, 'Three days later,

Lara found herself back in the same attractive and peaceful room, although this time it was early morning and she was waiting for Priscilla to arrive…'

Then her eyes fell on the third book, a blue Collins diary. The missing year. Her mouth dried as she scrambled for it, flicking through the pages. Dense, tight, grey pencil covered every available line on each page until the middle of February and then nothing except the occasional birthday reminder. She leafed back to the first entry, 1 January, and started reading.

New Year's Eve Party in our cellar last night. Got off with Sam in the sitting room. Fried eggs 5 a.m. Rob, James, Stella, Caroline etc, Sam and I went out…Lake Court until 6 a.m. Good party.

So detached. So unemotional. No reflection of what she'd actually felt at the time. Just the confirmation that she'd always been a bit obsessed about the time. She read on, to the entry for 3 January.

Sebastian's party.

Did not really talk to Sam—he got off with Jane R. Talked to Caroline and Tim. Couldn't get James to shut up. According to Ruth he fancies me! Help! I like Sam of course.

Who the hell was Jane R? She had absolutely no memory of the incident, and yet, according to this diary and therefore indisputably true (who, after all, would bother to forge in such an unattractive book?) Sam had kissed another girl, less than seventy-two hours after Jess and Sam's so-called significant night that really did mean something, honest. Jess sat back, as if winded. Here was irrefutable proof that her memory was totally fallible and completely unreliable. I don't remember that *at all*, she thought.

She read on, but there was no mention of Sam at all until

the following Sunday, when she'd written about YF: *Talked to Sam. James on the warpath—help!* Somehow becoming so upset with James about whether or not he'd stopped her and Sam from being together seemed trivial in the light of new evidence.

She had to face the fact that there were other reasons to be upset with James.

She started flicking through the other two notebooks again until her eyes alighted on two dense pages of blue-inked writing.

On Friday we went to Sam's house. Hints beforehand... catching his eye across the room, him sitting beside me, standing close to me, etc. We were in the kitchen with Anna and Rob and Sebastian was leaving. As Sebastian left the kitchen, he turned off the light as a joke, and then put it on again. Sam (who was sitting beside me) said he could turn it off again, which he did and in the 3-4 seconds that it was turned off Sam put his hand on my knee and thigh, etc. After that Sam looked at me and smiled and I am sure that no one noticed anything. We caught each other's eye, etc, but that is all. No real change in our relationship as I thought there could be...

This felt like one of the more honest things she'd written. The non-sequiturs made her smile. As did the 'put his hand on my knee and thigh, etc'. What did *that* mean?

But what struck her most was the diffidence of her younger self. If someone like Sam put his hand on her knee now, she'd make sure he knew whether she liked it or not. How might things have been different if she had reacted to his touch, had let him know even a tenth of what it meant to her? These isolated acts that had seemed so unreadable at the time now appeared unequivocal. She wondered how things might have turned out differently, if she had gone out with Sam during that last year or two of school. Not unrealistic enough to think they might have stayed together, certainly not in different cities through university, but perhaps long enough for her to gain some confidence in herself as a person.

And if she had gone out with Sam, been happier in herself, might the disastrous episode in that downstairs loo never have happened? She held her fists to her forehead. How helpful were these 'what ifs'? But then a thought did occur to her. Even if it had happened, maybe Sam would have noticed something, maybe he'd have come to find her? Maybe if she had talked to someone—anyone—it would have been dealt with at the time. Maybe the consuming, hot shame and conviction that it was her fault would have been challenged.

She really didn't want to think about how much of the anger she'd felt towards Sam that evening at James and Fiona's was deflected anger towards someone else.

She was so tired. She thought she'd dealt with all of this—her father, James, those boys at college, the whole lot—when she became a Christian. And forgiven them. And forgiven herself.

She put her head in her hands.

SAM

The phone rang. His pulse accelerated. Ridiculous. He was a grown man.

'I've found the missing link.' Jess sounded cheerful.

'You have? Is this good news for me?' *Do not screw this up.*

'That depends on your answer to this next question. Who was Jane R?'

'Jane who?'

'Jane R, and that may have been the correct answer. Does that name ring any bells?'

'Jane R.' *Tell the truth.* That was the most important thing. 'Didn't Rob's sister Natalie have a friend called Jane? Rutherford? Robertson?'

'So you don't remember getting off with her two nights after New Year?'

'No I don't. I take it we're talking about a particular New Year, and that you found the missing diary.' He was ultra-aware of his pulse tripping uncomfortably.

'My mother sent it to me. How can I have totally forgotten something like that?'

'Well, it obviously wasn't important. I can't remember it either. Where was this?'

'Sebastian had a party. In his cellar.'

'You're absolutely sure about this?'

'I have the documentary evidence, M'lord.'

He exhaled. 'In that case I plead inebriation. It's the most convincing line of defence.'

'That's your mitigating circumstance?'

'Give me a break, Jess. I was a teenager, for God's sake—'

'And ordinarily that would give you a special dispensation. However you are the one who's tried to convince me that what happened two nights before has stayed with you. Was special.'

'It was. I remember it. And I have no recollection of this other night at all.' He paused. 'Are you furious?'

'No. It's all such a long time ago.'

'I'm sorry, could you repeat that?' He laughed.

'I'm not obsessed with the past, I'm just interested. How it all fits together. The 'what if' argument.'

'OK.' *Good.* 'What are you 'what if-ing' about?'

'I don't know. What might have happened. I also found a long description of my feelings when you put your hand on my knee in your kitchen.'

'Amazing. I take it you still keep extensive diaries.'

'Of course. But it's different. Then I only wrote the baldest of facts with no emotion whatsoever. A severely emaciated version of the truth. Now I try to write what I think…'

'They're still powerful documents and could be used as evidence at a future date.'

'I also found the sweetest birthday letter you sent. I'll show it to you sometime.'

'See? This is positive evidence. That I was once, in the mists of time, capable of a romantic gesture.' He stopped, caught by the vehemence of his own tone of voice.

'OK,' she said. 'But you don't need to be defined by it. You make romantic gestures now.'

He pressed a palm against his chest. 'Meet me in Oxford. I've told Will I just can't stomach the happy family stuff.'

'You can't spend the whole of Christmas on your own.'

'So don't make me. Jess. You know you want to.'

'Don't count on me. I'm going to Brussels.'

'Why?'

'Because I've said I would. Because there'll probably be a new baby to meet by then. Because…'

'Would they understand if you changed your mind?' He had a swift sensation of her body pressed against his, his hand in her hair, the anticipation of a kiss.

'They're expecting me to go. Tell me about your day.'

At least they could conduct a civilised phone call again, Sam thought, when he put the phone down. This week of talking each evening had restored that. He had feared that he'd never be able to erase the damage caused the previous weekend, but now he felt as if their conversation was more realistic and less romantic. They were no longer gazing at each other purely as potential saviours who could solve all their problems and make them truly happy. Now there was an intimacy, an honesty to their interactions. He could show Jess who he really was, all of it. Maybe there would even be a time when he could tell her the worst of it, and the dull ache at the pit of his stomach—the one he managed to ignore most of the time—would finally ebb away.

JESS

Three days before Christmas, Jess rang Tom at work to finalise arrangements for him to pick up the children the following morning. She'd already left two messages on his mobile, and had no response.

'He's in a meeting. Can I take a message?' said a woman's voice.

'Is that Denise?' Jess felt herself tense.

'No. She's already in New York. Can I take a message?'

'Please ask him to ring Jess. It is important.'

Silence on the line.

'Of course. I'll pass it on.' The phone clicked off.

'Darlings, I can't tell you how much I'm going to miss you,' said Jess, holding on to her children like a drowning woman to a lifebelt. 'Have a fantastic time and see you on Saturday.'

'Mummy, I miss you.' Millie clung to Jess as tightly as she was being held.

'I know, darling. But we can talk every day. You can ring my mobile.' Jess caught the twitch of Tom's face. He was taking the children to his parents and wanted to be on the road. She turned to her son.

'Bye-bye, darling. I do hope Father Christmas brings you exactly what you want.'

'I hope he's gone to Hamleys,' said Ben. 'Everything I want is there.'

Jess hugged her first-born and felt grateful that from the maelstrom she'd managed to prise a morning to race into town. She stood up and met Tom's eyes.

'We need to talk after Christmas,' he said, his voice low.

'OK.' The old dread settled in the pit of her stomach. She had to remember that he no longer had the power to hurt her.

She saw the children into the car and waved to them till they turned the corner of the street. No time for sobbing. She grabbed her coat, bag and holdall and rushed for the tube to King's Cross and the Eurotunnel terminal. Her mother and stepfather were waiting for her on the concourse. Her sinking heart sank some more when she saw their eager faces.

'Darling, so exciting. Maria's in labour. Patrick's just rung.'

Jess took a deep breath.

Her mother smiled at her, but already there was concern starting in her eyes. 'What is it, darling?'

Jess focused on her mother, but felt Martin's gaze as he looked from his wife to his step-daughter and back again. 'Felicity?'

'I'm sorry, Mum.' She looked down to fiddle with the handle of her case, unable to watch the excited expression leech from her mother's face.

'What's going on?' said Martin.

Jess's heart fluttered. She pressed her palm to her chest. She had to do this. 'I'm sorry. Would you forgive me if I didn't come with you?'

'What?' said Martin.

'Jessica, be serious.' Felicity used her head teacher voice.

Jess took another deep breath. 'I am completely serious.

And I'm really sorry. I'd love to come with you, but I need to stay near the children.'

'Jessica, your brother's expecting you. It's all organised,' said Martin.

'I'll pay for my ticket. I'm really sorry, Martin.' She turned back to her mother. 'I have to stay here.'

'Darling. Where will you spend Christmas? I can't bear the thought of you being alone.'

'I won't be alone.'

'Where are you going?' said Martin.

'Mum, I'm going to see Sam.'

'Who?' said Martin.

'Where is he?' Her mother moved closer.

'In Oxford.'

'With his brother?'

'At his house.'

'Darling, they may not want an almost stranger descending on them for Christmas.'

'Mum, it will be fine. I was invited. I just didn't realise how much I want to go.'

'Oh, darling.' Her mother reached for Jess and gave her a hug.

Jess nearly broke down on her mother's shoulder. She pulled away, the blood rushing in her ears. If she didn't go now, the fear would paralyse her.

She hugged them both and started to walk away. The presents. She stopped and grabbed a plastic bag from her holdall. 'Here, Mum,' she called. There followed an awkward minute or two while her mother located two presents, amid Jess's protests that it really didn't matter.

'Don't be silly, darling.' Her mother reached for another hug. 'You must have something to open on Christmas Day.'

Jess plunged towards the tube, trying to visualise the

quickest route to Oxford. Sam had texted the night before to say he'd arrived. *I'm here,* was all the message said.

The tube train was crowded with chatty Christmas tourists. She stood, wedged in, her holdall between her feet. Sweat prickled her scalp. She felt dizzy and put it down to lack of food. She'd had only the tiniest bit of toast Millie had chosen to leave.

When she arrived at Paddington there was a fast train leaving in twenty minutes. She found a seat and texted Sam: *Are you there?*

Almost immediately, he replied: *I'm here. Where are you?*

Before she either leapt off the train or was violently sick, she texted back: *On Oxford train. Are you at the house?*

Yes, came the reply, a few moments later. Such a powerful word.

She spent the crowded journey picking her nails. She considered the contents of her holdall, but she had her only decent clothes with her. Had she known she was going to Oxford, not Brussels, the lack of choice would have forced her to pack identically. She even had the present for Sam in her bag. *Not that surprising,* she realised.

As they approached Oxford, she stationed herself by the door, searching for Sam through the glass until he slid into view, wrapped in his long coat and scarf. His face was expressionless but then he locked eyes with hers and raised a hand in greeting. *Here comes one of those edge-of-chaos moments. This way or that way. This way or that way.*

At last the train stopped. Sam had kept pace with her, opened the door and leaned down for her bag. His hand was warm. She stepped on to the platform. 'What are you doing here?'

'What are *you* doing here?' He kissed her. His lips were warm and gentle, ratcheting up her speeding heartrate.

'It's cold. Let's go.' He put his arm round her.

For a moment she tensed, propelled back to the mortification of James Gorton insisting on putting his arm round her at the cinema, sending waves of hot embarrassment flooding through her, hating the possessiveness of it. When she'd shaken him off, he'd used that hateful term, the one he'd used before, the one he'd use again. 'Prick tease.'

But this wasn't James. This was Sam. She had to stop her mind from racing back to those teenage years time after time. Or she'd never find peace with him.

She hadn't seen him since that dreadful interview in her kitchen, a month ago now. Hadn't touched or kissed him for nearly two months. And his arm felt so good, the weight of it across her shoulders, anchoring her to him.

'Thank God you're here,' Sam said. 'I'd have died of boredom. What changed your mind?'

'Well. Oxford's closer to the children. They're in Stratford with Tom's parents.'

'There I was, thinking it was my boundless charm.' His smile was irresistible.

'That too.'

When they arrived at Will and Diana's, he deposited her holdall at the bottom of the stairs. 'Cup of tea?'

'Lovely,' she said, forming her hands into fists to stop shaking from fear and cold.

'Go and sit in the front room. The paper's in there somewhere.'

'I'll close the curtains.' She switched on the side lights and drew the curtains, instantly warming the room up. A tall Christmas tree stood in front of the window, suffusing the room with the cool, fresh tang of pine needles.

Sam handed her a mug and sat down beside her on the sofa. 'I can imagine Woodham Road looking something like this, when I get my act together.'

'Yes.' She gazed around the warm, book-lined room.

He'd gone absolutely still, watching her. 'So…'

'You're wondering why I'm here.'

'Not particularly. I'm just grateful.'

She tried to think of something that wasn't a cliché. 'I thought maybe we could talk and try to work out a way to…' She stopped at the look of amazement on Sam's face. '*What?*'

'Well, I just assumed that, as you'd changed your plans and come to Oxford, that meant you were going to sleep with me.' He put his mug down.

Jess's heart lurched. She tried to think of something to say.

'You've got to admit that, looking at it from my point of view, it's practically a promise of sex.' He smiled lazily.

'I…I…' Coherent sentences escaped her.

His shoulders shook. 'You really should see the look on your face, Jess,' he gasped, between bouts of laughter.

'Sod you.' She reached out her free arm to swing at him, frowning so that she wouldn't laugh.

'Come here and give me what I want.' He pulled her against him, taking her mug and putting it on the table beside his.

His grip was firm and she wrenched herself back to see what would happen. He let go immediately, raised his hands in surrender. 'Jess. I'm joking.'

'I know.'

'I don't think you trust me. It's like being trapped in a bad movie.' He handed her mug back.

'What do you mean?' She wanted him laughing and holding her, not serious and sad.

'You won't have sex with me. I only want to have sex with you.'

Jess stood up. 'This calls for Jane Austen.' She walked over to the alcove crammed with novels, alighting upon a beautifully bound set of books. Almost immediately she found what she was looking for. 'Have you read this?' she asked, holding up a copy of *Sense and Sensibility*. 'Or seen the film?'

'Yes. Don't ask me to remember it, though.'

'OK. Elinor the heroine is talking to her sister. *'And after all, Marianne, after all that is bewitching in the idea of a single and constant attachment, and all that can be said of one's happiness depending entirely on any particular person, it is not meant—it is not fit—it is not possible that it should be so.'*

'Beautiful. Doesn't help.'

She faced him. 'Sam, I shouldn't have—'

Would you rather be in Brussels? Or London?'

'No.' A glimmer of a smile. 'Maybe somewhere hot.'

'Alone?'

She pursed her lips. 'Might be safer.'

'But not half as interesting?'

SAM

'You said something.' He pulled his mind back from the heat, from the imagined softness of her skin under that cardigan, enjoying the things she was doing with her mouth. What he might be able to persuade her to do with her mouth. Really, all he had to do was stretch out a hand and undo one or two of those shiny buttons. OK, so sex was out. But there was a whole world of other possibilities he was fairly confident he could interest her in.

'Food. We should go shopping,' said Jess.

He drove them to the supermarket, aware that something happened to Jess whenever they were in the car together. It wasn't because he was a bad driver. He wasn't.

They chose satsumas, raspberries and blueberries, carrots, parsnips and potatoes, organic beef and a free-range corn-fed chicken.

'Wine next.' He put several bottles of champagne, Pouilly-Fuissé and Saint-Emilion into the trolley.

'I wasn't planning to drink that much.'

'It's Christmas,' he said, regretting it the moment the word was out of his mouth. He watched her shoulders droop. 'Thought I'd leave a few bottles for our hosts.'

'That's a nice idea.'

'How about a pudding?' he said.

'Anything you'd like?'

'I meant a Christmas pudding,' he said slowly.

'Oh. OK. I'll find the ingredients for brandy butter. I'll meet you at the check-out.'

When she found him, he said, 'Do you think this'll be enough?'

She surveyed the mounds of food, her mouth twitching. 'I doubt it.'

JESS

Jess lay in a fragrant bath for a long time, delaying the decision about which underwear to put on. She was alone with Sam, miles away from the distractions of family life, faced with that flipping coin again. Heads, they Did It. Tails, they slept in separate beds. There was always that tantalising offer of all the other things they hadn't done, not to mention his willingness to experiment.

She could always jump on him and get it all over with.

They could spend the next three days in bed. Jess sighed. Bliss. Frankly, three days in bed rated as bliss, with or without the sex. Tomorrow she was just going to sleep until she woke up. And the next day. And the next day.

Before she went downstairs she rang Tom's parents' number and sighed with relief when Tom's father answered. 'Yes, they're just saying goodnight.'

Only half-past seven. Of course Clarissa would have them in a strict routine as soon as they arrived, but sending Ben to bed at this time was optimistic.

'Mummy, we went in the garden in our wellies,' said Millie, sounding heartrendingly young and breathless on the phone.

She talked to them both—Ben only after audible persuasion from his grandfather—and promised to ring them tomorrow. 'Can I talk to Daddy?' she said, at the end of the conversation, but Ben had already put the phone down.

Oh well, she could tell him about her change of plans tomorrow. He could always reach her on the mobile.

SAM

'This is excellent,' said Sam, indicating the beef with his fork. Two glasses of champagne, the heat from the oven and the warmth of the house were combining to relax them both. He tried not to stare as Jess unbuttoned her cardigan, exposing a little flushed flesh.

He topped up their red wine. 'Mm. Full-bodied. There's a description.'

Jess looked up. 'What?'

'You heard me. I have these thoughts. Any time you're near.'

'I see. I wish you wouldn't.' She sat back.

'Jess, tell me what you want me to say and I'll say it. We can go as fast or as slow as you want…' He stopped at the sight of her face crumpling into giggles.

'Sorry,' she gasped. 'That was mean, but I couldn't resist it.'

Grin at me again. Please. 'OK. Now that we're asking questions. What is it with you and driving?'

'What?' Her eyes connected with his.

'Driving. Something happens as soon as we get in the car. Is it driving in general, or is it me, or…'

She made him wait while she took a sip of the Bordeaux. 'Both. Driving in general, but you in particular.'

'Explain.' He sipped the nicely expanding wine.

'You have great hands.'

'I don't understand.'

'I will certainly deny this if you ever mention it in public, but there is something completely attractive about a man doing something physical, well. You do driving well. With your hands.'

He grinned. 'You find my driving sexy?'

'I didn't say that.'

'I just remembered that we really should go and pick something up. Now. In the car.'

'Idiot. I'm going to regret telling you.'

'You find me irresistible,' he said, the tension evaporating off him. 'You fall silent and hold your breath so you don't give yourself away. Or jump on me.'

'Shut up and eat your food.'

JESS

'I didn't mean to wake you. Thought you might like a cup of tea.' Sam stood at the top of the stairs, in jeans and a thick grey jumper, his hair damp from the shower.

'What time is it?' said Jess.

'Half nine. How did you sleep?' He put the cup down and sat on the end of the bed.

'I don't even remember turning the light off.' She sat up to reach for her cup.

'You didn't. I came up to say goodnight, but you were fast asleep, so I switched it off.'

She touched her fingertips to her lips. 'Sorry. I didn't mean to fall asleep. It was all that good food and wine.'

'Don't worry. What do you want to do today?'

'Do you have any suggestions?' She blushed, sitting in the double bed in her pyjamas.

'Well...' He caught her eye and grinned for a moment. He cleared his throat. 'Why don't we head into town and do some last minute Christmas shopping? Bargains, mind. Anything suitable for under a tenner.'

'That's a great idea.'

'You will say if you want to ring Stratford or anything, won't you?'

'I rang them last night, before I came downstairs.'

He hesitated for a moment, but she waved him on.

'Everything OK?'

'I think so. Didn't manage to talk to Tom about my change of plans, but he'd ring me on the mobile anyway. I'll talk to him later.'

'Does he know about me?'

'Not exactly. Sort of.'

Sam stood up. 'See you downstairs.'

'I will tell him where I am, today,' she said, to his retreating back.

Felicity rang Jess's mobile in the middle of breakfast, to tell her that after a long labour, Maria had given birth, without medical intervention, to a baby son, as yet unnamed.

'Does it make you feel broody?' said Sam, when she put the phone down.

'Not in the least,' Jess replied. 'Why?'

'Just wondered. Shall I drive us into the centre of town? Please?'

'No, walking is good, particularly if I carry on eating the quantities I put away last night.'

'Wimp.'

They separated in the pedestrianised shopping area and arranged to meet in an Italian restaurant for an early lunch. The place was already heaving when she arrived.

'You look cheerful,' she said.

'I've been successful. You?'

'Barely. I may need more time.' She really didn't want to be the person who bought him a scarf. Or gloves. Or boxer shorts. She didn't even know if he preferred boxer shorts or briefs. Oh, good grief.

They didn't linger over lunch, hassled by a harassed waitress and a queue of people.

'Shall I meet you in the bookshop?' Sam suggested. 'If you need more time.'

'Thank you.' Jess had the familiar feeling that everything had a double meaning.

He kissed her and let her go, while she tried to locate her missing stomach. Lust made her knees quiver. He caught her eye and grinned, as he turned away.

Oh hell, he knew precisely what effect he had on her. Why did she try to kid herself that she was somehow mysterious and unpredictable?

When she reached the bookshop he was reading in the fiction section, a shoulder against the wall, his hands expertly turning the pages. Her knees began to quiver. Pitiable.

He looked up, as if sensing her eyes upon him. 'There you are. Anything else you want to do?' He lowered the book.

She stopped an inch from his chest and raised her face to kiss him.

'Wha…?'

She was on her toes, her lips on his.

He followed her to keep the contact as she sank down on her heels, pulling her against him with his arms around her, kissing her back. 'Thank God. I'd given up hoping you might kiss me one of these days. What was that for?'

'Happy Christmas.'

'Kiss me again.' He bent his head, blotting out the light, as she let her eyelids fall.

'Oh,' she said, coming up for air. 'We're in a bookshop.'

'Shall we go?' He tucked the book he'd been reading back into the shelf. 'Back by the colleges?'

'Yes.' Their eyes connected. She had a feeling her yes covered more than the walk.

The moment Sam closed the front door, he caught her, kissing her for minutes, unwrapping her scarf, pulling off her gloves, unbuttoning her coat and his, and leaving them dropped on the floor beside their bags of shopping, before pulling her into the twilit sitting room and onto the sofa.

At last his arms were fast around her, her hands exploring the contoured muscles of his back beneath his sweater, feeling the breadth and height of him, absorbing his warmth, sensing the tension seep from her neck and shoulders for the first time in weeks. She felt her breath slow and deepen as his hands cupped her face, strong fingers in her hair, on her back, pulling her against his chest. His tongue darted into her mouth, sending quivers to her knees, making her wrap herself around him, as close as possible. He pulled her on to his lap, his hands round her waist, holding her tight, showing her how aroused he was.

His hands were undoing the buttons of her cardigan by touch, still kissing her deeply, concentrating on the kiss while his fingers explored. She could feel the heat of his palms through the thin jersey top, cupping her breast, finding the nipple beneath the lace of her bra, circling her other breast as she leant into him, kissing him back. *This is how I want to feel.*

He pulled back and looked into her eyes. 'It won't be for us.'

'What?' Through the fog of her mind she could hear the phone ringing.

He kissed her again, his hands on her waist, and she fell back into the sensations of his mouth and tongue and hands until he stopped moving.

'What?' she said.

'That's the children. Calling from Spain.' He rolled her on to the cushions and headed for the hall. Jess lay back on the sofa, fighting for breath, clenching her teeth, pulling down her skirt, fumbling for the buttons of her cardigan.

Half past three. The service of Nine Lessons and Carols would be on the radio and she had the brandy butter to make.

In the kitchen she turned the radio on, and set about softening the butter in a bowl. She was creaming butter and sugar together when Sam came in.

'Sorry about that. Emma wanted to chat.'

'Don't be. Is she OK?'

'Yep. Kate's evidently being her usual sunny self and Elizabeth has gone into holiday mode, which means she's got her head stuck in a book. I think most of that was wanting a little attention.'

'Where are they?'

'Near Gibraltar. Nigel is a fellow consultant, also divorced, with one boy who's Josh's age. He has an apartment on one of those resorts with golf courses. And if he plays golf, he won't cramp Elizabeth's style by being around too much. It will suit them perfectly.'

'What's he like?'

Sam shrugged. 'Very ambitious. Very like Elizabeth. Very tall. What are you making?'

'Brandy butter.'

'I can't imagine Elizabeth making brandy butter. She's very scientific about food. Sees it as fuel.' He flicked a finger into the mixing bowl.

'But you love food.' Jess batted his hand away.

'I know. It should have been a sign.'

'At least you could have a conversation about work. You share a profession. You and I couldn't talk in the same way.'

'No. But I don't want to talk about it in that way. Being a GP is about having the knowledge, but it's also about people. In hospital medicine, there are still a lot of doctors who don't see their patients as people. They're medical conditions. No emotions to get in the way.'

'Which must be essential to do the job well.' *I can't imagine what you see in me. I sound so different to Elizabeth.*

'But you understand why I was so cut up about that patient dying. She would have told me to get a grip and given me some lecture about being a much better doctor if I remained emotionally detached.'

'I can't believe that. She cares about her children. She still cares about you, I'm sure.'

'Yes, I think the emotional ties she feels towards them have taken her by surprise. But it's as if she can only deal with so much emotion. The more children we had, the more she severed her links with me.'

'I'm sorry.' Jess put down her wooden spoon and gave him a hug.

'That's much better,' he said, his breath warm on her neck.

'Find the brandy for me, would you?'

He extracted a bottle from the drinks cupboard. 'The person I really worry about is Kate. She's already cutting herself off, emotionally.'

'She's at the age when they do that anyway. You're her father and you can provide a balance for her, stop her from becoming too shut off. And I'm sure Elizabeth wants that too.'

'I hope so.'

Jess poured the brandy into a tablespoon and began mixing. 'Try it.' She daringly held out a finger of mixture.

'Delicious,' he said, when he'd sucked enough to put tremors in her knees. 'The brandy butter's nice too.'

When she rang Stratford, Tom's mother answered the phone. 'Ah, Jessica, how are you?'

Jess could feel the froideur down the phone. 'Fine, thank you. I've been making brandy butter and listening to the Nine Lessons and Carols.' Why did she still strive to prove to Clarissa that she had been the right sort of girl for her oldest son to marry? *Like me, like me.* What did it matter now?

Clarissa tutted. 'Can you get that in Brussels? Here's Millie wanting a word.'

'Hello, darling,' said Jess, listening to her breathy daughter telling her all about what a helpful girl she'd been for Granny. She sat down at the dining room table.

'We made brandy butter and I did the mixing,' said Millie.

'That's just what I've been doing, darling,' said Jess, feeling a clenched weight on her chest. 'How's Ben? And Daddy?'

'Ben's been helping Papa in the garden, and Daddy's been working, but he said he'd play a game with us later.'

'Does he want to talk to me?'

'I'll pass you to him,' said her daughter solemnly.

'Love you, darling, I'll ring you tomorrow,' she said, her voice breaking, but Millie had gone.

'Did you want something?' said Tom, his voice abrupt.

'I just wanted to let you know that I changed my plans at the last minute. I'm not in Brussels.'

'Not in Brussels? Where the hell are you? Don't you think that's irresponsible? What if something happened to one of the children?'

Jess had a strong sense of déjà-vu. She took a deep breath. 'For a start, the first thing you'd do is ring my mobile, which I've had with me the whole time. Secondly I'm in Oxford.'

'You're in Oxford? What the hell are you doing in Oxford?'

'I came to meet Sam Rushmore. His brother Will lives here.' She was convinced Sam would be able to hear her thumping heart.

'What are you talking about? I'm going to ring you on my mobile. Don't move.'

Jess let the phone drop into her lap.

'Are you OK?' Sam said.

'Tom's ringing back. He hates surprises.' Her phone rang and she scrabbled to put it to her ear.

'Start again. Who are you with?' said Tom.

'Sam Rushmore. Old friend. You went to his wedding. He came to ours.'

'What the hell are you doing with him? This is why you insisted on going to Millingham that weekend I had to be in New York, isn't it?'

'I'd made plans. It was difficult—'

'Well, just don't expect me to be flexible next time. Not if you're having it off with your boyfriend.'

'Tom. Please. I'm sorry this comes as a shock. I should have made more effort to talk to you when you came back from New York.'

'Yes, you bloody well should have. Have the children met him? Has he slept at the house?'

'They have met him, but he's never slept there while they've been there. It's not like that—'

'I'm surprised you managed to control yourself at all when we were married, given your past. How many others have there been since we split up?'

Jess swallowed hard. 'Tom.' She clenched her free fist between her knees, squeezing until the pressure across her knuckles was almost unendurable. Screaming and swearing at him would do no good. 'Please don't do this.'

'We need to talk when I'm in London.'

'Fine. How are the children?'

'Fine. I've got to go.'

The line went dead and Jess laid her mobile on her lap.

She was intensely aware of Sam's footsteps. He sat down beside her and took her hand. 'I'm sorry. I hope you didn't do that purely on my account.'

'No. I was going to tell him anyway. I had to tell him I was here.'

'He took it badly?'

'He likes to control things. I'm beginning to think that if we ever get the chance to re-introduce our exes they might get on extremely well.' She shrugged. 'When he's caught off-guard, his instinctive reaction is to lash out. He says things without thinking.'

'What did he say?'

Jess stood up. 'It doesn't matter. When he's calmed down, he'll know it's not true anyway.'

He put a finger under Jess's chin and tilted her face to look at him. 'Tell me.'

'Oh, some crack about all the other men I must have had, reverting to type, that sort of thing.'

'Bastard. How could he say that to you?'

'Because he's hot-tempered. And if I'm honest, the only reason I was so calm was because I feared you'd think less of me if I really laid into him.'

Sam eyed her. 'You are amazing.'

'I think we need a plan.'

'Why didn't you tell him we weren't sleeping together?'

'Because it's none of his business.'

'But he'd—'

'It doesn't matter anymore what he thinks of me. It matters a lot more to me what you think.'

Sam put his arms round her and kissed her. 'So, we need a plan?'

'Oh. Yes. What about going to Midnight Mass?'

After Midnight Mass at St Mary's, the University church in the centre of Oxford, Sam persuaded Jess to sit in the sitting room, by the light of the fire and a single table lamp. They sipped some of Will's superior whisky.

Sam stretched his legs out on to the low padded stool that doubled as a table, in front of the sofa.

'Do you mind if I take off my boots?' she asked.

'As long as you don't mind if I do the same with my shoes.'

It felt a self-conscious act, removing her black leather boots, but it also felt like a release. She stretched her toes out in front of her.

Sam slumped into the corner cushions, catching her eye. 'It's good to see you.'

'You say that a lot.'

'It's my "Here's looking at you, kid," line.' He nudged her ankle with his foot and she wriggled her toes.

'What time is it?' she said, to fill the suddenly dense silence.

'Time to play footsie.' Caressing her instep with his toes, he twisted round to face her on the sofa. 'Fancy a foot massage?'

He pulled her legs over his knees, bracing his feet at the end of the sofa to stop her from falling off. He cupped her left foot in his hands, strong fingers working across the arch to the ball of her foot.

'Too ticklish,' she said, when she got her breath back.

'Not a problem.' He increased the pressure just enough to stop the spasms. The feel of his fingers was exquisite. Erotic. His eyes were dark upon hers in the firelight. 'Sensitive feet, Miss Lamb.'

She pulled his feet into her lap, feeling their warmth through his black socks. A flashback of him emerging from the sea on Croyde beach, bronzed and firm, his feet gripping the sand, hair tousled by the breeze, grinning at her. Good job he had her pinned to the sofa. Otherwise, she'd have fallen off.

'What?' he said.

'I was imagining that your feet are still brown from the summer.'

'Is that so?'

'Yes.' She stripped one sock off, then the other, her hands pale beside his feet.

'Oh yes,' he groaned. 'Putty in your hands.' His fingers strayed up her calf. 'I take it you're not wearing socks?'

'Afraid not.' She wore woolly tights under her long skirt, but suddenly flesh on flesh had a lot more appeal. 'Maybe I'll go and slip into something more comfortable.'

He let her go and stood up, pulling her up by the hands. 'Don't be long.'

She ran upstairs and yanked off her tights, worrying about what knickers she was wearing. Bad sign. Middle of Christmas night, no less, and she was contemplating sex. No. She was imagining sex. Ninety-nine per cent of her conscious thought—and probably just as much of her unconscious mind—was absorbed by it.

She could hear him coming up the stairs. He would be here any second. She shoved her discarded tights under the bed with her heel and looked up.

SAM

'Knock, knock.' Sam handed Jess her glass. She looked relatively friendly, but she could be about to throw him out. 'Cold feet?'

'Hot feet. The relief of taking my tights off.'

'I see.' Encouraging.

She scooted further up the bed with her drink and he stretched out at the bottom, his head in his hand, watching her shadowed face. He put his glass on the floor, then captured a naked foot. 'Where were we?'

Her skin was soft and smooth under his fingers. He refocused on her face in time to see her bite her lip as he caressed her calf, working back down to her ankle.

She met his eyes. 'Give me a foot.'

'With pleasure.'

Her fingers were cool and firm on his feet, warm in her lap again. He pressed his heel a little, against her inner thigh, and enjoyed another of sharp intake of breath. She was so different from Elizabeth. He lifted her foot and kissed his way down her shin, appreciating the reciprocal pressure against his feet, the trailing of her fingers down his toes. He kissed around her ankle, and put his mouth on the swell of her calf, gently biting her flesh, his hands stroking behind her knee. She slipped her hand up the leg of his trousers, warm hands on his shin and calves.

'I had no idea feet were such an erogenous zone,' she said, her voice far away, above the rushing in his ears.

'Me neither.' Never had kissing someone's ankles been anything like this appealing. 'At the risk of sounding like a badly written pop song, I want to kiss you all over.'

She wriggled and he grabbed a foot in each hand, his thumbs under the instep.

She gripped his feet back. Her eyes locked with his. He rolled closer, a hand drifting up to her knee, under her skirt, further and further. He felt the muscles tense and then relax under his touch, watching her parted lips. He rested his hand on her hip, feeling the lace beneath his palm as he kissed her, grateful when she grabbed him and he leaned into her, twisting around to push the length of his body against her.

'Sam,' she murmured against his mouth.

'Jess.' He kissed her, while her arms circled his back, pushing his jumper up, pulling at his shirt and t-shirt. He arched against her, his body tensing and relaxing, feeling her body echo the pattern.

'I've been dreaming of your weight on top of me,' she breathed, against his lips.

'Have you now?' He increased the pressure of his hips.

'Oh, yes.' She answered his pressure, her eyes dark and certain.

He closed his eyes and kissed her.

An old, familiar panic welled up behind his eyes and he concentrated on not hyperventilating. Would she be very offended if he used the kissing of her, like people used paper bags, to stop himself from sinking into shallow-breathed oxygen-deprivation? It would be OK. The tightness of his erection proved that… But…

'Sam?' She leaned away from him slightly.

He opened his eyes reluctantly, dizzy with lust and panic. On his way upstairs, he could have detoured into the bedroom for one of the confidence-boosting blue pills. But he hadn't wanted to count his chickens.

'Sam?'

He shook his head, trying to throw off the dizziness, the rushing in his ears, the pressure of the darkness bearing down on him. 'Yeah.' He watched her mouth. *Brown paper bag. Helps.* He bent to kiss her but she put her hand on his chest.

'Are you all right?'

'Yes. Let me kiss you.' He reached her lips and savoured the soft pressure, flicking his tongue into her mouth as she opened under him. *This could work.* Viagra or no Viagra. His hand found her breast, firm beneath his palm, the nipple taut through her cardigan. He undid the buttons by touch, concentrating on kissing her, pushing the wool aside, feeling the hardness of both nipples under his fingers, itching for her skin against his, finding the edge of her top, peeling the lace of her bra aside, connecting fingers with the velvety softness of her breast, the hardness of her nipple.

All he needed to do was take one breath to get from her mouth to her breast. Another metaphorical paper bag, and he was still as hard as ever. Could build up to this. Take as long as he needed. He took a breath and plunged to her breast, his mouth around the peak, tongue circling and circling as Jess arched into him, her fingers in his hair, pressing him to her. Making the panic set in, making him think he wouldn't be able to breathe. He wrenched away, desperately trying to pull the oxygen into his lungs, wanting her mouth to regulate his breathing, but already registering her anxious face, knowing she'd stop him, knowing he couldn't breathe, that he could die, on this bed with Jess.

I deserved to make love to her and show her how much I love her.

As he thought this, the constriction in his lungs eased fractionally and he managed to pull more air into them. The darkness receded and the rushing in his ears slowed and he blinked and tried to smile at her stricken face.

'Sam?' she whispered.

'Sorry. Mini panic attack,' he said, holding on to her for dear life, rolling so that they lay on the pillows, facing each other. He reached out to tuck the hair falling across her face behind her ear.

'Are you all right?' she said.

'Yes. Come here.' He hugged her to his chest, his palms flat on her back, lazy fingers at the nape of her neck, in her hair, while his breath grew steadier, deeper, slower.

JESS

They lay like that for a long time, until Jess realised he'd fallen fast asleep and was not about to wake up. Eventually she eased herself out of his arms and got ready for bed. For a second she contemplated going downstairs to the other double bed. Then she tucked the bedspread over him and climbed under the covers. He looked breath-taking in the dim light, his hair falling over his forehead, hands under his chin. She wriggled one of her hands into his.

Ironic really, that she'd finally got to the point of thinking, OK, fuck this, well more to the point *fuck me,* and he'd started hyperventilating at her in such an alarming manner. She tried to imagine what he must have been thinking to become so panicky. The momentousness of the decision could get anyone down. With or without painful episodes in one's past, not to mention anxiety about how the equipment might or might not work.

She had expected to feel offended or hurt or unloved, but instead she felt warm and safe lying next to his solid presence. She stretched out her hand and switched off the light. In the faint, rosy glimmer of streetlight, his chest rose and fell while she listened to his steady breathing.

SAM

It took Sam a moment or two to work out where he was. The sight of Jess, lying on her side facing him, her hand underneath her pillow, stunned him. He tried to piece together what had happened the previous night.

Things had definitely changed in Jess. But, just as she became ready, he'd scuppered it all by having a panic attack. Maybe he could go and take that pill—and brush his teeth—and come back and persuade her to begin where they'd left off. But in the cold light of day, she had every right to change her mind, and then he could have a rather painful problem on his hands. So, he'd just have to be irresistibly persuasive.

Even as he considered this he felt his chest tighten a fraction. No. He could do this. They were meant to do this.

Jess opened her eyes and looked straight at him.

He smiled. 'Hello.'

'Hello. What are you doing in my bed?'

'I'm not exactly in your bed.' He disentangled his long legs from the bedspread. 'This was my bed long before it was yours and—is that an offer?'

She grinned. 'Happy Christmas. What time is it?'

'Happy Christmas.' He pushed himself up on one elbow and glanced at his watch. 'Time to bring you breakfast in bed.'

He brought her a tray laden with raspberries, blueberries, croissants and champagne, and watched her licking the crumbly pastry from her lips and fingers, sipping the icy bubbles. The doubt and panic of last night seemed a long way away.

By the time they'd put the chicken in the oven and prepared the vegetables, he was having to recite times tables just to keep from pulling her onto the kitchen floor.

'Do you mind if I ring the children?' she said.

'Of course not. I'll ring too.' He went into the hall for his mobile, but stopped when the silence caught his attention. There should have been talking.

Jess was sitting at the dining table.

He could make out Millie's chatter at the end of the line as he sat down beside Jess.

'Tell me about your stocking,' Jess whispered. More chatter.

'Yes, darling. I love you, Millie,' Jess said, her face contorting as if she were trying to keep control of herself.

'Hello, darling. Happy Christmas,' she said. Ben. Monosyllabic. 'What did Father Christmas bring you? And did you like your Bionicle? Oh, darling, that's lovely.' Sam watched as tears coursed down Jess's face. 'I'd love to be there helping you make it, too… Oh, darling, I love you too.' She pressed her free hand over her mouth as if to stop the sobs. 'Yes, darling, Happy Christmas.' She put the phone down on the table and put her hands over her face, her shoulders heaving.

'Don't,' she said, when he touched her arm. She bolted to the oven and took the chicken out to baste.

'Jess.' He watched her rigid shoulders, her clenched jaw.

She put the tray back in the oven. Their eyes connected, hers filled with fresh tears. 'I can't bear not to be with them. I've looked after them all year, with him pitching up only when it suits him, and now he gets them for the whole of Christmas. It's not fair.'

He blotted her tears with his handkerchief. 'It's not.'

'I know he has a right to be with them at Christmas. But I still want to see their faces. I want to know what Millie thought of the little angel doll I put in her stocking. I wanted to *see* Ben's face when he opened that big Bionicle. I wanted to be—'

'I understand.' He kissed her, to comfort her, to show her he was here, but she erupted against him, kissing him back fast and deep and full, holding on to him for dear life.

'I don't want to feel like that. I want to feel like this,' she whispered against his mouth. His hands were in her hair, moulding the shape of her skull, his mind leaping ahead to holding on to her as he entered her. The dizziness was there as the blood rushed from his brain, but he kept breathing steadily, while Jess pressed herself against him, her hands fighting for his skin, pulling his clothes aside, slipping under his shirt to press against his back.

His fingers dropped to her neck, her shoulders tense as bullets. He caressed her, waiting for a sign that she was relaxing. Her shoulders dropped and his hands stroked down to the fastening on her pink top. He stopped kissing her to undo the silver pin, resting his forehead against hers, parting the woollen jacket, his fingers exploring her breasts under her top. 'Jess.' He leant back fractionally to meet her eyes.

'Yes,' she said, that look of certainty still there.

'Are you all right?' His fingers felt for the wrap-over tie.

She kissed him, pressing her breasts into his hands, pulling him against her. 'Are you all right?'

'Yep.' He picked her up in his arms. 'I'm not doing this

on the kitchen floor.' He put her down at the bottom of the stairs. 'You'd better walk if you want me to still be breathing by the time we get to the top.'

When they reached the landing, he nudged her in the direction of the next flight of stairs. 'Give me two seconds.'

Thank God for forward planning. Thank God for condoms.

JESS

It had better be two seconds. She took the stairs two at a time, Sam already at the bottom.

'Pink lace.' He grabbed her, his mouth trailing down her neck, burning at her throat, stopping all coherent thought as she sank into the sensations. Fingers pushed into the cups of her bra, cool air on her skin, her nipples. Her hands finding his belt, undoing the buckle by touch as he brought his lips to her breasts, kissing between them, his tongue trailing across soft flesh. She pulled the belt free, fingers feverish for the button, the zip, her hand finding him hard, stroking him until he caught her wrist.

'Don't. I won't last long as it is.' He fell on top of her, on to the bed, kicking off his shoes, hands on her hips, stroking down her thighs, pulling up her skirt, into the top of her tights.

I should have worn stockings, she thought, as he stripped her tights off, pulling off his sweater and shirt. She pushed his t-shirt over his head, his strong brown arms yanking off her top, leaving her pale and trembling in his arms.

'Jess, you are so beautiful.' His hands spanned her waist, searching for the zip, finding it at her hip, yanking it down, shoving the skirt to the floor with his strong legs.

But she was beyond conversation, concentrating on rendering him naked as quickly as possible. Jeans and boxers, and her bra and knickers joined her skirt on the floor, but not before he scrabbled for his back pocket. He kissed her as he put the condom on, kissing her as he moved between her thighs, pushing into her, raising his weight off her, his hands braced either side of her head as he pushed, closer and closer, until she felt as if she'd come home.

'Oh, Jess.' He groaned against her mouth, raising himself up enough to stare into her eyes as he built a rhythm.

She watched him, as his eyes grew darker and darker. The exquisite weight of him, the flutterings darting around her body, wanting him closer and deeper, winding her legs around his hips, hands on his back, as he rocked into her tightly.

'Jess, I can't—' he gasped, against her mouth and she kissed him, deep and fast, as he shuddered and collapsed on top of her, his head against her cheek, feeling his quickened breath, his hammering pulse. He reached behind his back for her hand and interlaced their fingers, drawing deeper and deeper breaths to slow his breathing. 'Sorry,' he said into her shoulder. 'Couldn't last any longer. You're too dazzling.'

'Dazzling.' Slowly her conscious mind seeped back into her brain. She had the feeling she needed to do something, but she couldn't think what it was. And she didn't have the energy, even if she was beginning to feel a bit squashed, under his weight. 'Sam?'

'Sorry, here.' He rolled to one side, getting rid of the condom, curling his free arm around her shoulders, keeping their hands interlaced, pulling her into his chest.

'I have the feeling I'm meant to—oh, bloody hell.' She sat up. 'The chicken.'

'It'll be fine. In a minute.' He pulled her back down and kissed her. 'Thank you. You have no idea how much better I feel.'

'Not too panicky?'

'Better than could be imagined. I'm out of practise. I don't normally collapse quite so quickly.'

'It's hugely flattering. And more normal than I thought.'

'More normal?' he echoed.

'I didn't feel you were being a doctor.'

'I should bloody well hope not! Not when I'm in the throes of passion. So, normal is good?'

'Normal in a good way, but still heart-stopping.'

'Heart-stopping?' He grinned at her.

'The chicken.'

'OK. Shame to ruin Christmas lunch because we were too busy making love.'

'Don't start all that making love stuff.' She sat up and cast around for her clothes. Even after everything, she still wanted to cover up a little. He sat up too, and put his trousers back on, handing over her skirt and tights.

'So, I'm not allowed to say that even now, straight after we've finished, I want to spend the rest of the day and all night, and all tomorrow in this bed making love to you.'

'Absolutely not,' she said, elbowing her stomach as it fluttered and disappeared. She was trying to conduct a civilised conversation with a man who was not her husband while she tried to locate her knickers.

Sam pulled his t-shirt over his head, his brown torso giving her another stomach-fluttering moment.

'Looking for these?' He grinned, his face flushed, hair flopping over his forehead, eyes darker than ever. He held them just out of arm's reach as she leant for them.

She met his lips instead.

'Yep,' he said. 'Still want to make love to you.'

'Go and check on the chicken.' She managed to grab the pink lace out of his hand and put them on.

'Love you too.'

SAM

When Jess came downstairs, she looked calmer than Sam dared imagine. 'Everything's under control,' he told her. 'And I rang Spain and Millingham to say hi.'

'How are they?' said Jess.

'Fine. Kids are delighted with their presents.'

'And you?'

'Better than fine.' He searched her face, his mouth dry. 'You know my problem. I'd invested in some medication, just in case I needed help. More from a psychological rather than a physical point of view.'

'OK.' She looked down.

'Well, just so you know. I didn't have to use it.'

'You didn't?'

'No. It just felt right.'

She raised her gaze to look at him steadily.

'A little champagne with our smoked salmon?'

'Oh, I don't know. Look what happened when I had that last glass.'

Sam laughed. 'Well, if you have another and the same thing happens, you can just blame it on the champagne. Again.'

They sat at the dining table until mid-afternoon, enjoying their feast. At four o'clock, they settled down to watch *It's A Wonderful Life,* and ate a piece of Christmas pudding each, smothered in brandy butter and cream.

By the end of the film, Jess was sniffing, having wept through most of the second half.

'I'm going to run you a bath,' said Sam. 'Then let's go to bed and open some presents.'

JESS

Jess lay down, her head on a towel, and stretched her legs out beside the taps at the other end, her knees surfacing through the profusion of bubbles. When Sam opened the door, she stayed put, eyes closed, relatively relaxed.

'Sit up a bit, will you?' Before she knew what had happened, he'd joined her, stepping into the bath behind her, settling down into the water, now at a perilously high level. His hands began to lazily circle her shoulders and then her breasts, slippery with bubbles.

She relaxed against him, her head on his chest. 'I could get used to this.'

'The perfect Christmas Day. Next year, when we've got all the children with us, we'll be fantasizing about slipping off to make love, or have a bath together.'

'Sam, don't.'

His hands slipped to her midriff. 'You're going to have to marry me now.'

She turned her head so she could see his eyes. 'Are you crazy?'

'I have never been more serious. Marry me, Jessica.'

'Sam. Can't we just… Let's not…' She spread her hands over the bath water.

'Think about it. Properly. Not when I'm distracting you. I didn't mean to ask you in the bath, actually. But I know what it's taken for you to let me make love to you. So I wanted you to know. That I know.'

She kissed him. 'Shut up.'

'I've been having fantasies about doing it in the bath.' He pulled her up to her knees.

She squealed. 'The water will go everywhere.'

'Who cares?' he said, nudging her from behind, biting her shoulder gently, his hands cupping her breasts.

Her heart skipped against her ribs and her mind was fogging up again. She turned around, ignoring the sloshing water. 'I want to see you.'

'Whatever you want.' He kissed her lips.

Half an hour later she sat in bed at the top of the house, wrapped in a huge towel. Sam climbed the stairs with a tray of cheese and biscuits and red wine, and they opened presents.

Sam gave her the softest brown leather, fur-lined gloves, 'Because your hands always seem to be cold in those old woollen ones.' On that long ago snowy night, her hand had been warm in his, tucked into his coat pocket, but later on her fingers had been icy to the touch. He wasn't going to let that happen again.

She tried them on. 'They're gorgeous.'

'There's something else,' he said, producing a tissue paper covered box from the side of the bed. 'I wasn't sure I'd give you this. But things have changed.'

'Should I be nervous?' Her hands shook as she tried to open the tissue paper carefully and then ripped it off in her impatience. There was more tissue inside, and underneath that the softest midnight blue silk nightdress. 'It's beautiful.'

'Put it on and then I can rip it off you.'

She raised her eyebrows at him.

'Please. I won't look if you'd rather I didn't.' He walked

over to the desk, so she pulled the towel open and slipped the spaghetti-strapped nightdress over her head.

'Now, where was I?' Sam turned round and looked at Jess. 'Time to unwrap my favourite present.'

'Sam. It's just that… Having not done this in such a long time—'

'I have just the idea,' he said, letting his full weight fall on her again, bringing his lips to hers. She squirmed under him and he lifted his head to look into her eyes. 'Oh yes, do that again.'

'Shut up.'

'It's the silk. That's why I bought it really.' She twined her legs around him, but he was already slipping south, hands on her hips, stroking down her thighs, gently teasing the hem of the nightdress in the opposite direction until his fingers raked up and down her inner thighs, parting her legs, cool fingers stroking and sliding against her until she lost her mind.

Jess held on tight to Sam's shoulders through his robe, shoving it off him, hands fluttering across his smooth skin, into his hair as he slipped further down the bed, his fingers parting and sliding, the warmth of his hand everywhere as she wrapped her legs around him, pressed towards him. He kissed down her stomach, gently biting her inner thigh, opening her to his mouth, his tongue, the heat of him against her. With his free hand he anchored her to the bed with her hip, giving her something to push against as the waves of heat built up against his finger deep inside her, his tongue flicking, sucking her into his mouth, with no inhibition at all. She laced her fingers through his hair, eyes tight shut as her breathing deepened, the breaths expanding and rolling across her body, everything concentrated on what he was doing with his hands, his mouth, his tongue. Her thighs clenched, the pressure building and building as she pushed against him and he held her until she cried out his name.

Seconds later, he was kissing his way back up her body, pushing off the robe, pulling her into his arms as he slid hard inside her.

She jolted back to the present, her eyes wide. 'Did you—?'

'Of course. Jess. I. Knew. This. Nightdress. Would. Add. Something,' he said, as their bodies slid together, as he rocked into her, higher and higher, their eyes connecting.

Jess was beyond words, Sam's body hard against her, his hands in her hair, shaping her skull, pulsing inside her, pulling hard breaths into his throat, finally falling on top of her. She held him until his breathing steadied and he leant off her, his head on his hand, watching her face.

'Bloody hell,' he said after a while, drawing the duvet over them.

'Quite. Was that just the nightdress?'

'That was beautiful you. Nightdress or no nightdress. Although I can't deny that it added something.' He smiled. 'Which reminds me. No more.'

'What?' She felt a chill despite the warmth of his body.

'No more supplies. I thought I was pretty optimistic investing in a three-pack but we've just used the last one and I can't find anymore. You're going to have to be very well behaved until I find a chemist's tomorrow.'

'You want to be careful about issuing challenges like that,' she murmured, curling against him.

'Noted.'

SAM

'It's about time you gave me an answer to my question. The answer I'm looking for, mind,' Sam said. It was Boxing Day morning and they sat over a late breakfast. Jess had had to push him out of bed eventually, in the direction of a cold shower, when his constant erection had been pressed into her back longer than either of them could stand.

'Sam…'

'No point in pretending you don't know what I'm talking about.' He walked round the table, sat down and put his arms round her.

'I just… I…'

'Why don't you and the children come up for New Year? I'll have the children with me. We can have an experimental couple of days together. See how it goes.'

'It could put us both off for life.'

'Or not. I don't want to see you just one weekend in four, when we're both knackered and stressed out. If we're in the same place we can fall into bed together on a Wednesday lunchtime. If we want to.'

'How many married couples do you know who still make love on a Wednesday lunchtime?'

'Yes, but we'd still be in the first throes of passion. Newlyweds.'

'I read something about loving someone being about

choosing to continue loving them after you've fallen out of love.'

'But you can try to prolong the being in love bit too, can't you?'

'Still doesn't solve the geographical problem, though.'

'Look.' Sam leaned back and clasped her hands. 'We've made it this far. What's two hundred miles between friends?'

Jess was studying their joined hands.

'Really. Where there's a will, there's a way. Come for New Year. We'll have a bit of a reunion.'

She finally looked up. 'What do you mean?'

'See who's around. Rob perhaps. Caroline and Philip. James and Fiona if we're very lucky.'

She slipped her hands from his. 'New Year with all the children under one roof?'

'Go on. I dare you.'

JESS

It was not that she didn't want to take up his offer to spend New Year together. Now that she and Sam had finally consummated this lost love, this unrequited teenage passion of hers, there was a comfort to having reached a plateau in their relationship, even if she already felt the guilt seeping in from all sides.

His smile enhanced the warmth in his eyes. His face looked boyish in the morning light, more relaxed and quietly confident than ever.

There was nothing to do but smile back.

Yes, there were still things to say. Sooner or later she'd have to tell him at least something of what James had done all those years ago. She'd demanded honesty of Sam, it was only right to offer it in return.

Maybe she wouldn't have to see James at all. A houseful of seven people could prove so overwhelmingly busy she might be able to duck out of any proposed trips to the pub, pleading unavoidable childcare. And the rest of the time, there would be Sam. The solid, dependable, good-natured father and potential step-father. The lover of her dreams. The best friend she'd yearned for in her first marriage.

Ah. Tom. Whatever her issues with her ex-husband, she would try to protect the children's relationship with their father. Which did not mean running off to see her boyfriend in Manchester.

She looked up and gazed at Sam. 'Are you my boyfriend?'

Sam grinned. 'Boyfriend. Lover. Partner. Whatever you like.' He shrugged, lacing their fingers together. 'Best friend…soulmate…you know where I'm going with this…'

Acknowledgements

Thank you to the many friends, family and colleagues who have encouraged my writing. Thank you to several writers, particularly Susan Johnson, Caroline Lawrence and Sophie McKenzie, for being so generous with your time and advice.

Thank you to the enthusiastic and talented 2018-19 cohort of The Novel Studio at City, University of London, first readers of many chapters of *Like Me*, and tutors Emma Sweeney, Rebekah Lattin-Rawstrone and Kirstan Hawkins for your excellent guidance. Thank you to the first readers of the complete manuscript, Florence Rees and Anne Phipps. Thank you to Emily Pedder of www.thebookedit.co.uk for a fantastically helpful edit. All your feedback made it a much better book.

Thank you to Simon Avery of www.nicegraphicdesign.co.uk for the great book cover, to Caroline Goldsmith of Goldsmith Publishing Consultancy for all the meticulous work making the manuscript print and eBook ready, and to Philippa Makepeace of studiomakepeace@gmail.com for the terrific website design. Could not have done it without your kind expertise.

Thank you to the friends of my youth, especially Sarah Pickstone, Bronwen Roberts, Jane Scrivner, Kathryn Skelton and Sophie White. Please forgive my purloining various aspects of our lives together, and using them to create fiction. Thank you to my brother Benedict and my sister Emma, your kindness, humour and resilience this year has been essential.

Finally, thank you Aidan, Christian and Imogen. I am so grateful for your endless love and support in so many ways.

Coming in 2024
The Millingham Series: Book Two

ME TOO

Set in 2009, *Me Too* picks up the story of Anna and Rob, childhood friends of Jess and Sam. Anna is the only one of the old school crowd without children, and most of the time she can ignore the increasingly desperate voice in her head, reminding her that her arms are empty.

She would never have considered going it alone, but when she encounters Rob again, at the wedding of mutual friends, he sees her needs and desires in a way she can no longer ignore.

Why does a child need to be brought into a stable family situation? She's a competent professional. She could do it alone.

All she needs is a willing helper, and when she propositions Rob—perhaps because she remembers him as the gawky, lovable almost-Goth of their teens—their shared history gives her a certain sense of security. What could possibly go wrong?

About Katharine Light

Katharine Light was born in Glasgow and lived there until her family moved to South Manchester when she was ten. While in her teens, she began writing stories for her younger sister. These mostly centred around a naïve heroine and a 1980s pop star (some would say the hero was modelled on John Taylor of Duran Duran).

She did a degree in psychology at University College London, and after a year travelling, worked in corporate film production for several years, before taking a break to raise her children. During this time, she did two year-long writing courses with the Open University, and completed a first draft of *Like Me,* book one of The Millingham Series. She also started writing book three, with book two squeezing its way in slightly later. She wrote mainly during the holidays, and around her busy work for a local church.

During 2018 and 2019 she studied on The Novel Studio course at City, University of London, focusing on *Like Me*. She recently won the competition City Writes, with her short story *My arms are empty,* which is based on an episode from *Me Too*, book two of the series.

Katharine lives in South-West London with her husband and quite often at least one of their adult children. She loves singing, walking, painting, looking at art, and going to the theatre.

Author photograph by Alex Vanotti

Sign up to Katharine's author newsletter at:

www.katharinelight.com

Instagram/Threads: katharinelightwrites1

Facebook: Katharinelightwrites

X: @katelightwrites

Printed in Great Britain
by Amazon

32938400R00209